I0735468

Also by Andrea Gibb

Adult Fantasy:

The Sanarii Chronicles:
*Child of Kitarra*
*Defender of Kitarra*
*Prince of Kitarra*

Children's:

*From Schoenau*

# DEFENDER OF KITARRA

THE SANARII CHRONICLES
BOOK II

# ANDREA GIBB

www.andreagibb.com

**WIND&ROOT**

www.windandroot.ca

*To Micah,*

*Because regrets are heavy things.*

*Those who were strong are now weak,*
*With healing hands, the babes will speak*
*Light turns to dark and colors shift,*
*Two rivers join when two lovers rift,*
*Watch for the child of two thrones,*
*Born with magic in his bones,*
*A child lit by the stars,*
*Watch for him, for he shall be ours.*

THE HEERA MOUNTAINS
KARA
RODAN
THE SAND SEA
N

LONG ILSES
KITARRA
THE WANDERLING MOUNTAINS
WITHE
THE FERRY
WINDEKEEP
SPINNAE
KITARRA PEAK
ATTINGARD
KILEV
MARKEH
STANDING STONES
THE TARM
ALLATI
TAYEN'S VALE
MAHLAS
LITTLE HILL
FISHTOWN
STONYHILL
THE MIDLANDS
THE GREAT FOREST
OLD ROAD
THE KEEP
DWELLER'S KNOLL
CAER ANDRI
ULLIAN
CARTENEL
JULLAYAH
ALDERRIDGE
THE GREAT BAY

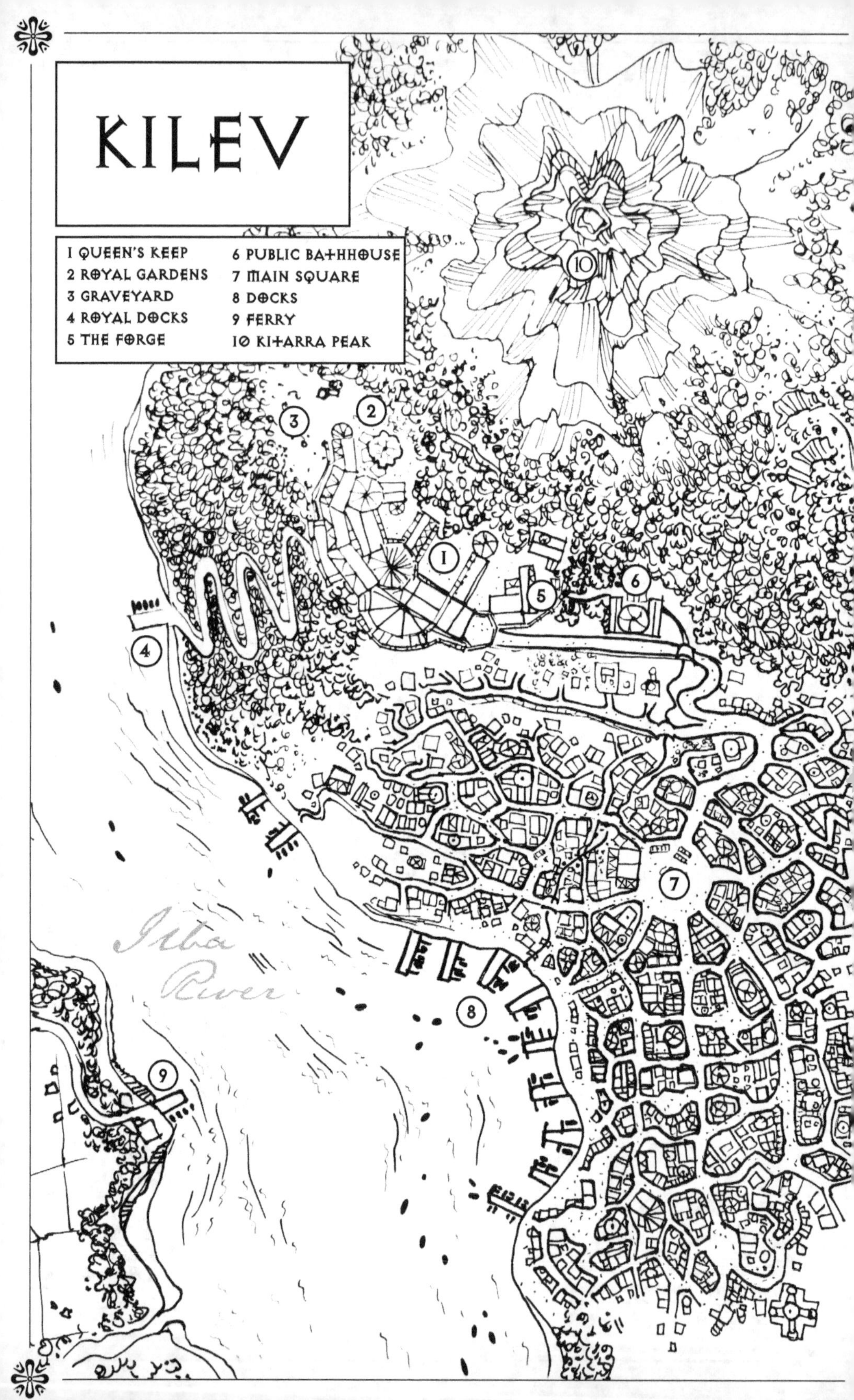

KILEV
1 QUEEN'S KEEP
2 ROYAL GARDENS
3 GRAVEYARD
4 ROYAL DOCKS
5 THE FORGE
6 PUBLIC BATHHOUSE
7 MAIN SQUARE
8 DOCKS
9 FERRY
10 KITARRA PEAK
Itta River

# KARA

1 IMAL'S PALACE
2 AIYAN'S HOUSE
3 THE MARKET
4 THE CHALICE
5 THE TOWER
6 BERIC'S HOUSE
7 WAFFA'S
8 THE BROTHEL
9 ASH ALLEY

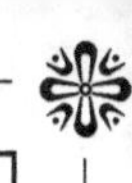

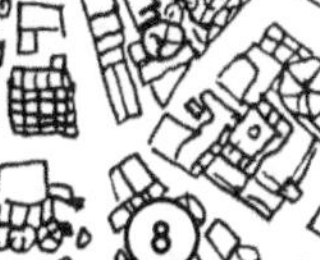

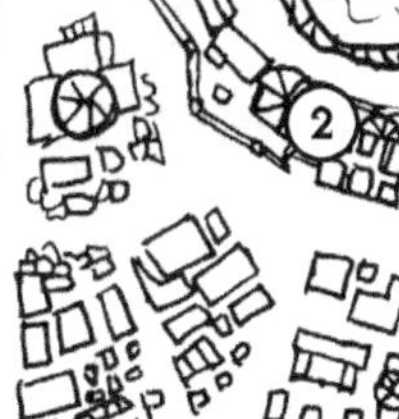

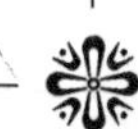

# CALYPSO

AND JUST LIKE THAT, she left. She was gone from the Great Forest and Calypso knew she would never come back.

Calypso perched high on a thick bough of the evergreen tree, but he felt watched. He peered down between the snow-laden branches to see Timur. The mountain cat's glossy green eyes made Calypso wish he could turn into something small and inconsequential, like a grub that could burrow into the moss and be forgotten. But Calypso was already forgotten, at least by those who mattered. Eva had not even looked back.

"You can't follow her," Timur said, his voice no less of a growl even though he shifted into the form of a man, standing in the snow, naked. The Forest provided for its children. Calypso would never feel the cold just as Timur would never feel the ice under his bare feet.

Calypso shuffled his feathers stubbornly. He didn't want to talk to Timur. To talk to Timur, he would have to change his form, and that was the last thing he wanted to do. Other forms felt tight, unnatural. He preferred a raven. He didn't like being a boy, all smooth skin and spindly arms and feet and fingers. And as a raven, he could *fly*.

Timur growled again. Calypso knew the old man had no patience for his brooding, but Calypso didn't really care.

"You have spent too much time outside the Forest." Timur shook his head. "Too much time inside that bird body," Timur muttered as he shifted once more and disappeared into the trees.

Calypso wasn't sure if Timur had intended for him to hear the comment, but he had, and he couldn't unhear it. Probably it was true. He had been raised outside the Great Forest as a raven. He always knew he didn't really belong at the Keep, but he never felt like he belonged in the Great Forest either. He was a foundling. An outsider. Nothing had changed when he realized he was a *velidar*.

*Child, come to usss.*

Calypso shivered. The voices were on the wind, in the trees, casting both light and shadow. He was compelled to follow the call, but his wings felt stiff, and his feet stuck with trepidation.

*Calypsssso …*

*Raven child.*

*Come.*

Calypso went. The trees whispered the path to him. He flew between tree and branch, over ravine and creek.

He landed on the moss, feeling the magic of the Forest wrap around him, assisting his change. Calypso imagined being embraced by strong arms would be similar to the feeling of the magic surrounding him, but he had never had the experience. One cannot properly hug a raven.

Before him was a ring of trees. Big, big trees. Taller and wider than any others—and that was saying something because the Great Forest was home to many ancient and immense trees. Even the air felt ancient. The insignificance of his fourteen years was an eye-blink in that space.

He walked between a gap in the trees into the clearing beyond. His fear was replaced by curiosity. Magic shifted around him and he was in a field of tall yellow grass. The bright sun absorbed into his dark hair first. He marveled at the sensation; a *velidar* couldn't feel the cold of winter, but he could always feel the warmth of the sun. He trailed his fingers through the grass—maybe the appendages were good for something.

*Come.*

Where the grass parted, Calypso met a perfectly circular pool, dark as the night sky and smoother than the most pristine glass. He knelt and looked into the water because he could not not look into it.

He saw a boy.

"Rhyl," Calypso said out loud. His voice was strange. He had never spoken with his human tongue before. It was a wormy, squiggly sort of sound. He moved his lips, feeling them with his fingers. He was supposed to be looking into the pool, the most magical thing he had ever encountered, and here he was, getting distracted by his human body.

Little Rhyl was still in the pool before him, happy, smiling, playing with a Kitarran child. Calypso's chest hurt.

Then the pool showed him something else. His human fingers dug grooves into the dark sand around the pool's edge. Tears leaked down his face. He rubbed them, leaving wet drops on the back of his hand. He had never cried before.

"Can it be stopped?" he asked the Allmakers when the pool had gone dark and empty once more. He could feel the old spirits with him, watching him. His nose was wet and sticky. He drew a deep breath through his mouth, but it caught on all his new emotions.

*Yes. Maybe. Nooo. It depends on the boy. And you.*

"Me?"

*Yes, raven child. You must be ready.*

"What must I do?"

# TAYEH

ONE YEAR LATER.

THE WANDERLING MOUNTAINS did have a certain beauty to them. The rocky outcrops, sweeping and intense. The plateaus of green. The ice fields that never saw enough of summer's warmth to melt fully. The vast expanse of rock and air was both calming and exhilarating. And quiet.

The landscape contrasted with the ferocity of the wind howling in Tayeh's ears even if he couldn't feel it rake his fur down to his skin—the advantage of being a spirit. The wind did not bite into Tayeh's skin. Nor did it move a feather on the great wings of the other Guardian.

Attin stood on the edge of a cliff. The cliff might have been a thousand feet tall, or only ten; the clouds below were too thick to tell. Attin's pure white wings were outstretched as if to catch the wind.

Honestly, Tayeh was shocked to find Attin in such a rugged, raw place. The Guardian was too … fanciful. In life, Attin had been a king, surrounded by riches, women, power. His hubris had imbued the culture of Allati with a greed that was Attin's legacy. Surely there was no place as opposite and stark and humble as the mountaintop. Attin had named his city after himself, after all. It didn't fit.

But perhaps even a Guardian could change. Not a reassuring thought.

"Tayeh. You came." Attin turned to Tayeh, his golden eyes filled with a decent amount of condemnation.

"I would not ignore the summons of another Guardian."

"Oh?"

Tayeh spread his hands. His presence was proof of his testament. Attin nodded, and his face softened, or at least appeared less angry. He sauntered over to Tayeh and sat upon a semi flat rock, his wings folded behind him.

"You took something of mine, Tayeh."

"She was never yours."

"Evangeline is of my blood. My people need her. You kept her from me, mentored her in the ways of the *sanarii*—my magic. How dare you? You and that fox-woman know only a scrap of my magic—of Eva's magic. The audacity ..." Attin let his annoyance fall between them to be snatched up by the wind.

"Her mother fled in anguish from your people. Your people would never have taught her about magic. They would see only a woman, useless, except for the children she could bear. And for that, they would have taken her soul, and her will, and for what? More pretty, fair-haired daughters to exploit? More sons to make into spoiled or embittered lords?"

Attin sighed in acknowledgment. "I have made mistakes. I have ignored my people at times. I have grown absent and lenient. The Shadow Guard is almost non-existent. I am accountable for that. But still, Eva should not have gone to Kitarra."

"You would still have healed her, knowing she would leave Allati?"

"Of course." The answer was instant. And reassuring. "You speak as if you have not asked sacrifices of her," Attin said. "Yes,

Tayeh. I know what you have done. The *simul rami* has shown me, and I have seen the pain you have caused her. Taking her husband and son from her? For what? So she could save a man hardly worth the effort? And fail? What game are you playing?"

"It is not a game. And if it is, I do not know the rules." The All-makers had insisted Arrain be saved, and Tayeh could not ignore the Old Ones. "Eva is in Kitarra now, with her son. You know as well as I that magic is stirring throughout the realms—and across the sea. Is it a coincidence that after searching this whole age, the vercuri are making their way to Kitarra once again? You know the legends as well as anyone. The rift is growing."

Attin looked out over the lonely landscape. "The vercuri must not fall into the wrong hands."

Tayeh grunted his agreement. "Eva has the power of the Old Ones."

"So, all these years, you have kept the truth about her magic from her?"

Tayeh nodded, feeling the doubt of it in his heart. "I taught her what I could, but there is so much she does not know." He had kept much from Evangeline—to protect her. If she knew the truth about her magic, it would destroy her. And she was so fragile. He needed her to be strong.

"Let me teach her everything," Attin suggested. "The world will need it, in the end."

Tayeh felt a war within him. He had caused her enough pain and anguish. Could he ask more of her? Did he have a choice?

"If I teach the mother, then she will teach her son," Attin continued, "and don't you dare pretend that is not the reason you are here."

Tayeh grimaced. "The boy will need a tutor, someone more than you or I."

"Yes. But until then, there is much he can learn from his mother."

"Fine. Teach Eva, if she will let you."

"She will."

"Why so confident?" Tayeh asked.

"Because the dark is coming, and she is my warrior daughter."

# CHAPTER 1

# MILA

"KAILE BROUGHT a body back with him."

"What did you say?" Mila was not sure she had heard Simirri right.

"A body."

Mila stared at Simirri. "Whose body?"

"He didn't say. Where are you going?"

"To find Kaile."

The War Commander was not in the habit of bringing dead people home with him. It was beyond strange, but then, there were strange sightings and stirrings in the lands around the Keep. People from Barrowsby had gone missing. There were stories from other towns close to the Great Forest that made most huff in disbelief, but the stories made Mila's heart thrum with unease.

Mila found Kaile in the courtyard talking to Will. She paused; Kaile was a mess. His clothes were caked in dark brown blood. His face looked like he'd aged ten years in the four weeks he'd been gone, his handsome features sharp and creased. He waved Will away when he noticed her approaching.

"Kaile, what happened?" Mila asked, fingering his ruined tunic.

The fabric was beyond resurrecting. The little stags she had embroidered along his cuff were drowning in the dried blood.

Kaile rubbed his hand down his face. "I need a drink and clean clothes. Come with me?"

It was a long walk up to the Lord of the Keep's chambers. Mila followed Kaile in silence. She didn't feel right asking courtesy questions about his time in Caer Andri, or teasing him about Simirri—not when his disturbing story hung between them untold.

Inside his chambers, Kaile poured them each a drink from his bottle of potent fire-wine. He took a long swig with an appreciative grimace before pulling off his blood-encrusted tunic.

"For the love of little green apples …" He sighed, looking at the blood from a new angle. "What a mess."

"Are you going to tell me what happened?" Mila took a sip of her drink. It warmed her throat and belly.

"Darryl and I rode ahead as scouts. We were attacked."

"Is he all right?"

Kaile nodded, sitting down in the chair opposite her with the grace of an ox. "Do you remember, long ago, when Tarran and Murryn were kids, they were attacked in the forest? I wasn't at the Keep then, but Eva told me about it."

"Of course, I remember." Mila would never forget the marks on her sister's hands, and the nightmares that followed. Or Tarran's remarkable recovery, thanks to Eva's magic. Mila had an idea where Kaile was going with his tale, and why he had wanted to discuss it with her in private with a strong drink to take off the edge. "This attack—you think magic was involved." There, Mila said it.

"The thing that attacked us was not entirely human."

Mila recalled Simirri had said "body," not man.

"I am hoping you can have a look at—at the body. You could tell me if it is one of—"

*Don't say it, Kaile.*

"—your kind."

He said it. Mila's gut squirmed like a thousand maggots had hatched inside her.

"I will look. But I can't imagine I will have answers for you."

Kaile nodded. "I know. Thank you."

The silence between them felt like the inside of a storm. There was more. She could see it in Kaile's drawn expression. His anger and fear greeted her nose like a perfume.

"I am sending Irri with a team to investigate the towns along the Great Forest," he said.

"Not Tarran?"

"No, not Tarran." Kaile met her eyes, hearing her unspoken question. "I cannot trust Tarran."

Mila's drink was suddenly heavy in her hand. "What happened?"

Kaile shook his head. "Nothing in particular. I just don't feel like I can trust him. He and Caeris are—I don't know what I am trying to say." He glanced at the closed door. "I am sorry. I know he and Murryn are ... involved." The word fell short of what Murryn and Tarran were. "Mostly it's just a feeling. But—" Kaile faltered.

"I know. Tarran has a good heart. But he is ... lost."

Kaile's face twisted in agreement. His brow pinched.

"What else is the matter, Kaile?"

"Serac is here, Mila."

Mila's heart jumped into a cold, dark cave.

"Don't worry. He can't hurt you. I won't let him hurt you." Kaile's steady gaze begged her to believe him.

"Thank you for that, Kaile."

Once, she had been the master of her secrets. She had kept them all hidden and locked away. From Murryn. From Eva. From everyone—Kaile being the single exception. Now, Mila felt like the deeper and thicker her secrets became, the harder it was to keep them tidy and contained. Perhaps someday her secrets would spill out, and the people of the Keep would chase her into the Great Forest with pitchforks. The Great Forest was a place of hidden things and forbidden magic—where else would a shape-shifter belong?

"Did you show Serac this?" Mila asked. The room was dim; one of the torches had guttered. She could see perfectly fine—a gift from her oldest secret.

The body was laid on a shroud, naked, bruised. There was a puncture on his sternum where Kaile had landed the killing blow. Mila covered her mouth with her hand. "He looks like a man," she said.

"When he died, the otherness left him. And no, I have not shown Serac."

"You know the Goddess requires any hint of magic reported to her Temple Master."

"How could I forget?" Kaile drawled. "I would have thought the strangeness was a figment of my imagination, but for Eva's tale—and yours." Kaile couldn't keep a slight smile from curling his lip.

"Is something amusing, Kaile?"

"No. Of course not. Just remembering fairer times …" But his smile grew even with the dead body before them and death creeping in from the shadows. Kaile's reckless good humor was what endeared him to Mila. She smacked his shoulder.

Fairer times indeed. Kaile had been an enjoyable lover, and he made her laugh, but that had never been enough for her. And Kaile didn't want a wife, or even a partner; he just wanted to have fun. Maybe it had been the wine or Kaile's good heart, but really, she had just wanted to tell *someone*. So she told him all her secrets. Secret one: her past as a rent girl. Secret two: Serac, her patron, had left her for dead. Secret three: Eva had rescued her and saved her life with magic. Secret four: that Mila was descended from the *velidar.* Secret five: she could turn into a wolf.

"Show me," Kaile had asked with that charming smile of his.

"I can't," Mila had replied. "My magic is … broken—you don't believe me."

"I do. I do believe you. You are magic, Mila. You don't have to prove it to me."

Kaile was such a flirt. But he had believed her. And he had kept her secrets.

Mila inhaled. She could smell old blood. Death. Violence. Fear. And, yes, magic, but not her kind of magic. The trace was faint. Kaile put his hand on her shoulder. His touch was reassuring, as he intended.

"I don't know what this is, Kaile. It does not smell like the magic of the Great Forest."

Kaile nodded, looking down at his feet.

"Are you going to keep this from Serac?" she asked.

"I haven't decided yet."

"I wish I could be of more help."

"Mila, without you, the Keep would fall to pieces."

"You know what I mean, War Commander."

# CHAPTER 2

# COTOCH

*Cotoch …*

The *varing* pulsed with Imal's call, but Cotoch ignored it.

He leaned on the stone walls of his tower, the only vantage point in Mahlas he could see the land and the town sprawling beyond. The wind whipped with the nagging persistence of an old crone. With the winter ice melted, the smell of the marshes that hemmed the lake was substantial; the ground of the Tarm was thawing and saturated, making the mud reign supreme. The grass remained brown and lifeless, but a few days of warm spring sun would turn the valley plain a green so bright, it would hurt his eyes.

His attention flitted to his city. Mahlas bustled with spring business. The smithy was alive with the drumbeats of hammers and tongs, smoke billowing into the air from the forge. A few women walked beside a mule-led wagon filled with wool newly shorn. But it seemed small to Cotoch. Paltry. Insufficient. He was the bird longing to fly and stretch his wings and feel the world move under his gaze. And Mahlas was his cage.

The wind died. A silence enveloped Cotoch, broken only by the sound of wings. Speaking of birds …

"What are you doing here?" Cotoch asked through gritted teeth.

Crea stood beside him, her black wings arching like a gate to the underworld. She followed his gaze out over Mahlas and the Tarm.

"I told you not to come back," he growled at the spirit woman.

"Cotoch—"

"No, Crea. One year has not changed my mind. Our alliance is over."

"But, Cotoch …" There was honey in her voice. Honey that might have once swayed the hearts—or at least the lusts—of men. But Crea was a spirit. Her influence was a joke. Cotoch had been a fool to believe her promises.

Cotoch turned to face her, wondering if his anger would quell her. These days, his anger was a living beast he had yet to tame. "You failed to deliver on your promise. You encouraged me to use the *varing*, knowing what would happen."

"I did not tell you to torture and kill your wife," Crea said in a bitter voice.

"You don't want me sitting on Kitarra's throne. All you want is chaos."

A light flickered in the woman's eyes. "Cotoch, I can teach you—"

"No. You lost your chance. I have my own army and my cousin's men. I don't need your help. I don't need Kitarra."

Finally, she seemed to sense his sincere hatred. She shifted her shoulders, her black wings stretching.

"You will regret not choosing me, Cotoch," she said. "Here, a parting gift." He instinctively caught the small token she tossed him.

"I doubt it," Cotoch muttered to himself, looking down at the trinket—a round piece of metal with bits of faded ribbons clinging to it. It looked ancient.

"Do you remember your mother, Cotoch?" Crea asked.

"No," Cotoch heard himself answer.

"Pity. She was a strong woman. For a slave."

Cotoch wished he could drive a dagger through Crea's heart. Then he would be rid of her. But one cannot kill a Guardian, a fucking echo.

"My father killed my mother."

"Is that what you think?" Crea crooned. "He loved her, in his way."

"How can you know that?"

"I am a Guardian." Her teeth stretched across her face. If birds could grin, that's what they would look like.

"What is this?" he asked, turning the trinket over in his hand.

"It belonged to your mother. It is her past. Her history. Your history."

"Why would I want to know her history? I never knew her."

Crea shrugged. "We are the sum of our history—our parents' legacy." And then she flickered into nothing, a shadow lost in the wind. Air rushed into Cotoch's ears along with the calls of his cousin.

*Cotoch ...*

He really needed to answer Imal.

"Sir?"

Cotoch spun to see his captain.

"What is it, Easra?"

"A messenger has arrived from Allati," Easra told him. "He is waiting to speak with you."

"Excellent." The token cut into his palm as he squeezed it. He put it in his pocket.

Cotoch's chamber was dim compared to bright, sunlit Tarm, but it didn't take long for his eyes to adjust. The man waiting to speak to him was dressed in the Allati style, long tunic matched with fitted leggings, all garishly decorated with embroidery and beading. The Allati liked to indulge themselves. Fine clothes. Lavish houses. Hordes of women.

"This is Lord Wilkim, son of Lord Tull."

The man stepped forward as Easra introduced him. He bowed to Cotoch, smiling nervously as he spoke. "King Ottella would welcome a visit from the Lord of Mahlas. He very much looks forward to discussing an alliance."

Cotoch smiled but did not feel the rush of excitement such a pronouncement should have brought. An alliance with the monarchy of Allati would be a great victory. It was what he had been hoping for since his visit the previous fall. But he felt nothing. "Thank you. That is most generous of your king. I look forward to meeting him again—"

*Cotoch. Answer me.*

"Thank you, Lord Wilkim. Easra, see to his comfort," Cotoch said rather quickly, waving the two men out of his chamber.

*Cotoch, you son of a bitch, where are you?*

The inaudible call made Cotoch's ears itch. He needed to answer Imal or everything might fall apart, well-laid plans or not. Whatever he did, he could not induce Imal's rage. He was not strong enough to withstand being the focal point of his cousin's sorcerer magic. Cotoch had lost too much in his folly, in his blind grasp for magic and power. He had had his heart's desire in his hands, and he had lost it.

Eva.

Illiah had Eva. Illiah had Kitarra. Illiah had a child destined for greatness. For power. The Kitarrans spoke of the child like a demigod, birthed from divinity. Foolish, of course. But even the Allati whispered jealously about Rhyl, the stolen prince. The Promised Prince. What a way for a child to grow up. He would be spoiled and insolent and likely unable to accomplish the most basic tasks. The Kitarrans would make him into a fool. Heroes were not forged in the laps of their mothers and the riches of their realm.

The little token was heavy in his pocket. He pulled it out, turning it over, then placed it in his drawer along with his stash of culla.

Cotoch locked his chamber door before opening the secret entrance to the crypts. There were other entrances to the tunnels below his house, all of them secret. His secret. But he had never been the master of the dark. He had merely been a tool, a vessel. Once, he had thought he understood the *varing*, the dark magic, but now he wasn't sure he ever did. Once, he had thought of himself as a great sorcerer; now he felt more like a pawn.

In the dark, Cotoch clutched the amulet in his palm. The magic vibrated along the hard sinews of his hand. As his only reassurance in a world of fickle, rebellious magic, he wore it always. The amulet made things clearer, made the magic almost visible. Perhaps if he had known the power of the amulet sooner, he would not have lost the *varing*. Now he needed the amulet, and her, to harness the *varing*.

"Where are you?" Cotoch spoke into the foggy, damp dark.

"Here." The voice was forced, pulled by the magic in the amulet that was Cotoch's only hope to regain the future of his dreams.

"I need more."

"There is no more."

"You lie."

Cotoch waited. His patience was not legendary. He squeezed the amulet with his mind, using it as a rope to draw the magic of the crypts to him. A shape appeared out of the dark. He held out his arm and felt the creature put her hand in his, a hand that felt like tree bark, dry, flaking, and fissured, not like proper skin at all. But it didn't matter. He closed his ears to the whine of pain that sounded more like trees bent in the wind than a living creature, a sound so far from human that it did not stir Cotoch's nightmares to life.

Cotoch felt the *varing* fill his mind, almost the same as it had before that day just over a year ago. The *varing* pulled from the old spirit's pain was slightly different from when taken from a mortal. But it worked. Cotoch's arms tingled with it. His mind saw things his eyes did not.

"That wasn't so hard, was it?" he said.

But the creature had retreated; the whining did not stop.

"Cotoch. You took a very long time to contact me." Imal's face was smiling, but Cotoch knew his cousin was not amused. Imal's rage was separated from his amusement by spider silk, a tenuous and invisible line.

Cotoch had no excuses to offer him. He would not admit weakness. He would never admit that he had lost control of the *varing*, and now his only access to his *candarii* magic was through a strange spirit creature who had been trapped in the crypts below his house for who knew how long. He could not tell his cousin how torture gave him nightmares that stole his courage and nearly his mind.

"Imal. What do you want?" No need for pleasantries.

"I want a man," Imal said with relish. "He is familiar to you, I believe. His removal from Kitarra would benefit both of us."

"Why do you need one particular man? Do you not have enough of them in Rodan to choose from?"

Imal did not appreciate flippancy. Cotoch didn't really care.

"Get me this man, and I will teach you how to use magic to create an army. Not just any army, an army that is under your complete and utter control. I will teach you how to take the will of any man and bend it to your own."

Cotoch was holding his breath and let it out slowly, careful not to let Imal see how intrigued he was. He knew Imal had control of the *daeum*—his army of monsters—in a manner Cotoch had only tasted. Yes, Cotoch had loyalty, but it was hard bought. Stone came to mind. Yes, the Kitarran had returned. Yes, he had succumbed to his addiction and was basically a slave once more, but still, Cotoch could—would—only trust Stone so far. To have an army under his absolute control would make his alliance with Allati very interesting indeed. He remembered how he had felt to control Eva. How it made his blood sing. It was something he would never forget. Still, he wasn't sure he was strong enough to use the *varing* the way Imal did.

"It would take a great deal of effort to find and then pluck one man from inside Kitarra. Kitarra is wise to me now."

"Yes, your greed for that woman led you to reveal your true plans." Imal was not wrong.

"The Kitarrans only know a little. They have no idea you and I are allies, much less kin," Cotoch said, trying to patch up his confidence.

"Are you sure? I have been learning a little about your Praedan magics—there are others who can see. These san-arr-i."

"Even if they knew everything, what can they do? I have an army that can easily match any force they throw at me."

"So, you will get me this man?"

"I can not promise."

Imal gave a long, drawn-out sigh, like a wistful, hungry dragon. "Do not forget, Cotoch, that my army of *daeum* is stronger than a rock-slide. You have seen what my army did to the Kitarran Isles. And it is not so very far between Rodan and Mahlas. You would feed my magic as easily as this man. You are my kin, so it would please me less … but …"

Imal let the threat hang heavy in the magic between them. Cotoch felt his loathing slide down his back and vibrate into his stomach.

"Give me one month."

"Done."

# MILA

IN HER SHOCK, Mila almost dropped her bundle of laundered clothes onto the dirty floor.

"Murryn! What in the name of the Guardians are you doing?"

Mila's sister sat surrounded by a carpet of red shavings that had once been her hair. What was left on her head was roughly cut, obviously with little thought. Murryn sat calmly surrounded by shreds and tatters, reading a piece of parchment. She lifted her eyes just enough to meet Mila's. Not a flicker of emotion betrayed Murryn's motives.

"Your hair," Mila wailed, stepping into their shared room. "Your lovely hair! If you wanted it short, why didn't you ask me to cut it? You look—"

"I found this in Tarran's room," Murryn said, ignoring Mila's indignation, waving the well-worn parchment at Mila.

Mila sighed. Murryn had been unpredictable of late. Volatile almost. And it was just hair. Beautiful, fiery hair that Mila had combed and dressed with love and care countless times.

"When did you sneak into Tarran's room? Actually—don't tell me."

"How do you do it, Mila?"

"Do what?"

"Keep everything inside so tidy. You keep your anger and hurts so hidden. Even when Illiah and Rhyl were taken—and later when Eva went missing—you were so calm. I want to set everything on fire."

Mila didn't know how to reply. "Practice?" Mila offered lightly.

Murryn glared at her. "Not funny. I am serious. I feel like I am being ripped apart."

"We all suffer grief in our own way, Murryn. Lindin puts his into training the recruits, Kaile into his responsibilities as War Commander. I have put mine into my work, in memory of Illiah and Rhyl—and Eva." Their names caught in Mila's throat. Every. Time. Brave Illiah. Dear little Rhyl. Eva, whose descent into madness caused Mila's heart to contract with guilt. Murryn's heart was broken by her lover; Mila's was broken by her own failings. She had failed Eva.

Mila rubbed her tears from her face with her sleeve. Sometimes her guilt leaked out of her eyes.

"I'm sorry, Mila," Murryn muttered.

In reply, Mila wrapped her arms around her sister, remembering the little slip of a girl she had been. Now Murryn was a warrior, her delicate muscles hard.

"I wish—never mind," Murryn said with a sniff of her own.

"What is that?" Mila gestured to the old letter.

Murryn handed Mila the note, her eyes still deadpan.

Mila took the note, recognizing Eva's handwriting. Cold fingers of regret constricted her heart. The letter was addressed to Tarran. There was no date. The parchment had deep folds caused by countless refolding.

*Tarran,*

*Your heart is hurting. This is not you. You are more than your revenge—so much more. I am leaving you this because I love you. And Illiah loves you. You will see us again. Caeris will not listen to me, no one wants to listen to me, but know they are alive, Tarran. I have seen them, and I know it in my heart. Kitarrans took them for reasons I do not fully understand. I am going to Kitarra to find them. Don't forget who you are, who you are meant to be.*

*Love always,*

*Eva*

Mila rubbed her cheek to find it wet once more. She gave the letter back to Murryn. Eva's words were full of Mila's hopes and dreams. Precious, fragile things that withered in the slightest chill. Mila had always known Eva had left for Kitarra. But Eva had left in the dead of winter. The mountains had been shrouded by snow and everything had been frozen. How could she have survived the journey? Everyone knew the Midlands were dangerous. Everyone said Eva was dead. Yes, Mila knew Eva had her magic and had trained as a warrior, but she was a woman, and Mila knew how susceptible her gender was to the power of men. Whatever might have befallen Eva was the stuff of nightmares.

Eva must have written the note shortly before her departure. She had been half mad, her belief that Illiah and Rhyl were alive some fiction created from her desperate desires and grief. It could not be the truth. Caeris and Kaile and others had seen the bodies. Illiah and Rhyl were dead. And how could a wife and mother lose her family without going mad?

"This letter made you cut your hair?"

Murryn shrugged.

"How is Tarran? Did you speak to him?" Mila asked.

Murryn gave a little nod. "He is different. I mean, he has been different since they were taken, but he is different again. Resolved, I think. He won't tell me, but it is as if he stands on the edge of a knife, always tense, always worried, always guilty."

"I think we all feel guilty about what happened," Mila said quietly. That day flashed in her mind with great clarity. She could still remember every detail of the Kitarrans' armor, their strange catlike features, long ears and tails and furred bodies. Even their voices. Little Rhyl clinging to his father, unafraid. Illiah looking into Mila's eyes with his last fateful message to his wife. *Tell her I love her.* But Mila never got the chance to tell Eva. Eva sunk into madness and grief, and nothing could console her. She became a ghost, unrecognizable. And then, like her dead family, she had disappeared, her tracks obscured by the falling snow.

"Yes," Murryn agreed, flicking a fallen lock of red hair from her shoulder. "But this is different. He feels guilty about what happened after."

"He told you this?" Mila asked, hopeful for her sister's sake. Murryn loved Tarran, and had been devastated when Tarran left to follow the king to Caer Andri. Murryn had wanted to follow him, but Tarran forbid her. Murryn was a determined woman. Tarran had said terrible things to make her stay behind. Mila did not believe for a moment that Tarran was indifferent toward Murryn. Tarran's heart was in his eyes when he looked at Murryn. Whatever Tarran's reasons for driving a wedge between himself and the woman he loved, he believed it was for the best.

"No. But I sense it," Murryn said.

"Oh, Murryn. Maybe you should let him go—"

"No." The word dropped like a stone. "I will not give up on him."

After a moment, Mila said, "Let me fix your hair. You look like a poorly shorn sheep. Or possibly a dog with mange."

Murryn said nothing but nodded, suddenly more like the girl barely entered into womanhood that she was. In many ways, Murryn was so fragile, innocent. At her age, Mila's innocence had been flayed from her soul like skin from a traitor. Relatively, a broken heart was not the worst thing Murryn could experience.

"Lord Serac is here," Murryn said quietly as Mila made a few decisive snips at what was left of Murryn's poor hair.

Mila waited. "I know. Kaile told me."

"I know what Serac did to you."

"How?" Mila had told no one, except Eva, and later Kaile. Murryn had been young and afraid; Mila hid as much of her painful truth from her sister as possible. Before, because Murryn was a child. And later, because Murryn could best almost any of the royal guards in single combat. With a temper like a summer squall, and twice as impulsive, Mila could not trust Murryn not to seek out revenge.

"Tarran told me."

Mila should have known. Tarran had been Illiah's spy, even as a boy. Illiah had known about Serac and trusted Tarran implicitly; it made sense that he would know.

"If he touches you, I will kill him." Murryn's voice was calm and sure.

"Murryn, it would be the death of you," Mila hissed. She did not doubt her sister's skill or her resolve. Both were qualities Murryn possessed inherently. "Caeris will execute you as a traitor if you touch Serac."

"If he can catch me," Murryn whispered.

Mila said nothing. She continued to work, making the most of Murryn's remaining fiery wisps.

"You look like a boy," Mila said when she had finished.

"Well, I never did get a figure like you," Murryn remarked smugly. Mila smiled. What Murryn would do with a pair of ample breasts, Mila did not want to contemplate. She would likely bind herself flat so her curves would not interfere with her fighting.

"Do you think they could be alive?" Mila mused. "Do you think Eva could get to Kitarra alone?"

"I don't know. We all know Eva was mad to attempt the journey in winter. But why did the Kitarrans do it?" Murryn pondered, not for the first time. "They never gave any reason. None at all. It never did make sense."

Mila agreed, but then she was not a strategist nor a warrior. She knew nothing of political maneuvering. She knew nothing about Kitarra. She wanted desperately for her friends to be alive, even if it meant they were prisoners in a faraway land, ruled by a strange race and a strange queen. If they were together, Mila knew they would be happy.

# CHAPTER 4

# ILLIAH

THE RAIN MADE THINGS DIFFICULT. A creek ran down Illiah's face. It was as if a river in the sky had burst its banks and flooded all of Kilev, drowning the very air he breathed. It was a rain to drown all rains. A rain to wash the streets of Kilev away like melting clay. It was a rain to turn his skin soggy and fingers stiff.

He wiped the wetness away with his sleeve, a pointless exercise because his sleeve was already soaked through. He needed to find shelter. Soon the dry bits beneath his cloak would surrender to the onslaught. Wet would slow him down, but it would cripple the girl. She was a thin, frail creature. And they had to keep moving.

Illiah turned to his ward, taking her arm, pulling her closer. Her small frame tucked into the meager warmth of her cloak like a snail into its shell. He gestured for her to stay close as he guided them along the dark street toward an overhang. The rain beat the cobbles like a drum, pummeling the earth with a vengeance. The deafening sound would hide the sound of their boots, but it hid the sound of approaching enemies.

The curtain of rain took all the remaining color from the night. Every flickering light was smothered in the living cloud that enveloped Kilev like a death shroud. But, at least what would hamper Illiah would hamper those following them. That also meant what helped him would help the enemy as well. Overhangs were safe—they were good hiding places—but they were obvious hiding places. Being obvious led to failure. The trick was to be both clever and practical, but not predictable.

Illiah strained his eyes, looking for movement, anything out of the ordinary. One of the houses along the streets opened its door. The light escaping from inside blinded Illiah briefly. He pulled the girl after him and ducked into an alley. If anyone had been watching, the light might have given them away. And Illiah assumed there were eyes everywhere.

A whoosh, the slight contrast in sounds, was all the warning Illiah had. His ward could not yell out a warning; that was not allowed. Illiah spun, drawing his latha. A shadowy figure came at him, exposed by the wet glinting blade in his hands. Then another. Two—no, four people circled them in the dark. An archer could be on the roof. Illiah pushed the girl back into the shadows behind an overflowing rain barrel. He twisted his hand on his latha, gripping hard against the wet, slippery handle.

Illiah was almost blind against the rain and the night. The attackers would be too. Illiah engaged his latha. But the blade did not extend when he flicked it open. He had no time to ponder the malfunction. He had practiced for this—a latha was designed to be an implement of death even if the blade would not open. It required a different technique to fight with a closed latha, but Illiah had practiced with that as well. The men came at him. Four men against one, and with a broken weapon at that. In his mind, Illiah heard a lament for his vercuri, his magical dagger that gave him enhanced speed and strength, but he shushed his longing and got to work. And besides, he had yet to meet a Kitarran who could best him. But four?

Illiah was not aiming to kill, just incapacitate. Knees. Gut. Groin. No, not the groin first—too obvious, predictable. Wrists. Wrists were good. Illiah focused on each, deflecting the blows directed at him until he could reach the weak spots. The first man was down already—Illiah had high-kicked him in the collar bone. He heard it snap. He brought his latha down on one opponent's knee, hearing a roar of pain. Illiah cringed. The other two looked less convicted in their attack. Their hands went up.

"Yield," they said in unison.

Illiah grabbed the girl's hand, pulling her deeper into the alley. Apparently, Illiah was not as familiar with Kilev as he had believed. Damn. Dawn was only an hour away.

*Don't be obvious, Illiah.*

The alley ended, but the roofs had wide overhangs, and Illiah felt confident that no one could see their location from the above. Illiah turned a few door handles, finally finding one that was unlocked. He was surprised that so many locked their doors in Kilev. Or was it this night? Because they knew he was trying to escape?

The building they entered was dark. Inside, the absence of the rain was like a cloak over his ears. His sound of his breath, and hers, was a rasp over metal. Their footsteps were crashing boulders. Illiah had one hand around the girl's and one on his latha as they went deeper into the building, which appeared to be abandoned, an old warehouse, perhaps. The next room was two floors high, with tall shuttered windows that let in what little light was to be had on a dark, stormy night.

Illiah found a corner and settled the girl into it.

"Are you okay?" he asked, reaching into his pack for his tinder box. As he lit a small light, he could see her face outlined in shadows. She looked fine. Curious, but still mute. Illiah set the little lamp down on the uneven, dusty wood floor. Next, he reached into his pack for his repair kit, laying it out carefully, but with urgency. In the dim light, he did his best to inspect his latha. Even broken, it was still a fine weapon. Intact, it was a force.

The mechanism was bent. Illiah grinned ferociously. Sabotage. It had to be. He always put his latha away in perfect condition. He wondered who had done it. Aisha? Mehmet? The queen herself? He couldn't think of anyone who could get close enough to his weapon. Selene? Unlikely. The queen's maid didn't have it in her to be a conspirator.

The girl watched him as he tinkered with the bent metal. It was also missing a pin, but he had several spares in his kit, a simple fix. Illiah stood, swinging the blades into the locking position. The resounding click was intensely satisfying. Illiah gave a flick, and the mechanism clicked, sending the blades into the resting position once more. Illiah tried it again. Blades out. Click. Flick. Blades in. And repeat. Each click was a victory.

"Onward," Illiah told his ward. She nodded, taking his hand.

When they exited the building, Illiah took a moment to get his bearings. A moment that included climbing up a tall wall to see the lay of the city below them. The light from the street lamps was streaky from the rain, but still gave some indication of the main roads. And Kilev, being built on a hill, meant that most places of height gave him a view of the city below. He hopped down, feeling energized that they were slowly making their way toward the docks and the boat waiting for them. The rain had even let up, now more a drenching mist than torrential waterfall.

The girl was much shorter than Illiah, forcing him to slow his pace. The alley opened up into a larger street, and Illiah realized his mistake. Too much space. Their shadows would be beacons against the cobbles. Illiah decided to turn around, head back the way they came, find a darker route. They had time.

It was fortunate that he turned; a few paces behind him loomed a man-shaped shadow. Illiah drew his latha and charged. The man sidestepped, ducking the blow. Illiah still managed to knock the man's sword from his hand. Easy. Except there were more of them. Several more shadows appeared from the alley. The girl yelped. Illiah spun. The first attacker raised a long dagger.

Illiah pushed the girl away from the melee, hoping the men would not snatch her. They didn't even notice her. They were intent on Illiah, circling him like slavering hounds. Illiah grinned. He had prepared for this kind of fight. He was not afraid of them.

Against his latha and his long reach, the men couldn't get near him.

"Yield!" Illiah hissed at them. They paused. "Yield!" he demanded again.

One man had lost his hood in his attack. Illiah did not recognize him, which struck him as odd. He thought he knew every one of the Peace Guards' faces.

Almost as one, the men backed away and fled.

It was intensely satisfying to watch them flee, but it wasn't over. He couldn't afford to grow comfortable or overconfident. How many times had he lectured vigilance? He needed to heed his own dogma.

More shadows appeared at the top of the alley. Illiah grabbed the girl's hand and ran. So much for dark alleys and discretion. He burst into the courtyard, discarding his secrecy. The strategy was no longer going to help them. He pushed the girl behind him once again and stood in the center of the courtyard.

He wondered if it was the same group of men—but no, he counted five. Two were Kitarrans, easily determined by their lofty height and pointed ears and swaying tails. With their superior night vision and agility, the Kitarrans would be the challenge.

Illiah raised his latha once again, and they came at him. He was fast. Even with the Kitarrans' superior senses and speed, he was still a match for them. They were playing with him, taking their time, not attacking all at once, his saving grace. His latha hissed in the night air. The rain had stopped, but the stones were still slippery. Illiah used it to his advantage, pushing his opponents faster and faster, making them stumble and slip. It worked—two men fell. Hard. Illiah would have laughed in triumph if his lungs weren't burning from exertion.

Illiah struck one Kitarran on the arm. The Kitarran fell to his knees, his long ears pressed back, his hands raised to yield, but Illiah was already facing the second Kitarran, the last of the group still fighting. Illiah struggled to keep his breath even in his ragged lungs, hoping his opponent did not see how fatigued he was. Illiah gripped his latha in both hands, holding it horizontally, punching end over end to break the Kitarran's defense. He couldn't block the speed of Illiah's attack. With a cut across his furred face, the Kitarran yielded.

Illiah wasted no time; he grabbed the girl and hurried into the night. Even as he did, he heard the long, mellow note of their pursuers' whistle, signaling to the rest of their group. Soon they would converge. Illiah and the girl needed to get to the docks. In their haste, she stumbled and rolled her foot. Illiah sheathed his latha and scooped her up. She didn't weigh much.

Illiah ran as fast as he could while carrying the girl who grew heavier with each street they crossed and each alley they passed. The streets of Kilev were slowly sloping toward the river. Illiah could feel his momentum increasing. He had to be careful, or he would drop and further injure the girl.

The quiet waves of the Ilba River glittered before them with the faint lantern light from the city. The sound of their gentle rhythm gave him hope. He put the girl down, tucking his arm under her shoulder. Illiah was thankful he knew the docks well; a stranger would see the maze of ships and wharves, and despair.

The boat rocked gently in its berth along dock number twenty-four. Everything was quiet. All Illiah could hear was the gentle lapping of the river against the sleeping boats and the solid piers. The wind had picked up. Small whitecaps were visible on the river in the faint light. Dawn was coming.

The girl made to get on the boat, but Illiah put out his hand to stop her.

"Wait," he whispered, knowing sound traveled over water like sunlight.

He took a jump-step onto the rocking boat, taking a moment to train his balance to the uneven footing. Sure enough, three figures convalesced from the small hold. Their blades flashed. A trap. Illiah had expected it. He had to be fast. Which is why even as he assessed, he was striking. Hard. He used the momentum of the rocking boat to his advantage, amplifying it with his own. He struck, aiming with his latha, but used his foot at the last minute to confuse his opponent, sending him into the murky water. The other two he cornered into the bow. One tripped and hit his ribs on the railing. The other put up his hands—her hands. She took off her hood, her gray pointed ears twitching. She bowed her head in submission.

"Kura," Illiah said, bowing his head. The queen's guard smiled slowly.

"Well done, Illiah."

"Thank you."

Illiah's young ward came up behind him, grinning, clapping her hands.

"Shall we go tell the queen that you passed your iudarii trial?" Kura asked, her toothy smile bright in the predawn light.

"The queen? Let's go tell my wife," Illiah countered with a grin, sliding his latha into the sheath at his back.

# CHAPTER 5

# ILLIAH

ILLIAH WAS SORE. And tired. But somehow it was easy to ignore those things because he had passed his iudarii trial.

There had been whispers about how disgraceful it was that the First Defender of Kitarra had not taken the trial. He tried to ignore how it rankled him. But it was true. He was a foreigner in a position usually held by a person who had proven himself—or herself—worthy.

Queen Arrah scoffed and told him he had proven himself worthy of the position many times over and to stop pouting like a youth with an itch to scratch. Eva was no comfort to his hurt pride; her pregnancy had claimed any opinion she had on the matter. She had spent months too sick to contemplate Illiah's prickly self-confidence. Thankfully, her pregnancy sickness had passed as the twins grew. Twins. Illiah had an inkling raising twins would be the real trial.

Yes, Illiah had passed the iudarii. Without a vercuri. His name would join the long list engraved in the Peace Guard's Hall of those who had taken the trial and passed. He could not dismiss the warm glow of satisfaction. The pride. Kaile would tell him not to let it go to his head—by the Guardians, he did not miss many things about Jullayah, but he did miss his foster brother.

For almost two years, he had lived in Kitarra, more than half that time as First Defender, a position of power only preceded by the queen. He had the ability to send a message to Jullayah, but what would he say? Jullayans would call him a defector. His dear brother, the king, would command him to return home, and he would not go. He would not leave his son. And if he could return to Jullayah with Rhyl and Eva, would he? The Kitarrans had kidnapped him and Rhyl, setting Eva on a quest that nearly killed her. The shadows of her journey shaded her eyes when she thought no one was looking. Illiah would kill Cotoch—someday—for raping Eva.

And still, after all that, Kitarra was his home.

What kind of logic was that?

Illiah's shoulder protested as he clenched his muscles. Must have been that hit from Kuni, the brute. He rolled his shoulders to loosen his muscles, chanting to himself that Cotoch's time would come.

After Illiah basked in the pride and affection of his wife and the queen, Eva told him to take a nap. He should be exhausted after spending the night awake, crawling through Kilev in the drenching rain, but his spirits were high. Sleep would not bow easily. Eva's advice was sensible, but instead, Illiah went to the infirmary to see the men and women who had sacrificed their skin for his pride.

It was an honor and a tradition, he was told, when the adversaries in the iudarii trial were injured, though mortally wounding an opponent would result in automatic failure and immediately stripped of any status. Any guilt Illiah felt for causing injury dissolved when he saw the beaming faces of those he had "vanquished." Mostly, the inflictions were scratches and cuts, bruises without a doubt—one broken collar bone. Fash was the one who took Illiah's latha on the face. Even with half his furry face covered in stitches, Fash was grinning so widely (albeit gingerly), Illiah had a feeling he would not hold a grudge.

"Someday, when you do your trial, I will be there to take your blade," Illiah told Fash, holding his hand over his heart.

"Oh no, my lord, you are not allowed—you fight mean," Diea proclaimed, holding a cool cloth to the cut on her arm.

"Really?" Illiah asked, slightly abashed.

"No. Not really. You were brilliant!" A round of cheers and whistles reverberated off the infirmary walls. Illiah noticed that most of those gathered were not injured; they were merely there to bask in the air of celebration and pride and camaraderie.

"Which of you were from the alley by Thirteenth Square?" Illiah asked. The attack at the Thirteenth Square had been a pathetic attempt. Illiah wanted to know if the men had been too timid to hurt him or just didn't have the skills—the latter Illiah felt needed to be discussed. Everyone looked at each other, their faces slightly mystified.

"The Thirteenth Square? Are you sure? I didn't think any of us went that route. Diea? You and Kura led the hunt."

"No, there was another group, before you. Three men," Illiah said.

"No. I led that attack. There were five of us," Vayn told him, gesturing to Fash and the others.

"Are you sure?" Illiah's gut clenched uncomfortably.

"Absolutely. Did someone else attack you? Someone not part of the trial?" Vayn glanced at Diea, his lips a thin line.

Illiah frowned. "Where is Clari?"

"With Juno." Diea rolled her eyes. "Clari!"

"Here." The young woman stepped forward from the dark corridor. She blushed, dropping Juno's hand. Illiah had not known the two were in a relationship. Wasn't Clari too young for Juno?

"Do you remember the men who attacked us in Thirteenth? The one with the dagger?" Illiah asked.

Clari nodded, her eyes darting around the room. She had yelled in warning, which was against the rules. "I think so. When you told them to yield, they ran away."

"Did you see any of their faces?"

"I did not." Clari frowned. "Who do you think they were? Could they have been sent to hurt you?"

Exclamations filtered through the room like a stink.

"No, wait," Clari insisted. "What better place would there be to attack Illiah than during a trial? The whole point of the trial is to fight at a disadvantage. And everyone knows you are not aiming to kill—another advantage for them."

Her sensible words slid like ice water down Illiah's spine. It made sense. Eva was going to be livid. Maybe he didn't need to tell her. But he looked around the room and knew that there would be no way to stop the rumors now. His soldiers were loyal, but they were young and liked to talk.

"Clari, I don't want to contemplate what else goes on in that mind of yours," Illiah said with a rueful smile. "But that theory makes a lot of sense. As distasteful as it is."

That had the attention of the room. Illiah's soldiers suddenly looked less like young men and women and more like the brutal killing force he was training them to be.

"You really think they were assassins?" Vayn asked what they were all thinking.

"I don't know. If they were assassins, they failed miserably. I was going to berate whoever it was for their lack of skill against a latha."

That made his soldiers laugh, as Illiah intended. "Do not worry," Illiah continued. "That is my job. Now, go fix yourselves up. The queen is celebrating tonight, and you are all invited."

They clapped. Fash gave a great hoot that stretched his stitches, making him groan, inciting more laughter from his fellow guards. Illiah grinned, despite the trickle of unease inching toward his heart.

When Illiah told Eva about the attack, she looked like she was going to vomit. He almost reached for a bowl. It had been a few weeks since she had last retched, but Illiah was not confident in her proclamation that the worst of her pregnancy sickness was behind her. She was carrying twins, after all. Illiah felt a tinge of guilt about that. Not that he was really to blame. It took two, as she liked to remind him.

"You all right?" he asked, still eyeing the bowl.

"No, I am not all right! You are saying someone tried to assassinate you. Clari is right; it was clever to do it during an iudarii trial. Everyone was expecting violence and shadowy villains on the streets of Kilev. And you would not know one attacker from another. If I wanted to kill you, I might try it on a night like that. It was so dark and rainy and awful." Pregnant Eva tended to prattle.

"You have thought about how you would assassinate me?" Illiah asked, trying to keep a smile from his lips. Pregnant Eva also glared at him. A lot. It amused him. Which was why it was so fun to antagonize her.

"I am now," she said, her voice full of prickles. Then her face softened. "I really don't like this. You should keep Ari with you."

"Hard not to." Illiah glanced over at his uandian, his loyal dog, who was close by watching him with dark amber eyes. Her ears twitched forward hopefully.

"Do you think it was Cotoch?"

Illiah sighed, a long, grating sound that made Eva's brows arch. "I don't know. Why now? He hasn't stirred for a year."

"Stone would tell me if he was planning something." Eva sounded so sure, Illiah's heart twinged as something vile rose like a beast within him. Jealousy and anger were not comfortable emotions. "How can you know what Stone is thinking and doing? He abandoned you, Eva. How long was he working for Cotoch before you saved him? Obviously, his allegiance is to that fiend, not to you."

Eva glared at him. This time, it was not amusing.

"He would tell me."

"How? How could he possibly send a message to you even if he had a mind to?"

"I don't know. I just know that he would try."

Illiah lowered his voice. "I don't understand how you can be so loyal to him after what he did."

"He didn't do anything."

"Exactly! He ran!"

"You can't know what he was feeling."

"True. But what kind of man runs from his son?"

"Illiah, please," Eva said, her eyes wet. Illiah had pushed too hard, said too much. He took her hand and squeezed it, thankful that she let him.

"If it wasn't Cotoch, who was it?" she asked.

Illiah was fairly certain it had been Cotoch's men. But for her sake, he said, "I don't know. I have people looking into it."

Eva's face was etched with her grief and sadness over her amourii. Illiah wrapped his arm around her, kissing her neck.

"I am sorry. I know you care about Stone."

Eva nodded but didn't speak. Illiah hated to see her cry. There was nothing he could do to stop her tears; every one was a shard of steel in his heart. Well, he could keep his mouth shut.

"I wish Tarek were here. I wonder what the Iron Wolves might have heard about Cotoch," Eva muttered.

Illiah agreed, but they hadn't seen or heard from Tarek since the previous autumn when he had appeared in Kitarra looking for Eva. Illiah had tried, and failed, to recruit Tarek and Elish. The nomadic life suited them; they had no interest in serving Kitarra, but they had promised to visit from time to time, as friends.

"Anyway, enough of this. I need to change. I can't wear this to the ceremony." Eva squirmed out of his arms. "Did you tell them?"

"No. I want to surprise them," Illiah said loud enough so she could hear him from her dressing room. A smile spread across his face at the thought of his young soldiers getting their official designations within the Peace Guard.

"The invitations went out to their families this morning. They will know soon enough. Lord Susor is arriving within the hour," Eva told him.

"He played it close."

"He doesn't like you," Eva all but shouted.

"Thanks for the reminder." Illiah felt slightly dreadful at the thought of talking to Lord Susor, Aisha's father. Susor was not pleased with the responsibilities Illiah had hoisted on his young son.

But Illiah had too few like Aisha—the young man was skilled, and a natural leader. The decision had been made as the First Defender. As a father, Illiah could understand Susor entirely. Rhyl was just a child. It was easy to forget Illiah would see him grow up to be a warrior. And not just any warrior—the warrior that would somehow save all of Kitarra from an evil they knew next to nothing about. Suddenly he didn't feel guilty or apprehensive about Susor's visit. The Lord of Withe had nothing on Illiah.

"Aisha will be happy he came," Eva said, her voice muffled by fabric. Illiah wondered if he should go help her dress, but likely she wouldn't appreciate his version of helping.

"Is that what you are wearing to the celebration?" Illiah asked as she reappeared.

"Why? Don't you like it?" Eva smiled, running her hands over the gauzy fabric and her bulging belly, her rounded breasts. Illiah pulled her next to him and kissed her. He ran his hands over her curves, feeling her lean into his touch.

"Shows a lot of skin," Illiah murmured against her exquisite neck.

"It's the Kitarran fashion."

"Yeah, but Kitarrans have fur! You do not," Illiah said, moving from her neck to her lips. She gave a little yelp when he squished her belly as he leaned against her.

"The babies don't like that."

"Excuses." Illiah sighed, smiling at her.

"My lord, my lady," Anfru, Eva's manservant, appeared at the door. Illiah really needed to have another talk with Anfru about knocking. "My lord, Turk is waiting in your study to see you. My lady, Lord Susor has arrived."

"Excellent. Help me finish dressing, Anfru, then I will go meet him," Eva said, but she smirked at Illiah. Illiah regretted that Eva had not asked for his help—but then that would likely have set the day back at least an hour. He sighed and went to find Turk.

Turk was grinning ear to furry ear. He clasped Illiah's hand in his great paw. "Congrats, Illiah. I hear you did exceptionally well in your trial. Bellah sends her regards."

"Thank you, my friend." Illiah found the warmth in his voice constrained as he told Turk about the assassins—or whatever they had been. Turk glowered.

"It must be Cotoch," Turk muttered. "The foul cur."

Illiah thumbed his bottom lip. "That was my first thought too, but …"

"But?"

"You have heard the rumors. Not all of Kitarra is happy with a foreigner as First Defender. And since Eva's arrival, her close relationship with the queen—you know what they whisper about us. They call us manipulators—conspirators against Kitarra."

Turk waved a dismissive hand. "Only a few. There are always those who harvest their bitter seeds so they can grow bitter plants. And I can't imagine they would ever act on their ideals. The people, your soldiers, they love you. And Eva. And Rhyl. Only a fool cannot see what you bring to Kitarra."

"Still. I would feel better if I knew who was behind this."

"You didn't see the men's faces at all?"

"I did, but there wasn't much to go on."

Turk nodded. "I will see what our birdies overhear. But in the meantime, doesn't the celebration start within the hour?"

Illiah noticed that Turk was dressed particularly well, his gray tunic hemmed with dark blue thread, his fur slicked back and combed.

"I suppose. But they can't really start without me, now can they?"

"Ha! Your wife will not thank you for making her stand longer than necessary with that cargo she is hauling around."

"Hey, don't call my unborn children cargo!"

"Don't you?" Turk countered with another laugh.

"That was just to irritate Eva," Illiah told his friend.

"Honestly, why that woman crossed the continent to return to you is beyond me," Turk teased.

"True love, mate," Illiah replied with a grin.

Turk shook his head with a laugh. "You two are a strange couple. You know that, right?"

"I do. We do."

Turk gave a great huff of laughter, slapped Illiah on the shoulder, and said, "Guardians help us if those twins have your sense of humor!"

CHAPTER 6

# MILA

MILA MANAGED to avoid Lord Serac for three days. But when Serac proclaimed a grand feast be held in honor of the Black Goddess, Mila, as Head Stewardess, could not avoid it without reflecting poorly on the War Commander. She hoped Serac would not recognize her. Maybe he wouldn't remember her at all.

But her optimism abandoned her as she sat in the great hall for a grand feast she could not avoid.

It was as if Serac had been waiting for her; his eyes found her the instant she walked into the room. On the curve of her neck. On her skin where her breasts swelled against the cut of her dress. In her soul. Serac had always been in her soul. All it took was his lingering look, his serpent's eyes consuming her, and she knew she would never be rid of him.

She needed to disappear. To fly. To run. For the first time since she was a child, she yearned to embrace the magic in her blood and take her other form. The yearning shocked her—where would she go? She had no other home, and she would not for her life abandon Murryn.

Murryn was absent from the feast. She and her cohort of friends were somewhere by the stables. No one would notice. Murryn was not the Head Stewardess. As a mere soldier, she had no obligation to attend.

As Mila sat and tried to eat, she told herself over and over that Serac could not hurt her. Kaile had vowed to keep her safe, to protect her. But seeing Serac in all his glorified power made it hard to imagine Kaile could do anything if Serac chose to hurt her. Even as War Commander, Kaile was subservient to Serac, the king's cousin and closest adviser and friend.

Fear rose real and putrid in Mila's gut. Something shrunk inside her—her courage perhaps. The truth was no one could protect Mila if Serac chose to claim her. Going against Serac was a death sentence.

A little part of Mila's mind called for logic and gave her hope, whispering that Serac was leaving the next day. One more day and he would be gone, back to Caer Andri.

The feast concluded without incident. Mila retreated, counting the hours until Serac's departure. She went to the stables to look for Murryn before heading up the many steps to her room. She was greeted cheerily by Murryn's friends. Pungent fumes wafted from the skins of stolen ale behind their backs. They told her Murryn had gone off to bed. Mila didn't mention anything about the pilfered ale, though she was tempted to, just to see the panic on their faces.

When Mila reached the top of the stairway, it was to discover that Murryn was not in their shared room. Mila frowned. But she was not her sister's keeper. Not anymore. Murryn was a grown woman who could best all of her male counterparts with any weapon she could get her hands on. Murryn could take care of herself.

Maybe Murryn had backed Tarran into some dark corner to confront him. Mila wasn't sure if Murryn was brave enough to do it. Or, more likely, if Tarran was brave enough to face her. Murryn was awfully competent with her daggers.

Mila dressed for bed and waited for Murryn, hoping her sister was taking care of her heart as well as her skin and not doing anything rash involving a particular young man. Tarran was in her thoughts as she lit a few candles and took out her embroidery. Kaile had brought her a box of beeswax candles, an expensive gift. She began a pattern of amber-colored foxes that would go nicely on Kaile's dark red tunic.

It was getting late, and Murryn had not yet come up.

The door creaked open. Mila thought she had locked it. She looked up from her needlepoint. Her tongue froze. Her body followed.

Serac closed the door behind him. The lock clicked home.

"My dear Mila, how I have missed you."

*Run,* her mind screamed. But there was nowhere to run.

*Change.* But exposing her magic to the Temple Master was incarcerating herself to a life at the Temple. And the dead space Serac's presence reopened in her soul almost swallowed her courage.

"And think how surprised I am to find you here? Working under the guise of Head Stewardess no less?" Serac didn't sound surprised, despite his words. But Serac had always been a snake, a manipulator.

Once, Serac had not been a monster. He had been the handsome nobleman who showed his favorite whore affection, brought her gifts, and made her believe that love could be found at the end of a coin. She had been so young—a beaten culla-addled whore looking for a prince to save her. In the end, she had been rescued by a princess, a woman, not a man. Memories of Eva's compassion gave Mila's courage a breath of life.

"I thought the culla would kill you in the end," he said.

"Well, it didn't. Now leave," Mila said, finding her tongue.

Serac almost smiled. A single brow raised in a familiar expression. It made Mila angry to see Illiah's face hiding in Serac's; how dare they be kin when Illiah had been good, kind, and brave, and Serac was a masochist.

"I am not going anywhere." Serac came toward her, his eyes, his body, full of intent.

"What do you want?" Mila knew what he wanted, but she needed to distract him.

"You were always the best, my favorite. So, tell me, Mila, what *do* I want?"

Mila put down her embroidery, her hands surprisingly steady. She forced herself to look up at him, cocking her head. She reclined on the bed, her back to the wall. Her heart rattled in her chest cavity, but she managed to attain a supine pose and began untying the laces of her night-dress.

Serac smiled, coming closer. "Once a whore, always a whore."

"I thought I loved you once, did you know that?" Mila said, keeping Serac's eyes on hers. He smiled, and for an instant, Mila saw the Serac she had first met, the young Temple Master, new to Caer Andri, new to his freedom, his dark eyes filled with something her younger self had thought might be heroic. But if that man had ever truly existed outside Mila's culla-induced fantasies, he had perished that night Mila had almost died.

Serac unlaced his tunic and lowered himself over her like a trap.

His breath felt like a blade on her neck. She put one hand on his cheek, tracing a finger down his throat, remembering with awful lucidness the places he liked to be touched. With her other hand, she reached under her pillow for her knife. Her fingers clawed with desperation but precision. She felt its handle, smooth and comforting. It had been a gift from Illiah to keep under her pillow—for sweet dreams, he'd told her.

To keep Serac distracted, she put her hand against the skin of his stomach. Where once his skin was smooth and muscular, she could feel the hard edge of multiple scars. He grabbed her wrist, stopping her from touching his mutilated skin. Fear laced through her gut. Her magic slipped. Her eyes began to shift. She could see beyond the dim light of her room. Beyond skin and feature, to the space between life and energy. She saw something writhing inside Serac's soul that made her lungs catch in revulsion. Evil and hate and despair traveled through his hand into hers. The physical feeling his magic invoked made her stomach roil. Tendrils of Serac's dark magic curled like smoke toward her, as if sensing her magic.

Mila told herself not to panic. Serac had never been aware of her magic, perhaps because the culla had all but extinguished it. She waited one heartbeat. Then another. But Serac didn't notice what was happening in the space around them where magic lived. He removed his shirt, his eyes flashing with anger and lust. Long-healed welts decorated his skin, ugly and cruel.

"A gift from Illiah—the cur," Serac said, following her gaze, his lips curling. "But now who is the victor? Illiah is dead."

Mila clutched the handle of her hidden dagger like a lifeline. Serac leaned down as if to kiss her. She would only have one chance. Long ago, Eva had given her a lesson on the weak points of the body. And Illiah had told her that if she ever had to use the dagger, not to hesitate. Hesitation would kill her.

With Illiah's and Eva's advice in her mind, Mila took all the force she could muster, using every hurt, every bit of anger, and slashed the knife up across Serac's throat, pushing deeper and deeper. The blood came faster and faster. It was a sharp knife. It did its job well. Too well. Serac's bloodless, lifeless body slumped onto her bed, pinning her legs. The tang of iron was thick in the air.

She was acutely aware of every point her body touched Serac's. The hot, damp blood soaked into her clothes, sticky and slick on her skin. But her heart was numb. Calm.

A knock came at her door.

Her heart changed course, trying to leap out of her chest.

She had just killed the king's last living kin. She was a traitor, a criminal. In other words, a dead woman.

There was no place in her small room to put a body. Gods, a body. The blood. It was all over her. Her hands and face were covered with it. Her clothes were drenched. The stains would never wash out.

"Who is it?" Mila's voice sounded unrealistically calm. How was that possible?

"It's Murryn. Is something wrong? Your voice sounds strange."

Not so calm, then.

Mila slithered out from under the dead man with speed enviable by an eel and unlatched the door with hands roughly cleaned on her linens. She opened the door a crack, looking out at her sister. Tarran was with her.

"Mila." Murryn was observant; she must have seen blood splattered on Mila's face. She pushed her way into the room. "Mila,

Mila, Mila!" Murryn looked at the body. The blood. Tarran was silent but closed the door quickly behind them, locking the three of them in the room with Mila's crime.

"He tried to—" Mila's voice came out as a sob she hadn't known was building inside her.

Tarran took her by her shoulders, looking into her eyes, rooting her. Something softened in Tarran's face, something good and warm.

"Don't concern yourself with him. He was a monster. We need to get out of here."

Murryn was already packing. Mila was missing something.

"Where are we going?"

"Kitarra." Tarran's eyes were less soft and filled with fiery determination.

# CHAPTER 7

# EVA

ILLIAH WAS ASLEEP. Eva sat up slowly, hoping he wouldn't wake. The sky, barely warming with the return of the sun's light, was just enough for her to make out the shape of Illiah tucked under the blankets.

Eva put her hand on his warm skin, wishing she could run her hand over his muscles and feel them tense under her caress. Her husband was strong in so many ways. She loved it when that strength was employed by holding her, fulfilling her. She bit her lip to stop herself. She didn't want to wake him—he needed to sleep. It had been a late night. All of Kilev had celebrated Illiah's successful *iudarii* trial and those promoted from trainees to Peace Guards. Illiah had been so happy.

Eva closed her eyes, finding the thread of the *simul rami* that linked her to Illiah. He would not wake when she touched him with her *sanarii* magic; she had done it before. Her heart lurched. The taint of *candarii* magic still grew and stretched inside Illiah's soul from when, almost a year ago, the *varing* had enthralled Illiah. Eva pushed her *sanarii* magic into that bit of darkness and covered it with her own light until it dissolved.

She opened her eyes. The taint was gone, for now. Illiah was still asleep, none the wiser. Secrets were vile things, but she could not tell him the *varing* kept returning to reside in his heart. Not when she could wash it away with her *sanarii* magic.

Eva rose, as silent and stealthy as she could be with her bulging, pregnant belly that made every movement awkward and ten times as difficult. Ari, Illiah's dog, woke as soon as Eva opened her eyes. Ari merely gave a little wag of her tail where she lay on the bed of furs. Talo's and Rhyl's uandians slept with them in their adjoining room and did not come to greet her. It was still early, even for Rhyl and Talo. Eva wrapped herself in her warmest robe and thickest slippers and embraced the quiet of the early morning as she made her way to the archives.

The quiet of the sleeping palace made Eva's ears itch, ears that were more accustomed to the shrieks and giggles of children than the hush of a room built of ancient stone.

The archives of Kitarra were a collection of glorious old rooms shrouded in tomb-like silence and forgotten mysteries, set against the mountain in the back corner of the Queen's Keep. But unlike a tomb, and Kilev had enough of those, the light came in gently through skylights designed to bring in enough light to make lanterns unnecessary but indirect as to not touch the precious manuscripts and scrolls. The archives were only usable during the day; Eva would never have the courage to bring a candle anywhere near the dry manuscripts.

The tall shelves were laden with scrolls and books and dust. A ladder wheeled around the room, allowing the peruser to access even the highest shelves. She eyed it wishfully, knowing if she needed something from the high shelves, she would need to enlist

Anfru. Her pregnancy affected her balance. Was there anything it did not affect?

The table in the center of the room was littered with her spoils—bits of enigmatic wisdom, scraps of archaic journals and records. Anything that mentioned magic. She settled into her place at the table and delved back into her study.

"I thought you would be here this morning while the rest of Kilev sleeps off its boisterous night," a voice came from behind her.

"Good morning, Anfru."

"I brought breakfast," he said, sliding a tray of warm food onto a small table close by; she didn't want food by the precious documents. "Don't forget to eat it."

"You are a marvel," Eva told him, but her attention was already focused on the records before her.

After a while, her bum began to twitch uncomfortably from her stillness. She shifted slightly. Her eyes moved from the old paper before her to the parchment beside her covered in her own scribbles. In the center she had written:

*Those who were strong are now weak,*
*With healing hands, the babes will speak*
*Light turns to dark and colors shift,*
*Two rivers join when two lovers rift,*
*Watch for the child of two thrones,*
*Born with magic in his bones,*
*A child lit by the stars,*
*Watch for him, for he shall be ours.*

The prophecy. Eva had studied those words until her eyes bled. Not literally, of course. But she had stared at it long enough that the shape and meaning of the words had disappeared to become nothing more than squiggles of ink. Very unhelpful squiggles.

*Those who were strong are now weak,*
*With healing hands, the babes will speak*

That part made sense. It spoke of the Kitarrans themselves, a race much diminished by the death of their babes, their inability to reproduce, and their high suicide rate. The two were not unrelated. But why so many Kitarran babes died was a mystery. The history of Kitarra was full of large families. Arrah's grandmother had been a child of eight, not uncommon a few generations ago. But something had changed.

*Light turns to dark and colors shift,*
*Two rivers join when two lovers rift,*

She could almost touch the meaning of the next two lines. But even after much thought and headache, it was still elusive. Two rivers. Two rivers of magic? When the thing made of *varing* had taken over her mind, she had seen the two rivers. The *simul rami*, the river of light, and the *varing*, the dark river. But what did that have to do with two lovers? Magic and lovers were in separate states of being. Perhaps a metaphor? She had explored that too but came up dry.

*Watch for the child of two thrones,*
*Born with magic in his bones,*
*A child lit by the stars,*
*Watch for him, for he shall be ours.*

Of course, it described Rhyl perfectly. The reason why Tayeh had brought Illiah and Eva together to conceive the child, and why the Kitarrans had risked war to get him. And it wasn't just his lineage that made Rhyl a candidate for the prophecy. He would be a healer, a *sanarii*. But still, how could one man save them all? From Eva's own experience, she knew using magic was taxing. She could only draw so much from the *simul rami* without damaging herself. Rhyl was descended from Crea, through Illiah, which meant something—Eva wasn't quite sure what. And there was nothing (that she had found) that alluded to what or who Crea had been in life before becoming the spirit woman she was now.

Kitarra's archives had very little information about the *sanarii* or the *candarii*, and what they did mention was unhelpful.

She kept coming back to the two lines.

*Light turns to dark and colors shift,*
*Two rivers join when two lovers rift,*

Out of the whole prophecy, the two lines confused her. As if they were separate somehow, and ominous.

*Dwellor's Knoll. The invaders. Illiah... The revenant on the beach. Illiah. Illiah. Illiah.*

Her scribbles were in the margins, circled and gnawed at by her dry nib.

But no matter how much Eva studied the prophecy, it did not yield explanations. It did not explain how Rhyl, or anyone else, was going to bring balance and eradicate the threat of the *varing*. Almost a year she had been in Kitarra, and there was no trace of the ghost made of *varing* that had attacked them on the beach. Stone had destroyed it with one of the nine magical artifacts carved from a fallen cendari branch—a vercuri. But the thing Stone destroyed had been a thing of magic. And destroyed was not the same as killed or gone forever.

Eva sighed in frustration. Not for the first time, and certainly not for the last.

She turned to another script she had found. The writing was old, almost impossible to decipher, and messy. It had taken her some time to read each word until it made sense.

*And so a revenant was found. It looked like a little boy who everyone believed had been murdered. Only something was amiss about it. Later it became apparent that it was not the boy, but an echo of the boy, made of varing.*

Eva's eyes focused on the word *varing*. It was only the third time she had seen it written. The writing was someone's translation of a much older text. Someone else had been curious like she was. Someone who could make something of the ancient language. Someone with too much time on their hands and an unhealthy curiosity for dark magic.

Then she focused on the word *revenant*. Eva recalled the thing that had looked like Serac but could not possibly be Serac.

"Anfru?" Her voice was a thunderclap swallowed by the stone.

When he didn't answer, Eva looked up to see he was gone. A ripple cascaded across her pregnant belly; her voice had woken the sleeping babes currently residing inside her. She stretched, feeling them push against her ribs; one stretched its foot toward her pelvis, the other decided to try her stomach. She held her breath until the twins resettled.

"A couple more moons, dear ones," she murmured. "You are not ready to come out yet."

Maybe Anfru went to get her more food. Eva turned back to her study, flipping the page of the old text, hoping for more answers. Always hoping. Each page she turned, each new book or scroll was another chance to find the key. Or anything—a hint, a scent. Anything that would help her understand what Kitarra needed from Rhyl. Her child.

The queen had told all she knew, which was not helpful. An old evil. Kitarra dwindling. Babes stillborn. Dark magic gathering and tainting the good and simple. The prophecy. Damn the prophecy.

There were dark spots in Kitarra, Arrah had explained. Sites of strange and violent doings. Eva had listened, her skin crawling. People who would go near the dark spots would suddenly find themselves obsessed with evil thoughts, haunted by nightmares. Those who lived close were often the victims of unusual crimes. A series of violent and out-of-character murders. A good man turned into a rapist. A faithful mother and wife abandoning her family. Those places were not safe. And they were growing.

But why? What caused it? It reminded Eva of Dwellor's Knoll

all those years ago. She would never forget that day when her sword had been bloodied for the first time, taking the lives of those poor, crazed men.

Eva closed her eyes, and all she could see was Illiah and the *varing* lingering in his heart. Her head hurt.

Where was Anfru? He was almost constantly close by. He didn't trust that she would wait for him if she needed to climb the ladder.

At first, Eva had been unsure about having a manservant. But when she found out she was pregnant, Arrah had insisted. Loudly. And over the past few months, Eva had grown used to Anfru's quiet nature. She had come to rely on his counsel, his steadfast nature. She still couldn't quite wrap her head around the idea of devoting one's life to serving another, but she appreciated Anfru's dedication, regardless.

And with Anfru around, it meant fewer duties for Selene. Illiah pressed that Selene had gotten over her infatuation with him, but Eva still didn't trust the young woman. If Eva had had her way, she would have banished Selene from her life, from the palace—but even Eva knew it was not her place, and Arrah did value the woman's help.

Stone had pledged his life to Eva out of honor, but Anfru owed her nothing. He just liked following her around, making her snacks, making sure she didn't trip down stairways or get winded going up them, fetching books from high places.

Eva heard his soft footsteps but didn't bother to twist to see if it was him. Movements not planned in advance required far too much effort and complaining from her unborn children.

Anfru had a bowl of berries, the first of the season.

"How did you know I was just thinking of crawler-berries?" Eva exclaimed, her mouth watering. "Thank you."

Anfru shrugged, his bony shoulders almost brushing his large ears. His eyes twinkled as they always did under her praise. He leaned over her as she plucked a berry from the tray, looking at the page before her.

"I know that writing—the one in the margin," he said in his quiet voice.

"Really?" Eva asked, her mouth full.

Anfru met Eva's eyes. "It is Prince Arrain's hand."

Eva was not prepared for the jolt that ran through her. Stone—Arrain—studying the ancient writs, looking for the same clues as she was. Arrain, the scholarly prince who had become an exiled warrior. And Anfru would recognize his writing. When Eva had found out that Anfru had once served Arrain and Emri, before their deaths, she had been pleased and honored that he would offer his services to her and Illiah—mostly her. Illiah had multitudes of men and women at his command.

Through Anfru, it was as if a small piece of Arrain and Emri was with her. Like she could share their world after all. Not as the wistful young girl she had been when she met Emri, but as a counselor to the queen, a mother of Kitarra's chosen one, a foster mother to Arrain and Emri's son.

"When do you think he wrote this?" Eva asked, swallowing her mouthful.

Anfru pursed his lips. "Long ago. Before Emri, I imagine. In his youth. Yes. I do remember him coming down here quite often for a good year, obsessive almost. But then Emri came over from the Isles and Arrain was instantly enamored with her. The texts took less of his time then, but he did not forget them. He kept a journal. I don't know where it is now."

Both joy and grief warred inside her as she imagined young Arrain meeting Emri, wooing her with his eccentricities and strange humor. How different was Eva's Stone from the prince who had loved his princess and lost her? A pressing weight of regret shrouded her heart. If she had only followed Stone into the forest that night …

"Did he ever talk about it to you?" Eva asked, pushing her regret aside.

"Likely he did, but Arrain had many passions. I do not recall anything about magic—plants, yes. But not magic. We could look for his journal?"

"Yes. But where?"

"In his apartment. I don't think the queen ever had it cleared out after they died."

Eva had had no idea. The Queen's Keep was massive. Eva had never come across the room Anfru spoke of.

"Where is Arrain's room?"

"You want to go there? Now? Shouldn't you rest? You went to bed at midnight, up at dawn."

"Anfru—I am not a child."

Anfru gave Eva his disapproving face, which was like his normal face, but his mouth was just a hair straighter.

Eva stood, her back, her knees, her babies, protesting. Anfru took her elbow. Eva grimaced at the need of it.

"Pregnancy does not last forever," Anfru cooed.

If Illiah had said it, Eva would have barked at him. But Eva could never yell at Anfru; he was too soft, too good.

Eva was quiet as they walked up the twisting stone stairs. The air warmed as they rose out of the rocky depths. She didn't want Anfru to notice her tight belly, the pain that made her breathe slow and steady. It was not labor, but it would still alarm him. The last thing she needed was Anfru reporting it to Illiah, and the lot of them ganging up on her, forcing her to abandon stairs. Illiah would present a perfectly reasonable argument and she would have to acquiesce to his sound logic. The Queen's Keep—and Kilev—was built on a mountainside. It was either up or down. She refused to be hobbled to her room for the next few months.

Arrain and Emri's apartment was not far from the rest of the royal apartments. Eva had passed it countless times and never known what was behind the closed door. She had assumed it was a closet. Or immaculate guest chambers. The Queen's Keep had enough of both.

Anfru opened the door. Dimness greeted them. The room smelled stale and stuffy. The curtains were drawn tight. Anfru took several long strides across the room to let in the sunlight. Dust motes followed him in a lazy parade, sparkling in the newly invited sun.

Eva's throat tightened. It was a cozy space. Practical. Books everywhere. Weapons. A big bed, empty of mattress and linens.

"Did—did she die here?"

"Yes." Anfru's voice was as tight as Eva's. It was not an easy place for him to be either. He had been devoted to the prince and First Defender.

Eva went over to the bare bed and touched it. She closed her eyes. She didn't need the *simul rami* to imagine the lifeless body of Emri, the midwife cradling a babe thought dead, and Arrain fleeing, blinded by tears, running to find them in the spirit world, then, just seconds too late, Talo taking his first breath. But it would be too late. His father was gone, his heart blinding him to the truth he would not know for nearly six years. And by then, that version of Arrain was dead.

Eva opened her eyes. Tears trickled into her nose. She wiped them away with the back of her hand with an unladylike snort.

"I wonder if Talo has ever been in here," Eva said.

"Do you think it would do him good?"

Eva shook her head. "It didn't help me when my parents died. I was afraid of the emptiness of their room for a long time."

"I forgot you lost your parents at a young age as well."

Eva drew herself up, looking around for the journal. Anfru followed her lead. There were stacks of books. Of course. Arrain had been a scholar. Her Stone, her Arrain, was fierce and feral, but Eva could see how a scholarly life had once suited him, before the grief and guilt. "What does the journal look like? Do you remember?"

Anfru shrugged. "Not much different than any journal."

"Not helpful."

"One cannot be constantly perfect." Anfru's dry voice made Eva laugh, but it came out wet and shaky.

Eva looked beside the bed, between the frame and a little lamp table. She kept her books in a similar place. Eva gave a triumphant exclamation and bent to scoop up the treasure. Eva winced as the babies squirmed and fought against the sudden constriction of their accommodations.

"Careful, milady."

Every time Anfru called her "milady," Eva forced her emotions to ignore how the title reminded her of Stone. It was not a commonly used appellation. Stone—Arrain—must have learned it from his manservant, though manservant did not accurately describe

Anfru. Anfru was more than a servant. He was … well, he was Anfru.

The journal was thick, with a spine like a tree trunk, the pages wavy from use. Eva thumbed through it, feeling a forest of emotions. She had a strange notion that she would get more answers from the journal than from wrestling with the old dusty books, that the key to her questions was in the same place as a considerable part of her heart. That Stone should have her answers was unnerving yet made a kind of sense. Their bond, their entwined destinies, still pulled at her thoughts, even after he had abandoned her, breaking his oath of honor.

"I want some quiet to read this," Eva said looking around the room with a last lingering glance. She and Illiah were the only ones who knew the truth that Stone was Prince Arrain—or had once been Prince Arrain. And Eva thought it best if it stayed that way. Maybe she would tell Talo, when he was older.

Beyond the silent archives, quiet was an endangered creature. Rhyl and Talo were adept at appearing with a gust of noise the moment Eva began to think about how soothing it was to sit alone. Not that she really minded. She had lived seasons without hearing her son's voice, his cries, his laughter. Every moment with him was precious.

But those moments made studying the prophecy impossible. One could not study and mind two young boys at the same time. Luckily, she was not the only who could entertain her son and Talo. She didn't know where the boys were, but she knew they were off having fun, well looked after. Kitarra loved Rhyl and Talo.

Their family chambers were empty. Quiet. Her dear ones were probably breakfasting with the queen and some of her guests after the ceremony. Eva did not feel guilty for missing out. She sent Anfru to find out where they were, to see if they were missing her. Maybe Illiah was in council. Eva wondered if he had found any answers about the men who had attacked him during his trial. If it was Cotoch, why attack Illiah? Leverage? If Illiah heard anything, he would tell her.

She wanted to *see,* to use the *simul rami* to find answers, but pregnancy weakened her. And Cotoch was wreathed in dark magic and darker memories that she did not want to touch.

Eva propped herself up against pillows in the bright light of her room and opened the journal on her lap, letting her eyes adjust to the fine, scrawling script, her heart pounding with a kind of homesickness. She didn't hear the door open.

"Mu-ha-la." The singsong voice, followed by a metallic click, made Eva grin. She turned as much as her stomach would allow to see Illiah holding out his latha, unfolded in all its splendor, the newly honed steel glinting in the same light that illuminated the journal on her lap. An impish grin danced on Illiah's face. Eva rolled her eyes. "You snuck out this morning."

"I couldn't sleep," Eva told him, then changed the subject quickly. "Really, I am surprised you haven't brought that thing into our bed at night."

"I can do that?" Illiah replied, his grin stretching, something Eva would have thought impossible.

"No."

Eva turned back to the journal. A series of clicks meant Illiah was folding and unfolding his latha.

"Go play with Aisha or something," she told him. "You are in my light."

"Aisha is busy running around the city under the orders of the First Defender. He never has time to play with me anymore."

"Well, the First Defender is a bit of a hard-ass. Not to mention—" Eva's words transformed inelegantly into an unintelligible protest as Illiah came up behind her and wrapped her in his arms, sinking his teeth into the skin of her neck, making her nerves shiver with delight. "Stop! You are making the babies upset. They are kicking me!"

Illiah gave her neck a few consolatory kisses, rubbing his hand on her stretched belly.

"No news?" Eva didn't want to mention "'assassination attempt."

"No," Illiah replied slowly. Evasively. Illiah did not like to talk about Cotoch, especially with her. She let it slide.

"What is that?" Illiah asked, coming around the couch and sitting beside, gesturing to the journal.

"It's Prince Arrain's journal."

Illiah was quiet.

"Arrain was something of a scholar," she told him.

"So I have heard." There was an edge to his voice. Eva pushed down her annoyance. Maybe if Illiah had known Stone as she had, he wouldn't judge him so harshly. But maybe Stone deserved it ... Abandoning her, his amourii. Abandoning his son. Yet she couldn't find an ounce of anger in her heart for Stone. Only pity.

"Anything helpful?"

"I just found it. I was about to read it when you traipsed in here to show off your latha. Again."

"I am not showing off." Illiah sounded petulant.

"Lord Susor is requesting a word with you two," Anfru came and announced.

Eva snapped the book shut, forcing down another growl. Illiah patted her belly and gave her a sympathetic look.

"The guests will be leaving soon, and you will have more time," he crooned.

"I know, I know," Eva said, rubbing Illiah's long fingers through her own. "I just know this is important. I feel it in my gut—time is running out."

Illiah held her eyes in his steady gaze, pulling her into the deep crevices of his trust. "We will find answers, Eva. We will not let our son fall into a destiny that will destroy him."

"I know," Eva said, biting her lip against the strong emotion she could not yet identify. "I know."

# CHAPTER 8

# COTOCH

"SIR, WE FAILED."

"I see that," Cotoch said, looking at the line of empty-handed warriors. He was not pleased, but then he hadn't really expected them to succeed in taking Illiah during the iudarii trial. Still, if they had ... He still had time, but in the back of mind loomed Imal's threat. Cotoch could not escape the idea of being that man's captive, locked, festering in the dark.

"Easra?" Cotoch hailed his captain. He had another plan in place.

"Yes, my lord."

"Prepare the men. We leave at dawn."

Easra gave a tight nod and was gone from Cotoch's sight.

Cotoch stalked off to his chambers and locked himself in. He pressed his hands against the table, leaning into it until the wood pressed against his palms. He knew what he needed to do, but he didn't want to do it. He didn't want to go into the dark.

He swore once and stood up straight, clutching the amulet that hung around his neck.

The door built into the wall of his chamber was not obvious to anyone but him. It led him down, down, until the dark was absolute, and the smell of damp and rot filled his nose. He didn't need light; he knew the passageway intimately. He trailed one hand along the wall of rock, the other still clutched his amulet.

He counted twenty steps down and came to the place beneath his house—the crypts and corridors that were his private dominion.

He couldn't see, but the amulet would lead him where he needed to go.

"Where are you? Come to me." His voice was harsh in the dense air.

"Here."

Cotoch could smell dawn on a spring day. The amulet pulsed slightly as she approached.

"I am leaving," he told her.

"Where are you going? Allati?"

She spoke to him more and more these days. He wondered about it but was not sure he wanted to ask her why she was curious about the doings of the sunlit world.

"No, not Allati."

"Kitarra, then?"

"For a time. Then I am going to Rodan, to see my cousin."

She was silent. Then she put her hand in his. It was not a human hand. It was hard and flaky like bark and cold like damp moss. He wanted her to recoil from his touch. He wanted her to run and hide and weep. Her meek acceptance felt like he was taking her soul, not just her pain.

He used the amulet to pull the *varing* from her. Its hostile magic moved through her strange hand into his, moving under his skin, filling his veins with its potency.

He dropped her hand; he didn't want to hold it an instant longer than necessary.

"You think you will succeed," she said, her voice barely more than a whisper, weakened from what she had given him.

"I will."

"If you do—" She stopped herself.

"If I do, what?"

A strangled noise escaped her lips. She was shaking. Her head moved back and forth. It happened sometimes. The spirit woman would not die; Cotoch had tested her limits many times. But she did not remain unaffected when Cotoch took her magic. She often collapsed into spasms for a few days after.

Cotoch turned away, leaving her and her strangeness in the darkness.

# ILLIAH

ILLIAH DIDN'T LIKE INTERRUPTIONS, but when Tolmi stormed into his council, breathing like a ragged old crone, Illiah bit off any budding reprimands about the intrusion. Tolmi was the picture of health and strength, a soldier regularly fawned over by the ladies with his broad shoulders and sculpted muscles, an endurance athlete the like of which Illiah had never met. The man's winded state gave Illiah pause.

"My lord," Tolmi gasped. "Markeh is being attacked from the Tarm—Cotoch's army."

The split second of silence that followed his statement was as thick as Kitarra Peak is tall.

"The garrisons?" Illiah asked.

"Gone." A wealth of pain was in Tolmi's eyes. "Dead."

A lesser man would have cursed; Illiah was not going to waste his breath. He put his hand on the young man's shoulder. "You did the right thing by coming straight here. You could not have saved them."

Tolmi nodded, almost believing it.

"You are sure they are from the Tarm?" Turk asked.

"Yes. I snuck close enough to see the likes of them—they were not the invaders. They wore Cotoch's colors."

"Did you see how many men?" Illiah asked.

"At least two thousand."

"Good man." Illiah gave Tolmi's shoulder a reassuring squeeze, catching Turk's and Aisha's eyes from down the table. They would be thinking the same as him: two thousand men. Markeh was a small village, but Illiah's garrison stationed there had been nearly three hundred. It was a border town, not far from the coast; every such town had a strong garrison stationed there. Three hundred men and women—soldiers—dead. A village destroyed. And two thousand men. Illiah had seen Cotoch's armies—they were a force, a force Illiah had spent the better part of a year preparing to face.

"You are dismissed, Tolmi."

"But, sir—"

"It is a hard ride from Markeh. Rest. I will call when I need you."

Tolmi nodded, deflating slightly.

Illiah turned to Aisha. "We leave at sundown."

"Yes, my lord." Aisha gave a terse bow and went on his way to rouse the soldiers. This was why Illiah needed Aisha. Who else would take on the task of gathering an army in one afternoon?

"You need to stay here, Turk," Illiah told his general.

Turk glowered.

"I need you here. In case—"

"In case you don't come back. Right," Turk said in a grating voice. "Be careful, Illiah."

"I am always careful. We have been training for this. I have the soldiers."

"I know. Just keep your head." Turk gave Illiah a meaningful look.

"I always do." Illiah shot his friend a smile. Turk did not return it.

Illiah had been expecting a move from Cotoch since, well, since he sent Cotoch's failed assassin back with a bleeding stump of an arm, even before he'd learned that Cotoch had imprisoned and raped Eva. Over a year ago.

Part of him had yearned to invade Mahlas. Attacking Cotoch's city, razing it to the ground—he dreamed of it sometimes. It was a rotten thing to ache for a man's death. And the part of him that woke from his nightmares, heart pounding in fear, whispered that if he killed Cotoch, he would cease to be Illiah and become something more sinister, more terrible. Something like Cotoch himself.

And yet not a day went by that Illiah didn't think of Cotoch, wanting nothing more than the man's neck beneath his blade, or his hands—he was not picky. But he couldn't tell Turk that.

But Cotoch had been quiet. Mahlas had been quiet. Eva had watched with her *sanarii* magic as much as she could, but she was weak from pregnancy. When she did look (entirely without his consent or blessing but his wife was a wild creature, who rarely listened to his logic), she reported that Cotoch had managed, somehow, to put barriers up against her magic. Eva had done the same, as well as she could. It was not a familiar skill for her, but she had to try to keep Cotoch's *candarii* eye away from Kilev. Away from her and Rhyl.

Illiah went to find Eva and the boys. There would be no time for proper farewells.

Eva didn't get up when Illiah entered their chambers. Her hand caressed her belly abstractedly. By her expression, she had heard the news.

Illiah knelt beside her, one hand on her belly, feeling his twin babes twisting beneath; his other hand cupped Eva's cheek. He smiled as she melted into his touch.

"You are leaving."

"I have to."

"I know." Eva kissed him, arching against him, her bulging belly pressed against him. Was it wrong that his body didn't care? That he felt his longing for her in every sinew of his being? Armeria, his uandian, sensed the closeness and came to beg for some attention, putting her head on Illiah's knee.

"Good girl," Illiah said to his dog.

"You should take her," Eva told him, her fingers tangled in the dog's fur.

"No. Battle is no place for a dog. She should be here with you."

"Illiah, what if it's a trap?"

"You think Cotoch would wage war to get to me?"

"I don't know. It just feels wrong."

"There is no evidence that Cotoch was behind the attack during the trial—"

"But there is no evidence that he wasn't."

"Eva, I have to go."

"I know. I—I just—I can't lose you again."

"You won't."

"That's a fool's answer."

Illiah couldn't reply because the large chamber suddenly shrunk as two boys and two more dogs filled the place with their bubbling energy. Talo was getting tall, but then so was Rhyl. They were both skinny; their constant movement made it impossible for anything other than brass and wit to stick to their bones.

"Daddy is leaving," Eva told the boys. They groaned as one.

"Why?" came Rhyl's piteous wail. "How long?"

"Where?" Talo asked.

Illiah answered, "To the border, and I don't know. I will be back as soon as possible."

"Good thing you have a latha now, Daddy."

"Yes," Illiah said with a laugh. He hugged the boys close and kissed them both. Then he gave Eva another kiss, and another kiss for her belly, and then he left. His family. His dear ones. It was too easy to leave them. In his head was Cotoch. And in his heart was the yearning for revenge.

CHAPTER 10

# ILLIAH

MARKEH WAS A BURNED HUSK. The buildings were smoldering ruins of black. Smoke curled into a cloudless sky, a gray snake against the looming mountains to the north. Illiah scanned the desolation, looking for a house left unscathed, a street unplundered, livestock left alive. But Cotoch's army had been thorough. Illiah's border garrison had failed.

Cotoch's army, a writhing mass of men and tents and horses, was just beyond the worst of the mud and ash. Looking at the size of the enemy's camp for himself, Tolmi's estimate was correct. Two thousand men. Where was Cotoch in the press? Was the so-called lord even there, overseeing the destruction of his whims? Maybe he was back in Mahlas, smugly watching with his *candarii* magic. Illiah hoped not. He wanted the vile man within his reach.

But if Kitarra was what Cotoch wanted, why had he waited almost a year, until now, to attack? Why not strike when Kitarra was at its weakest after the Isles had been lost? Kitarra was no longer a wounded animal. Kitarra had teeth and claws and was prepared to fight. Illiah had had time to train his soldiers and build his garrisons and form his divisions.

Cotoch had taken Markeh, but that was where it ended. Illiah's men would be the tide that pulled Cotoch's army out to sea. Here. Now.

Unless Eva was right and it was an elaborate plan to trap him. Unlikely. Moving a two-thousand-man army required a great deal of effort—Illiah had personally experienced this. Why would Cotoch go through that trouble just for him? No, this was part of a bigger plan—whatever that was. It was only Illiah's inflated pride that made him suspicious of a trap designed for him alone.

Illiah looked behind at his five divisions. Each was made up of two hundred men and women, fifty archers, fifty on horseback, the rest foot soldiers. They moved in tight formation. Behind the soldiers stretched the line of wagons and camp workers, but Illiah could hardly see them ambling through the dust churned up by the soldiers and horses. His soldiers. He wanted to think the warmth coursing through his chest was courage, but it wasn't. It was the anticipation of seeing Cotoch's men bleed into Kitarran soil. He pushed down his excitement with his shame. How many would die today? At his command?

"Sir?" Aisha hailed him.

"Sheridan."

Aisha gave a tight nod and moved off to spread the command through the host.

Illiah's scouts had returned with more details about the enemy and the lay of the land. Sheridan was the tactic Illiah decided they would use. Illiah had several, all named after islands lost to the invaders. Sheridan would arrange the horsemen as wings on either side of the center of Peace Guards armed with lathas. The second line would be archers; the reserve would be the remaining foot soldiers armed with swords. He had used the tactic years ago in Jullayah, only on a smaller scale—and without the latha-bearing Kitarrans. It should work well on the nearly flat, open plain that surrounded Markeh.

Was that the reason Cotoch chose Markeh? For its wide, flat plain, perfect for battle? With few hidden dips and ridges, no side had the advantage. It would be an even fight. Still, there were always unknowns, and Cotoch was a *candarii*—what tricks did he have up his sleeves that Illiah could not predict? Illiah's men and women were well trained, strong, ready. Many had lathas and the skills to use them. The last six months of their lives had brought merciless tests and trials. And his Kitarrans, few though they were, had strength and speed and quick healing beyond any human. Yes, they were more than ready to put their hard work to the test.

He thought wistfully of the time, hundreds of years back, when the Kitarran army was almost entirely comprised of Kitarrans. One well-trained, catlike Kitarran could easily contend with ten, maybe even twenty human men. The Kitarran armies of old would have been unparalleled.

"They know we are here." Aisha was back. He was right; Illiah had already noted the churning movement of the enemy. They were preparing for engagement. It would happen before nightfall.

Yes, Illiah's soldiers were well trained, but blood and death were different foes in real life than in theory and practice. There was nothing that could prepare a soldier to watch a comrade fall, gutted and bleeding, crying, begging for life. Or going home to tell a family their loved one had died. And Illiah, as their commander, held their lives in his hands.

"Sir, your maps are ready."

Illiah tore his eyes from his enemy. A table was prepared with Illiah's maps, and notes of tactics were there as well as drink and food. His division captains stood around, waiting.

"Sheridan?" Captain Vox confirmed with a sly grin. Illiah was not the only one chafing at the bit for blood.

Illiah nodded. "We have more men than Cotoch—and women," Illiah added, giving Captain Jasmin an apologetic look. Jasmin replied with a half smile and a shrug. She was a tall woman, but slight. She had been a Peace Guard in Withe for twenty years before Illiah recruited her to be one of his captains. "But our soldiers have not been tested. We cannot assume we have the upper hand. We must fight with determination and discipline.

"Aisha. Vox. You need to watch for holes in the fighting line. Watch your distance with your archers. We want them to do their work without hitting our own."

"Where will you be, sir?"

"I will be with the left wing, leading the sweep, if necessary." It would also be an ideal place to watch for Cotoch, but Illiah didn't mention that to his captains. Revenge was not something he added to his tactics.

"First Defender, they are approaching!" A scout rushed at them, his face flushed. They turned as one, and sure enough, Cotoch's army was in position and approaching.

"I thought we would have more time," Jasmin muttered.

"Get to your divisions," Illiah said tersely. A steward held Penn's reins, and Illiah vaulted to the back of the big black. Penn leaped into a gallop at Illiah's silent command.

"Formations!" Illiah roared, cantering down the line. Satisfied with the positions, Illiah joined the horsemen of the left wing. He inspected the enemy, their armor, their drawn weapons. The distance was too far to see their expressions, their faces. He could not see anyone who was obviously Cotoch.

Then the noise of battle began. The sound of a thousand boots upon the earth. Hundreds of horses' hooves crushing the vegetation. The shuffle of leather armor and metal weapons. The sound of a hundred lathas pulled from their sheaths, opening with a hundred metallic clicks, like a hundred insects. The breath of men and women wondering if it was about to be their last. The beating of thousands of terrified yet battle-ready hearts. Illiah did not believe that anyone could go to battle without fear. Some hid it better than others, but the fear was there, always.

Penn stamped and snorted but did not move. He would wait for Illiah's command, like any good soldier.

Illiah lifted his arm and brought it down. The fighting line moved ahead—Aisha's and Vox's divisions. A hailstorm of arrows followed, landing on the outskirts of the enemy front line. Instead of quelling the enemy, the arrows spurred them onward. They picked up their pace as if safety lay in the throe of the fighting line.

The clash came quickly—the first meeting of blade to blade and hand to hand and blood to blood.

"Wait!" Illiah commanded the left wing. The right wing, beyond the latha-bearing foot soldiers, moved. They would force the enemy toward them without circling them entirely. If the enemy decided they were losing, Illiah wanted them to retreat. A caged man could be a dangerous beast.

Penn tossed his head, and Illiah checked him. Not yet.

He watched the battle, trying not to focus on the blood, the thrust, the slash of steel against flesh. The death. If he focused on each man and woman, it would destroy him. He needed to see his divisions as a whole, to spot a weakness before it became catastrophic. What he saw was satisfying. His soldiers fought well; they held their courage, and more importantly, their formations.

A lone enemy horseman caught his attention, standing on a rise above the enemy horde, observing.

Cotoch.

Illiah could almost see his sly disdain from his position just outside the fray. Cotoch who had raped Eva. Cotoch, a sorcerer, an evil man fit only to nourish the trees with his corpse. Illiah's battle was not in the press, it was with that man. He spurred Penn forward, around the clash of men, away from the battle, toward his real foe.

Cotoch saw him and took flight. Coward. But Penn was fast. Illiah held his latha in one hand, reins in the other, raised out of the saddle so Penn could fly. His sword was attached to his saddle in case his latha was lost or broken. Illiah reveled in the sound of his warhorse's hooves leaving tracks in the ground, in the sound of air rushing past his ears. His hand tightened on his weapon.

A small copse of trees crowned the hill where Cotoch had vanished, and too late Illiah realized his mistake. Beyond the trees, in a small dell, was a host of men, waiting. Illiah could not count, but he knew there were too many. A trick. A trap. Illiah was an idiot.

It was too late to retreat. They had him surrounded. He gritted his teeth and charged. The men swarmed, thick and angry. Penn reared, stamping, snorting, his massive body a weapon. Illiah used his latha, but he could not block the massive spear that struck his horse in the chest. Only his quick reflexes kept him from being crushed as Penn fell, legs sprawling, then still. Illiah had no time to reflect on the death of his loyal beast. The men pressed around him. He was the caged beast now, and he would show them how dangerous he could be.

The latha was a tool of destruction. With it, Illiah's reach was doubled, and the curved blades could gut a man with less effort than a sword. The two blades curved around Illiah, almost like armor. Blood sprayed across Illiah's face, in his hair, sticky on his neck, his hands, forcing him to grip the handle of his latha with all his strength.

But still, the men came at him. Illiah heard a cry and managed to spin, only to see Aisha enter the fray. The Kitarran must have seen Illiah leave the primary battle and followed. It was against Illiah's orders, but maybe with the two of them, they could get out of the mess Illiah had created. Or maybe Aisha would die because of Illiah's stupidity.

Sometimes skill is not enough. Illiah pondered this absently as a sword struck his left arm. The pain lanced up his shoulder into his head. He didn't drop his latha, but it was enough to make him pause and allow the enemy to land a blow on his shoulder. The man could have killed him. Instead, Illiah dropped to his knees, his head foggy, his arms numb. His latha was knocked from his hand. Illiah lunged after it, but it was too far, and his arms were unresponsive. He fell in the dirt. Another blow landed behind his ear, and blackness greeted him like a lost lover.

CHAPTER 11

# MILA

MILA JUST WANTED to lie in a proper bed, eat a decent meal, and never walk again. Her shoes were at war with her feet. Her leg muscles had long ago given up protesting; now they were just numb. They had left their horses behind in Jullayah when they crossed the river. The boat they had found had only enough room for their packs. Mila's shoulders had ached for the first while, but she was used to it now. Or maybe that was because they had eaten most of their food and their packs were lighter. She didn't know. She didn't care. She just wanted to get to Fishtown.

Tarran had surprised her with his detailed knowledge of the Midlands and the rangy settlement called Fishtown, but then she remembered Illiah had sent him on a scouting mission the summer before he had been killed—or taken, as Tarran believed—so it made sense. Tarran hadn't gone alone; Murryn had gone with him. The two had returned from the mission locked into a serious relationship. Mila had always been suspicious that had been Illiah's goal all along.

So Tarran and Murryn knew the Midlands a little. And they had a connection in Fishtown, but that did not make it safe. The

Midlands was a dangerous place, especially for strangers who had not proven themselves. Reputation was everything in the lawless land, Tarran explained.

They had money, stolen from someone's coffers; Mila didn't bother to ask whose. Tarran had many skills, and it did not shock Mila that being an excellent thief and pickpocket was one of them. In Fishtown, they hoped to get supplies, perhaps horses, to see them to Kitarra.

Kitarra. Mila still couldn't wrap her mind around their destination. But where else could they go? Jullayah was not safe for them. Mila could not imagine anywhere but the Keep as her home. Already, she missed the Keep, the stairways, the misty hills, her friends. Kaile. Talamir and Freya and their children. Scrub the cook. Mila pressed her hand against her eyes. The truth was, she didn't have a home. She could never go back to the Keep, to Jullayah. Not ever.

Would Kaile know in his heart that Mila had murdered Serac in self-defense? Or had Kaile condemned them as traitors and sent men after them? Kaile's men would never search the Midlands for them, they were safe now. Mila would never know how Serac's death affected Kaile or Jullayah. She could only look forward to Kitarra. At least in Kitarra they could find answers. She would settle for that.

"We are almost at Maclais's border," Murryn told Mila. To Tarran, she said, "We should stop here, rest, and go on in the morning."

The surrounding landscape had become a blur to Mila. She didn't care where she was, so long as she could sit, take off her pack, and rest her feet.

"I should go ahead and scout the town, just in case," Tarran said.

"I will be back in a few hours." He leaned down to brush his lips against Murryn's, his face shifting with the simple joy of it, but only for a moment. His cold, calculating shield came up, and he was off into the sparse forest of twisted conifers.

Mila and Murryn sat huddled together, nibbling on tasteless dried fruit and wafers. It began to rain softly, a late-spring rain that didn't penetrate the evergreen canopy above. It was quiet, almost peaceful. Mila dozed for a time. When she woke, Tarran still had not returned. She realized she was alone with her sister for the first time since leaving the Keep.

"I heard Tarran talking in his sleep last night while I was on watch," Mila mentioned. "He was speaking a different language."

"Oh?"

"Why would he speak a different language?"

"He learned it as a child."

"Where? Allati, Kitarra, even the Midlands—they all speak the same tongue."

Murryn sighed. "Tarran is not from any of those places. He doesn't like to speak of it."

"Which is why I am asking you instead of him," Mila muttered.

"You are too considerate, Mila," Murryn said with a watery smile.

"I killed a man."

"No, you killed a monster."

Mila could not argue with that.

"Tarran came from a land called Rodan. He came to Jullayah with the invaders—as a slave."

"A slave?" Mila felt colder saying the word.

"Yes. He was taken from his family as a young child and sold, sent across the sea. When Illiah defeated the invaders, he took pity on Tarran and gave him the chance to live a new life."

Illiah had been everything to Tarran. Father. Brother. Mentor. Savior. His death had crushed something inside Tarran. No wonder he was desperate to believe that Illiah was alive. A new understanding of Tarran's grief clicked into place. "That is why he is so loyal—and so broken by—" Mila did not say *death*, but Murryn heard the unspoken word. Her face turned stony.

"They are alive, Mila. I know they are."

Mila wanted to share her sister's optimism, but she couldn't. Hope was dangerous. Hope was a feather in a wind storm.

"Which is why I feel compelled to find Illiah." Tarran's voice came from the grass as he slipped beside Murryn. Murryn looked torn between amusement and scorn that Tarran got past her sentry. Tarran gave her a quick kiss on the lips. "Maclais will welcome us into Fishtown. We have his protection," Tarran told them.

"A good thing?" Mila asked.

"A very good thing."

Fishtown was … smelly. With a name like Fishtown, it was only to be expected.

It was a primitive place, low buildings clustered around a bay. Spring sunshine sparkled off the blue water. Docks lined the water like shorebirds. Boats bobbed in the bay. Fishing boats, Mila guessed, because everything smelled like fish. She had never seen the ocean before. The salty air stuck in her nose, and she was sure she would never forget it.

Walking through the town made Mila glad for her riding clothes.

She couldn't imagine wearing a skirt through the muck and dust, both equally evident, contradictory as it was. The people regarded them stoically, and Mila remembered that they had Maclais's protection. Maclais, she had been told, was the master of Fishtown. At least at the moment. It was about reputation, Tarran reminded her. If a bigger, meaner lot ousted Maclais, then the town would change ownership. But Maclais had been in power for a decade—a long time by Fishtown standards. Mila didn't want to contemplate his methods.

Maclais's house was also the town inn. It was a big building, built with timber and stone and thatch. They stepped inside to a bustling hall, the smell of ale and bread and cooked fish mingling alongside the sounds of laughter and music.

A great voice boomed across the hall, matched by the massive breadth of a man who launched himself through the crowd toward them. His face crinkled with a grin. His cheeks were rosy, which, by the smell of the place was likely from an excess of spirits.

"Tarran, my boy! Murryn, my little firefly!" His grin faltered a little as he laid eyes on Murryn's hair. "My little firefly, what have you done with your hair? You look like a lad! Not that this one cares, eh?" He thumped Tarran on the back. Even with Tarran's darker skin, his blush was obvious.

"Maclais, this is my sister Mila," Murryn said.

Maclais's ruddy, expressive face calmed as he studied Mila. He held out his big hand for her, and she took it. He brought it to his lips. "Did you know you have the Forest in your eyes?" he asked, almost absently. "Are you a lady of the Dark Wood?" Mila willed her hand not to tremble in his. Then Maclais grinned again—he was missing a few teeth—and Mila knew he was only teasing.

"My lady, welcome to Fishtown!" He dropped Mila's hand to drape one arm over Tarran's shoulders and the other over Murryn's. "Davis! Food! Meat! Wine! Ale! We have honored guests!" The aforementioned Davis appeared out of nowhere, a slip of a man with a balding head and bright gray eyes, but a ready grin.

"Mac, how dare you not tell me Tarran and Murryn were coming! I would have prepared the wedding room and taken out the best linens to air," Davis said mournfully.

"Davis that is not necessary," Murryn began, blushing hard.

"Nonsense, Davis, just food. Bring food!" Maclais repeated, waving the little man away.

Food was brought and eaten and enjoyed with much relish and laughter, mostly Maclais's, and mostly at Davis's expense, though Mila could see that affection was the underlying motive for the teasing. The man bore it like a whetstone.

After the meal was finished and another round of wine had been poured, Maclais sobered and leaned across the table to Tarran.

"So, my boy, what brings you back to the Midlands? I know my hospitality is revered and reputed, but still, I find myself surprised to see you here with your fair ladyfolk." Maclais winked in Murryn's direction. She did not appreciate the term "fair lady," and Maclais knew it.

"We ran into a spot of trouble in Jullayah." Tarran glanced at Mila. Mila gave Tarran a shrug. She really had no qualms about him telling her story. Not now. Not when she had already lost almost everything.

"What kind of trouble?" Maclais asked with a curious gleam in his eye.

"Mila murdered someone—a bad man. A rapist. But the man

also happened to be King Caeris's cousin," Murryn explained. Maclais's brows rose, indiscernible under the wrinkle of his large forehead. Then he gave an appreciative guffaw.

"What a pair of women you have here, Tarran. You better watch yourself." Maclais jabbed Tarran in the chest with a muscular finger. Then he sobered once more. "Do you mean Serac?"

Mila nodded.

Maclais huffed. "I knew the bugger. His slippery eels would come to Fishtown every so often to purchase ragwood. Never liked his people, but I will miss his business."

"What is ragwood?" Mila asked.

"The weed they turn into culla powder to feed their rituals at the temple," Maclais said

"That is not all they do with it in Jullayah," Mila said bitterly.

"'Tis a nasty herb, that is for sure," Maclais agreed. "But it has its uses. Lining my pocket, for one." But he didn't laugh. "So Serac is dead. And you three are on the run. Where is it you are running to?"

"Kitarra," Tarran said without hesitation.

"Kitarra? With their prudish queen and silly tree-rituals?" Maclais waved his hands around his head.

"We have friends in Kitarra," Tarran answered.

*We hope we have friends in Kitarra* was Mila's cynical thought.

"So you hope to travel through the Midlands, through the Tarm and up into Kitarra?"

"That is the plan," Murryn said.

Maclais's eyebrows sunk, and he looked like another person with his face lined and pointed. "The Tarm is not safe for 'friends of Kitarra.' I would beg you to go a different way."

"Oh?"

"The Lord of Mahlas, Lord Cotoch of the Tarm," Maclais spoke the name and title with sarcastic flair, "is an ambitious man. A strange man. Rumors tell that he is at war with Kitarra. You should not travel through his land."

"What about a boat? Can we barter passage?" Tarran asked.

"A Kitarran boat has not been seen in Fishtown for over a year. I would not hold out hope for that," Maclais said. Tarran growled.

"What about a Fishtown boat?" Murryn asked.

Maclais shrugged. "There might be one crazy enough to take you up the coast, but it would not come cheap."

Tarran looked at Murryn and Mila. Mila nodded. They needed to try, at least, if it would save them months of travel overland through Allati.

"Davis will show you to your rooms, and in the morning, you have my permission to beleaguer the boatmen with your desperate request."

"Thank you, Maclais," Murryn said, taking the older man's hand.

Maclais waved her off. "All right, off with you younglings. Procreate. Practice for those sweet little babies you will make. And you, forest girl," Maclais said with a hand on Mila's arm, "good work. Serac was an evil sort, from what I heard. You should not feel sorry for killing him."

"Who said anything about being sorry?" Mila replied.

"Maclais says they rarely leave the safety of the bay."

Mila followed Murryn's gaze out to the wide bay dotted with boats. Murryn's short hair looked like sparks in the sunshine. She wore a rough-spun vest over her thick tunic, her trousers a copy of

Tarran's. Murryn did look like a boy. She walked like a boy too, but Mila knew it was an adapted posture. Mila couldn't pass for a boy even if she cut her hair and bound her chest. Her hips were too wide, her waist too small. If Mila had a flake of gold for every time a man commented on her pleasing figure, she would have enough to buy anything her heart might desire. Too bad one couldn't buy silence.

"Which one is the ship?" Mila asked.

"Not sure. Tarran said he would meet us here."

It had taken Tarran and Murryn two days, but they had found a boat to take them to Kitarra. "For every coward, there is a warrior. For every cautious fisherman, there is a madman," Tarran had told her with a sideways smile.

"So our captain is a madman?" she had asked.

"That, or maybe just greedy," Tarran had replied with a shrug.

Tarran appeared between them, slinging his arms over their shoulders, his coils of hair almost golden in the sun.

"Ready?" he asked.

"As ready as I ever will be," Mila replied.

"That is the ship," Tarran said, pointing to a boat moored just down the dock.

If Mila could have run back home to the Keep, she would have. Tarran's face was a carving of resolve. And Murryn would follow Tarran to the ends of the earth. Literally, it seemed.

The ship was different from the bay vessels. It was longer, taller, thicker, generally sturdier-looking, which was a relief. Besides the small rowboat that had taken them across the Great River, Mila had never voyaged by boat. Neither had Murryn. Tarran knew boats, which made sense now that Mila knew he had been a slave on one from another land.

A man appeared on the deck of the ship as if he dissolved from the mast and sail. There was something weathered and woodish about his brown eyes and wind-roughened skin. "Ah, there is the boy," the man said, jutting his chin out at Tarran.

"Captain Seagrass," Tarran answered tightly. Tarran hadn't been a boy for a long time.

"We are ready. Just setting the sails and rigging—we set sail before the sun reaches the zenith. The tide is ready for us. Is that all you brought with you? And the women?" His brown eyes twinkled over Mila and Murryn.

"Yes, you said it was only a few weeks to Kitarra."

"Aye, aye. It is almost summer. The warm wind will pull us right. Come, Cutless will show you to your places."

Cutless appeared to be a young man, about Tarran's age, but skinnier and more weather-beaten. Like a shore tree, contorted and gnarled by the perpetual ocean wind. Cutless took Mila's bag, gesturing with a long finger for them to follow. He only had three fingers on the one hand.

"Got caught by bandits," Cutless explained, noticing Mila's glance. He gave her a roguish smile that was not as charming as he seemed to hope. "They took my first finger for my insolence, and the other out of jealousy." He gave her a ludicrous wink. Mila ignored him.

The ship's hold was small but bigger than Mila had expected. There were hammocks for the crew, squeezed into the cramped space, elbow to elbow. Cutless offered them each one. He gave them the rundown of ship life, winking as he told them about expected— and unexpected—duties.

Murryn took a step toward the scrawny deckhand. "What exactly are you implying?"

Cutless opened his mouth to say something clever, but Murryn took another step toward him. In her hand glistened her small, curved neck knife where an instant before there had been nothing. "Are you implying that as women aboard this ship, you 'expect' us to suck your small, weather-bitten cocks?"

Cutless gulped as his aforementioned weather-bitten cock was cradled by Murryn's knife.

"No! Not at all. That would be rude of me. Disrespectful. I would never—" His voice trembled a little, and Murryn smiled, tucking her knife away so fast it might have just dissolved into her skin.

"Good. Glad we got that squared away," Murryn said.

"Well, this is going to be fun," Mila remarked when Cutless had bowed his way out of Murryn's reach.

# CHAPTER 12

# EVA

THE HOT POOLS, the gardens, the walls of the palace, the sounds of the city faded into memory. Before Eva, the twisting, sloping forest climbed the mountain toward the spire that was Kitarra Peak, which was invisible, hiding behind a crown of clouds. At her back was the cendari tree.

The cendari tree had held Eva's affection from her first day in Kilev, and since then, it had become one of her closest companions. Eva had known trees with power. The giants of the Great Forest had hummed with the *simul rami*, warm with the presence of old wisdom. Right from the first, she knew the cendari tree was an old being. Eva could sit nestled in its roots and feel the *simul rami* pulse loudly in her ears. She could touch the smooth, gray bark with her fingers and feel it flow into her veins. She could almost talk to it, only a tree's language does not work well with words, so Eva used pictures. She asked the tree to find Illiah. She closed her eyes and searched. It would tax her pregnant body, but she couldn't lose Illiah again.

A battle lay before her. Cotoch's army was slowly succumbing to the sheer numbers and skill of Illiah's divisions. But where was Illiah? Where was her First Defender?

Staying with the battle was difficult; holding on to the vision in the *simul rami* was like clinging to a slippery rope. Her own weight, her weakness, pulled her down and away. But Eva needed to know Illiah was whole and sound. Battle and death traveled as comrades. Why should her husband be immune to death when others were not? Why should his soldiers die and not him? *Because I need you.* It too was a selfish thought.

"Eva!"

A jolt trembled through her body. Being taken abruptly from the *simul rami* was always uncomfortable, sometimes painful. Her stomach was ill for a moment, her body still. Only when she felt the twist of her unborn children did she relax. The babes were okay. Next, she turned, preparing an angry word or two for the interruption.

But her words died in her throat when she saw Anfru's expression.

"It's Rhyl and Talo," he said, his eyes brimming with something terrible.

Eva stood too fast; her belly pinched, her head spun. Anfru caught her arm, rooting her. "What happened? Where are they?"

"I don't know." Anfru's face was anguished. "Pudding and Crackers were found dead, poisoned."

"Selene," Eva whispered. Selene had betrayed them—she felt it in her bones. Eva would kill her. But death was too good for the traitor.

"I am afraid to contemplate if it was her," Anfru said. "But … she is missing as well. I don't know what to think." Anfru was visibly shaken; he was no warrior. His strength was in wisdom and calm and understanding. It was why Eva respected him dearly.

"I need to *see*," Eva told him.

Anfru helped her settle once more at the base of the tree. The roots pressed against her like a comforting embrace. She closed her eyes, nails digging into the bark, her will delving into the *simul rami*. She begged the life-magic to show her what she needed. Her heart hammered in her chest.

She searched, but she could not find them. She could not find Rhyl or Talo or Selene. The children's link to the *simul rami* was thick and clouded. They were alive; a dead person felt different. A memory felt different. But something was obscuring her, something that felt like *candarii* magic.

Once again, she came out too fast, but this time under her own volition. She needed tools to focus the *simul rami*, to break the barrier put around her children. The cendari tree was not enough.

"If I am right about Selene, we should search her room," Eva said. Why had she not suspected the woman before? Right, because Illiah was fond of reminding Eva her paranoia was based on jealousy, and Eva had let him persuade her of it. *Damn it, Illiah. Fool.* Selene had amused his affectionate heart and made him feel guilty about her misguided affection.

Eva moved as fast as her swollen body would allow with Anfru holding on to her elbow. They didn't speak.

Eva had never been in Selene's room. She had never befriended the woman who was in love with her husband. How could she? She was too callous.

Selene's room was richly decorated. Not surprising. Selene was a merchant's daughter. She liked pretty things: fine dresses, jewelry, art.

It was not hard to find what Eva was looking for. The gold basin hidden in the closet of clothes was smaller than the one Cotoch had

had in his chambers, but it was a similar shape. A memory slammed into Eva's thoughts: Cotoch speaking into his gold bowl to someone who knew Illiah. Why had she not realized before? Why had she forgotten? It had been Selene. Selene was Cotoch's woman. An apprentice? She was too old to be his daughter … A lover? Eva wanted to hurt something. She wanted to destroy something. Her nails dug into her palms and she bit back a scream.

Eva collected herself and poured water into the gold basin from a pitcher. She took a hair-clip from the table. Eva hoped the object was imprinted with some of Selene's essence. It would help her focus. She put it into the bowl. Then she *looked*.

Blackness filled the bowl, choking Eva. She backed out of the *simul rami* with a curse. Selene was protected by *candarii* magic. Eva could not see her past or her present. Eva would never in a hundred lifetimes forget the feeling of being trapped with the *varing*. It was proof, in a way, that Selene was a sorcerer.

Eva looked once more, this time prepared for the onslaught of *candarii* taint. She used her will like a needle's point and pricked the blackness, calling to the *simul rami*, welcoming it through the fog. The tiny prick of light, of magic, grew and Eva managed to grasp an image of Selene. She was in the forest, which was not helpful. Rhyl and Talo were with her, unhurt, but obviously scared and confused. Eva reached and tried to make the vision widen, to discern their location. She couldn't; the blackness collapsed around her connection to the *simul rami*, until finally there was nothing left of the boys or Selene, only sparkling water in a gold bowl rippled by her ragged breath.

"Selene has the children," Eva said. Her forehead beaded with sweat. She hissed as a pain in her belly made her pause. "In the forest somewhere. She must be taking them to Mahlas."

"The babies?" Anfru asked. Eva realized she was almost doubled over, her hands on her belly, her face pinched from anger, fear, and pain.

"I am fine. They are fine. It is just false-labor pains."

Anfru bit his lip, clearly torn between her preservation and the situation at hand.

"But I don't know where in the forest they are. When were they last seen?" Eva asked.

"Three hours ago. But the bodies of the dogs are cold."

"Where is Arrah?"

"Questioning the servants with Turk."

The queen's council room was down a long, gentle flight of stairs. Stairs. Anfru cupped Eva's elbow as she moved down, step by awkward step. Each impact rippled painfully in her belly.

Arrah was questioning Yolina, the young serving girl who usually brought the boys' breakfast. Yolina's face was red and puffy from crying. It was clear she was devastated by the news. No one was that good of an actor.

Eva wanted to break into sobs herself, muttering curses and screaming at anyone who was near her. She had promised herself she would be strong. Logical.

"Arrah, it was Selene," Eva interrupted. "She took the children. They are alive, in the forest, but I don't know where."

Arrah looked aged. Exhausted. Turk thanked Yolina, who rushed out of the room with a few hiccupping sobs.

"That is our suspicion." Arrah rubbed her temple with a long, clawed finger. "But I hoped it was not true. Can you find them?"

"I can't. Sorcerer magic is blocking my sight." Eva slumped into a chair. Turk leaned forward, his usually cheerful face grave. "I think Selene is working with Cotoch. I found a gold basin in her room, similar to the one Cotoch had. She is a *candarii*, I am sure of it. I think she is taking the children to Cotoch."

"The attack on Markeh—it is too much of a coincidence," Turk muttered.

"A distraction," Eva agreed. "Have you heard from Illiah?"

"No," Turk said. "I will send my fastest soldiers into the forest with a tracker. We will find them, Eva." Turk put his big hand on her shoulder. Eva covered his hand with hers.

*I am not alone this time.*

Turk gave her shoulder a squeeze, nodded to Arrah, and left. He would send a message to Illiah. He would search the forest. The Queen's Keep and all of Kilev was already being scoured for clues.

"How far do you think she could get with two small children?" Arrah muttered quietly.

"I don't know. Alone? Not far. But if she had help? I don't know."

"If she is working with Cotoch, she won't hurt them."

"No. They are too valuable as leverage," Eva agreed.

"We will get them back, Eva," Arrah vowed.

"Yes. And I think I know how," Eva said, standing up.

Eva could not rely on Illiah. He was in the thick of battle. Turk was capable, but Selene was devious, and Eva feared this had been planned far in advance. Eva needed … Stone.

No, this time, she was not alone. But still, she could feel a vast emptiness opening inside her.

The halls of the Queen's Keep were silent. The Queen's Guards had the Queen's Keep locked down. Everyone was being questioned. No stone would be left unturned.

*Tayeh, I need you.*

Eva had not spoken to Tayeh since before Illiah and Rhyl were taken. She had not been able to bring herself to search for him. And he had not revealed himself to her. Although Eva believed Tayeh had never meant her harm, he had manipulated her. He had never cared for her beyond her magic and her birth status. He was not her father. He was not family. He was a Guardian whose only purpose was to preserve the balance of magic. At any cost. She had just been his tool. His pawn.

But, despite her history with the Guardian, she put everything into the plea. Her desperation. Her grief. Her fear. If Rhyl was the child of the prophecy, and if Tayeh had contrived for him to be brought to Kitarra, then Tayeh would not dismiss her call. There was too much at stake.

Just before her chambers, an old Kitarran sat on a stone bench, gazing at the city and river lands below. He turned to look at her. Eva stopped in her tracks. Her heart fluttered with something akin to joy. Strange … what had happened to her anger? Her betrayal?

Tayeh shifted on his seat as if inviting her to join him, his amber eyes bright and unearthly. And kind. And sad.

"Tayeh," Eva whispered, sitting carefully beside the Guardian.

Tayeh smiled at her. "Eva."

Sobs suddenly choked her throat. Old tears and old grief mixed with the new, all fighting to surface. Eva wiped her nose on her sleeve and sniffed noisily.

"I need to reach Stone," she said.

Tayeh nodded. "I can show you how. But, Eva—" He stumbled over his words.

"What?"

"There are things—things I have not taught you. About your magic."

"No shit."

Tayeh almost smiled. "I am sorry."

"Teach me now."

Tayeh nodded, his hand on hers, his touch like sunlight. "I will teach you how to find Stone. Attin will teach you the rest."

CHAPTER 13

# EVA

EVA LEANED her head against the cendari tree. Tayeh sat across from her.

"Let's recall that *sanarii* use the *simul rami* within them to heal others, but to use their sight, they must command the elements. Water and Earth hold the past, Air, the present. Fire can be used in many ways. It is the most malleable of the elements. It can be destructive. It can bring life. A *sanarii* can also manipulate the elements in a tangible way." Tayeh's rhythmic way of speaking brought back a hundred days of Eva's childhood she had spent under his tutelage. "A *sanarii* can make it rain, create fire, call wind, and make the earth tremble. Not all, but some have the power of the Old Ones—like you."

"You never told me I have the power of the Old Ones. You didn't think I was worthy of that power?" Eva asked, unable to keep the bitterness from her voice.

"No. That was not it. You were—you are—worthy. I love you like a daughter, Evangeline."

Eva's heart bled a little, desperate to believe him. But she couldn't think about that now. She needed to find Stone.

"Do you remember when you were a child, and I told you about raw magic?" Tayeh continued.

"I remember you warning me about it."

"The *simul rami* is the vessel that holds magic, the energy of the world, but magic is permeable. Dark and light magic float around us, in the very air we breathe and the water we drink. The magic not contained inside the *simul rami* is raw magic—unpredictable magic."

"Like the *varing*."

"Yes."

"But a *sanarii* cannot control the *varing*."

"Correct."

"But a *candarii* can use the *simul rami*. I saw Cotoch using it to talk to someone with a gold basin—Selene, I assume—but she is *candarii*. Stone is not."

Tayeh held up his hand. "Back up a wee bit. Raw magic is the magic of the Forest Folk."

It had been over a year ago, but even a lifetime would not erase the memory of when the Forest Folk had come to Eva and infused her magic with theirs.

"Can I contact Stone in a dream space like when the *velidar* came to me in the Forest?" Eva asked hopefully.

Tayeh huffed. "Not exactly. I wish Lula were here to teach you this, but I will try my best. Each *sanarii* has an element with which they work the best, an element they can call to them. You have two."

Eva remembered the countless times the air flowed through her fingers, over her arms, around her body, humming with the *simul rami*, begging her to command it. Something stirred within her.

Something long forgotten, the feeling of heat and wind and air and smoke. The feeling of fire on her fingertips and ash in her lungs.

"Yes, Eva," Tayeh said. Each word dropped like a boulder. "Your kin elements are Air and Fire."

And she remembered.

"Air and Fire. A dangerous combination," she whispered. "I did it. I started the fire that killed my parents, didn't I? That is why you never told me this?"

Tayeh closed his eyes, defeated. Eva touched her face and found it wet. She wiped her eyes. Her parents had died because she had called the fire with the wisdom of a seven-year-old girl. Fear and grief wrapped around the logic in her memories.

"Was I right to keep it from you? I don't know anymore," Tayeh said.

"It would have been a hard burden to bear. Terrible. As a mother, I think I can understand your choice to keep it from me," Eva told her guardian. She would do anything to spare Rhyl pain and grief. But in the end, was that her role as his mother? She could not protect him. Obviously.

*Breathe. Just breathe.*

"I wanted you to know the truth," Tayeh said.

"We don't have time for your regrets! I need to find Stone, now!" Her desperation clawed at her sanity. "How do I use Fire without burning myself or everything around me?" Eva shivered despite herself, her hand on her rippling belly. "How do I use Fire and Air to create a dream space to contact Stone?" Her head hurt.

"I cannot teach you to control Fire. I know you do not want to risk your babes. And I cannot teach you to create a dream space—"

"Then what can you teach me?" Eva wailed.

He gave her a sad smile and touched her shoulder with one big hand. "Do you know why the Kitarrans are dying, Eva?"

"No." Eva closed her eyes. This was taking too long—she needed to find Stone.

"Each Kitarran carries a piece of the *simul rami* within them. Before birth, it is poisoned with the *varing*, and the babe dies; it is the only time the *varing* can infect a Kitarran. As a *sanarii*, you can connect to the *simul rami*, and therefore any Kitarran in the same way. And you are more powerful than you know."

Eva bit her lip. Did Arrah know this? Is that why Emri's first child died? Were Kitarrans really immune to the *varing* after they were born? The questions raced across her mind, but she silenced them.

"You do not need to create a dream space to contact him because he is Kitarran. You have felt this connection to Stone before," Tayeh reminded her.

"Yes, I guess I always sensed it … Tayeh, did you tell Arrah to leave me behind, hoping I would find Stone?"

"I did."

"But he abandoned me. In the end, I couldn't save him. In the end, he did not want to be saved."

"Yet here we are. Do you believe he will help you now?"

"Yes. Without a doubt."

"Then I was right in my decision," Tayeh said, though his voice grated at the admission.

Tayeh reached into one of his pockets and brought out the gold bowl, the one Eva had used as a child to connect to the *simul rami* for the first time. She took it from his hands, feeling like a little girl learning her first lesson about the *simul rami*. It was already filled with water—how, Eva could not fathom. That had always been her task. As a child, Tayeh had always asked her to fetch water for the seeing bowl. She remembered walking back to the glade in the Great Forest, every step measured so as not to spill a drop.

"First, you need to connect to the *simul rami* absolutely," Tayeh instructed. "Once you are there, you can navigate the river of magic. You must find Arrain's core—the part of him that is his alone. His own bit of raw magic."

"What if I get lost?" She wasn't sure if it was possible, but sometimes the *simul rami* felt enormous and alive, like it would embrace her in its light and she would never want to leave.

"I will be here to help you find your way back."

Eva swallowed. "What about my babies?"

"They should be all right."

Eva nodded, shifting the bowl in her hands. "I am ready."

"Then use the bowl."

Eva looked into the bright water. The *simul rami* pulsed up the roots of the cendari tree into her spine, down her arms, and through her fingers into the bowl. She thought of Stone, his white and gray fur, his yellow eyes, his lilting smile. His laugh. He had a good laugh.

"You must get inside his head, or you will be nothing more than a whisper, a figment of his imagination," Tayeh said, breaking Eva's concentration.

"What if Cotoch senses it? If he knows I can talk to Stone, he will kill him."

"*Candarii* cannot sense the presence of *sanarii* magic. And even if they could, I don't think Cotoch would have the training to do it."

It was not the most reassuring speech Tayeh had given her. But what choice did she have? And she knew Stone would risk his life to save the boys.

The gold bowl was warm in her hands. The tree behind her pulsed, as if urging her forward. She closed her eyes, letting her consciousness sink into her connection through the *simul rami*.

As she navigated the twists, the light, the ripples of energy that was the *simul rami*, she realized it was not the first time she had wandered down its branches to Stone. She reached out to the thread of magic she knew led to Stone and followed it. And there he was, a bright point in the river of magic.

She couldn't see where he was, not really. She was just there, inside his mind. She had healed Stone once. This was almost the same. She wrapped herself around his core of raw magic, his heartbeat loud in her ears. The dark stain of the culla coursed through his body; he was Cotoch's slave once more. He had broken his oath. Eva had no choice but to trust him. She called out to him with her magic and hoped.

CHAPTER 14

# STONE

STONE SWUNG HIS SWORD, moving through the series with ease and strength and speed. He could feel every pair of eyes in front of him devouring his technique, hoping it would stick in their minds and soak into their muscles. It wouldn't. It would take practice. And more practice. Oh, and yet more practice. Stone grinned as he finished, knowing he had made it look effortless.

"Your turn," Stone told the line of young recruits. They began. They faltered. Their courageous expressions melted toward defeat. Stone stopped them and started again, this time slower, going through each step, correcting their form where necessary. A collective sigh of relief came over the class.

They worked on the series all morning, until the men sagged under their fatigue, and their eyes glazed over, and Stone knew there was nothing else to teach them until they had a break and nourishment. They went off to the mess hall with sighs of relief. The kitchen smells had been permeating the practice ground for nearly an hour. Cotoch fed his soldiers well. Good food meant strong muscles and sharp minds.

"You there, hold up." Stone pointed his sword at the man's

collarbone. The young man was Jullayan, a recent exile from those parts. Dark hair. Dark eyes. Sinewy. Hard. The Jullayan looked at him with the venomous contempt of a cornered asp before his face slid into an expressionless mask. Stone had noticed the particular look from the corner of his eye earlier and wondered what he had done, besides the grueling practice, to deserve the youth's derision. "You are better than this class. Why are you holding back?"

The man held his chin up for an instant before lowering his gaze. He shrugged and tried to look small. A trick. He wanted to avoid attention. Stone's attention.

"What is your name?" Stone asked.

"Irri."

"You are Jullayan."

The man nodded.

"What are you doing in Mahlas?"

Another pointy-shouldered shrug. "What are any of us doing here? Starting a new life."

Stone narrowed his eyes at him, sensing a lie. Stone had gotten better at spotting lies, a remnant from his time with Eva. Sometimes he could swear she put thoughts in his head. That she was watching him from Kitarra. The idea made him shiver in revulsion. She would not be pleased with what she saw. Wasn't there an idiom about eavesdroppers not liking what they heard? *Yeah, go ahead, blame Eva. Like she got you into this mess.* Stone's self-deprecating sarcasm was not as fun when there was no one to share it with.

"Can I go? Am I dismissed?" Irri sulked.

Stone nodded. He let the boy take a few steps, then Stone pounced, his raised sword ready for a fake blow. Irri swiveled, blocked, moving with a speed and skill none of the other young men in the class had. Stone grinned, victorious. "We need to talk, I think."

Irri glowered at him for the deception. His mouth opened and he spoke, but Stone could not hear the words because a splitting pain blossomed in his skull. His reality tilted and faded. His feet felt like they had fused into the hard ground of the practice yard.

*She* was in his head. Fully. Overwhelmingly. He could even smell her human smell mixed with the scent of her *sanarii* magic.

*Stone.* Eva's voice was unmistakable.

It was like his mind was split in two. One part saw Irri, standing before him, his mouth moving slowly, so slowly, like time had made its own rules and no one knew what they were. The other part could see Eva. Her face, strained and worried, her hair a mess of starlight, her eyes bright, pleading, full of a thousand emotions and shades of blue and green.

*Stone?*

*Yes, but—but I think I have finally gone mad,* he managed to say.

*You are not mad. I am using my sanarii magic to get inside your head.*

Stone was at a loss for words. Almost. *Creepy,* he said.

*Stone, Talo and Rhyl have been kidnapped by a woman named Selene. I believe she is working for Cotoch. Another candarii. But I can't find her. I think she is taking the children to Mahlas.*

*What do you want me to do?*

*I want you to save them and bring them home. I want you to come home. And I don't know who else to ask.*

Stone wished she had left the last part out. It made him feel like the rotten apple in the basket.

*Where is Illiah?*

*He is in Markeh. Cotoch invaded Kitarra with an army. There was a battle. I have not yet heard any news.*

Eva floated in Stone's mind, but in reality, it was Irri standing before him, his lip turned up in disgust. Stone put his hand to his temple, hoping he wouldn't fall over.

"Did you even hear me?" Irri asked.

Stone held up one finger.

*That sounds … like a terrible coincidence. Cotoch's army invades Kitarra, Illiah leaves with a host of men, then the children go missing?* Stone mused. Cotoch had left with a fuck-ton of men, but Stone had thought they were headed to Allati.

Kitarra. Not good.

*Stone, I need you. Why did you leave?* Eva's voice was fading, but her grief was crystalline.

*You know why.*

*Not good enough.*

Silence.

*Please, save the boys,* Eva begged.

*You don't need to ask, milady.*

*Stone, I miss you.* Then she was gone. His head was put back together, but it felt quiet and empty, and, by the Old Ones, it hurt.

Stone shook his head, trying to focus his eyes, but it was like being blinded after looking too long at the sun. Eva's words had been clear, but now they were slipping from his memory. Through the splitting pain in his head, he could see Irri glaring at him.

"Wouldn't expect much else from a fucking turncoat," Irri mumbled. Stone grabbed his shoulder.

"Boy, you need to watch your tongue." *Even if I deserve it,* he almost said out loud. Irri shrugged Stone's hand from his shoulder, his face dark and hostile. Stone let him go. He would deal with him later.

Children. Fuck.

Stone did not know Cotoch's mind or his plans. He had never fully regained Cotoch's trust. And he preferred it that way.

*Coward.*

He preferred to pretend that he did not loathe Cotoch with all of his being. He took the culla Cotoch offered in exchange for his services. With the numbing liberties of the drug, it was too easy to mute his emotions in Cotoch's presence and forget what Cotoch had done to Eva. Stone had once vowed if he ever saw Cotoch again, he would kill him. But in reality, he had crawled back to Cotoch and begged for forgiveness. And culla.

Gods, his head hurt. Or was it his heart?

CHAPTER 15

# STONE

STONE HELD the small vial in his hand and studied the pinch of gray powder inside. He pulled out the stopper and tossed the contents into his mouth, feeling the culla dissolve on his tongue. It tasted a little sour and a lot like shame.

Not a minute later, he felt the drug move through his body. Once, the culla had made him feel invincible, alive. Now it gave him energy, but something was lacking from its release. His heart was still heavy; the culla was not holding up its side of the bargain.

Stone lay on his bed. For the first few minutes, the culla made his head spin and his arms tingle. He closed his eyes, his mind racing around what Eva had told him—how she had told him. Last time he had seen her, her magic had become weak and useless. Evidently, a temporary condition, and somewhere along the way she had learned to burrow into his mind like a parasite.

He could not recall anything about *sanarii* being able to mind-speak. The culla made his heart race, and each thought came and went with speed and clarity, but there was no wisdom attached. Each thought was born and tossed away.

His mind found itself in a dark place.

*Arrain.* A voice called his name. For an instant, Stone thought it was Emri. But no, Emri was dead. Even in his mind and memories, his wife was dead and buried. Or so he liked to tell himself. Nor was the voice Eva's. Maybe it was his conscience.

*Arrain.*

No, the voice was not his own. It was coming from below. From somewhere deep, like in the earth, not within himself. Stone opened his eyes and felt … something. A something he could also smell. Moss and dew and dirt. Crisp air on a fall morning. The culla did strange things to him sometimes. But this felt different. There was magic involved, but not Eva's magic. Old magic.

"Where are you?" Stone asked out loud.

*Down in the dark where he keeps me.*

Stone shivered. He had pretended, like many who lived in Cotoch's sprawling house, that there were not strange doorways that led to deep, dark places in the dusty corners of the old building. And he had pretended it was not a coincidence when an enemy spy or someone who had earned Cotoch's wrath disappeared—not unlike the vague and unsettling rumors about Sandra, Cotoch's wife.

*He will be back soon. He brings death with him.*

Stone assumed "he" was Cotoch. Stone spun, feeling a watchfulness from the corner of his room. He saw it—her?—for an instant. Dark green skin like tree bark. Hair like moss, or maybe feathers. Skinny like a sun-starved seedling. Round eyes black as pitch. Sad eyes.

One of the Old Ones. The spirit disappeared as soon as he saw it, like shadows coalescing without the sun.

"What do you want?" Stone asked.

*I want you to kill him. I want … I need you to kill him …*

"Cotoch?" Stone whispered.

*No. The other one. The one who brings pain without death. Darkness without stars.*

"What is his name?"

*I cannot speak in names.*

"You spoke my name."

*But you are not like them. You have worn death, and death has made us kin.* The voice faded, its strength spent.

Stone did not like the sound of that. Not one fucking bit.

CHAPTER 16

# EVA

THE GRASS WAS GOLDEN. The wind had died down to a breeze and smelled like sweet herbs. Eva stood upon the crest of a hill: below stretched the valley plain, the Tarm. Above her, around her, spread the branches of a cendari tree whose leaves flickered like music, bells, or quiet drums, or the beating of a lover's heart. She reached out her hands to touch the leaves. Her arms were green and covered with moss, her fingers patterned like tree bark.

Eva turned to see Illiah beside her. It was Illiah, but it wasn't Illiah. He smiled at her, his green eyes bright, laughing, like a boy without a care. Happy. She couldn't remember the last time she had seen such peace on his face. She cupped his cheek with her hand and closed her eyes to kiss his lips, her breath mingling with his. She felt the kiss along her body, down to her toes, like warm water rushing over her. Drowning, she reflected, would be an easy way to perish.

Illiah dropped her touch and moved away. Eva opened her eyes. The sun and its golden caress was gone. Illiah stood with his back to her, looking at the valley plain below. The grass of the Tarm was brown. The wind gusted through the branches of the tree and tugged at her hair, but still, she did not feel its chill upon her skin. She called to Illiah. He turned to her and Eva felt fear like a thunderclap.

Illiah's face had morphed. Part animal, part plant, part rotten. His hands were claws and bone. His mouth was filled with sharp teeth. His lips stretched into nonexistence. His skin was black and oily, dripping dark blood from wounds torn across his skin. He was a nightmare. He was consumed. The smell of sour ash was thick on the wind.

In Eva's hand was a spear. It was long and lithe, taller than she, and made entirely from wood. A flash of light rippled down the length of the smooth spearshaft. The wind howled. The thing that had been Illiah stepped toward her. She had no choice. She plunged the spear point into the his chest.

Horrified, she turned to flee, to find comfort in the cendari tree, in the *simul rami*. But the tree was black. The leaves turned to ash, the limbs rotting and severed. Eva recognized the dead tree. She had rested under its black limbs as she fled Mahlas with Stone in the dead of night. As soon as her consciousness took hold of the memory, it shifted into another. A burning building pushed up against a cliff, flames towering up toward trees of immeasurable height and Eva screaming and crying and pleading in the terrified voice of a little girl.

Eva woke from the dream. Her nose was stuffed, and her cheeks were wet. Armeria leaped onto the bed, sensing her distress, whining, putting her cold nose on Eva's arm, licking her skin. Eva wove her fingers into the dog's fur, smelling her familiar doggy smell.

A dream. A dream. Only a dream. A nightmare. A memory.

She pulled her blankets tight around her throat, her body

shivering. Armeria tucked herself close, the dog's comforting body heat soaking through the blankets. But still, Eva shook. Memories filtered through her grief. The dream had felt familiar. Like the thing that attacked Illiah years ago by the Keep, dragged away by a creature of the Forest. She would never forget how it looked and smelled and felt. And then again, it had taken shape along the river a year ago. The Serac monster on the beach that Stone had killed with a vercuri. Both times, it had taken Illiah's mind, his body. Dark magic wanted Illiah like a hound slavering for meat. It did not make sense, but she felt it as a certainty. Eva could not protect him. She never could.

And somehow she knew if the dark magic consumed Illiah, terrible things would happen.

"Milady?" Anfru's quiet voice shocked Eva from the thoughts her nightmare had birthed. His voice shook a little.

"What is it? Talo and Rhyl?" Eva asked. Her beating heart pressed against a thousand knives.

"No, Eva. It's Illiah. He has been taken by Cotoch."

CHAPTER 17

# STONE

STONE USUALLY ate alone. Sometimes Rory or Hawk would share his table, but the rest called him a turncoat, a betrayer. Even among exiles, there was honor. And Stone had none.

The mess hall was always loud, always busy, full of boys trying to become men, and men trying to *be* men. Cotoch kept them well in line. There was very little ale or other spirits. Now and then, a few wenches and a keg of ale were smuggled in and kept hidden until the captains found out—the usual stuff. Most of the young men were from Allati, naturally. The Allati regarded their sons as competition for the women. Unless they were of noble blood or firstborn, they were usually exiled at a young age. Mahlas welcomed them with open arms and gave them occupations and food, and Cotoch fed their dreams and ambitions handful by deceptive handful.

Stone was pretty sure Cotoch believed in his philanthropy. He believed he was a good lord to his people. And Stone ruefully admitted that in some ways, he was. But there was something else going on in Mahlas—Cotoch was a sorcerer.

No one had seen Lady Sandra for nearly a year. There were rumors that she had left Cotoch and returned to Kitarra, that the turbulence of their relationship, which was no secret, grew to the point of fracturing their union. Stone didn't quite believe it. Sandra had been too ambitious to go back to being a merchant's daughter, to beg coin and riches from her parents. And Cotoch had never flinched when Sandra took her own lovers. The timing of her disappearance coincided with Eva's escape. Sandra was the reason Eva had been able to escape, which would have enraged Cotoch.

Stone had never liked Sandra, so why did he care if she was gone? He didn't.

There were rumors that Cotoch was looking for a new wife. A small group of men had just arrived from Allati. Stone had a feeling alliances were being made. Was Rhyl's kidnapping part of it? Stone wished he had Eva's ability to snoop with magic.

There were no rumors about a kidnapping. It had been a week since Eva's infiltration into his head and still not a whisper wafted around Mahlas, which was strange. Usually, Mahlas was a cobweb of intrigue and loose tongues. Could Eva be mistaken? Maybe it was the Allati who had taken Rhyl. But why would the Allati want Talo? Collateral? Stone's gut clenched like a constricting snake. Talo was the least of the prizes; what if they hurt him? No. They wouldn't hurt Talo. He wasn't Kitarra's chosen one, but he was the prince.

Stone's food tasted off. He shoved his plate away.

The young Jullayan walked through the hall, looking like a gloomy shadow.

"Irri," Stone hailed. The man swiveled, a drink in his hand. "Sit with me a moment." Irri glanced around the hall, no doubt wondering if he could disobey. Stone was his superior, and a Kitarran warrior. Surely someone would have warned the newcomer to watch out for Cotoch's pet?

Irri came over and sat beside him on the bench, hunched over his drink, waiting with bored, heavy eyes.

"Where did you train?" Stone asked again, putting a growl into his voice. The sound was enough to make most recruits wet themselves, but Irri just glowered at Stone, resolute. "You are too good not to have been trained somewhere."

Irri opened his mouth, but a shout came from the door.

"Lord Cotoch is back! And you gotta see who he has with him!" The man spoke with a Mahlas accent, a born child of the city. Second generation. Stone heard the victory in the man's voice and died a little inside. Silly analogy. As far as Stone knew, death didn't want him.

He shared a look with Irri, and they both rose, following the crowd out into the courtyard to see what the excitement was about.

The expanse of the courtyard spread out between the training buildings and Cotoch's main house. The cobbles were invisible under the feet of a few hundred men. The air filled with shouts of victory and gleeful rage. Cotoch sat in the saddle grinning, not like a boy with a toy but like a cat with a mouse. Stone saw him, a lord, a man of cunning action, a man hundreds would follow and pledge their lives to. A force.

Cotoch caught Stone's gaze, holding him with his dark eyes. Stone swallowed hard. He had let himself become a slave to this man. Again. His cowardice crept along his spine, but it was not alone; the faint buzz of the culla robbed his shame of its potency. Stone noticed the corner of Cotoch's mouth twitch into a triumphant smile as Stone dropped his gaze.

Cotoch raised his arms for silence. "Behold, our victory!" Their victory was in the form of a prisoner. Tied and gagged and slumped on a horse. Dark hair slick with rain or blood, shoulders stooped with pain and exhaustion. Stone could tell the man was injured. There were a few other prisoners, on foot—a Kitarran and two young men. Their eyes spit daggers.

"Illiah," a quiet voice breathed at Stone's elbow. Stone caught Irri's eye. Irri realized he had spoken out loud.

Stone turned back to Cotoch's prisoner with more perception. "By Attin's sagging nipples," he whispered.

It *was* Illiah.

Stone had only spent a short time with Eva's husband, and with his swollen and muddied face, Stone had not immediately recognized him. But now that he looked harder, there was no mistaking Illiah's proud features. Stone grabbed Irri by the arm and propelled him away from the crowd into the building at their back.

Irri did not protest, but his shoulders squared, his eyes darted, looking for an out. Stone found the darkest, smallest corner he could squeeze himself and Irri into.

"Who are you?" Stone demanded, twisting Irri's arm. Literally. The young man cringed in pain.

"A better question would be, who are you?" the youth spit back.

Stone pressed harder, but the boy stopped cringing and merely glared at Stone with dark, hateful eyes, swallowing his pain. Stone had to give it to him—the boy was tough.

"I know who you are, Arrain," Irri hissed.

Nothing could have hit Stone harder than hearing his real name from the lips of a waifish stranger from Jullayah. And that was saying something because Stone had had both a *sanarii* and an old spirit in his head.

"Your fur is different, whiter. But I know it is you."

"What are you talking about?" Stone growled.

"I know you—knew you. Years ago when I was more boy than man. An orphan. I was sent on a mission for my realm." Irri let his Jullayan accent slip from his voice to be replaced by an accent that matched Stone's. "Emri trained me. Do you not remember?"

Stone spent a significant amount of his energy trying not to recall the days and weeks and months before Emri died. He reluctantly remembered, but it was not with clarity. The culla messed with his head. He vaguely remembered the spies Emri was training to infiltrate Jullayah to get close to Eva. It had been done in secret. No one knew but Emri, a few of her most trusted guards, and Arrain, of course. Emri did not keep secrets from her husband.

"I am not that man anymore."

Irri gave Stone a look that spoke to the obviousness of the statement.

"You know Illiah," Stone whispered. "There is nothing you can do for him. Cotoch will not let him live." The words tasted like shit. "But if I can trust you, I need your help. What was Illiah to you?"

"Illiah was my friend. A good man. A brave man. I am from Kitarra, but I would die for him."

"Good. But it is not Illiah we need to save. Rhyl and—" *My son.* But he could not say it out loud. "The Kitarran Prince has been kidnapped. Do you know Illiah's wife, Eva?"

"The men say you betrayed her."

*Ah, so this is why he hates me.* Loyal little fuck.

"I failed her," Stone admitted. "But I will not fail her in this. She has gotten a message to me saying that Cotoch's spy has kidnapped the children and is bringing them here. We need to get them back to Kitarra. Can I trust you?"

"You already have, or I would be dead, wouldn't I?"

Stone shrugged a nod.

Irri laughed harshly. "But can I trust you, turncoat?"

"In this, you can," Stone said. "I will die before I let Cotoch have Eva's son and Talo."

Irri glared with malice—as if Stone had spent every day of his life drowning kittens.

"But Illiah—the others."

"We can't help Illiah. The others? I don't know. But the children are more important."

Irri nodded, but it cost him.

Stone gripped his shoulders. "You knew Illiah?"

"Very well. Rhyl will know me, I think. It has been a long time."

"That will be good and bad. But mostly good. I don't want Rhyl giving you away. But they don't know me at all. And I need them to trust me."

"What do we do?"

"We need information. See what you can find out." Stone glanced up to see that their small corner was no longer undiscovered. Captain Easra was coming over to them, smirking. Easra had moved up in Cotoch's ranks over the last year. Easra knew Stone despised him and loved to remind Stone that Easra was now Cotoch's go-to person, instead of Stone. Time to improvise. Stone took Irri by the collar and hit him.

"Watch your tongue, boy." Stone shoved Irri aside, not even giving him a second glance. He heard him scamper off.

Easra raised a brow. "The lord wants to see you," he sneered.

"Of course he does. He can't fuck around without an audience."

But inwardly, Stone couldn't begin to wonder what Cotoch wanted of him. Easra shook his head, muttering sharply about rabid dogs that needed to put out of their misery. Easra knew nothing about misery.

# EVA

A COLD TEAR dripped down Eva's nose. Another followed it. Eva couldn't bring herself to wipe them away.

Her room was bright. Sunlight came in through the tall windows. The marble walls glinted amidst the rich fabrics and tapestries. Once, the sun had been beautiful. Now, it was too bright. Too real. Too quiet. She would have traded every sunlit day for her room to be filled with the laughter and bubbling voices of Rhyl and Talo, and to feel Illiah's arms wrap around her.

She could not find Illiah. His thread within the *simul rami* was shrouded in dark like Rhyl's and Talo's. But Eva did not think he was dead.

A ripple of pain flowed through her belly. She winced against it, curling like a dying spider. She had to be careful; her body was heavy with her twins. The last few weeks, testing out her magic, reaching out to Stone, had weakened her. The babes would die if they were born too soon.

In the silence of her rest, her thoughts were not good company. A tempest of tears shook her body. She forced herself to breathe, in and out. In and out. Armeria stirred from her place beside her, giving Eva's arm a thorough licking.

With effort, Eva reached up to grab Arrain's journal where it sat on the table beside her bed, opening it to a random page.

*The midwife confirmed that Emri is pregnant. It is terrifying for both of us. Emri and I have both seen our siblings born still and dead. Emri's mother died in childbirth, like so many Kitarran women. I wonder if it is the varing's effect on us Kitarrans. Not even we can escape the evilness of it.*

*The babe died … Emri is alive. Our hearts hurt. It was a little girl. We buried her beside her grandfather.*

So much grief. Poor Arrain. Eva had hope, a gift Arrain never had. Eva believed in Illiah, in his strength. She had to. She knew no other way forward. Even without the vercuri, Illiah was still a force. And Stone—Arrain—he too had strength, even if he didn't know it. He would believe in himself before the end. And Rhyl and Talo had the blood of their fathers—and their mothers. They, too, were strong. Cotoch did not know the force of love and determination he was playing with. Yes, Eva should have killed him, but she did not believe for an instant that he would win.

"Milady?" Anfru hadn't knocked, he had opened the door quietly to see if she was awake. "There is a messenger, one of Illiah's soldiers."

Eva snapped the book shut, sitting up in the bed. "Bring him."

"Her."

Eva gave her head a little shake. "Right. Bring her."

A young woman came in, her boots flecked with mud, face covered in grime, eyes sunken with fatigue.

"My lady, Lord Illiah has been taken by the enemy." When Eva did not answer, the young woman continued, "It was a trap. Cotoch baited him—"

"And Illiah took it." Illiah's hatred for Cotoch rivaled only her own. And Illiah was a man of action, a man of justice. He could not make Cotoch accountable for what he had done to her, and oh, how it had gnawed at him. Long ago, it had been Serac who had been beyond his reach, then it was Cotoch. Still, Illiah was a smart man. He should have seen it. Why had he not seen it?

"What happened?" Eva's voice was calm. That strange calm, so at odds with the waves of her riotous emotions, frightened her

"Lord Illiah broke from his position with his men, riding across the plain. No one knew what he was doing until he was beyond our reach. His horse was too fast. Aisha followed him and a few others, but they were taken."

Another shard pierced her heart. Aisha. Lord Susor would be anguished. "Who were the others?"

"Antoli. Grip."

Eva did not know them, but she needed to hear their names.

"Cotoch was gone before we knew what happened. Before we could get enough soldiers together to go after him. They retreated, we pursued, but we never caught up with him."

"But Illiah was alive?"

The young woman's lips quivered, reminding Eva how very young she was. "We think so, my lady."

"And Aisha? The others?"

"We think they were all taken alive."

Were.

Eva nodded. Her hope was a dagger. It would cut her if she let it slip.

"What do we do?" the young woman asked, her eyes brimming with that same dangerous hope.

"We can't help Illiah, not now. Illiah would tell us to focus on the children." Eva could not say it without a sob catching in her voice.

The warrior nodded; she would have heard about Rhyl and Talo. All of Kitarra was swarming with anger over their abduction. Cotoch was a fool not to realize he was playing with wildfire. There was nothing Kitarra loved more than those two boys.

"Milady." Anfru reappeared. Eva hadn't even noticed he had left. "Another messenger has arrived. From Cotoch."

"Help me dress, Anfru." Eva reached out her hand for Anfru.

"What do we know of this messenger?" Eva asked as Anfru draped her Kitarran gibrar over her shoulder. The Kitarran robe was only worn by royalty. It had been a gift from Arrah. Beyond its significance, it was both comfortable and beautiful.

"He is from Mahlas, born and raised," Anfru told her. "No ties to Allati or Kitarra. He claims to have an important message from Cotoch and begs an audience with the queen."

So many hats did Anfru wear. Counselor. Manservant. Conscience. "But not with me?"

"Not that I am aware."

Eva pinned her hair back with two gold clips. The woman

looking at her from the reflection of the tall polished mirror looked like a warrior mother, a queen. The gibrar did its job well.

Anfru led Eva to the queen's tertiary solar, a room that high-lighted the beauty and expertise of Kitarran architecture with its pronounced, curving beams. Wood framed the elaborate glass windows. The quantity of glass spoke of wealth and riches more than any textile or polished floor.

Queen Arrah sat, her back straight, her hands resting gently on the arms of her chair. It was not exactly a throne, but it was regal. She had two Queen's Guards behind her, both women, and her two uandians at her side. Armeria walked beside Eva as she went to sit in a chair beside the queen. Eva tried to walk without waddling and failed. The chair took up space where the First Defender would stand, but Eva could not stand long enough to look regal or imposing.

Eva shared a look with Arrah. The queen's sad eyes were crisp, merciless.

"Bring in the messenger," Arrah commanded, shifting a little in her chair.

More Queen's Guards escorted the messenger who was a man of middle years with nothing exceptional to note. Eva would not have picked him out from a crowd. There was nothing offensive or aggressive about his countenance. Only the knowledge that he was Cotoch's man made her want to reprehend him.

"Queen Arrah," the man said, his voice surprisingly pleasant. "Lady Evangeline." He nodded to Eva. "I bring tidings from Lord Cotoch. He has your princes and your First Defender, and if you move to attack Mahlas, they will die."

Arrah looked at Eva. It was not new information. Attacking Mahlas was beyond foolish.

"What does Cotoch want from us?" Eva asked.

"He offers a trade. You, Lady Evangeline, for your son and Kitarra's prince." The man's eyes rested on Eva's bulging belly.

Eva raised a brow. "What of Lord Illiah?"

"He is not part of the bargain."

A silence fell over the atrium, heavy and uncertain. Eva could feel the queen radiating with outrage. Eva felt nothing. She was cold, empty.

"You may leave," Arrah commanded. "You will be shown hospitality. We will send for you when we are ready. Uya, show this man to the east wing," Arrah commanded. Uya nodded, taking the man by the elbow. He looked put out that he was being dismissed—perhaps there was more he had to say. But Eva was done with him, as was the queen.

With the enemy gone, Arrah leaned toward Eva, giving her arm an affectionate pat.

"Dear one, you can't consider it."

Eva exhaled slowly. She could consider it—was considering it. She would give anything for Rhyl and Talo. Her freedom—her life—was a small price to pay. Infinitesimal. But she would not condemn her unborn twins. And there was still hope. There was still Stone.

Eva had not told Arrah the truth about Stone. She had only told the queen that her amourii, her Kitarran exile, was in Mahlas and that if needed, he would give his life to rescue the boys. It was cowardly to keep the truth from Arrah. And worst of all, Eva could imagine being in her place, believing her son to be dead. Part of Eva longed to tell Arrah that Stone was Arrain, her son, but it wasn't her secret to tell.

"You still believe your exile can save them?" Arrah pressed, her mouth thin.

"Yes."

"You have a lot of faith in him. I hope it is not misguided."

"It is not, I assure you." As Eva spoke, her gut tightened; a tiny part of her knew the lie in her words. She wanted to have the utmost faith in Stone, but he had broken his promise, his honor. He had chosen the path of a coward. He had chosen fear over loyalty. Grief over love. Maybe he did not know another way.

# CHAPTER 19

# STONE

"COTOCH, I see you have found a prize," Stone said by way of greeting.

"Stone, you are a cur," Cotoch muttered, but he was still grinning with his victory. Stone knew Cotoch had long since given up threatening him using proper titles and all the respectable phrases and manners that went with it.

Easra's frown was all kinds of ugly where he stood at attention. Easra would never address Cotoch as Stone did. He didn't have the balls for it. Or maybe Easra was just the smart one.

Cotoch poured wine. White. From his pillaging, Stone guessed. Stone had expected Cotoch to cause more trouble since Eva had taken refuge there, ending his alliance with Kitarra. But he hadn't. Cotoch had sat brooding in Mahlas—until now. Maybe he hadn't been brooding so much as planning.

And still Stone had sided with Cotoch. For what? The culla? The culla.

"Come with me," Cotoch said. He did not need to adjust the tone of his voice to sound commanding. It was in his eyes, his cadence.

Stone obeyed and followed Cotoch through the house, each

passageway darker and older than the next. Stone had never been in this part of the house before. Stone wasn't sure what was more disconcerting—the dark, ageless stone walls that emitted dread and pain like a visceral sensation, or the fact that there were more and more secrets about Cotoch he did not know. Maybe the rumors were true. The words of the Old One haunted him: *Down in the dark where he keeps me.*

Stone was walking blind and barefoot into the viper's nest. With the life of two boys in the balance, Stone's chest tightened, and an old anxiety boiled in his bones. Would this be the day death finally claimed him? When he most needed to live? If so, it would be no more than he deserved.

The damp stone seemed to soak up any light, any hope. Away from the warming fires of Cotoch's house, the air was cold. There was no way Cotoch's father had built the tunnels or the crypts; they were centuries old. Had it been a temple? An ancient Kitarran fortress? Even with his Kitarran eyes, he couldn't see much of the architecture concealed in shadows, but what he could see did not strike him as Kitarran. It was so old.

"I need a test of your loyalty, Stone." Cotoch's voice was loud in the dark. Stone pushed the lump of fear down deep. Not failure, not yet.

"Loyalty? Have I not given you reason to trust me? Done everything you asked?" Stone argued.

"A war is coming. I need to know you are on my side. Or—" Cotoch glanced behind him where his guards trailed in the darkness. "Or you do not leave the dark." Stone noticed how death was not part of the bargain. Of course not. Fate wanted Stone alive.

Cotoch's cold eyes shone with dark magic, and Stone felt like a fool. Cotoch was not a ruthless leader bent on the survival of his people, he was a sorcerer. For once, Stone had nothing to say. No quip or curse. He had a dreadful notion of how Cotoch was going to ask for his loyalty.

Cotoch put the torch he had been holding into a wall bracket and unlocked a dark door before them. The torchlight brushed the circular walls, fading into a ceiling so high and dark it looked like a night sky devoid of stars and moon. The torchlight was bright enough to outline Cotoch's prisoner.

*No* was Stone's first anguished thought. *Not this.*

Illiah sat hunched on the stone floor. His lip was split, and there was blood on his chin, his neck. His hands were bound behind his back; tight ropes bound his feet. He looked up with lucid, hate-filled eyes that met Stone's and hardened. Stone could feel Cotoch watching him.

"You know this man?" Cotoch confirmed.

"Yes. He is Lord Illiah, First Defender of Kitarra." Stone made sure his voice was emotionless. "Eva's husband."

"Yes. Her lover. Her mate."

"You want me to loosen his tongue?" He had done it enough for Cotoch in the past. Hurt a man to get information. He knew the pressure points on a man's flesh. He had a feeling Illiah would not cow easily. He was a strong man.

Cotoch nodded. Illiah stiffened as Stone approached. He took Illiah by the cuff of his blood-soaked shirt and tossed him to the ground. It would hurt, but Stone could have thrown him much harder; the force would not likely break any bones. Then he picked Illiah up again and sat him on the hard ground before landing a blow on Illiah's chin. The punch was not enough to knock him hard, and the poor man's face was already wet and stained with blood. Stone hoped Illiah would get the message and pretend that it did. After two more blows which looked worse than they were, Illiah lay on his side, gasping. Stone was pleased; Illiah was a good actor.

Stone turned to Cotoch expectantly.

Cotoch shook his head slowly. "I have no questions for him. That is not why we are here."

What did Cotoch mean by that? Did he know about Arrain? No. Not likely. If he hadn't known six years ago, he wouldn't know now.

Stone shrugged as if his pointless cruelty was of no consequence.

Cotoch approached Illiah and crouched to look him more or less in the eye. Illiah lay with his head on the hard stone, meeting Cotoch's eyes with equal malice. The tension of the room permeated into the walls, an invisible storm.

Cotoch unclasped the sword at his belt. Stone ignored the injustice in his heart. The fine sword was beautifully crafted. It had spent some time in Stone's keeping. Illiah's sword, a weapon fit for a prince, a blade ever eager to deal out death. Stone had tested its ruthlessness.

"Your sword is mine. Your latha is being smelted down. Your wife will never forget that I have claimed her, and before the end, she, too, will be mine. Your son is mine. Ah, yes. You did not know, but even as we speak, Selene is on her way here with young Rhyl and Talo. Kitarra should have guarded its treasures better. What a realm of fools." Cotoch's sharp words filled the damp stillness with his victory. Illiah remained quiet. A lesser man would have screamed and wailed and begged to know the truth. But Illiah didn't. There was no fear in Illiah's eyes, only anger, hate, and frustration. Stone suspected Illiah's helplessness was more painful than any wound Stone could inflict.

Cotoch waited, but still, Illiah said not a word, which Stone knew would infuriate Cotoch more than he let on. Cotoch clipped the sword back to his hip. He handed Stone a dagger.

"Kill him," Cotoch commanded.

Stone could not afford to hesitate. Even a sliver of indecision would give away his heart, and he would never see the day and save the boys. He would never see his son. In two long steps, he was before Illiah's bound and helpless body, kneeling on the hard stone, heart pounding. But he could not show his fear or his absolute disgust at what he was about to do. He could not let Cotoch see the shaking in his hands.

Illiah looked up at him, his eyes unafraid. Stone blocked Illiah's face from Cotoch with his body.

"Get the children home," Illiah whispered. Stone gave him the barest of nods and put the knife to Illiah's throat. He thought of himself in Illiah's place and wished with all his heart he was the one under the knife. His nostrils filled with the smell of earth and dew.

*He needs to die,* the voice of the old spirit said for Stone's ears only. But the faint, magic-tainted words shook with anguish.

"Kill me," whispered Illiah.

# CHAPTER 20

# EVA

*Come with me.*

The voice was leaves rustling in a summer wind. Water pouring over rocks. A lifetime of sunny spring days. Eva had heard the distinctive voice before. She would never in her life forget it.

Over a year ago, Eva had stood over Cotoch, a dagger in her hands, the smell of his dark magic in her nose, and her body aching with what he had done to her. She had wanted to kill Cotoch then, but someone had stopped her. Someone with that same voice had begged for Cotoch's life. Eva had stayed her hand and fled with Stone instead of killing Cotoch.

Now, she wasn't sure it had been the right choice. Cotoch had taken everything from her.

For a year, Eva had questioned her memories of that moment. Had she imagined the voice in her head and the comforting smell of the forest in her nose as she contemplated gutting Cotoch? Had it been her conscience warning her that killing Cotoch would have stained her soul for eternity? No, she had come to believe it had been something other. And now the same voice was calling to her, pulling her.

She had tried to see into Mahlas, to find Rhyl and Talo and Illiah. But all she could see was darkness, walls of dark magic closing around them. Then she sensed it—moss and green and living things, but also darkness, another cage. The *simul rami* led her deep under Cotoch's house. She could smell damp moss and earth. She was plunged into a mind that was not her own. Invisible chains surrounded her. And longing, a thirst for light and air and earth.

*Come with me.*

Eva's eyes were the spirit's eyes. Her beating heart was that of the rocks and hidden creeks. She was no longer entirely Eva, *sanarii*, wife, and mother. She was something other. Something as old as the earth itself.

She watched Cotoch come down into the dark. Something broke and shuddered inside her as he approached. Her hands which were not quite hands trembled like winter-crisp leaves. Cotoch was not alone—a tall Kitarran followed him. A Kitarran with fur that gleamed silver in the torchlight accented by stripes and spots that danced like shadows. Eva saw what the spirit saw, felt what the creature felt, but she was also still herself, and she recognized Stone.

Cotoch's focus was on a hunched form before him. A man. It was Illiah, bound immobile and injured. At Cotoch's command, Stone hit Illiah, tossing him to the floor. Stone could have been washing dishes, or tending a fire, for the lack of expression on his face.

"Kill him," Cotoch commanded.

Stone took the dagger from Cotoch without hesitation and put it to Illiah's throat.

Eva screamed. She lunged. But she did not own the body she inhabited—if she could even call it a body. She could not command it. She was there by invitation, and her mouth felt like it was filled with cotton, and a warning was in her mind: *You cannot fight this.*

"Stop."

Cotoch's voice rippled against the dead stone. He smiled. Illiah's breath came out in a ragged sigh of relief as Stone released the blade from his neck.

"Unfortunately, it is not I who will kill you, Illiah." Cotoch jerked his head meaningfully toward Stone. Nothing changed in Stone's expression, but he stood and followed Cotoch away from the prisoner, taking the torches with them.

They left behind absolute darkness. Eva reached out with the *simul rami* and the strange spirit's magic, and moved to find Illiah in the dark, giving him some of her magic, healing some of his injuries. They weren't as bad as she'd expected. Stone must have been playing Cotoch when he tossed Illiah around. Of course, he was. Eva could trust Stone.

*You must leave this place. And him.*

And suddenly, Eva knew the reason she had been brought to the dark to see Illiah. She was given a chance to say goodbye. Why or how, she could not say, but she knew it with certainty. But she couldn't. Wouldn't.

Abruptly, the spirit pushed her away. Eva could sense the *varing* taint the *simul rami*, and she knew she had to leave. The old spirit was shrinking into the stone, into the shadows, filled with fear. Eva could feel it bone deep.

*Leave,* it commanded.

"Who are you?" Eva asked. But there was no answer because Eva was alone in her body, in her mind. The dark, the *varing*, the old spirit, Illiah, were gone.

CHAPTER 21

# COTOCH

"I THOUGHT we had agreed to wait. The timing of this is not ideal," Cotoch muttered, sipping back his wine with less relish than he preferred. The relief he felt at Illiah's capture was beyond what he had expected. He felt like a god. Powerful. The man had fallen into his trap like a hungry fox. Seeing Illiah bloodied, beaten, and helpless was a balm over Cotoch's aching soul.

And then Selene had turned up with two little princes.

He turned to Selene, who sat straight-backed, beautiful and serene, watching him with a flash of annoyance.

She has grown into a beautiful woman, Cotoch thought. If he had a daughter, would this be what she would look like? Would she be as haughty? Something akin to regret pierced his heart and made him take another sip of the piquant wine.

"It was the perfect time," Selene challenged. "With your attack on Markeh, everyone in Kilev was distracted. It was easier than I thought to get the children away from the palace."

"And how are the little treasures?"

"Shaken. I calmed Rhyl, but Talo is less malleable," Selene replied. "But they are too young to do anything other than cower."

"What do you think they will do?" *They* were Kitarra. The queen. Eva.

Selene shrugged. "I think they will listen to your messenger. Eva will do anything for her son. And Arrah will do anything for her grandson. But—"

Cotoch pushed the feeling of excitement down. He could not afford the disappointment if Selene was wrong.

"Eva is pregnant," Selene told him. "With twins. She won't risk her unborn children."

"Twins?" The idea was repulsive. Eva, her lithe form, stretched and bulging with not one, but two babies. But at the same time, he felt a stab of jealousy for Illiah, which was ridiculous. Illiah was not enviable now, locked and abused in Cotoch's crypt.

"The men say you are leaving in the morning," Selene stated.

"I am taking Illiah to Rodan, to your father. Hence the poor timing."

Selene straightened, her eyes narrowing. Her sharp inhale revealed her dismay.

"To Rodan?" Her voice quivered a little. "Am I invited?"

"No. If your father wanted you home, he would have told me."

Cotoch poured himself another glass of wine, offering Selene a drink with a gesture. She shook her head. Her expression melted into something forlorn and young.

"You didn't think you would get to keep Illiah, did you?"

Selene shot him a glance that told him she had hoped for that. Very much.

"I have something more for you. I have made alliances in Allati. I want you to go there. Together, we can take that realm for our own."

"Allati?"

"Yes, my dear."

"But the Allati have hunted our kind for hundreds of years."

Cotoch laughed. "The Shadow Guard is almost gone. The Allati wouldn't know a *candarii* if it sat across from them at the dinner table. Can you imagine if *candarii* were as easy to spot as the pale-haired *sanarii*?" he thought out loud. Then he shook his head. "Think of it, Selene. A throne. Riches. Power. You have been a servant for too long; you were born to rule." Selene was the natural daughter of an emperor. Cotoch could see he had her at that last bit.

"What about the children?"

"They stay here, guarded and taken care of."

"You wouldn't hurt them?"

"You wouldn't have brought them here if you thought that."

Selene glared. "How do you know me so well?"

"We are blood, Selene."

"Can I see him before—before you take him away?"

Cotoch regarded his niece. He wondered if he should deny her. It was for her own good, after all. Illiah would go to Rodan, and there he would die. Why dwell on what one couldn't have? Like he should talk.

Cotoch sighed. "Fine. Come."

He took his wine glass and told Selene to grab a torch. She held it gingerly, trying to make sure it didn't drip on her gown. Yes, Cotoch thought, Selene would not settle well in Mahlas. She liked her finery. She liked being powerful. She would do well in Allati.

Cotoch led her down to the crypt. The cell was down deep, but not near the deepest part of Cotoch's secrets. Cotoch nursed his wine as they walked down, down, down.

"This is an awful place," Selene remarked. "But I can feel the *varing* here. It is strong."

This made Cotoch pause. Was it a mistake? He had never thought about what it would be to take another *candarii* here, to where he had harvested so much pain and death. But still, Selene did not have the amulet.

Illiah's cell had a door, but it was the absolute darkness and the chains around his wrists that kept him trapped. And his injuries— not life-threatening—were undoubtedly debilitating.

Selene thrust the torch into Cotoch's free hand without comment. She crouched down beside Illiah, her dress dragging in the dirt. She ran a finger along his face. Illiah opened his eyes, squinting against the torchlight.

"You should have chosen me, Illiah." Selene's voice was honey-sweet.

"I would never have chosen you, Selene," Illiah replied in a hoarse, hopeless voice. Then he said, "Am I dreaming?"

Selene smiled her father's serpent smile. "No, Illiah."

Realization dawned across the wretched cur's face even though he could barely open his eyes.

"You betrayed us," Illiah croaked.

Selene laughed, a light tinkling sound that Cotoch knew would entrance the idiotic lords of Allati.

"The children," Illiah hissed. "Why?"

"Men are such fools," Selene said bitterly. "If you had chosen me, you would be free." It was not true, but perhaps Selene believed it.

"Who are you?" Illiah said, shifting, trying to move. He failed. Cotoch hoped Illiah was not too hurt. Imal would not appreciate his prize being damaged beyond repair. Cotoch made a mental note to bring his healer to see Illiah before their journey in the morning. Cotoch smiled inwardly. Cotoch couldn't decide which was more amusing: Illiah's fear, or Stone's absolute subservience. Stone would have killed Illiah.

"I was born in Rodan, across the sea," Selene told Illiah. "My father is an emperor."

"Then why are you here? In the dark?" Illiah spat.

She had no answer for him. Illiah closed his eyes, lying his head back on the stone.

"Cotoch has offered me a throne," Selene said. "I would have preferred you. But my *candarii* magic didn't work on you. Maybe I will have better luck with an Allati prince. Goodbye, Illiah." Selene patted his cheek. Illiah winced as if her touch hurt him. "Say hello to my father for me." She stood and swept out of the room, leaving the torch for Cotoch. Cotoch knocked back the rest of his wine and followed the girl up into the light with no regrets.

# CHAPTER 22

# ILLIAH

PINPOINTS OF YELLOW hovered in the darkness behind Illiah's eyelids. Yellow eyes filled with fear and anger and pity. Illiah opened his eyes; the image blinked out of existence.

The dark was sludgy. Illiah stretched carefully. His body hurt in too many places to catalog, but the pain was not lancing, just oppressive. Like the dark. His clothes felt damp and crusty.

By the Guardians, it was dark. By the Guardians, he wanted a fight.

Selene had betrayed Kitarra. Selene had betrayed him. How could she?

*Say hello to my father for me ...* That was what Selene had said—at least that is what he thought she had said. Selene's words slipped through his memory into the surrounding abyss.

He sorted through his options. His body hurt; moving was a calculated risk. He couldn't see his injuries; he might be bleeding. He couldn't see an inch; there might be a crevasse. Something inside him screamed from the deep recess of his remorse. He was trapped. And if Cotoch's plan was for him to waste away in the dark, he would waste away in the dark.

Eva had once described the feeling of being surrounded by Cotoch's *candarii* magic. The choking blackness, her mind being pushed into a box. Like drowning in magic, she had told him. Illiah had been taken by dark magic, not once but twice, and he didn't remember it at all.

Illiah wondered if the oppressive, sightless murk he was trapped in was similar to what Eva had felt. He wept to think of it. Hot tears fell on his face, tickling his nose. He wiped them on his shoulder because his hands were bound. The movement hurt. Everything hurt.

"Eva … I am sorry. I was a fool," he said to the dark. His voice sounded like tree bark rubbed over gravel.

"You are fortunate to have the love of one so strong," a voice spoke from somewhere behind him. The voice was like the creak of a tree in the wind, the sigh of a brook over pebbles. Illiah could smell moss and damp and something else … sunlight, perhaps.

Illiah sighed. He was going mad, it seemed.

"Yes …" he agreed with his madness.

Something brushed across his brow in the dark, making him start. Pain made his breath catch. There was something there. Something that was more real than his mind could create.

"I too had a love like that. The kind of love that moves mountains and stars and rivers." The voice trailed away like the ending of a tragic ballad.

"Who are you?" Illiah asked.

"I am a prisoner. But unlike you, I made my own cage long ago." The voice faded as if the speaker had walked away. The voice had not belonged to a human or Kitarran; it had sounded more ethereal— more *other.* The smell left with it, leaving behind the lingering stench of rotting damp and his own excrement.

"You are stronger than most. It is why he wants you."

The strange voice had come back.

"What does Cotoch want of me?" Illiah heard himself ask. He was not sure if he spoke out loud or in his mind. He couldn't feel his tongue. Whichever it was, the spirit creature answered anyway.

"No, not him. He really does want you dead—the other one, he wants you for your magic." The voice sounded decidedly female. "Yes, you have magic. Why do you think you are so fast? So good with a sword? Cunning, you have been called. The vercuri? Yes, the vercuri was helpful to you, but can't you see? You have magic without it. You harvest it from the pain of death and injury, the pain of the heart. You are a *candarii*. You have been using the *varing* without knowing it."

"That is not true." The words stuck between Illiah's tongue and the roof of his mouth. Beads of sweat broke across his brow at the very notion that he was a sorcerer like Cotoch. He had never sought out death. Murder disgusted him. What he did, he did to save his people, his loved ones. He was a tool to bring peace and justice.

*But you failed.*

That voice was his own.

"Like him, you are descended from the same *rauna*—or god, if you prefer the term." The voice was definitely female—and angry. Bitterness flowed through the dark like smoke.

"Is that what you are? A *rauna*?"

"Not really. I am older. And more of the earth than Them—" Illiah heard the capital T in her words. Did she mean the Guardians?

The Allmakers? The *velidar*? Illiah's head felt like lead. "Or at least, I was. I think They have sought out the trees and the earth. I don't know, I have been down here a long time. An age." The sadness in the voice made Illiah shift and look around. But there was nothing to see in the dark. Only a sound that reminded Illiah, oddly enough, of shuffling feathers—like Calypso when he settled on his roost for the night. Strange, Illiah hadn't thought about Eva's pet raven for a long time.

"What is your name?" he asked.

"Tsuga," she replied with a sound that was more heartbeat and leaves rustling on branches, but he heard it as "Soo-gah."

He reached out his hand toward the sound and was surprised when he touched something silky and smooth, tenuous as spiderwebs—feathers. Then his fingers touched roots and moss, then flesh, then wind. The wind told him she was gone back into her dark cell where he could not follow.

He woke to screams. The old spirit, the thing of feather and wood and flesh, was being hurt. Illiah knew the screams of pain, the cries of fear and fate and hope. Her pain was his pain. Her anguish was his anguish.

"Cotoch!" Illiah screamed into the dark. "I will kill you. I swear upon the Allmakers that I will kill you and flay your skin from your muscles, and you will scream as she screams, and you will know her pain. And I will take it. I will take you." Illiah had no way to know if Cotoch heard him.

Illiah's stomach roiled. His throat burned from retching and screaming. He thought of Cotoch hurting the immortal creature over and over in the dark. A creature that could not die, but could feel pain. Eventually, the sounds died down, and there were just small whimpers in the dark.

Illiah sobbed into the near silence.

The creature was wrong; Illiah could not be the same as Cotoch. It was impossible.

# STONE

STONE DID NOT see Cotoch's convoy leave. But then, Cotoch *was* the master of shadows. The prisoners were gone as if they had never been.

But Illiah and his men were not dead. They were headed across the sea with Cotoch and a contingent of Cotoch's favorite guards, to the strange land of Rodan. Stone wondered if Rodan was the Forgotten Lands, a place, Kitarran legends told, where humans had been birthed by the Old Ones many ages ago.

Stone mourned his inability to rescue Illiah, or even to die trying. Saving Illiah, Eva's beloved, would be a good way to die. But he couldn't. His duty was to the children. He had promised Illiah as much. At least Cotoch had stopped Stone's hand from delivering the fatal blow to Illiah's person. At least his claws were not stained with Illiah's lifeblood. He would have done it. He would have twisted the knife and let Illiah's blood pool at his feet and watched the life drain from the eyes of a good man.

"Hey! Stone!"

Stone turned away from his inattentive watching of the guards-in-training to see Rory walking across the courtyard, his brow furrowed, his steps fast and heavy.

"What?"

"Cotoch is gone, but he left me with orders to organize an escort to take Lady Selene to Allati."

"Who?" The name sounded familiar.

"Selene. The young, pretty woman who arrived yesterday." Rory sagged under Stone's vacant expression. "Cotoch's spy from Kitarra? The one who kidnapped the princes. By the old spirits, Stone, you have been taking too much culla."

Rory was not wrong.

"You did hear about the princes, right? Bold move," Rory huffed.

"They are here?"

"Yeah." Rory jerked his head toward Cotoch's sprawling house.

"Who is this woman, exactly?"

"Cotoch's niece," Rory said sharply. "Cotoch planted her in Kitarra years ago. Must be a clever woman to have gotten close to the queen. Rumor says she was the queen's most trusted servant."

Stone firmed his stance to keep from teetering. How could he have never known this? He had been close to Cotoch before. But he had not known about a spy in the queen of Kitarra's employ. He had not known Cotoch had a niece. Maybe the culla had clouded his mind and he had merely forgotten.

"You are well informed," Stone remarked.

Rory's mouth went thin. "Yuri told me."

Cotoch's old mistress was now Rory's mistress. Humans and their lusts. Whatever.

"You said she is going to Allati?" Stone clarified.

"Yes. And I need your help," Rory begged. "I can't get this done before tomorrow, not without you. And I need you to come along."

"Errr ... the Allati really don't like me, remember?"

Rory cursed long and elegantly.

"I can't come with you, but what do you need me to do?" Stone offered.

"I need you to select men for the escort. You know them far better than I."

They spent the morning discussing the logistics of the journey, but at the forefront of Stone's mind was the two boys and how to smuggle them out of Mahlas. With Cotoch gone, this woman soon to be gone, Rory gone, and Irri in his back pocket, it felt possible.

"What is Cotoch planning to do with the princes?" Stone asked as they sat for a meal in the mess hall.

"Leverage? I don't know." Rory shrugged and blew on his hot stew.

Or a bargain? Stone did not say it out loud. Rory didn't know Cotoch's obsession with Eva or the details of Stone's relationship with the *sanarii* princess. Would Eva trade her freedom for her son? Yes, Stone was sure she would. His resolve quenched into steel. He imagined watching Eva as Cotoch's wife, under Cotoch's control, sharing his bed, bearing his children. No. He would not let that happen.

"There." Rory pointed out the archway that led into the courtyard. Stone followed his gaze.

A woman walked across the courtyard. She looked like she had just stepped out from the Kitarran court. Her dress was rich and beautiful. Her hair shone like autumn leaves. Her back was straight, her chin high and prideful. At her side walked a young boy of about five or six, his hair the color of starlight, his eyes studying his feet. Stone's chest tightened—the culla had not taken all his emotions after all.

Cotoch would want the boy because he was a *sanarii*, like his mother. A child born for greatness but raised under the thumb of a *candarii*, coveted by both Allati and Kitarra. The child of the prophecy, clearly. Even if Stone were not familiar with the boy's mother and father, he could see the boy was special. He looked *other*, plucked from the Great Forest, wreathed in magic.

A few steps behind them walked another boy. If the woman and Eva's son were out of place in Mahlas, this boy was more so. He was tallish, thin, his ears overly big, his long arms hugging himself even though his Kitarran fur would keep him warm against any weather. His big blue eyes looked around the courtyard, begging for something, hoping for something. Stone lost himself in those eyes briefly. Emri's eyes. His son. A hundred perfect what-ifs assaulted him. Then a hundred regrets descended and ate them. Stone realized his hands were shaking. He closed them into fists.

Rhyl looked up to see that Talo had trailed behind. He reached out his hand, and Talo took a few leaps to catch up, securing his hand in that of his friend's. They clung to each other like leaves in a storm.

Stone needed to find Irri.

*You should kill her,* Eva's angry voice whispered in Stone's mind.

*Are you watching me?*

*Through you, I can see them.* Her voice was filled with heartache—and hope. *I want her dead.*

*Do you think I enjoy taking lives, Eva?* "Do you think I am a monster?" Stone realized the last bit he said out loud. His mind was silent, but it ached from her piercing magic.

The mess hall dimmed as the torches lining the walls guttered, then fanned, glowing and stretching toward the low ceiling. Stone watched them; some instinct for self-preservation was screaming inside him. A wriggle of unease wormed its way past his culla-flattened emotions. No one else seemed to notice the strange dance of the fire.

"What did you say?" Rory asked, his mouth full of stew, his brows pinched.

"Nothing."

"Hey, you all right?"

"Just a headache."

Rory grimaced. "I heard the culla was nasty stuff."

Stone took a spoonful of stew he could not taste. The torches resumed their usual placid dance. He glanced back to the window, but the boys were no longer in sight.

Stone had never felt so alone.

# CHAPTER 24

# ILLIAH

A HEALER CAME and forced Illiah to drink something that tasted bitter and oily. He gagged, then spit it up, unfortunately mostly on himself. His head spun like the world pulled him around in a dance.

When he woke, his face was pressed against a rough wood floor. But there was light. Compared to the absolute night of his former prison, the dim light around him was blinding. The air was different—tangy, salty. The ocean. Yes, that was the smell.

His arms were still bound, his feet still hobbled. He tried to sit, but the floor shifted, knocking him over. His jaw hit the wood hard. He was on a boat. His stomach roiled, a gift from the healer's brew or the waves. Illiah had his bet on waves. He needed a bucket. Too late. He spewed bile onto the floorboards; the smell rose to greet him. He moved a little to avoid it congealing in his beard. Thirst gnawed his thick tongue like a dog on a bone.

He lay still, trying to ignore the smell, trying to discern with his ears the manner of his floating prison.

The creak of the wood under the strain of oars in action was foremost in his ears. Then came the grunts of effort as the oar was pulled through the water, and the release as it was drawn up and back. Repeat. Repeat. A layer of shouting ebbed and flowed above it.

The voices of men grew louder and clearer, along with booted footsteps descending into the hold that was Illiah's prison. Visitors. He couldn't make out their words. It took him too long to realize it was because they spoke a different language. It was the tongue of the invaders. This time it was not the kindly Kitarrans pulling him from his life, it was a devious monster whose currency was in pain and suffering. A little voice in Illiah's head whispered that he would never see the shores of his home again.

It made a terrible kind of sense. Cotoch's ambition was vastly more far-reaching than Illiah had first imagined. The man was a spider. His web touched more than just the Tarm. Cotoch had somehow contacted the invaders. Had he been responsible for the attack on Jullayah as well? The Isles? Selene had mentioned her father, the king across the sea, Illiah recalled. He could almost see the pieces fitting together, but his head hurt, making the pieces lopsided and crumbly. He cursed Eva for not killing Cotoch when she had the chance.

The men talked, voices rough, amused, cutting. He couldn't see them. Illiah could not see any passage to the sky, only dim, drab light that must come from the only access or perhaps through the slats of the wood. There were crates around him, tied down but piled high enough to create a barrier between him and the rest of the ship's belly.

Illiah pinched his eyes shut against the dizziness that threatened his concentration—he could hear three men approaching. They stopped. They laughed, but not at Illiah. There must be others in the hold. Other prisoners to torment. Illiah heard boots contacting flesh and grunts of pain.

Illiah tried again to stand, to move, to shout, anything. But his body was as helpless as a newborn babe.

The men came and gave him a swift kick in the gut and it was Illiah's turn to groan into the floorboards. He bit his tongue against the wave of sick that would make the ocean proud.

Illiah glared up into their faces, trying to etch their scars into his memory. He would find them. One day, when he escaped, he would find them. He would find Cotoch. He would end them all.

They could see his anger, his lust for revenge, and they laughed. They left, and all that remained was the sound of the oars and oarsmen above. Pull, release, pull, release. Exhale. Inhale.

"Illiah?"

Illiah stiffened. Hoarse as the voice was, he knew it. Something in his heart broke.

"Aisha?" he managed.

"Yes, sir."

"You were captured." Question and fact.

"Yes. And Antoli and Grip. They got put onto the oars."

Illiah closed his eyes. His fault. He had run into that stupid trap, heart pounding with the promise of revenge. And his loyal men had followed. He had betrayed them with his folly and his arrogance. And now … and now they were slaves.

Illiah tried once more to sit and assert his strength—for his men. But knifelike pain pressed against his ears, his eyes, pushing him down like a hundred stones.

Something happened above on the oars. Loud voices in the heinous tongue lashed out. Illiah couldn't see, but he knew someone was dying up there.

A sob caught in Illiah's throat. Then another. Cold tears dripped from his eyes onto the wood already saturated with despair.

# CHAPTER 25

# MILA

"SHIP AHEAD!"

The ship deck burst into a flurry of movement. The vibrations of twenty booted feet across the deck of the ship made Mila wince. The crew moved in organized chaos, a dance without music. Some of the crew prepared to raise sail to increase their distance from the unknown ship. The rest went for their weapons.

Seagrass stood still among the storm, gazing down his eyepiece, a strange device he had proudly won from a Kitarran captain in a game of cards—a story he had told at least three times.

"Not Kitarran!" the captain called, his voice successfully competing with the ocean wind and the waves and the sound of his men. The brief lull surrounding his proclamation was followed by an increase in the frantic activity. "They have the weather gage," Mila heard Seagrass mutter. "This is going to be a shitstorm."

Two weeks of sailing had not given any more indication whether Seagrass was mad or just bold and greedy. He was a man of many moods and tendencies, but he was an excellent sailor. They had weathered two storms so far without note. And his crew, only sometimes drunk, always followed orders.

It wasn't until Tarran and Murryn appeared at Mila's elbow that the first trickles of fear raced down her fingers, making her palms itch. Together they watched as the other vessel crept closer.

Seagrass put down his eyepiece and turned to Mila. "Best go below, my dear. This could get messy."

"Who is it?" she asked.

"It is not Kitarrans. Strange ships have sailed these waters the last few years. But never worry, my men are the best, and Tarran and Murryn are here to lend us their blades."

"Go below, Mila," Tarran told her. "You will be safer there."

Mila nodded. She had killed a man, but she was no warrior. She hated the helplessness of it. Her hobbies had never included swords or knives. Maybe they should have. Maybe Eva and Murryn had it right, and a woman should learn to fight. Fighting was not the only tool for survival, Mila thought absently.

Mila was the only person below deck. The only person not fit to fight or be of any use in battle. The entire crew was ordered above deck with swords and bows and knives. Mila felt discarded, as useful as the barrels of dried meats and vegetables and grains she huddled beside. Surely there was something she could do? But it was too late to ask, and the pattering of activity on deck gave her the feeling that she would just get in the way.

Above the shouts of the men, Mila could hear Seagrass's booming voice. The boat itself seemed to answer with creaks and groans, as if telling its captain it was trying its best.

Time passed slowly. The shouts continued. Mila had the feeling that the boat was under sail and traveling fast, but without a horizon or the wind in her face, she couldn't be sure. For a while, the shouting died down, and she wondered if she should go above.

"A second boat!" This was Seagrass again, his voice loud enough to permeate the wood ceiling that separated Mila from the mayhem above.

The shouts continued, and the boat listed making the barrels shifted a little. Mila thought she could hear the lapping of water close. Mila's arms shook from her taut muscles.

The ship righted itself. The sound from above changed. Shouts became angry, defiant. Then the shouts turned into screams. Mila had never heard the violence of war. And she would never forget it.

Feet pattered down the steep steps into the cabin. Murryn appeared, breathless and bloodied, her eyes wild.

"They are taking the boat," she hissed, pushing Mila down farther into her crack between the barrels.

"Where is Tarran?"

"Fighting. I saw him at the prow. Then I lost him in the press. I needed to come down here. Tarran can fight for himself; you can not."

Murryn was right. Mila couldn't even use her magic. She did not know how. She was useless. Good for nothing. It was her fault they were in this mess. She had killed Serac. She was the murderer. But Murryn was the one protecting Mila, again. Because Mila could not defend herself. Useless.

"Thank you, Murryn," Mila whispered.

Murryn nodded, her eyes fixed on the stairs, waiting. A hound at the hare's hole.

They came, their footfalls like falling stones. The ease of their pace spoke of victors walking over a dying battlefield. Mila could not understand the language they spoke. Murryn crouched, her knives out, one in each hand. When the men were close, she sprung her trap. One man was dead instantly, blood gushing across the dim cabin. There were more; Mila could see four dim shapes from her hiding place. They did not seem concerned over the death of their comrade. They laughed as Murryn slashed and darted around the small space like a gnat looking for skin to prick. Murryn was a superb fighter, but seeing her against four large, grown men gave Mila a whole new appreciation for her sister's skill.

The men's laughter died as they struggled to overcome Murryn. What had been a game for them was no longer. But the men were joined by more. The ache in Mila's heart told her she was about to witness her sister dying in a glorious attempt to save Mila's life. She could not allow it.

Mila called to her magic. She reached deep within to find her other half, her other form that was innately fierce and dangerous and deadly. But it didn't come. It was there, not sleeping exactly, but trapped, bound by knots she did not know how to unravel. She had pushed it down so often and so deep that now, in her time of need, it would not obey her. Her failure would be her sister's death.

A backhand punch to Murryn's face sent her sprawling across the blood-slick wood. Mila screamed. The sound ripped from her chest, pulling all her fear and frustration with it. But still, her magic did not come.

The men saw Mila and yanked her roughly from her hiding spot. With their raised scars and brutish eyes, their faces were awful to look at. And they smelled as bad as they looked. Worse. They grabbed her roughly, pulling at her clothes, fondling her breasts, her hips. Mila knew what would come next.

A voice shouted from the stairs—their leader by the way they straightened in his presence. He sauntered over to the dimly lit scene where he eyed Murryn sprawled, half crawling on the floor toward her fallen knives. He put his foot on her wrist, making her grunt in pain. He looked at the dead men. He only had one brow, the other a lump of scars, and it rose in obvious surprise. He jerked his chin to the men, and they went to work binding Murryn's hands.

It was a testament to Murryn's extensive injuries that she did not strike or lash out. The man looked Mila over, touching her face, pulling at her shirt to expose her breasts, but in an assessing way, like one would measure the quality of meat on a pig to see if it was ready for slaughter. Mila glared at him, wishing she could claw his scars open.

He gave a command in the strange language. His men looked crestfallen. He had taken away their prize. Mila let her heart hope, just a little. He gave the order again, emphasizing his command by punching the man closest to him. The man coughed, trying to stand straight, but Mila had seen the metal knuckles their leader wore.

Murryn groaned, fighting to stay conscious. Mila tried to keep Murryn in her line of sight, but the massive girth of the men made it impossible. They took Mila by the arm and pulled her along with them up into the daylight.

Seagrass's ship was a battleground. The deck was bright with blood. Already the seabirds roosted in the masts, waiting to pick through the feast below. Mila gingerly stepped over corpse after corpse. She recognized Seagrass, his face pushed into the deck boards, dead.

She looked around for Tarran. Her relief escaped as a sob. He was bound, his eyes blazing, but he seemed uninjured. Mila caught a glimpse of Murryn as she was half dragged, half carried up on deck. Her head lolled, but she could almost stand.

Tarran shouted something to the leader in the strange language.

The leader turned and looked at him sharply. Mila's heart sank. It could only mean that the men were from Tarran's land. Slavers.

The leader crouched in front of Tarran, turning his face with a hand covered with dried blood. The man stroked Tarran's ear, resting his long, dirty finger on the tiny hole prick at the top. The leader spoke something else to Tarran, but he sounded pleased. He patted Tarran on the head, then shouted orders to his crew.

They were forced onto the slaver's ship, along with a few survivors from Seagrass's crew. Young men, mostly. Cutless was among them. A second ship of equal size held off the port side some ways. Seagrass's crew had never stood a chance.

All the captives were forced below deck. Mila was shoved through the hold with Tarran and Murryn. Their guards rambled in loud, coarse voices, a string of sounds Mila could not understand—did not want to understand. The smell was overwhelming. Sick and excrement and despair mingled with salt and tar and rotten things. As Mila's eyes adjusted from the light of the sun on the ocean to the cabin, she could see that the hull was filled with people. The dim light unveiled dirty, gaunt faces. The whites of the captives' eyes glinted in the near dark. One prisoner sprawled in the open space where they were being led; their captors kicked at the person viciously. Mila heard a grunt of pain, but little else.

Murryn, Tarran, and Mila were put together in a corner separate from the other captives, chained and bound to posts. The guards left them after gesturing to a bucket and a pile of moth-eaten blankets. From the smell and the conditions of the other captives, it was luxurious.

Mila waited for the footsteps to retreat, then turned to assess Murryn. She was starting to come around. She had a bruised head and an injured wrist; already her face was a swollen mess. But Mila didn't think anything was broken. Tarran curled himself around Murryn, which was awkward with his bound hands.

"These men are the *daeum* from Rodan. The same men who invaded Jullayah years ago. The ones who killed my family," Tarran said quietly. "They are taking us back to Rodan, where we will be sold as slaves. Mila, you are lucky, they plan to sell you as a virgin— if they touch you, your value is less." The distaste in his words was thick as mucus. "They think Murryn is a boy."

"If they find out Murryn is a girl, they will rape her, won't they?"

Tarran's amber eyes were dangerous. "They will rape her regardless of her gender if her face is pretty enough. But I have hope— that man knew my name, as if he was looking for me. I think they will bring us to Rodan unharmed."

"Why would they be looking for you?"

"Because I was sent to Praedan—that is what they call Jullayah and the other realms—against my master's bidding. He was not a man to be crossed. Perhaps he is still looking for me."

"But that was years ago," Mila hissed.

"You do not know what kind of man he is," Tarran mumbled. He closed his eyes, looking more like the little boy Mila had first met than the warrior who had risked everything for love.

CHAPTER 26

# STONE

COTOCH'S HOUSE was blessedly quiet. Selene, Rory, and their escort were on their way to Allati.

Irri continued to gain Stone's trust by reporting what Stone had discovered about the schedule of the children and their guards. Cotoch had left for Rodan, ensuring that Mahlas was still heavily guarded. The children were no exception. Extracting them would leave a blood trail, that was certain. Stone didn't like it but could see no other option, and he would kill a thousand men to save Rhyl and Talo. The thought was unsettling but no less true.

Irri and Stone planned the escape. It wasn't that complicated, just risky. They only had one chance. If they were discovered, it was over.

The sun dipped below the horizon. Stone went through his pack one last time, sorting his weapons and what he would need to get the children to Kitarra. Food, water, blankets—what else did children need? He looked at the vercuri he had kept hidden for months, the one from Tayeh's Vale. It had saved Illiah's life once by killing a *revenant* of dark magic. Stone couldn't leave it behind.

*Stone.*

Stone grit his teeth against the onslaught of Eva's magic.

*This hurts.*

*Sorry …*

Stone didn't think Eva really meant it.

*I will meet you at the border. We are waiting.*

*We leave tonight. Please don't do this again. It's too painful.* He couldn't afford to be compromised by a headache.

Eva was gone.

He took another dose of culla. He needed to make one stop before he rescued the boys.

The hallways of Cotoch's house were constantly patrolled. Jakil was in charge of Cotoch's house guards. Stone did not like him—a mutual feeling. Naturally, Jakil's men didn't like Stone either. They always watched him like a fox among the chickens. So if he wanted to break into Cotoch's study, he would have to do so undetected. His fur was not the best color for blending into shadows, and he was not exactly a small man, but he was patient.

Dagger in hand, Stone crept down the hall, down the stairs, toward Cotoch's chambers. The darkness was nothing to a Kitarran. When had the shadows become so comfortable?

His heart raced, but perhaps that was just the culla in his veins.

There were three guards outside Cotoch's room. In his absence, Cotoch must be paranoid and mistrustful of his house staff. Stone wasn't the only junkie who would want to get into Cotoch's hoard of culla. But he was the only Kitarran junkie.

Stone watched the guards, hoping they would disband. They didn't.

The three guards fell under his dagger with three soft thuds, without the time to utter a cry for help, just as Stone had planned.

He stepped carefully over the blood oozing across the floor, tail raised to keep it from dipping into the crimson pools. He snuffed the torch in the hall to keep prying eyes from the scene.

There was a lock on the door, but Stone had always been good at picking locks. It only took him a moment before he opened the door, rushing into the room. He needed to be fast—he had to get to the children before the guards were found.

He exhaled in relief to find Cotoch's stash of culla in its usual place. He took the jar and dumped the fine gray powder into a leather satchel, tied it tight, and stuffed it into his pack. He resettled the pack on his shoulders.

Next, the children.

Stone followed a trail of blood and dead bodies to the chamber where the children were kept. None of them were Irri. The young man was efficient—and skilled. Everything was going according to plan—so far. *Don't get cocky, coward.*

"Stone," Irri whispered from a dark corner to get his attention. Irri breathed hard; he had only just finished the guards.

The door to the children's room was locked—from the outside. Irri scanned the hallway, a dagger in each hand—not a good spot for swords.

"Key?" Stone turned to Irri. The pressure in his ears was almost drowning him. He told himself to calm the fuck down.

Irri delved into the guard's pockets, coming up with a ring of keys.

It took two agonizing tries, but the third key fit, and the lock sprung, and the door unlatched. They slipped inside—

And were met by two pairs of wide, brimming, desperate eyes.

The commotion outside their door must have woken the boys. Or perhaps they had never been asleep.

Rhyl saw Stone and visibly relaxed. Of course, the boy would see Kitarrans as his allies. Stone had thought of himself as the enemy for so long, he had never stopped to think that a child, with no prejudices, would see him as something else. The realization hit Stone like an avalanche, almost bringing him to his knees.

Behind Rhyl and his beacon of bright blond hair, round blue eyes scrutinized him—Emri's eyes. Those eyes hit Stone right in his soul, and this time, he was brought to his knees.

"Are you—are you—here to take us home?" Rhyl's question was so quiet, Stone almost didn't hear it.

"Yes, I am a friend of your mother. But we must go quickly and quietly, and you must close your eyes," Stone told them both. He tried smiling. They didn't smile back. "Rhyl, do you remember Irri?"

The little boy studied the young man in the near dark. "I think so."

"Good. All right, Rhyl, you climb on Irri's back. Talo, you climb on mine. We must run."

The two boys nodded. It was not ideal; the boys had to cling to the packs, but there was no other option. They would need the supplies to survive until they could get to Kitarra.

Talo's arms cinched around Stone's neck. The poor boy was terrified.

"Ready?" Stone asked. He felt Talo nod. "Let's go. Don't forget to close your eyes." Stone had no way to know if they did, but it couldn't be helped. Maybe the darkness would hide the horrors of the night from the children's memories.

The halls were silent. Death had already feasted. Irri had been thorough, but the guards would be changing soon.

Irri and Stone had memorized their route. They met two servants in the hall. They had to put down the boys and dispatch them. It did not go well. There were shouts, and a strangled scream of the woman was cut off by Stone's dagger across her throat. He lunged back to avoid the blood.

There was only one more thing to do before they escaped into the night. They would not outrun Cotoch's guards unless the guards were too distracted to notice their absence. Irri nodded, taking a torch. Stone did the same. They dragged the fire along the hallway, letting it catch on anything that might burn, and most of Cotoch's house was timber.

They scooped up the boys and ran into the night. The narrow cat-track was still the best way to get out of Mahlas undetected. The path wound up the hill, at the top, the dead tree stood sentinel.

Stone's body was infused with culla, making it impossible to feel his protesting muscles and the air catching in his lungs. He watched Irri to gauge when they needed to rest, but for his slight size, the young man climbed the hill behind Stone like an ox.

Stone readjusted Talo on his back as he glanced up at the dead tree, black branches against the black sky. He had a strange notion the tree was watching him.

They kept their pace through the dark, making their way along the mountain's base toward Kitarra instead of into the forest as Stone had with Eva. He hoped it was not a mistake. Speed, not secrecy, would be their ally. They had an army waiting for them. They just had to get to it before Cotoch's men got to them.

Cotoch's men would ride hard, but they couldn't push their horses indefinitely without killing the poor beasts. And there was nowhere on the Tarm to find fresh mounts. Stone estimated they had five days until Cotoch's men caught up to them. Five days to reach Eva. Likely less. Was it doable? He was about to find out.

They kept their pace until the children began to whimper. Only then did they stop and rest. They wrapped the children in blankets, and Stone thanked the old spirits it was not raining.

"I'll take first watch," Stone told Irri. He wouldn't sleep, not with the culla still in his veins, not with his son sleeping so close to him, not with the Tarm plain spread before him and death chasing after them.

The children slept. Stone watched the clouds burst and part, revealing the stars here, then there, a great, infinite game of peek-a-boo. The moon was not yet risen. Just as well. The less light, the better.

Irri turned and shifted under his blanket.

"You should sleep," Stone chided.

"Can't." Irri sat up, careful not to disturb the boys who slept in a pile beside him. "At least the horrors of the night have not kept the boys from sleep," Irri muttered.

"Children are resilient."

"Yes," Irri said thoughtfully. "You are not going to sleep either, are you?"

"Nope."

The wind rustled the grass. A night-bird called out across the plain. A chorus of frogs began as if by design.

"Do you want to know why I left Jullayah?" Irri asked.

"Because they were rooting out spies, and your cover was compromised? Likely by a young, pretty girl who got it out of you with a combination of sex and wine?"

Rivers would freeze over from the blast of winter in Irri's gray eyes.

"I am teasing."

"You have a poor attitude," Irri hissed. "I don't even want to tell you now." But all Stone had to do was remain silent and wait until Irri was done twitching. Stone had a feeling Irri's reason for leaving Jullayah coincided with his inability to sleep. Something about his eyes spoke of haunted thoughts.

"Lord Kaile sent my men and me on a mission to a town—the name is not important—located along the edge of the Great Forest. The cliff along the Great Forest makes it impossible to go into the Forest—no one can climb it."

"So I've heard."

"Yes. And supposedly, the cliff works as a barrier both ways—nothing can come out of the Forest either." Irri eyed Stone in a way that foretold that was not at all how it worked. "When we got to the town, everything was silent. The only people we found were locked up in their houses, doors barred, starving. They warned us not to stay out of doors at night. The terror in their eyes was enough to convince us. So as night fell, we barricaded ourselves inside. A few of us stayed up in the watchtower, which was hardly taller than the small, rural houses. We watched, expecting to see bandits or rogues terrorizing the poor simple folk for who knows what sadistic reasons.

"Anyway, I was up on the tower. It was barely even twilight when they came—two of them. I still don't know what they were. Shadows. Animals. People. Nightmares. At first, I thought of ghosts or spirits, but they were solid. Flesh and blood. I could hear their footfalls, the sound of their claws dragging over cobbles. They saw us up on the tower and fixed us in their gaze like prey. Their eyes were human. Other parts of them seemed human, some parts animal. They were just so wrong.

"When I was a child, I lived in the mountains near Withe. My family were herders. One day a panther struck our herd—I watched it take down one of our aura. So fast. So accurate. These nightmare creatures were like that. They leaped onto the stone, trying to crawl up the tower. They tore the first door from its hinges. We didn't fight—we fled, locking ourselves inside the inner chamber as the creatures rammed their bodies against the wood. We placed every bit of furniture we could against the door, our bodies included, and prayed until morning."

Irri waited.

"Well?" Irri said, disappointed by Stone's nonreaction. "You don't believe me?"

"I think there is some truth to your story," Stone said after a moment.

"Some truth?" Irri huffed indignantly. "I remember the stories. The legends told how Kitarrans were created from the people of the Forest to protect against dark magic."

"Legends, yes."

Irri riled. "Legends! If those creatures were not created by dark magic, then I am the bastard son of Tayeh. The dark magic is here! That is why I am going back to Kitarra. The time of darkness is here. And Rhyl is the child of the prophecy."

"Shhh. Calm down, don't wake the children," Stone scolded in a whisper. "You are right. Emri—" Gods, when was the last time he had uttered her name? He couldn't help but glance where Talo lay sleeping. "Emri and I were tracking the dark magic—before.

It was in Kitarra too. Dark places where people went mad and violence festered with unusual potency. But there were no such creatures." Stone thought of the thing he had killed with the vercuri—not a creature, but not a ghost either. "Which is why we sent spies like you into Jullayah in the first place, because Kitarra needs Rhyl."

"He is just a child."

"I know."

"What are we going to do?"

"For now, get this boy back to his mother. As for the rest? I don't know."

Irri hung his head.

"What happened to your family?" Stone asked. "I find it hard to imagine a herder leaving the mountains to become a spy."

Irri looked up, grim painted all over his face. "They died in a wildfire along with our herd and half the mountain. I had nowhere else to go. I went to the Forge. I was asked to work as a spy—told I was a natural at it."

"At deception?" Stone asked with a grin.

"Something like that. Maybe they just wanted to get rid of me." Irri's voice trailed into silence for a moment. "Your wife was an amazing woman. I remember how Kilev mourned after her death—and yours. When the new First Defender asked me to go to Jullayah, I was more than honored."

"And now Kitarra is without a First Defender for the second time in a generation. Illiah is gone, taken. He was the First Defender." Stone saw Irri's grief. He had been a spy, but his admiration for Illiah had not been a lie. "Have you heard about the Isles?"

"A little. But I find it hard to imagine."

"That invaders destroyed every settlement on the Long Isles? I can't believe it either—yet, it is."

"Surely not *every* settlement."

"I heard there were few survivors. I fear what we will find when we get … get to Kitarra."

The word *home* almost slipped past his lips. Home. Stone wasn't sure Kitarra would ever be his home. Home was a foreign concept. He looked past Irri to where Talo slept curled beside Rhyl. Two small, furry ears poked above the blankets.

Home. The place terrified Stone.

# STONE

AT THE FIRST HINT OF DAWN, they were moving once more.

When the children tired, they put them on their backs. When they could walk, they walked. The more distance they put between themselves and Mahlas, the more Rhyl and Talo talked and had a skip in their step.

When night fell, and darkness made travel difficult, they found dells or thickets to hide in until dawn.

Stone felt like he was in a paradoxical dream where one half of his heart was petrified with fear that at any moment, he would hear the rattle of armor and the thunder of horses' hooves as Cotoch's men descended. And the other half of his heart soared and delighted in every glance from Talo, every smile, every gesture that was both familiar and achingly perfect. Talo was Arrain's sweetest dream made real.

But Stone was not Arrain, so how could he ever deserve Talo's affection?

By the third day, Stone felt twitchy. Like a spider was creeping up his back, but he couldn't reach it to brush it away. If they had kept to the trees, they would have stayed hidden but it would have slowed them down. And they needed haste more than secrecy so they had chosen the open plain; Stone hoped it had not been a mistake.

"Stone, how much farther?" The little voice was on the brink of tears.

"A little way yet." Stone turned away from the horizon to tussle Rhyl's hair. "Are you tired? Should I carry you?"

"I'm fine."

"Talo?" Stone asked his son. The boy raised his blue eyes from the ground, looking less sturdy than his brother who was not a brother.

"I'm fine." But Stone didn't believe it. He reached out his hand. Talo took it. "I just want to go home."

"I know," Stone agreed. "Me too."

Stone glanced at Irri. Their eyes met, sharing a look of concern. They needed to find the Kitarrans. Eva's army was on the move; they would be under their protection soon. But guards from Mahlas were behind them, a day, an hour, a minute, he had no way to know.

*Stone, they are coming.*

Eva's voice pierced his thoughts like an arrow. Stone looked up the road and down.

*We are not far ahead, but Cotoch's guards come from behind. You* must *hurry,* she urged.

*How long?*

*Not long. Move!*

"We need to move. Now. They are coming." Stone crouched down and let Talo scramble up on his back. Irri did the same for Rhyl. "Run."

And they ran.

# CHAPTER 28

# STONE

"THERE. BEHIND US."

Stone's stomach dropped. The smudge of dust in the distance was unmistakable. Guards on horseback.

"Keep moving!" Irri hissed, hiking Rhyl up higher on his back.

Stone kept his eyes forward, hoping against hope to see the Kitarran host ahead of them. Where were they? They should be close. Eva said they were close. Gods, he could not let Cotoch get the boys. He could not fail this time.

"Stone, they are gaining," Irri said, a note of fear in his voice. Stone ground his teeth. He could see the riders were getting closer. There was no way they had not been spotted. "Where are the Kitarrans!?"

"I don't know." Stone didn't like the well of panic drowning his logic. It felt too much like hopelessness—and he would know. "Come, get into the long grass. We have to get out of sight."

The tall grass was better cover, but the stalks tended to twist and tangle, constricting the ankles.

"This is horseshit." Irri said what Stone had been thinking.

"The Kitarrans will come," Stone said, feeling less than sure.

The boys were silent. Talo's arms squeezed Stone's neck tighter as he clung to Stone's back. Stone could hear the hooves of the horses.

"Get down," Stone said to Irri. They crouched in the long grass. "Talo, go to Irri, sit with Rhyl, and stay low and quiet as a mouse."

Talo nodded, his blue eyes wide. He crept over to his friend, and they huddled together.

Stone peered through the grass, ears pressed back. He took out his blade, as did Irri. Stone really wished he had a latha. His latha. But Mistura had been lost the second time Stone had died.

"They are turning off the road. They found our trail," Stone hissed to Irri. "Boys, I need you to tunnel through the grass, that way. Just keep moving. We will be right behind you."

Talo and Rhyl nodded, and their smaller bodies shuffled through the grass like weasels.

"How many?" Irri asked.

"Not sure. Too many."

Irri's jaw hardened. He was young, but he was not a coward. His will was sharp as his blade and equally unyielding. *A good man to have at your back,* Stone reflected. And to think he had been unwilling to trust him.

The horses were loud now. Their hooves pounded the grass flat. Stone gave Irri a meaningful look before lunging out of the grass at the closest horse. Stone was a Kitarran warrior. His reach was long. The rider had a sicara, the jagged blade pointed right at him. Stone's long legs propelled him to the height of the rider; his long tail balanced him as he used his momentum to drag his blade down the rider's leg with one hand while slashing out with the other. The rider fell, dead.

Stone swept the host in one glance, estimating there were about sixty men, but only twenty or so were mounted. Only twenty. Out of sixty. Sixty men. Fuck.

Stone struck and leaped and struck again. The horses bolted without their riders. Irri took down several. For a human, he had a long reach. The men swarmed, and Stone fought, giving everything to his blade. He let the battle surge take him. His ears were numb the sounds of death and pain. His mind calculated distance and speed while aware of the threats coming at him. His peripherals burned, announcing danger looming beyond his focus.

The cry of a child broke through the mechanism of his battle-mind, a scream of terror only a young child could render, a sound to break the heart and destroy the mind.

Stone ran toward it. The grass had been trampled into a bloody clearing. Talo lay still and crumpled, his tawny fur barely discernible amongst the summer grass. Rhyl perched over him like a bird of prey protecting its young, screaming in grief. Tears streamed down his face. Cotoch's remaining men paused before the child. For an instant, Stone wondered why.

Then he felt it. A ripple of power and magic moved through the grass like a torrent. Or a snake. Hunting. Searching. The crescendo of Rhyl's cry rose, and the magic pulsed stronger. Then, with a silent release of pressure, the magic was gone. Cotoch's men slumped and fell like puppets cut from their strings.

Cotoch's men were dead. Rhyl had killed the enemy with magic.

Rhyl's cries of grief morphed into a scream of defiance like the bravest and most desperate of warriors. It was a terrifying sound coming from a six-year-old boy.

Stone leaped to Talo and cradled his son's limp body in his arms. He was dead. His son was dead. Blood matted his fur, dripping from his ears. A blow to the head. A second, an instant from a wayward hoof. Stone wanted to scream, but he couldn't. Nothing came out. Nothing. Nothing. Nothing.

Rhyl reached for Talo, his little fingers desperate. Stone watched numbly as Rhyl sobbed, his head against Talo's, his eyes squeezed shut as if trying to dismiss the nightmare.

"Rhyl," Stone garbled out the name between sobs. Rhyl ignored him. The wave of magic came once more. But this time it was subtler, like a gentle breeze. It twisted like long, thin fingers, reaching, embracing and came to rest over Talo's body.

Talo's chest moved as he took a breath. Then another. And another. Rhyl opened his eyes and sat back, looking exhausted and wan, eyelids fluttering. Irri appeared and took Rhyl in his arms just as the boy fell unconscious.

Talo opened his eyes. They were clear and bright. Stone pulled him close to his chest. Talo nuzzled into his shoulder.

"I saw Mummy," Talo whispered. Stone's eyes released a lake of tears. His body ached as he sobbed into Talo's fur. "She knew you would come back for me."

And Stone could almost see her, looking out from Talo's eyes, a shadow, a dream. An old pain pushed against his ribs.

"Stone, we need to get out of here," Irri said, breaking the spell. "We need to keep moving."

"Are you all right? Are you hurt?" Stone asked Irri, shoving his emotions aside, untangling one arm from Talo to grip Irri's shoulder. Irri was painted with blood; the question was not unreasonable.

Irri shrugged. "A few scratches. You?"

Stone returned the shrug. He didn't think he was hurt, and even if he was, it would mend quickly. His pain was blinded by the glare of his son's almost-death and the shroud of invisible magic that followed Rhyl like a swarm of wasps.

Rhyl was limp in Irri's arms.

"Is he all right?" Irri asked, panic rising in his voice.

"I think so. It's the magic—you felt that, right? He will be all right," Stone repeated. Eva suffered from the same affliction when using magic.

"I did feel it," Irri said, shivering.

"I want to go home," Talo whimpered, his lips quivering. Stone squeezed Talo's hand.

"I know. Come, we are almost there."

Talo took a few wobbly, tired steps.

"We can't go any farther. There, up behind that hill." Stone pointed in the fading light. Talo crawled on Stone's back once more, and they made for the spot.

The hill was sheltered, with scrubby bushes that would cover their tracks and keep them hidden from those on the plain. Irri grunted as he placed Rhyl carefully on the ground. They wrapped the boys in blankets. Stone tried to feed Talo, but he wouldn't eat. Stone couldn't blame him. He had no appetite either—but he did feel the sting of the culla leaving his veins. He needed another dose, but he couldn't do it in front of his son. He just couldn't.

"You stay with the children. I will go and see if I can find the Kitarrans."

"You haven't slept for days," Irri protested.

"Just stay with the children. I will be back before midnight."

"Fine," Irri grumbled. "Just make sure you come back."

~

Away from Irri and the boys, Stone took his dose before roaming out into the night.

The air smelled better under starlight, and when the moon shone down on him, it reminded him of his childhood. He kept his eyes trained on the road ahead; he did not have time to admire the mesmerizing stars spread out across the ceiling of the Tarm.

A flicker of orange light became Stone's destination. As he approached, he could see it was not one but several fires. A camp. As soon as he realized it, three tall shadows materialized from the grass. One was taller than the others, pointed ears and pointed teeth gleaming in the starlight—the Kitarrans.

Stone put out his hands in surrender and gave a huff of laughter that was part sob. "My name is Stone. I need to see Lady Eva."

"Come with us," they commanded, not lowering their weapons an inch. "Keep your hands where we can see them."

Stone did as he was bid and let them herd him into their camp. They shoved him inside a tent lit with torches and importance.

A Kitarran looked up from his map. His tawny eyes bored into Stone. He was not alone.

"Stone!" Eva's voice was real and did not hurt his head at all. His heart, on the other hand …

"Eva," Stone breathed her name as a sigh. She rose from her seat of cushions and furs awkwardly, her belly leading the way. She was heavily pregnant. A large white uandian followed her, its tail wagging slowly.

"The boys! Where are the boys?" Eva's eyes were wild.

"Safe. Resting. Come, I will bring you to them," Stone said to the Kitarran Eva shared a glance with.

With only Eva's giant belly between them, Stone wanted to touch her, to hug her, but he wasn't sure he had that right. Not after everything he had done.

"I am coming along—" She planted her hands on her hips.

"You can't—look at you!" he told her.

"I agree, my lady. We will fetch the children," the Kitarran said.

Eva growled.

"I will be back in an hour with the boys, Eva," Stone said.

"Promise?" She took a step toward him, her eyes imploring.

"You know what that is worth ..." Stone muttered as he turned to follow the other Kitarran who was gathering guards into action. He looked back over his shoulder to see Eva watching him. Her pale hair reflected red in the torchlight.

"The children are about three miles east, hiding with my accomplice—a man named Irri. We were attacked at sunset," Stone told the man once they were out of Eva's earshot.

The man introduced himself as Turk, the Second. He gave a quick nod, his mouth a thin line, and motioned to his men. "Let's go."

Stone wanted to float in the relief washing over him. But until the children were safely ensconced by the Kitarran army, he would not allow himself to feel like he had succeeded.

It was past midnight when Stone returned to Irri and the children.

"Stone! You scared me half to ..." Irri's voice trailed into silence as he saw the host behind Stone. He grinned, his face boyish in his relief. "You found them! You really found them."

"Have a little faith, Irri." Stone punched Irri's shoulder playfully.

Turk moved to the children. Talo was waking, blinking slowly up at Turk.

"Turk," Talo said in a sleepy voice. Turk wrapped Talo in his arms, lifting him, holding him close, eyes closed in relief. The relief in Turk's expression was real and obviously deeply felt. Talo had a family, a life with people he loved. How could Stone think he deserved part of that?

"What is wrong with Rhyl?" Turk asked, releasing Talo, noticing that Rhyl had not woken with the growing commotion around them.

Irri eyed Stone.

"Magic. I think he will be all right, but we should get him to Eva," Stone explained.

Turk nodded.

"Are you okay, Talo?" the Second asked kindly. "Do you want to come with me?"

"I will stay with Stone," Talo answered, putting his little hand in Stone's. Stone felt like he had grown wings.

# CHAPTER 29

# EVA

THE DAWN AIR WAS COLD, but Eva's body was covered in furs, and she could feel two warm bodies close to hers—three, since Ari the dog was sleeping on her feet. Talo had fallen asleep with her arms around him. Rhyl was still unconscious from using magic, but he would be all right. Eva's eyes stung as tears of relief threatened to return. The boys were safe. Whole. For that moment, that was all that mattered. The rest could wait.

Eva could hear the camp stirring with preparations to leave— they would reach Kilev in a few days. They would be home, safe within the walls of the Queen's Keep where only the most trusted guards and servants would attend them.

She looked beside her where Stone had been lying, close, but not too close. He was gone. Her heart leaped with fear.

Slipping from the bed without waking the boys was no small feat with her big, pregnant belly, but she managed. She shivered and pulled her thick cloak about her. Wasn't it supposed to be summer?

She emerged from the tent searching for Stone's distinct form amongst the bustling guards and servants dismantling the camp.

The weight of her unborn babes pressed down between her thighs; it was not a new sensation, so she ignored it.

"Eva."

She turned to see Stone and melted with relief. He carried a tray of steaming food.

"Or should I call you Muhala—'great mother'—like the rest of them?" He smiled. Behind him lurked Irri, whom Eva had not spoken with the night before. Her heart swelled at the sight of the two men, both dear to her in very different ways. "You all right, Eva?" Stone asked.

Eva gripped the post of the tent to keep upright. She nodded, took a breath, and the false labor faded away.

The three of them went inside the tent. The children slept. Eva looked at Rhyl, watching for the rise and fall of his chest. If what Stone had told her was the truth, then her son was lucky to be alive. Eva had questions for Tayeh about her son's magic—about her magic. What other secrets had he not told her? Could her son really use his magic to take a life? Could she?

"Irri," Eva said, pushing the questions aside, reaching for a mug of hot tea. "Stone tells me you were a Kitarran spy for all those years."

Irri looked at his hands. Shame and anguish were his defining features. "Yes, my lady. I am sorry for the part I took in your grief."

"Oh, Irri. Thank you for saving the boys. I am so happy to see you." Eva wrapped her arms around the thin young man.

"I only wish I could have saved Lord Illiah," Irri said quietly.

Eva said nothing, but smiled weakly, for Irri's sake.

"I told you she wouldn't eat you," Stone said to Irri. "He is terrified of you, you know."

Irri glared at Stone.

Eva almost smiled. "Irri, I have forgiven the Kitarrans for what they did. Kitarra is my home now, my people." She couldn't help but glance at the sleeping children. "But you are too young to be a spy." Her motherly instinct agreed, but she remembered Tarran had been Illiah's spy at only eleven years old.

"The Kitarrans knew that Illiah was recruiting youth, so they sent me to be recruited."

"Clever." Eva bit her lip. "Can you tell me any news from the Keep? When did you leave?"

Irri's face darkened. "Not long ago. I wish I had better news to tell you," he began. He glanced at Stone. "Kaile sent me on a mission. There have been—hauntings is the only word I can think of—along the Great Forest. Towns terrorized, people turning violent. I saw it with my own eyes, a creature of nightmares ..."

Eva exchanged a glance with Stone. His yellow eyes were pinched and worried.

"I knew I had to come back to Kitarra to bring my news. Whatever is affecting Kitarra, is affecting Jullayah as well."

"I can't say that I am surprised. I felt it years ago. Whatever it is—this darkness, this *varing*—it tried to take Illiah years ago, before we were wed. Then last year, it tried again, but Stone destroyed it."

"Eva ...," Irri began, but he swallowed hard.

"Illiah has been taken by Cotoch," Stone told the news Irri was afraid to speak.

"I know," Eva whispered. "I know what happened. I saw it." She looked at Stone directly. Stone's eyes brimmed, and Eva could see her own pain mirrored in his face. She reached out and grasped his furred hand. His tail twitched, but he did not let go.

"Cotoch has taken him across the sea, Eva. To Rodan, the land of the invaders."

Stone's words were difficult to hear. Eva's ears were muted by her heart beating through its cracks. Stone pulled her toward him, and she sobbed against his soft arm. The comforting smell of his fur was thick in her nose.

"Cotoch left?" she asked when she had wrestled her grief into silence.

"For now."

"With Cotoch gone, we should attack Mahlas," Eva growled.

"No, Eva. That would not solve anything. Cotoch has already made alliances with Allati. And Mahlas is home to many good, honest people just looking for a home. I will not let you destroy that."

Stone was right. Eva was not a murderer. She was not a war monger. But her heart screamed for revenge.

"Selene went to Allati," Stone told her.

"I need to warn my brother. I don't know if he is strong enough to withstand her poisonous claws."

"We will send a runner. Hopefully, they will get to Vagar before Selene does," Stone assured her.

"Irri, tell me, how are Kaile and Mila and Murryn? How is Tarran?" Eva had wished many times her magic was strong enough to seek out her friends. Still, she had seen glimpses, but she wanted to hear Irri's perspective, Irri's tales.

"Kaile is a good leader. But … when I got back from my mission, I learned that Lord Serac was dead. He had been visiting the Keep. I was told Tarran and Murryn were responsible, but they had fled with Mila to the Midlands before I got back. It created quite a stir, as you can imagine."

"You are serious?" Eva blurted in her surprise. Stupid question. Of course, Irri was serious.

"Who is Lord Serac?" Stone asked, curious.

"He was Illiah's cousin and Temple Master. A sadist. A rapist," Irri said.

"He held me captive for a few weeks at Crea's temple. It's a long story," Eva told Stone. "He raped and tortured my friend Mila and left her for dead. I have no doubt that her sister, Murryn, would kill Serac to protect Mila—that girl is a force."

"Yes, that she is," Irri agreed. "I hope they are all right."

"If Tarran is with them, I have hope. That boy is all kinds of clever."

"Mummy," came a plaintive, sleepy voice.

"Rhyl, sweetheart, you are awake!"

Rhyl ran over to her on unsteady feet, launching himself onto her lap. Eva untangled herself from Stone and wrapped her arms around her son and kissed his forehead a few times for good measure. He still looked like he was half dreaming. She closed her eyes, savoring how real he felt, how perfect. Talo woke and crawled out from under the furs, creeping over to them, his tail low, his huge eyes glancing up at Stone.

"I'm hungry," he announced, trying to crawl beside Rhyl on Eva's lap. There wasn't room, not with her belly and her son. Stone reached out and pulled the boy toward him onto his lap. Eva smiled as Talo leaned against his father's broad chest, his expression calm—and safe.

Something wondrous wove around Eva's grief-filled heart. How could she feel so happy and so sad at once?

# CHAPTER 30

# COTOCH

COTOCH REGRETTED his decision to leave dry land a mere two days into the voyage to Rodan. It wasn't that he was seasick—thank the old spirits he did not suffer that affliction—no, it was merely the tiny compartments, the press of men, and Imal's *daeum* warriors made poor company. The terrible food, the lack of enjoyable, clean women—his list was long. Cotoch had observed the warriors on many occasions, but he had not spent time close to them, living with them, breathing the same air. He could have easily done without.

He had been given his own cabin—infinitesimal, yes, but his own. And he was given a serving maid, a mangy, flea-bitten, likely pox-riddled old whore, too stringy and leathery to tempt even a *daeum*'s insatiable appetite (he tried not to feel disrespected by this). He was given one bucket of clean, warmish water a day for washing and a glass of wine with his dinner, but he doubted the wine barrel would last the voyage. He was not looking forward to when it ran dry.

Cotoch disliked the manner of sailing. He detested the wet spray on his face above deck and the stale air below. He despised all the ropes and manner of pulleys constantly in motion to keep the boat afloat. He suppressed fears of deep, dark water but often woke feeling like he was suffocating.

And dying of boredom seemed more likely than drowning in a storm.

The *daeum* seemed to agree. A few days into the voyage, a strange boat was spotted on the horizon, and the *daeum* went in like a falcon after a pheasant. They took the ship and its occupants, shoving most of the survivors down below to stew. In Rodan, they would be sold as slaves. A select few were given the honor of entertaining the *daeum*. The *varing* leaked from their festivities, and Cotoch, with nothing better to do, harvested it.

He filled his washing bucket with salt water and looked into its depths. It wasn't as clear as his gold bowl, but it worked, and it gave Cotoch something to occupy his time.

He looked to Kitarra, to Eva, to the queen. But there was little to see. The magic in Kitarra was strong enough to block him from seeing Eva. But he still tried, imagining her heavy with child, sad, angry. He imagined caressing her with his *varing*, smoothing away her grief and her anger, watching it slide from her eyes replaced by desire, by love. For that one night he had had her, she had loved him. He imagined the *varing* moving through them like a chain, linking them, making her his.

Cotoch wished he could have killed Illiah.

Would Eva give herself up for her child? His messenger would be in Kitarra by now. He fully expected Queen Arrah to execute the man and send his head back in a bag, but she would hear him first. And so would Eva. And Eva would think about the bargain. She would give in eventually, he decided. She had the spirit of someone who would do anything for those she loved.

Cotoch used the *varing* to see Mahlas, to find the boy, to see Rhyl, the child that should have been his. It was unfortunate timing, him leaving for Rodan just after Selene brought the boy from Kitarra, but Selene had always been a tad impulsive and opportunistic. And there was something about the boy …

The *varing* showed him the little prince, and he was not at all where he had left him. Stone was with Rhyl and Talo, the turncoat. Cotoch should never have trusted the cunt. Stone had taken the children from Mahlas; Cotoch fully assumed Stone was taking the children back to Eva. Another man who looked familiar was with Stone, but Cotoch could not remember his name. They were running through the fields of the Tarm.

Cotoch kicked the bucket. The vision hovered in his mind. Water sloshed around his feet. He nearly hit his head in the small space. He growled a lengthy curse.

Below the cabins and stock rooms, there was a small, damp hull, where the bilge pump lived along with the rats. It was where slaves were kept—the pump could also be used to clear the result of too many bodies crammed into too small a space for a long time. Not a bad system, really. It was where the *daeum* had stashed Illiah.

Cotoch lowered himself down the ladder into the dark. Anger made his movements stiff. And he had to fight against the rocking of the ship. He almost tripped—his inefficiencies added to his inner rage.

A lantern illuminated Illiah's prison amongst the barrels

(apparently the *daeum* knew the human mind, like a plant, withered without light)(Cotoch had known that already).

"You." He crouched down next to where Illiah sat motionless and hunched.

Illiah looked up at him, his eyes darker than the shadows behind him.

"What do you want?" Illiah's voice crackled like worn hide.

Cotoch answered by grabbing Illiah by his filthy shirt and punching him in the side of the head.

"You," Cotoch repeated, his voice alien to his ears. He had not felt such rage since the night he dragged his wife down to the crypt and pulled the *varing* from her body. He struck Illiah again, and again. Illiah did not fight back. Illiah's eyes rolled back, black and hopeless. *How dare he?* Cotoch raged. Illiah slumped to the floor. Something black—death, perhaps—oozed from his face. The smell of iron and ash rose above the other, horrible smells. Cotoch's heart pounded in his chest. His legs felt invisible as the ooze slipped onto the floor and rose, like a nightmare, a shadow made of magic.

The blackness materialized from Illiah, and it stood tall, changing, shifting, until it resembled a man made of *varing*.

"Cotoch." It spoke in a voice Cotoch knew and wore a face Cotoch scarcely remembered as his father's—his nightmares had taken his father's actual features and twisted them long ago.

The boat pitched, and Cotoch tripped again. The light swayed from the rocking lantern. But the man resembling Cotoch's dead father did not follow the movement of the boat. He was a ghost, but he was not a ghost.

"Father," Cotoch said, faltering into Rodan, the language of his childhood. Then he shook his head. "No. You are not my father.

My mind has gone mad on this fucking boat, with these fucking monsters."

"Has it?" The ghost cocked its head and reached out with one long arm, grasping Cotoch's wrist, squeezing hard, pressing Cotoch's tendons against his bones, making his lungs forget draw air. Cotoch had never felt anything so real. The man who looked like his father did not let go, he pulled Cotoch close and blew into his face, a sick, black breath that no living creature could create.

"What are you?" Cotoch gasped.

"I am whatever the *varing* has touched. I am the dark river. I am the lost. I am the taken. I am the night." As it spoke, it looked less and less like a man, less like Cotoch's nightmares and more like dust and vapor. The hold it had on Cotoch's arm grew less tactile, less strong. Its eyes were the last to leave, the last to shift from human to magic to dream.

Cotoch was alone with Illiah whose shallow breathing indicated he wasn't going to die quite yet. Cotoch swallowed. His anger evaporated along with the ghost. What had he been thinking? If he killed Illiah in his rage-induced violence, Imal would take him in recompense. He hoped the *daeum* had a healer on the ship.

The walls of the boat seemed to close around him. His lungs felt like he was a hundred feet below the surface of the water. He scrambled up the stairs and gasped the cold air above deck, and the blessed wind pulled at his hair.

He was surrounded by monsters. If he wasn't careful, those monsters would pick away at his bones, bit by bit, until there was nothing left but his will to die and his regrets.

CHAPTER 31

# STONE

SEVEN YEARS. And Kilev had not changed, at least not on the surface. The streets Stone passed on their way through the city to the Queen's Keep were still a myriad of shops and market squares. The Queen's Keep looked like a flower frozen in time, its bright walls contrasting with the evergreen forest at its back. The golden branches of the cendari tree peeked out behind its walls. Kitarra Peak loomed over the landscape like one of his ancestors turned to stone, ever watchful, ever present. Stone found the sameness of the city comforting.

The docks still stunk like fish. The market was still as colorful and messy and chaotic as Stone remembered. Stone was thankful he could not see the Forge where it was tucked alongside the Queen's Keep. The Forge held too many memories of Emri.

Stone found himself quiet as he walked, muted by a jumble of emotions he did not have the energy to untangle. Talo and Rhyl did not walk—they bounced and hopped like squirrels, pointing here and there as they wound through the city streets. Stone almost expected them to grow wings and fly through the city, up to the palace in their excitement about being home. Citizens stopped to watch them, their faces gleaming in relief and joy to see the princes.

"Where is Mummy?" Rhyl kept asking, even though Eva was only a short way behind them in the wagon. She could not walk up the winding streets. The boys, on the other hand, could not sit still. But it was no surprise he wanted to keep close to his mother.

The boys prattled on about their home, their things, the pools—then they would fall silent because something was still missing. Eva, in all her bravery, had told them the truth: Illiah was captured and might not be coming home.

Stone blinked, and they stood before the Queen's Keep. He blinked again, and they were following two sprinting boys toward the heart of Kitarra's matriarchy. A crowd had been steadily growing around them, eager to welcome the two princes home. The press of well-wishers could not enter the Inner Keep where the royal family and their servants lived. Stone was not sorry to close the doors on them and move forward with only Irri, the boys, and Eva.

Stone silenced the memories whispering to him from the familiar hallways and nooks.

A tall, slender, sober man greeted them. His gaunt face broke into a wizened grin as he welcomed the boys home. He crouched so they could wrap their little arms around him. Stone's heart was pounding; his feet were lead, his tail brushed the floor.

Anfru, loyal Anfru. The man who had been Arrain's closest servant, his dear friend and counselor. How could Stone have forgotten his serious, somber brown eyes, his narrow, square shoulders? His hair was now heavily grayed; almost none of the brown was left. His eyebrows were bushy, full of character, odd on his narrow face. *It's me, Arrain,* he wanted to say—to shout. He wanted to shake the old man until Anfru saw him, knew him.

But nothing of the sort happened.

"Lady Eva, welcome home," Anfru said, looking at Eva but inspecting her belly.

"Thank you, Anfru. I am fine, see?" Eva proclaimed, but Stone sensed an edge to her words. He had been watching her for the past few days. She hid her emotions well, but there was something else, a pain that was more of the body than the heart.

Talo took Stone's hand and led him forward, almost skipping, his little whip of a tail swaying side to side, eager to show him his room, his sword, everything. Rhyl decided it was time to run, and Talo dropped Stone's hand to follow. The boys took off like wild horses.

Stone wanted to run too, but catching Anfru's gaze, he suddenly felt like he was eight years old and found running down stone staircases in the dead of night carrying an armful of stolen treats. He grinned despite himself and saw something he hoped was disbelieving recognition in Anfru's eyes.

"Anfru, please get Irri situated. Food, a room, anything he might need," Eva said. "Arrah will want to see him later, after he has rested." Anfru nodded, gesturing for the young man to follow him. Irri was worn off his feet and looked grateful for Eva's suggestion.

Stone followed the two boys into their chambers. Talo's and Rhyl's voices rose in pitch and happiness. Stone felt his cheeks stretch in a grin. Eva's large, white uandian Ari bounced around them, her tail like a tree in a storm, catching their excited energy. Stone paused and looked around the room. Illiah's absence was like a toxic thorn in Stone's heart.

Eva turned her eyes to Stone and held them. And held them.

"Stone," she whispered. "Stone," Eva said again, her voice sharp this time. Sharp enough to make the boys tense beside her. Her expression flashed and fluttered for a moment. Stone took a few steps across the room to her side. She looked like she was about to faint.

"Eva, what's wrong?" Stone asked.

Eva took a breath. "I am fine." It was unconvincing.

"Are you in labor?"

"No," Eva scoffed. "It's too soon."

Stone raised his brows. In Stone's opinion, Eva looked large enough to deliver. Did he just say that out loud?

"I am carrying twins, remember?" Eva growled.

"Ah. Right."

"The babies are almost here?" Rhyl asked, a hopeful note in his voice. The boy did not miss much.

"Boys, do you want to see Mua? She has missed you so much! Take Ari with you, but come back quickly. Then we will have something to eat, and maybe Stone will take you swimming."

The boys grinned, nodding their heads. Then they bounced out the door, the dog on their heels.

"Stone," Eva repeated, softer this time. A tear slipped down her cheek. It was the first time Stone had been alone with her.

"Eva." Stone was at her side without thinking. He caught her tear and cupped her face in his hand. Then he sat beside her and wrapped his arms around her awkward frame. She leaned into him and sobbed against his fur. Stone could almost see the fissures and cracks running through Eva's heart. Her husband and son, taken, again. Her husband beyond help. The risks she put herself and her unborn babies through. Betrayal and abandonment. He held her tighter and tried to keep her together with his will.

"I am sorry," he whispered.

After what felt like an age or perhaps a blink, Eva stopped shaking. "You brought them home."

Stone allowed himself a contented sigh.

"And now you are home," Eva added. "How does it feel?"

"I don't know. I can't feel very much these days."

"The culla."

Stone expected Eva to rant and break away from him, to accuse him of being a fool and a coward. For breaking his promise. For going back to the man who raped her. But she didn't.

"What happened to Rhyl and Talo …," she said. It was the first they had spoken of it in more than hushed tones. "Rhyl's magic. Talo dying. How could he have brought him back? It's impossible."

"How could Rhyl kill those men?" Stone countered, feeling a darkness spread through the chamber as he mentioned it. "But he did. I don't think it was his intention. I think it was fear and desperation—a dangerous combination in anyone, much less a magically gifted child."

"The Guardians told me he would be something special, that the child of Illiah and I would be a mix of *sanarii* and *candarii* …"

"But *candarii* cannot kill like that. I have never heard of anything like it."

Eva was quiet, thoughtful. She stiffened beside him and he realized it was not pensiveness that held her tongue.

"You are in labor," Stone stated.

"No. The babies are too small. And … and how can I do this without Illiah?" There was a note of panic in her voice. Then she bit her lip, her body arching slightly.

"When are they due?" Stone asked.

Eva had to take a deep breath, then another, before answering, "Another moon, at least." Her face scrunched and then she exhaled long and slow.

"Uhm." Stone put his hand on her belly. A convulsion ran through her body. It could be false labor, but her face suggested otherwise. "Can you even speak?"

Eva shook her head.

Stone waited.

"Something is trickling down my leg." Her voice rose in pitch. She glared at Stone as if it was his fault her water had broken. "Go find Anfru—tell him to get the midwife," Eva hissed after her body relaxed from the contraction. She barely got the sentence out before another contraction imprisoned her.

Stone's stomach churned. He fought the urge to flee—not that blood and gore bothered him, it was birth. He closed his eyes, remembering Emri's black fur drenched with blood. But he nodded, content to have a task, hoping Eva would be all right on her own for a moment. Babies took time, right? Still, he picked up his pace, jogging through the corridors.

Anfru was no longer with Irri. A guard told him Anfru was with the queen. Stone had never seen so many armed men and women patrolling the royal hallways. He could feel their curious glances slide off his back.

The queen was in her atrium. The tall arched ceiling of glass let in the sun, warming the air inside with little need of a fire. The room was filled with tender plants, most of which originated in the Isles. Fruit trees that only grew on sunny slopes. The brick floor was warm under his padded feet.

Stone's mother was dancing, one hand held by Talo, one by Rhyl.

A court musician played a lively beat; everyone was smiling, from the piper to the queen to Rhyl and Talo. Delight echoed through the room, reminding Stone of many wonderful childhood moments.

Not all his memories of the room were happy. He remembered the day his mother scolded him for fighting with another child— Stone couldn't remember the other boy's name. He remembered how his mother told him with tears in her eyes that his father was not going to get better. It was his mother's favorite room, where she found comfort and courage. It was no surprise it was once more a place of joy, and family.

Arrah saw him and paused her twirling. Her smile slipped, just a little. Her face blanched then narrowed in consternation, then recognition. A mother knows her son, despite his bleached fur and darkened stripes and traitor's heart. Stone's wits returned, and he turned to Anfru.

"Anfru, Eva is in labor. Please get the midwife," Stone said. Anfru paled, hurrying from the room.

"I knew that journey would be too much for her," the queen clucked.

Stone nodded.

Arrah kissed the tops of the boys' heads, still regarding Stone. "You are Eva's amourii," she stated. Talo flopped across her lap, tired from dancing. Rhyl tugged on Talo's leg like a puppy.

"Yes. I need to get back to her." But instead, Stone took a few more steps toward his mother. She looked so much older than she did in his memories. Her eyes were heavy with sorrows. But there was a strength to her like a cendari tree.

"Her babies are early," Arrah said, her voice frosty with concern.

"Will my brothers be all right?" Rhyl asked.

"Brothers?" Arrah smiled away her fear. "We will do our best. Artesia is a very clever midwife. She will help your mother as best she can."

Talo looked unconvinced. Stone wondered if Talo knew the manner of his mother's death. Had he visited the little grave of his sister? Stone took Talo's hand and squeezed it.

"Do not worry, Talo. Stay with Mua, keep her company, distract her so she does not worry about Eva's babies," Stone said, smiling at his son.

"I will," Talo said with a smile, his blue eyes crinkling.

Stone's eyes shifted to his mother's. Stone put his hand on her shoulder.

"How is this possible?" Arrah whispered, not talking about Eva at all. A sob escaped the queen.

"I really have to get back to Eva. I will explain later."

"Explain what?" Talo asked.

"Everything." Stone used his long arms to tussle both boys' heads at once.

# CHAPTER 32

# STONE

STONE FELT like an unneeded pair of feet in a crowded room. And the memories nudged at his sanity. He blinked, and it was not Eva in front of him, but Emri, trapped in her pain, her body strained, and the blood ... So much blood.

"Stone?" Eva's voice cut through Stone's trance. He blinked again. Eva's blue-green eyes pleaded with him. "Where are you going?"

Stone had taken a few steps toward the door.

"No. You stay here. I need you," Eva said through gritted teeth. "You are my amourii, and you are staying right here—if it kills you. Maybe watching my babes being birthed ... will ... finally ... spell—" Pain eclipsed her words for a moment. "Your end," she teased.

Stone sighed and smiled at her. "Fine. I'll stay."

"I'm cold," Eva said, even though the fire blazed and the chamber was warm.

Before the midwife's apprentice could move, Stone took three blankets and wrapped them around Eva, tucking her in like a babe. The midwife, Artesia, gave Eva a warm drink that she had been preparing. Eva took it and grimaced at the smell.

"Gurdy root," Stone said with sympathy. "Tastes better than it smells."

The midwife, a short Kitarran woman with an air for getting things done, gave Stone an appraising look. "How did you know?"

Stone did not answer.

Eva glared at him with the full strength of the sun, but she could not talk. Her work had just begun.

Eva didn't scream until her body forced the first baby out into the world. Stone had never felt so useless and obsolete, watching her push and strain. The first baby came, slimy and slippery. The midwife scooped it up and placed it straight into Eva's arms. Eva clutched the babe against her bare chest. Eva cried. The relief on her face was magic. The baby was small but not as small as Stone had expected. It wriggled and mewled and finally gave a good cry. The cord was clipped and tied.

"Is the baby supposed to be red like that?" Stone asked the midwife. But the midwife was busy preparing for the second baby.

"He is okay," Eva said, her body shivering between contractions. "Take him." Eva handed Stone the baby, so small, so new and raw. Full of life, full of potential.

With the help of the midwife's apprentice, Stone wrapped the baby in the blanket, rubbing the slime and birth muck from his little body. Snug in the wrappings, the baby boy was already trying to eat his fingers, moving his head, looking for something to suckle. Stone found that he was smiling.

The second baby arrived. The midwife announced that it was another boy. Like his brother, he was lifted, limp and covered with birthing tissue, to Eva. He wriggled with less fervor than his older brother. Eva put her hand on his forehead, her eyes closed. Stone held his breath.

"He is all right, just fatigued," Eva said, holding her second baby close. Her face was lined and exhausted, but with the babe on her chest, cradled in her arms, she looked like a goddess.

Eva expelled the rest of the birthing tissue. The midwife checked it, and nodded, declaring it a good birth, especially for twins. Soon the mess was taken away, and Eva lay comfortably on the bed, stitched up and propped by pillows upon pillows and furs. Anfru brought food and drink, his face smiling and relieved. Stone nestled the babies, one on each side of Eva.

"Two boys," Stone said, settling beside them.

Eva smiled, her face glowing despite her exhaustion and pain. It had been a short labor, but intense. And two babies.

"How are you going to tell them apart?" Stone asked.

Eva laughed, but it made her wince in pain. "I don't have the faintest idea."

"You could tattoo one of them," Stone suggested.

"Stone! That is a horrible idea."

"Just kidding. Partly. Seriously though, they are identical."

"This is Bren. This is Aralis," Eva told him, nodding to the babes in turn.

"Good names."

"Artesia knows of a wet nurse for them—I don't think I can manage on my own."

"You are not alone," Stone assured her.

"They have Illiah's dark hair. Rhyl's hair was white right from birth."

"So no magic, then?"

"Not children of the prophecy." Eva yawned.

"Go to sleep. Rest. I need to go see my mother," Stone murmured.

Eva closed her eyes, nodding. "I am glad you are here, Stone."

"Me too." And he meant it.

The palace slept. Rhyl and Talo slept, blessedly safe in their own beds with Ari at their feet. Eva slept beside her babes, a nurse ready to help her if needed.

Stone hoped that for the first time in a long time, his mother slept in peace, knowing her son was home, not dead as she had believed for so many years. For a time, his mother's joy, the light in her gray eyes, made Stone's heart soar. For a brief moment, he felt like he was home.

Stone did not sleep.

As the darkness of night fell and his thirst for culla grew, the feeling of reunion, of home, sloughed from his heart. He took a dose, letting the powder sit on his tongue long enough to taste the bitter herb. He cherished the taste as much as he found it repulsive. He counted his vials. He had enough for one more month, but after that? He didn't know what would happen.

A month after his return to Cotoch, he had tried to withdrawal from the culla. Another failed attempt at death—at chivalry. Why did he feel the two were connected? The aches and the sick had been like a stone crushing his heart. He had felt his blood drying in his veins, and his heart slowly lignify. His stomach purged itself of every bit of food or drink. He thought he would die of hunger. Of drowning. Of pain. Of heartache.

The yearning was what undid him. Succumbing to the culla, feeling the drug move through his body and his heart with fire and promises, was the thread that stitched his torn pieces into some semblance, some version, of himself.

Stone left the confines of the chamber and walked out into the night. He pulled the fresh night air into his lungs, then exhaled long and slow. He looked out over Kilev. Lights indicated that there were others, like himself, who could not sleep.

He felt like a liar. A pretender. He was no hero. He was no prince. How could he come back to Kilev, back to his mother, back to Eva—back to his son—and expect to be the man they needed? He was a traitor. A failure. An addict. A coward. Arrain, who was once a son, a husband, a leader—that man was dead. He had died by his own hand, leaping over the cliffs.

"Emri, what must I do?" he spoke into the night. He did not get an answer—he had not expected an answer. If his dead wife watched over him, she found him repulsive and shameful. She would not answer him. Not if he screamed and wept until his throat bled.

# ILLIAH

THEY DIDN'T WANT HIM DEAD. But they did want him weak and helpless. Cotoch did not come back to torment him, but the others did. The monsters grew bored as the journey lengthened. How many times had he been kicked across the hull of the ship until he spat blood into the wood, and he couldn't lift his head from the floor? Illiah couldn't count.

What they fed him was pitiful, and what he ate came up soon after with each pitch of the boat. His ribs pressed against his skin. His muscles deserted him like fleas on a dead rat. The beatings were just enough to keep him from being able to stretch comfortably or use the bucket efficiently.

He was alone. He didn't know what happened to Aisha after that first day. Illiah could not see beyond his tiny prison in the hull, and it was impossible to follow the commotion and movement of men on the ship. None of the voices he heard belonged to any of his men.

He clung to his anger. His hate. But sometimes there was only pain. And weakness. And shivering. Then they would feed him something hot, and his body lapped it up. Several days of being decently fed and almost warm would pass. He would feel his strength returning. And then they would beat him.

Days and days passed.

Illiah imagined Cotoch's death countless times in countless ways. Cotoch had been in league with the invaders all along. Had he commanded the attack on Jullayah all those years ago? Illiah thought of his dead brother, Aralis, and every man Illiah had sent to die. His only solace was the memory of every invader he had killed. His memories blurred from blood to tears and back again. It became difficult to decipher nightmare from dream from memory.

But it didn't matter. Cotoch was responsible for all Illiah's suffering. For the death of his loved ones. For the shadows in Eva's eyes. His wife, whom Cotoch had violated. And his son. His little boy in the hands of that monster.

Stone would rescue Rhyl and Talo or die trying. Illiah had to believe that Stone was the man Eva believed he was, that Stone would prevail where Illiah had failed. Illiah had to believe Rhyl and Talo would be all right. The alternative would drive him mad.

A morning came. At least Illiah thought it was morning—it was difficult to tell from the depths of the ship—when Illiah heard the raucous sound of many sea birds. It was the same sound that encompassed the docks in Kilev when the birds flew inland to feast on what morsels the fishermen threw into the water.

He strained to listen beyond the birds. What he heard sounded … different. The lapping of the ocean waves had changed. He could hear scattered voices, creaking, wracking, shouting. The ship deck above his head was a smattering of footfalls. They were preparing to dock.

Illiah's usual tormentors came down to get him. Illiah had named them Butt and Nose—one had a long, pointed nose often dripping mucus, the other scratched his butt more often than not. They spoke a bit of his language, enough for him to know they wanted him on his feet.

Illiah drew a painful breath and rose unsteadily. They took him by the elbows and half dragged, half carried him up the steep ladder onto the deck.

Illiah had not seen the sky for what could have been years, but maybe it was only a few weeks. He didn't know. He didn't care. Time was irrelevant.

The sky was brilliant and blinding and dishearteningly familiar. The ocean below was the same blue as its counterpart. Such an unreal color. Illiah felt his horizon slipping. Nose yanked him back to his feet. His perspective had been slipping because *he* had been slipping. He was too weak to stay on his feet.

The docks were not unlike Kitarra's, with a stream of people, boxes, and crates, unloading, loading and unloading. But the smells were more of the ocean. Briny and oily.

The city that rose from the docks was nothing like Kilev. As Illiah squinted against the glare, all he could see of the city was a mishmash of texture and blocks without height and sophistication. His eyes refused to focus. The sun had never felt so close, so malicious. It bore down on him with vengeance, distracting him quickly from his assessment of the new land. Illiah shook his head, reeling. Butt yanked him back upright.

Illiah wanted to look behind him to see if his men were being herded from the ship like he was. Had they survived the journey? Where were they? Illiah tried to look, but the sun was too bright, and his cruel handlers pushed him forward too quickly. He stumbled. Nose caught him in an iron grasp but cursed and cuffed his cheek, making Illiah's eyes water. Illiah tried to command his legs to walk, but it was like the waves of the ocean followed him, and every step he took was wobbly and angry. With each step, it became harder and harder to stay upright. His vision blurred and swam. He retched onto the dusty street.

Illiah didn't see the building he was dragged into. The change of light and temperature told him he was inside, away from the sun that had become his enemy. They took him down. And down. And finally dropped him on the ground like a sack. It was cool, and Illiah embraced it like a long-lost friend.

When he could move, he saw he had water and some gruel. A bucket for his waste. They had cut his bonds. After weeks, his feet and hands were free, and he had not even felt it. He rubbed his raw, red wrists. They felt bony and alien.

His prison was big. Tall, arching ceilings of rock. Rock everywhere. There was even a window, looking out onto the water. Heavy black bars framed the bay, pitted, rusted, but impervious. The sun rippled off the bright, blue-green water, reminding Illiah of something. Something he could not quite reach in his mind. Eva's eyes. Yes, Eva's eyes were blue and green and just as impossible to reach.

# CHAPTER 34

# AIYAN

ONE KNOCK. Two knocks. A pale-faced slave appeared as the door opened. The slave slunk into the shadows as Aiyan walked into the house. It was an elegant house. They usually were. Filled with pretty things like pottery, tapestries, wine, and slaves. The rodaeri of Kara were predictable in their tastes. Boring.

A man who was not a slave appeared in the ill-lit hallway. He saw Aiyan and froze like a leaf in the Heera Mountains in winter.

"You," the rodaeri hissed.

Aiyan was impressed the man had the capacity for speech. Usually when he was recognized, speech dissolved along with bladder retention. No one could look death in the face without feeling the icy fear of imminent dissolution.

The hallway darkened like a cloud obstructing the sun. Aiyan paused. The cloud was a group of armed slaves swarming toward him, blocking him from his mark. Aiyan had not been prepared for guards. And he was always prepared. Someone must have warned his prey that he had been targeted. Maybe it was Imal testing Aiyan's skill. It was not beyond Imal's devious nature to order a hit, just to see if Aiyan would fail.

Aiyan would not fail.

The guards were not *daeum*; they lacked the crazed fearlessness that Imal's enthralled army possessed. They were just men, and men were weak and frail. The hallway was narrow, not the best place for an ambush, but it gave Aiyan the advantage. His daggers gleamed long and sharp in his hands.

Aiyan was a concussion of swift movements aimed with precision to leave maximum damage. A dagger thrust to the throat—the soft place between collarbone and neck. The inner thigh. Lifeblood poured on the thick, lamar rug. With each wave of movement, a guard fell.

From the corner of his eye, Aiyan glimpsed the rodaeri with death marked on his back. Aiyan took down the last two guards and pursued. Seeing the defeat of his guards, his last hope for life, the rodaeri ran.

Sometimes, Aiyan wondered if he could run forever, so fast and efficient were his honed muscles. His prey dove through rooms, hallways, finally out a window into the street. The poor man was breathing hard. He wouldn't get far.

Aiyan growled. A chase down the street was not what he wanted. He liked a clean kill, preferably in the dead of night, with no witnesses. He liked to cloak his persona in mystery; the unknown led to fear, fear led to mistakes, and Aiyan wanted his enemies to make mistakes. It made his job that much easier.

Fortunately, Aiyan soon caught up with his prey. Unfortunately, there were witnesses. He grabbed the man's shoulder, throwing the poor cur off balance. Aiyan pounced and punctured the man's neck. The man didn't even have the chance to beg for mercy, which was Aiyan's preference. Imal's *daeum* liked to see the powerful become weak, to hear their prey beg and burble like snot-nosed children. Aiyan needed no such encouragement to do his job.

Aiyan watched as the last spark of life left the man's eyes. All that was left was meat. He shifted his gaze into his magic and saw that the man's dicidium was gone. Extinguished. It was done.

He looked around to see that the witnesses had fled. He was alone in the alley with the dead rodaeri.

He cleaned his bloody daggers on the dead man's tunic. Aiyan took a moment to inspect his coat; the indigo was clean, mostly. There were several spots along the shoulder. Aiyan had faith that Cliff would be able to get the blood out of the cream embroidery.

He took off his coat and folded it neatly. Then he did the same for his thin linen tunic and trousers until he stood naked in the dusty street. Next, he placed his sandals and his daggers on the neat pile. Cliff would retrieve them later, and as property of the Wolf, no one would touch them.

Naked, Aiyan pulled his magic around him. Stepping into his wolf form was like slipping on a soft robe. It covered him, comforted him, warmed him.

He took the body of the dead man in his mouth, feeling the flesh sink around his teeth, tasting the tang of blood on his tongue. He shook the body, ripping at its flesh with teeth and claws. Within moments, the man looked like he had died horribly at the claws of an animal, rather than the quick death by an assassin's blade.

Aiyan dropped the body at Imal's slippered feet. Imal leaped a little to avoid the blood—the emperor was overly protective of his velvet, gem-studded slippers. Aiyan couldn't blame him; the body was a mess. Ripped skin. Torn limbs. Blood and gore coated the body more than the clothes he had been wearing when he died. The victim looked like it had been dragged through the streets of Kara to the palace. Because it had. Aiyan had wanted to use poison. Imal wanted a blood trail. Literally. He wanted this man's death to be a statement.

Aiyan licked his lips with his long wolf tongue. His jaw was tired from dragging the corpse. Aiyan, as a wolf, was not a large animal, but he was strong. *Heera* strong. But a dead man was a heavy thing.

Imal's eyes were bright. He reached down and took the man's curly hair in his fist, lifting the face to look at what was left of the man's once-pleasing features. There wasn't much; the face was barely recognizable.

"Do you know who this is?" Imal asked Aiyan.

Something uncomfortable, like ice or apprehension, slid down Aiyan's spine. He kept his face smooth as glass as he shifted to his human form to answer his emperor. Nudity didn't bother him, and if it bothered Imal, the emperor never mentioned it. "Ro Tranio."

Imal's mouth curved with a small, poisonous smile. "Yes. But he has another name—Miyamoto. I searched for him for a year—me! The most powerful sorcerer in this forsaken land—only to find Miyamoto was one of my most trusted rodaeri."

Aiyan shrugged. "The slave resistance will die with him," he said, wondering if it was the truth.

Imal nodded, standing up slowly. "True enough. I wanted to torture him, but sometimes even a tyrant should show restraint. Ro Tranio was well liked. If it got out I tortured him to death, it would just cause more trouble. More fuel to the fire, so to speak. And I can't kill all my rodaeri … or can I?" Imal's rodaeri were slaves he had raised to power, given them freedom. Or so they believed. No one in Rodan was free.

Aiyan looked at the mess of the man he had killed. Miyamoto had been clever and brave—if a fool could be brave. Fighting against Imal was a fool's bravery. With his death, Imal would spread fear through the nobility of Kara like a wench-born disease. It was a talent of his.

"Put the body on the steps," Imal commanded. "It's a shame his face is a bit obscured by—all that. Still, they will know who it is. Also, Madra is back in the city. I need him dead."

Aiyan did not know why Madra needed to die. He didn't get to ask questions; no one questioned Imal if they wanted to live. Maybe Madra had asked too many questions.

"Yes, my emperor," Aiyan replied as he hoisted the body onto his shoulder. The dead man had been muscular in life, and taller than Aiyan, but Aiyan thanked his *heera* magic that the extra bulk did not weigh him down. He would not show weakness in front of a predator like Imal.

"Aiyan." A soft voice made him pause in the hallway. He twisted, looking around the awkward load he carried to see Allia. Her face was impassive, her head held high. Her long, dark hair braided in the fashion of a *heera* wisewoman. Her eyes didn't even register the mangled corpse—all she saw was him.

"Allia." Aiyan shifted the weight, wondering what he could say to her. "You are pregnant."

"It's not Imal's, if you were wondering," she told him.

Something sickened inside of him at the wrongness of the young woman before him, from her misused hairstyle—she was no wise-woman—to the round belly of a child she would never love, to the way she looked over Aiyan's blood-smeared, naked body with lust in her eyes. If he looked at her dicidium it would be brittle, and red, and poisoned. But the child … would it survive its mother's pain?

"Good day, Allia," Aiyan told her, feeling the body shift slightly from his shoulder; the blood was wet and slippery. Allia said nothing, but Aiyan felt her eyes on his back as he walked away. He was always walking away from Allia.

Aiyan put the body where Imal commanded. He could feel the eyes of every passing slave and rodaeri on his naked body. He let their disgust slip off his shoulders like oil. The body would decompose. Its fluids would seep into the stone and deepen the stains already marring the grandeur of the palace steps. It was not the first body to be displayed there as a warning. It would not be the last.

The body was a message that spoke of control and fear. Ro Tranio's family had been close to Imal's. His father had been comrades with the first emperor, Imal's father. If Ro Tranio could feel Imal's wrath, then no one was safe, no matter how well they kneeled before Imal and his sorcery. Tranio's death would be felt keenly through the rodaeri.

Something within the city was stirring. It was restless. Angry. Maybe, finally, Imal had gone too far. He let his *daeum* monsters run too often unchecked—too many casualties. Too much hurt. The balance had tipped long ago. Aiyan wasn't sure it could ever right itself. Gravity was pulling the city of Kara into chaos.

Aiyan stepped back to look at the dead man. The buzzards would pick him clean, and his bones would disappear. Human bones could be made into all sorts of things. Tools. Jewelry. Weapons. Slaves were not picky.

Aiyan gave his head a little shake and flexed his fingers before shifting back into a wolf; he didn't want to walk naked through the street. As a wolf, he was faster. And dried blood itched less on fur than bare skin.

# CHAPTER 35

# MILA

HALF OF THE PRISONERS were dead when they reached their destination.

The air had warmed, making the compartment hot like midsummer. Mila, along with Tarran and Murryn, pressed close to the cracks in the ship and breathed what fresh air they could entice inside. The other captives, bound en masse, had no such luxury. Tarran explained that the heat meant they were getting close to Rodan.

And one day, the boat came to a stop. There was a great commotion on the deck. The captain came down, followed by three men who were not *daeum* soldiers. Two carried lanterns for the third, who pressed a delicate cloth over his nose as he inspected what was left of the captives. He pointed to some and muttered.

Mila could not understand his words, but his meaning was clear enough. He was sorting the people for market.

Last, they came to Murryn, Tarran, and Mila. The captain said something, pointing to Tarran. Both lanterns illuminated Tarran's face. Tarran squinted in the light, which had become alien to them after so long in the near-dark. More words were exchanged.

Mila dared not ask Tarran what they were saying.

The lantern turned toward Mila, then Murryn. Compared to the *daeum* captain, the man inspecting them could have been another species entirely—a butterfly compared to a spider—with his embroidered clothes and smooth skin. He turned and headed back toward the daylight.

Tarran said something to the captain, trying to grab his arm, his tone urgent and pleading. Murryn's eyes flicked between the *daeum* and Tarran. The captain shrugged him off, pulling Mila to her feet, dragging her away from Tarran and Murryn. Tarran shouted and tried to follow but he was weak from the sludgy food and lack of sunlight and filthy conditions. The captain knocked him to the floor with a single blow.

Murryn didn't try to fight. She crouched beside Tarran, her face livid but sickly with her old green bruises that her body was too weak to heal.

"It's all right," Mila shouted back to them. "I will be all right." Then she could no longer see them.

Her head was fuzzy. Her feet ached. Daylight flooded over her as she was pulled up on deck. The fresh air smelled sweet and tangy. The warm breeze caressed her pallid skin. She had lost count of the days since she had felt the sun; how she had longed for it. But this sun was hot and oppressive. As soon as she felt it on her skin, she wished for solace from its pounding glare. The air was hot and thick. She let the men pull her and concentrated on not falling as she was blindly herded ashore.

Her eyes adjusted. Before her, a city sprawled this way and that. The city was stone, mostly. Rooftops were shaded with canopies of colored canvas. Her lungs sucked in the hot air—and the smell. In the boat, she had smelled damp, excrement, and sick for months.

The city air was like a garden for her nose—the sea, horses, spices, fish, heat, sand.

Mila was put with the remaining captives in the back of a large wagon. The tall sides were barred with wood to prevent escape but open so Mila could see the city as they drove through it.

The streets and alleys were pressed with people walking, riding, pushing carts, carrying goods. There were peddlers and trades-men. Children in rags. Covered litters carried by men with tanned skin and bulging muscles. There was music. Laughter. Shouting. Screams. Wails of babes. Dust. Dust everywhere.

The first Kitarran she noticed made her start. A woman, she guessed, with tawny fur that looked patched and dry—a slave. She wore a collar around her neck tied to a rope held by a man.

The wagon jostled and bumped along. The captives wept openly. How they still had the capacity for tears after everything, Mila could not fathom. She couldn't find tears for herself. Tears came with hope, and Mila had none.

She had been sold before. As a child, after her father had died, by the man who called himself her uncle. *What else was a man to do with two orphan girls?* Uncle said. Mila would never forget that day she was sent with Murryn to live in a brothel. How much their freedom had been worth, Mila never found out.

Then as a young woman, she was sold again—to Serac.

Mila watched the strange city pass and thought of that night she woke in Eva's room and was given a chance to start a new life. That night she had learned that someone cared. Someone who saw her for what she was—a person, deserving of a good life. She thought of Tarek and Mahone, of Darys. Of Illiah and Kaile. Good people. Her friends.

Were there good people in this strange new city? Were there kindly, brave souls amidst a culture of cruelty and carelessness? Mila studied the faces of those they passed and wondered if any of them had been rescued.

The wagon creaked to a stop, and they were herded like livestock into stalls of stone that looked recently cleaned, the rocks wet and blessedly cool to the touch. But the smell on the air was of death and cruelty and awfulness. Each stall was three walls of stone and one wall of barred metal. The occupants could see out, and others could see in. *We are put to market,* Mila thought.

They were not given food or water. The day waned, and Mila realized that the morning sun was nothing compared to the violence of the zenith. The heat was relentless. For a while, it angled right into the stone stall and made the place feel like an oven. They huddled against the wall and waited for it to pass.

The sound of voices and shuffling feet could be heard—a gathering of people. Mila was thankful. Maybe it meant they would get out of the heat. And waiting for her fate was intolerable. She had waited on the wretched boat for weeks. And now all she wanted was the torturous waiting to be over. *Careful what you wish for, Mila,* she berated herself.

Finally, they were called to the stage of sorts. A man announced bidders and took coin. Mila knew an auction when she saw one.

Mila tore her eyes from the crowd as she was hoisted up the rough steps to the stage. They stripped her of her dirty clothes, exposing her body to be inspected by the crowd. Mila had no shame to offer them. Nakedness was nothing.

The auctioneer set a price, and the bidding began immediately. Arms raised, the price rose. And rose. Mila could not fathom the amount, but there was a murmur of surprise through the crowd. Part of her raged. She had spent her adult life valued for her body and how her body made others feel. She was considered exceptionally beautiful and womanly and desirable. She had never hated it more than at that moment.

She didn't see the person who bought her, but she was hustled away from the crowds, her dirty clothes shoved into her hands. Her mind buzzed with anger. Who needed hope when one had hate?

CHAPTER 36

# AIYAN

AIYAN'S DECISION to visit the Market in his wolf form had been nothing short of idiotic.

The smell. Rotting corpses and acrid urine. Unwashed bodies confined into too small an area. The inexpensive and liberally applied perfume of a wealthy room-slave. These were passably tolerable as a man, but in his wolf's body, with his sensitive nose, the smells were almost blinding.

And the din of people, clanking chains, shouts, and wails were all sounds that assaulted his senses. The sounds were sharp in his wolf ears. Shouts mingled with cries of grief laced with the drawling talk of rich men looking for a deal. The talk of fools. The talk of slaves watching with disdain and amusement as their unlucky peers were dragged onto the dais to be sold. As a man, Aiyan could tune them out. As a wolf, the crescendo of noise made his head ache. And the din made it difficult to pick out signs of danger. It made his wolf half edgy.

But as a wolf, he was unmistakable, obvious. Everyone avoided him, hoping that by ignoring his presence, he did not exist or represent a threat to their person. They were wrong. Aiyan was always a threat. But there was already enough death and despair on market day.

The small but deliberate break in the crowd between him and the other market goers gave him a clear view. It meant he could afford to stay in the shade while observing the slaves led to the raised platform where the whims of those gathered would decide their fates. And it was hot, especially in wolf form with fur and his paws on the stone, even in the shade. Those in the open square had no such escape from the beating sun.

The wealthiest rodaeri often brought slaves to support awnings to shade them or a group of small boys to fan them. But today, the square was exceptionally crowded. There was no room for such luxuries. With new blood from Praedan, those gathered jostled to get the best vantage points—and to be as far away from the Pit as possible.

Usually, Aiyan avoided the Market because he despised every aspect of it. But with the shipment from Praedan, he could not miss the auction.

Aiyan glanced at Tilley, who was returning from her inspection of the slave stalls. Her furry, striped shoulders slumped. Her tail hovered just above the ground. She saw him watching and her back straightened; her face became a mask.

It was useful to have at least one of his slaves accompany him, and though Tilley was young, she was adept. Aiyan wondered if all Kitarrans were as clever and competent. Tilley stood well behind him, discreet. If she had something to say, she would have said it already.

The auction began. Men and women were sold. Then came an old man. Knobby knees, crooked from a life of hard labor, skin leather-tight with malnutrition, skinny as dried grass. Though he might not be as old as he looked. Working the fields, under the Rodan sun, could take decades from a man's body. Aiyan was not surprised when no one offered anything. There was more meat coming. The man was seized roughly by the market guards and tossed into the Pit.

The Pit was at the center of the market square. Round like the moon and dark like despair with a stench like carrion. Death lived in the Pit like a thriving, choking weed. Any rodaeri had the right to throw a slave into the Pit. It was a well-accepted form of disposal for those who would not work, could not work. No one wanted a useless slave. Hence the smell of rotting corpses. There was always a wide berth around the Pit. Similar to the distance the people kept from Aiyan.

"Look, the fucker pissed himself!" A wealthy, favored slave laughed along with his companions.

The slaves mocking their more unfortunate peer had never been on the platform, never been presented before a crowd hoping someone would pay enough to keep them from the Pit. They had been born into slavery, born into the house they would spend their lives and the master they would serve until death. They were fools. In an instant, they could find themselves being sold, their lives relying on a rodaeri's purse.

They were such shits.

Porthos, the cur, had not announced the arrival from Praedan until the last minute to dissuade any chance of being bribed—or if Aiyan had his way, blackmailed. The Market Master wanted to get the best price possible, which meant every slave from the new world would be auctioned off without prior inspection. Imal allowed Porthos autonomy, so long as he gave Imal first pick for his *daeum*. Porthos tithed painfully to Imal, but he still had a large house with as many fresh, pretty bed-slaves as a man could want. The *daeum*, Praedan, and Imal had made Porthos a rich man.

The price of a Kitarran had risen to a small fortune. The price of a Praedan slave who could speak Rodan's tongue had tripled. A Kitarran slave who could speak Rodan's tongue was impossible to purchase for less than a fortune. Aiyan had several fortunes, so naturally, he owned all of those things.

Aiyan didn't need new slaves, not really. But his curiosity outweighed his distaste in the location. And there was always a chance—no, he wouldn't let his thoughts go there.

The auction continued, and the new blood was nowhere to be seen. Maybe it was just a rumor created by Porthos to create a stir. It would not be out of character for the seedy Market Master. No, Porthos would bring the meat from Praedan out last. Aiyan resolved himself to wait until the end of the auction. And if it were just a ruse, Porthos would get a piece of his mind—or his teeth.

After the skinny old man, only three more unsellables were thrown into the Pit. One was a child. Its mother was sold, but the buyer did not want the child—no one else did either. Aiyan let the sounds of its cries permeate into his mind, captured and crystallized along with countless others.

Finally, the new blood was brought out. Prices went up. Bargaining became loud and intense. Praedan slaves looked no different from Rodan slaves, and soon enough, they would become indistinguishable except for their accent. But still, they were an easy sell for the Market Master. Even after his tithe to their emperor, he would still have enough coin after the day's sale to drown himself in every tavern between the Ash Alley and the Tower.

A young Praedan woman was brought onto the platform. The announcer's description whipped by Aiyan briefly, something about a virgin, unspoiled. The words were dust in his ears because something flickered around her. Something that did not make sense. Aiyan unfocused his eyes and let his mind, his magic, find the place between the light and the energy of life that revealed the dicidium, the little slice of magic that resided in every living thing.

Someone bumped against Aiyan, forcing him to lose his focus. Aiyan turned and snarled, flashing his sharp canines. The clumsy rodaeri paled instantly and disappeared in a hurry. Aiyan had a talent for making people disappear, of their own volition, or with his knife. Aiyan turned back to inspect the woman on the stage.

This woman's dicidium was vibrant and black. Not the black of oblivion, but black made of every color mixed, glints of blue and purple, glistening green. It was not possible.

Because she was not Kitarran, that meant there was only one explanation for her unique dicidium. She was like him. A shifter. But what were the colors of a *heera* shifter doing in a woman from across the sea?

Something rose inside him, desperate, ugly … a yearning. It was the only word he could think of to describe it. It was the same feeling that rose when he looked up at the moon on a quiet night, wishing for moss and dirt beneath his paws. He pushed the uncomfortable sensation down, deep, deeper, but it was a fight.

With his emotions under control, Aiyan looked at the woman again, this time without her distracting dicidium. She was pretty. Beautiful with her long curling hair, dark and mysterious. Her dark eyes could have been blue or black or an entire night sky. Aiyan had a fleeting thought that he had never seen a woman so beautiful. And her will sparked like diamonds in her eyes. She was strong. Unbroken.

She would be sold as a whore, without a doubt. Foreign, beautiful. Even rodaeri who kept a host of bed-slaves would pay dearly for a night with her. Aiyan glanced at the man who raised his hand to bid at the ludicrous price Porthos put on the woman. Aiyan was not surprised to see Dart, one of Nulla's men. Dart was as recognizable as Aiyan himself but had an entirely different reputation. He saw Aiyan watching him and winked.

Nulla never came to the Market herself. She hated it more than Aiyan did. But it was well known that if Nulla had her bid in the game, she would win. She always did. Aiyan watched the other interested parties back down, letting Nulla have her prize.

The auction concluded, and Aiyan's curiosity was far from satiated. But he could not indulge himself in finding answers; he had a job to do. The Market was only the beginning of his unpleasant tasks for the day.

# CHAPTER 37

# ILLIAH

"LORD ILLIAH." The accented voice was thick with amusement, and something else that Illiah stumbled over for a moment. Propriety. That was it.

Illiah's skin grated against the stone floor as he turned his stiff body toward his visitor. He had not heard footsteps approach. He had not heard the door to his prison open. The cool stone floor, the clean breeze from the ocean, the absence of the rocking waves, had lulled him to sleep. Or he had passed out. He didn't know.

Illiah struggled to comprehend the man standing over him. Dark hair. Hawk nose. Cotoch. No, not Cotoch. But almost. The man's face was similar to Cotoch's, but his fashion was different. Rich. Colorful. Layers of fabric. A forest of garments and stitching. The man's black hair was tinged with gray, so he was older than Cotoch. But not an old man. A man in his prime.

"Who—who are you?" Illiah managed.

"My name is Imal, Emperor of Rodan. Imal the Gracious. Imal the Conquerer. Imal the Snake. Imal the Perceiver. Take your pick. I have many names."

"Sorcerer," Illiah said, trying to pick his head up from the stone floor.

Imal inclined his head. "An old word, but applicable, I suppose."

"What do you want?"

"What do all men want?" He came two steps closer. "Women? Riches? To become more powerful than one's enemies?" He winked at Illiah. "Right now, what I want is you, but …" He regarded Illiah from another angle, the movement birdlike. "My men have been rough on you." His sigh was patient but grating. "That is unfortunate. I don't like waiting, but I am afraid our fun together must wait until you are feeling better. I will send a healer and some food. Do not worry."

Illiah managed to lift his head from the ground, propping himself on his elbow, just in time to see the back of Imal disappear through the prison door. Illiah saw the glint of light off weapons in the darkness. Guards, no doubt. Illiah could not imagine what this emperor could gain by keeping him as a hostage. But then, his head was aching, and rational thought had abandoned him somewhere in the hull of that ship.

Shortly after Imal left, a few young women came with warm water and food and soft linens. The smell of herbs and soap filled the prison as they washed Illiah and eased his bruises. They fed him like a child, one spoonful at a time. Illiah's hungry body took their nourishment, but it felt like a betrayal. A warning rang in Illiah's mind. Imal was not giving him kindness—something else behind his actions. Illiah's instincts screamed in warning.

# CHAPTER 38

# MILA

MILA COULD NOT get the sound of wailing children out of her head. The sound followed her beyond the horrid market, lodged in her heart like a festering sliver.

She had been sold to a young man with a pretty face. She had glimpsed him from a distance as the final call came down, but his fair features told her nothing about what she might expect from her enslavement. After, she had been taken to a building with thick stone walls and plenty of rooms complemented with locks and chains and floors covered in foreboding stains. Slavery was as ugly a thing as Mila could imagine. Worse. They had thrown an old man into a pit.

Mila would have vomited had she had anything in her stomach. They had not fed her all day.

A woman, aged but dressed in clean clothes, led Mila past the more ominous innards of the building into a small room with a drain in the floor. There was a large basin of clean water, and soap—glorious soap. Mila didn't need encouragement to wash her dirty body.

Once she had scrubbed clean, the older woman nodded in

a satisfied way but did not offer her new clothes. Mila was led, naked, into a large room.

Bolts of fabric lined one wall. A slew of old women sat at the long tables, some sewing, others creating metal jewelry. They all bent over their work, fingers moving like ants, squinting in the inadequate light of a few high windows and a score of ill-placed lamps. It was not what Mila expected.

Mila could not understand a word that was spoken. The woman squeezed Mila's arm painfully to get her attention, her wrinkled face devoid of patience. They gave her new small clothes and a dress, telling her with impatience to put it on. The dress reached down to her toes, the airy fabric soft and clean. The woman looked her up and down, put in a few pins, then gestured for her to undress again. The pinned dress was given to a sewing woman to make the adjustments.

Mila understood that she was to sit and wait while the women altered the dress. A second woman came with something in her hands. Mila craned her neck to see what it was, but the woman gave her cheek a hard slap and berated her in a stern voice to stay still. Or least that was how Mila interpreted it. She wondered what would happen if she disobeyed. Her mind wandered back outside to the market square and that awful pit.

A sharp pain lanced her through her ear, making her eyes water. She bit her lip to stop from crying out. The woman pointed to a red ruby earring in her own wrinkled ear. Mila noticed every woman in the building wore one, all red rubies. A tightness in Mila's chest made it hard to breathe. Tears streamed down her cheeks. The earring was a mark of a slave. A brand. A chain.

The woman held a small polished mirror for Mila to see her

stone. It was meant as a kindness, and Mila thanked the old slave. Mila's stone was not red. It was blue with veins of green and yellow and white, polished to shine like marble. It was beautiful, but still the mark of a slave.

Her dress was returned, the adjustments complete. Mila pulled it on and did the laces up the front. The style was unlike any she had seen or worn. It was tight across her chest and loose about her shoulders and hips. The fabric flowed around her like a cloud.

She was taken to another small room—a closet really—and locked inside. The walls were dirty, and there was no bench or cot. The floor was despicable. Mila wondered why they bothered giving her a clean dress at all. The waiting was worse. The door was solid but for a tiny window, and she was not tall enough to reach it.

Boredom became her enemy. All she could think about was Murryn and Tarran, her mind moving from one terrible notion to the next. Mila had survived being a slave before. She had survived being raped and beaten—Murryn could survive it as well. Murryn was strong. But the thought of Murryn enduring what Mila had, and would likely again, made her clench her fists to keep from clawing at the walls.

The sound of the lock clanging and the door opening was a welcome distraction. Mila wiped her face on her arm. The slave, a man this time, waved her forward, his eyes impassive. She recognized him as the man who had bought her. She had been bought by a slave? She noticed the stone in his earring was the same as hers. Ah, they must have the same master. She followed him out into the sunlit street.

"Welcome to Kara," the man said. His accent was thick, but if she paid attention, she could understand him. The relief that he could speak her language was as welcome as the open air. "My name is Dart. Follow?"

Mila nodded. Dart had slanted eyes and skin like bronze and a face like a woman. His eyes were lined with charcoal, and his clothes were bright and airy, exposing his chest and his lean, sculpted muscles. He walked like a woman.

"You are a whore?" Mila asked.

His eyes widened, feigning offense. Then he grinned. "I am. I work for Nulla, your new mistress. And as a whore, you will find no better place."

"Whores in a city of slaves?"

"Ah, but no one has the kind of whores Nulla does. She is a— what is the word?—expert. Yes. An expert in lust and desire and— how do you say it?—transcendence."

"Bullshit."

"Bull-shit?" Dart asked, not understanding.

"Dung. Excrement. A falsehood," Mila clarified tersely.

Dart laughed. "Yes, you are right. But our patrons don't know that. All they know is that at Nulla's, they pay for something they cannot get anywhere else."

"She sounds like a clever woman," Mila stated begrudgingly.

Dart shrugged. "She is a survivor."

Mila drew a deep breath that stunk of city and dust. She was a survivor too.

At first, Mila thought Kara was a beautiful city. Dart pointed out a few landmarks, the emperor's palace, the bay, the Tower—the *dae-um*'s stronghold. The estates of the great nobles—the rodaeri, they were called. The streets were dusty but mainly clean, often covered by airy awnings of brightly dyed canvas that kept the hot sun from backing the stone streets. The buildings were plastered and painted as well, the colors and designs unlike anything in Jullayah. Mila wondered how they created their dyes; the array of colors was mesmerizing.

Then she looked closer at the people. Many were dressed in bright colors, echoing the designs found on the buildings. Mila could see their hunched shoulders, their eyes blinded to anything but their task. On the side of the street, a girl was kicked by a tall man. No one stepped in to help her. Almost all the people wore stones in their ears. Turquoise, rubies, quartz, silver.

"What do the gems mean?" Mila asked.

"They mark ownership. Ours are black opal." Dart tilted his head so she could admire his earing. "They mark us as belonging to Ro Jeka."

"I thought you said Nulla was my mistress."

"Yes, but Nulla is owned by Ro Jeka. She has the same stone in her ear as you."

"I see."

"Come along, you are falling behind."

They walked in silence the rest of the way. The more Mila looked, the less beautiful and exotic the city appeared. Like a wench discarding her elegant dress to expose her pox scars and stretch marks. The shadows emanated despair and longing. The bright colors became masks, falsehoods—filigree covering blood and violence.

The brothel was exactly what Mila expected from the little Dart had told her, and her own assumptions. Some things were universal.

The building was ornate, beautiful. It spoke of luxurious and mysterious pleasures. The sign was small, almost easy to miss. Shades darkened the windows. There was no way for someone on the street to know what went on inside.

Dart took Mila around the back of the building through a few twisted, covered alleys. The back door was simple but locked. Dart took out a long key. "To keep out the riffraff," he told her with a sideways grin that would be irresistible to the right clientele.

The door opened to a little courtyard framed by two tall walls on one side, and tall buildings on the other two. The door was the only way in and out. The low, arched door leading into the building was plain compared to the elegance of the front.

After the bright sunlit streets, inside was dim. The door opened into a large kitchen where a few servants moved around slowly, chopping vegetables and stirring pots on a large fireplace. Mila's mouth watered from the smell. Food. Real food.

"Food will be sent to your room. We don't eat in the kitchens," Dart told her, taking her by the elbow.

"But—"

"No. There are rules," Dart said sharply. Mila followed Dart up through the house, her stomach aching.

"Here, this is your room. The bathing chamber is through there, and it is shared with Cresa. Cresa?" Dart called, poking his head through the curtained door. He came back shaking his head. "She is still sleeping. Late night."

Mila looked around at the fair-sized room. The window was tall and open; only a thin curtain kept the sun out. Mila wondered if the temperature stayed warm in Rodan all year. There was no fireplace. For furniture, there was a large bed, naturally, but also a table and chairs, a couch built for lounging. Was she supposed to entertain as well as fuck? Dart pointed to the bell on the wall that would call her slave.

"My slave?" Mila repeated.

"Yes. You have your own slave." Dart pulled the bell. It was soon followed by a patter of footsteps along the hallway, and then a small person poked their head into the room. Dart said something sharp in Rodan to the child, a girl with large round eyes and pale blond hair. A pretty child. In a brothel. Mila felt ill. Something inside her was dying already.

"What did you say to her?" Mila asked.

"That she should be quiet in the halls. Our patrons do not want to hear little girls running errands when they are deep in their pleasures," Dart replied. "Letti knows your tongue, but she doesn't really speak. Letti, fetch"—Dart turned back to Mila—"what is your name?"

"Mila."

Dart frowned. "It's a bit dull. Nulla will find you a better one." He turned back to the girl. "Get Mila food. She is very hungry." The girl nodded and skittered off. Mila did not hear one footstep in the hall. "Well, good day, Mila. I must prepare for the night ahead."

"Dart?"

"Hmm?"

"When do I—when do I have to start?"

"I don't know. Nulla will decide when you are ready. She will want to prepare you—advertise you to get the best price for your debut."

"Wonderful."

"Sarcasm?"

"Yes, Dart. Sarcasm."

Dart left her with one last pondering look.

The girl came back silently, carrying a heavy tray. Mila made a point to thank her before succumbing to the variety of food. The meat was red and hot and went down like water. The wine was like blood. It made her dizzy.

The door opening made Mila start. There was no lock, and there had been no knock. Mila swallowed her annoyance with a gulp of sweet wine.

A woman entered who could only be Nulla. She was beautiful but younger than Mila would have thought. Her long, golden hair was coiled elegantly on her head, and her ruby-red dress was covered in shimmering red beads. The jewelry about her wrists was dainty, like stars. Sure enough, she wore a slave earring, the same as Mila's.

The woman took a few steps to stand in Mila's personal space and placed a finger on Mila's jaw as she inspected her new property. "You are very pretty. Dart was right; he has a good eye. Are you a virgin? You are not with child, are you?"

"No and no," Mila replied, feeling her indignation rise.

"It's just business. You will learn that my house is the best you could hope for," Nulla said, her brown eyes narrowed.

"You speak my tongue well."

"I am very adaptable. Are you?"

"Yes."

"I believe it. I see it in your eyes. Something wild." Nulla smiled slowly. Mila clenched her fists. Nulla was right; Mila could feel it rise within her. Her wildness. Her otherness. Her magic. She hadn't felt it so strongly for some time, not since the night she killed Serac. "What do you know about sex?" Nulla continued.

Mila held Nulla's eyes. She smiled as Nulla shifted uncomfortably, if subconsciously. "I was a whore when I was young," she told Nulla.

Nulla nodded, breaking the eye contact to pour herself a glass of wine. "You don't look like an old whore."

"Thanks,'" Mila said. "I'm twenty-three, but I have not been in a brothel for seven years."

Nulla gave her a look that seemed envious. Mila pitied her. "Well, you are now. Understand?"

Mila nodded.

"Good. In five nights, your 'maidenhood' will be bought," Nulla said, as if she was done with their conversation. "But if you do not perform, I will sell you. I am a businesswoman, after all."

"Naturally," Mila replied.

# CHAPTER 39

# AIYAN

AIYAN WASHED THE BLOOD from his hands, scrubbing under his fingernails relentlessly, turning the water of his bath pink. He could morph his human body into a wolf's, he could see the aura of a person, but his magic could not erase the physical remnants of the day's work. And as he scrubbed and bathed, all he could think about was the woman from the Market. Death, mauling, blood, the taste of the dead man in his mouth, were all pushed to the back of his mind as he recalled her face, her dicidium—her magic.

The mysteriousness of her dicidium plagued his mind. It meant she had magic—the same kind of magic as Aiyan—but how? He needed to know. He needed to understand.

The woman had been bought by Nulla. He had heard that in five days, Nulla was hosting a party of epic proportions to introduce her newest exotic pet, selling her virginity to the highest bidder. Nulla loved a production, and so did the rodaeri of Kara.

Aiyan caught his reflection in the mirror and forced himself to look. The dark lines of his *heera* mark looked fresh and new on his wet skin. The black ink embedded with lines and whorls in his skin followed the drips of water down his body. The marks of a war-rior. The mark of the *heera*. How was it a woman from across the sea could have the same magic as him? *Heera* magic was as old as the roots of the mountains to the north and the grains of sand in the dessert to the west. Perhaps there were *heera* in Praedan.

Aiyan gripped the basin. She was not for him. She was destined to be a whore, to sell her body. When her soul broke, her dicidium would shift and dull, like every other slave in Rodan.

Blood scrubbed from his skin, dust from Kara's streets washed from his hair, Aiyan made himself an herbal brew that forced his stubborn mind and body into sleep. The brew would make his mind blank, keep dreams from subverting his sleep. He took a measure more than his usual dose.

Hands clasped his shoulders, shaking him awake. Aiyan's heart hammered. Sweat instantly beaded on his forehead. But it was only Day. The slave took a few rapid steps back in case Aiyan decided to pounce. Aiyan forced himself to relax, knowing his servant must have had a good reason for waking him in such an abrupt manner.

"I am sorry, Ro Aiyan. I know you don't like to be touched, but—"

"What is it?" Aiyan cut him off, waving his apology away with a flick of his hand.

"Imal sent a message."

"Fuck." Aiyan groaned. "I forgot there is an ascension today. When did he send it?" It was not wise to keep the emperor waiting.

"Not long ago," Day said, his long mouth sagging. "But I had a hard time waking you." His words were lined with reproach.

"It was just a sleeping draught, Day," Aiyan said, pulling himself up. His body protested. Perhaps he had overdone the dose, just a little.

Day nodded, but his frown only deepened. "Your clothes are laid out."

"Thank you," Aiyan said absently. He was unsurprised to find his thoughts still consumed with the woman from the Market. He wondered if she could change into a wolf or something else. Did Nulla know her latest acquisition was rife with magic? No, if Nulla knew, she would have told Imal immediately. If Imal knew the woman had magic, he would claim her as his own. That was not the kind of secret Nulla could keep from the emperor. Not if she valued her life—which she did. And the woman from Praedan was Imal's type—beautiful, delicate pale skin, large eyes, curved body. Aiyan was fairly certain her eyes had been blue, like the flower of a midnight poppy—a rare color in the natural world.

Aiyan grimaced and pushed his palm into his forehead. He could not get her out of his head.

Aiyan decided that in five days, he would go to Nulla's party. With that decision made, he could attend the emperor with a clearer mind. And being around Imal was like balancing on the tip of a needle over a bed of burning coals.

Thanks to the effects of the draught, it was later in the morning than Aiyan was accustomed to rising. The sun was hot overhead. His house was far enough from the palace that by the time he stepped into the cool shadows of the stone masterpiece that was Imal's home, beads of sweat trickled onto the silk of his collar. He pulled his long hair away from his neck, tying it back with a cord he found in his pocket. The cool palace air kissed his sweat-damp skin.

A *daeum* appeared from the shadows to greet Aiyan with a solemn bow. Aiyan always felt that there was something statuesque about the *daeum* guards, that they were just husks of stone waiting for their master's command, their eyes void. But the illusion of stillness only lasted until they sensed violence; then the *daeum* became very much alive. They inhaled blood and exhaled pain. They were monsters who had once been men—boys. They were nightmares and tragedy.

The guard spoke not one word but led Aiyan to whichever exquisite crevice of the palace Imal was residing in at the moment.

"Aiyan! My friend, welcome." Imal rose from his gilded chair, holding his equally extravagant cup carefully so his drink did not spill. In the chair next to him sat his cousin, Cotoch, Imal's kin from Praedan. Cotoch looked just as uncomfortable as the last time Aiyan had seen him. The man from across the sea was not taking to Kara's charms. Aiyan couldn't blame him. Imal seemed oblivious, but then, Imal did not care for anyone's comfort but his own. For Imal, comfort was just another weapon, a lure to keep his subordinates in line. "How did it go?"

"It went smoothly," Aiyan replied, taking the drink offered by one of Imal's slaves. "Madra is dead. Gojik will take his place, but he has decided to cull Madra's slaves. He sees them as liabilities." An image of Madra's dead body, prostrate and bleeding, flickered across his mind's eye. Imal's methods were messy and brutal, and eventually, he would have no more rodaeri left. What then, Emperor? What then?

But Aiyan was no adviser. Imal did not have advisers. He listened to no one.

Imal frowned. "Such a waste. If Gojik were a better man, he would have been able to sway the slaves' loyalty or drive them into submission through fear. I have seen both work. But Gojik is lazy. We knew that. And a rich man can always find more slaves."

"Yes, Gojik's laziness is his greatest asset," Aiyan drawled.

Imal laughed. "Yes, the man is easier to control than a *daeum* soldier, so long as you are me." Imal grinned. "Speaking of the *daeum*, you know what today is?"

Aiyan nodded.

"You always look so glum, Aiyan. It is a good day. The next set of boys are ready to become warriors. My warriors." Imal took a relishing sip of his drink. It was not wine; Imal did not drink on ascension days. Aiyan glanced at Cotoch, who had yet to join the conversation.

"How many?" Aiyan asked.

"Thirty."

"A good number."

"Yes. Strong, strapping lads, for the most part. It is such a pity I cannot change the Kitarrans. What a force I would have then." It was a wish Imal had revisited so many times, Aiyan was almost surprised it had not come true. Aiyan nodded sympathetically, but inwardly he was relieved Imal had given up creating *daeum* Kitarrans. That had been ... messy. The Kitarrans were immune to the *varing*—at least those who had survived Imal's attempts. Aiyan suspected it was because their dicidium was different from a human's, a different speck of magic that pulsed, bright and alive. Something Imal's *varing* could not penetrate.

"There is something else," Aiyan mentioned, "You look too gleeful for merely an ascension and the death of Madra. Those are common-enough affairs."

"Ah, how observant you are." Imal's eyes twinkled like a little boy's. "My prize is finally ready." Imal turned and shared his wide grin with his cousin. For the first time, a genuine smile stretched across Cotoch's face. He looked uncomfortably like Imal.

Over the past year, Aiyan knew communication between Cotoch and Imal had been almost nonexistent. Cotoch had refused to answer Imal's summons. But finally, Imal had given his cousin an offer he couldn't refuse. A challenge he couldn't revoke. And now Cotoch was here, in Rodan, and he had brought something with him. Something that had made Imal exceedingly happy. And in return, Imal had promised to teach his cousin about the ascension.

Imal's eyes glinted like he was at the height of his wine and magic, but he had had neither. With his *heera* magic, Aiyan could see the *varing* flow around Imal.

"Revenge is like honey to a wasp." Imal looked pointedly at Aiyan. Aiyan's chest tightened as his memories responded to Imal's remark. Aiyan wrestled for control over the riot of emotions threatening to leak out of his expression.

"Agreed," Aiyan muttered.

Imal laughed. "Come, Cotoch, Aiyan. The time has come."

There was nothing Aiyan hated more than the ascension, but he knew refusing Imal was not an option. Imal liked an audience. Aiyan had watched it before, and he would again.

"Do you think I am the wasp, Aiyan?" Imal asked as they walked to the ascension chamber.

"You're certainly not the honey. Nor the honeybee."

Aiyan noticed how Imal's bark of laughter made Cotoch jump.

Aiyan looked at the poor curs, taken from their homes, beaten, subjugated, raped. The boys were almost men—young, gangly things with lumpy throats and childlike faces and hard, sinewy muscles. Their hair was cut to almost nonexistence. They wore the same bland trousers all *daeum* trainees wore. Their expressions always seemed desperate—starving. Not starving for food—starving for light, companionship, peace. Maybe the ascension was a mercy to their souls. It was certainly not a mercy to the world.

Aiyan forced his mind away from the thought. Hardened it.

The boys watched Imal like one watches a predator over the rise of a hill, hoping the wind did not shift.

It was unfortunate that the first ascension of the day went awry. The first boy was more man than the others, his thick, muscled neck and his height an indicator of the brute he would become. His eyes already held a hint of the *daeum* madness; some came into their cruelty more naturally than others. The young man sat in the stone chair, eyes fixed on Imal's. Imal smiled to see his bravery. Aiyan knew Imal hated the snivelers. Even when two large, *daeum* guards strapped the boy's hands into place, he still retained his courage.

The boy's head was a comfortable height for Imal to rest his hands, one on each cheek. A weighted silence filled the room as Imal let his magic move. Only Aiyan could see the vines of *varing* slip from Imal's fingertips and crawl inside the boy's nose, his ears. Rotten, slimy tendrils that mixed in the boy's *diciduim* and took over, corrupting it.

The *varing* was kin to *heera* magic the way oil was kin to water.

The boy in the chair began to scream; the noise came from him with the force of an anvil. There was no crescendo, no gentle rise in volume. Aiyan's nerves jolted. Imal almost released his hold before leaning into his sorcerer magic like a lifeline, trying to salvage the boy's mind. The boy started to shake, straining at his bonds. The ungodly scream went on and on. Aiyan could not believe a human could make such a sound.

Imal called his guards. It took two large men to snap the boy's neck, putting an end to the noise. The stone echoed with the resounding silence of Imal's failure. Imal did not like to fail.

"Well. That was regrettable," was all Imal said, giving his shoulders a shake. He called for the next boy.

The next boy had soiled himself waiting in the hallway. Aiyan could not blame him. He could only imagine the terror permeating through the boys as they listened to that awfulness. But in moments, the ascension had taken, and the boy's eyes were hard and uncaring, no longer touched by terror. The *daeum* made terror their weapon, using it more effectively than any poison Aiyan could concoct. Imal took his dagger and began the first ritual cut along the boy's cheek. The boy did not even flinch as the dagger cut through his lip, his blood dripping onto his lap.

One by one, Imal took the remaining boys and bound them to the cold stone chair and used his dark magic to transform them. The fear in the boys' eyes dissolved, becoming hard and cruel and empty.

Aiyan glanced at Cotoch from time to time. The man's face was a calculated mask, but Aiyan had a wolf's intuition, and he could smell the man's fear—and disgust. Interesting. It seemed Cotoch was not a living reflection of his cousin, after all. Imal gave Cotoch a chance to practice the ascension for himself, but it didn't work. Cotoch lacked conviction.

Aiyan preferred to imagine that in becoming *daeum* soldiers, the boys, as they had been, were dead, that their souls had been eclipsed by dark magic. But Aiyan knew, rare as it was, that a *daeum* could break free from the confines of dark magic. He knew that somewhere deep down, that broken boy was still there, caged and lonely.

Thirty was a fair number. Imal was weak by the time the last ascension was finished. Not that he showed it. Imal did not display weakness, not even to Aiyan. But Aiyan could see it. Imal's *varing* was almost gone; he would need to recharge. He would need sleep. There would be no late-night parties for him tonight, no slaves warming his bed. It was one of the few times Aiyan knew Imal would be indisposed.

It meant Aiyan would not be sent to kill anyone that night.

# CHAPTER 40

# ILLIAH

AFTER DAYS of careful ministration by Imal's healers, Illiah could sit without feeling off his axis, and he could wash and use the bucket accordingly. He managed to walk the length and breadth of his prison and crane his neck to the arched ceiling. The floor undulated. Illiah tripped and skinned his knees like a toddler, weak and unsteady. His prison was not as terrible as the hole in the ground where Cotoch had kept him, or the rocking hull of the damp boat. Illiah's stomach heaved just thinking of it. No, this prison was almost kind.

On the sixth day, Imal returned.

Illiah stood, his eyes level with the emperor's. Imal smiled. He looked over Illiah and nodded approvingly.

"Excellent. Now, we begin." Imal's eyes changed. The approval left, leaving a void of lust and pain and anger. A knife was in Imal's hands, its blade shining like a star.

Two men came from behind Imal. Their faces were scarred and etched, their hair long and matted. They took and held Illiah by his arms. Illiah struggled, applying every move, every trick he could remember, his heart bursting with the helplessness of his situation. He was a child compared to the power of the men as they held him effortlessly. He had been sick, beaten, and malnourished too long.

Imal pressed the tip of his long, cutting knife against Illiah's chest and drew the blade across it. At first, Illiah felt nothing, but then a fiery pain flickered across his skin, lancing up into his neck and down his arms. His nerves rang and screamed. Fear constricted his lungs. Illiah pressed his teeth together to stop from crying out.

"Pain is power," Imal hissed.

Then Illiah saw his pain, a trick of the mind, perhaps. He saw a thin, black, bilious smoke, oozing and cognizant, leave his body and rise into the air and into Imal's waiting mouth. The air smelled like iron and heat. Illiah could smell fear. Or vomit. His vomit.

He didn't know how long Imal cut him. He felt like he poured a river of blood and pain into the stones. He screamed eventually. When he opened his eyes, he was alone. Blood dripped from his wounds, smeared across his chest. If he moved, every inch of him begged for peace, every cut and bruise came alive, tormenting him. The stone cradled his broken body. He looked up at the ceiling. Black, smoky shapes flitted there. They were waiting, he decided. Imal had not taken them all. What were they? They watched him. He watched them, not caring that his mind had broken.

The healers came and tended to his wounds, easing his pain with salves and compresses, and Illiah slept.

The next day Imal came again.

Illiah thought he had known pain. He had been wrong.

Illiah thought he had known fear. He had been wrong.

A cycle formed. Imal came. The healers tended to him. Illiah began to heal, to grow stronger. Then Imal came again. Then the healers. Then Imal.

He lost track of the days.

# CHAPTER 41

# EVA

*Illiah, where are you?*

Eva stood on the bluff above the Queen's Keep. The river twinkled like a blanket of stars below. The city lay below her like a tumble of rocks after an avalanche. Behind her, the Peak was clear and crisp.

She had tried using the cendari tree to find her husband. She had tried the air. She had used fire, but she could not find Illiah. She didn't know what else to do. She didn't know which way the wind had taken him. But she could not believe that he was dead. She remembered once, long ago, when they had been apart for an entirely different reason, and she had shared his dreams. There was a connection of more than heart and emotion between them. She could not give up.

But—and there was always a but—what if she was merely deluding herself? What if she was just a fool, a woman hoping for her love when the truth was simple, if horrific? People died. Illiah was no more invincible than the next man asked to give his life for his realm. Fate no longer needed him. Rhyl was what Kitarra needed—what the Guardians needed. Not Illiah.

Already, Kitarra moved forward. Lord Susor, Stone, Turk, even young Irri, were leading the realm forward. Their prince had come back to life; Arrain was alive. Talo had a father. The children were home, safe and guarded. A miracle had happened. And how many miracles could one hope for?

Rhyl and Talo were safe. The twins, dear Bren and Aralis, were born early, but healthy. They nursed well from the wet nurse and were growing fast. Yes, she could not ask for more miracles. And yet …

Stone had told her that Illiah had been sent across the ocean. Eva appreciated the way he told her the plain truth. There had been too many lies between them, he reminded her. Once they had kept secrets from each other, but not anymore. Not even when the truth was like salt on a wound.

Stone encouraged Eva not to give up on Illiah. He said it with his heart in his eyes. Arrain had given up his wife, his son, his life, and he knew the price was too high. And fate was too cruel.

"He is alive," a deep voice like velvet spoke beside her. For an instant, Eva thought of Vagar, her brother, whose voice was somewhere between the growl of a predator and the purest note of guitar. But it was not Vagar; that was impossible. It was Attin. His white wings fanned behind as if he had just landed from a great height. He was exactly as Eva remembered. Handsome. Bright. His golden eyes glowed like a sunset.

"Do you swear it?" Eva asked.

"I will show you." Attin's smile was an unfurling rose. He held out his hand. Eva took it without hesitation. Like with the cendari tree, the gold bowl, wind, and fire, she felt the *simul rami*. All the elements that linked her to the magic of the earth ran through him like he was a sculpture of magic and energy and light.

She closed her eyes and let Attin guide her. They flew along the river of magic, but it was the real world coming into focus below them. The water glistened, and Eva realized it was the ocean, not the *simul rami*, that she was gliding over. At the end of the ocean, there was land. A city of dust and sun rose from its shore. The *simul rami* pulsed, and Eva found herself in the dark, under the city, surrounded by arching stone. Illiah sat on the bare stone floor, his arms around his knees, his eyes vacant. His beard was shaved, his hair trimmed. He looked clean. His clothing was new and soft. The long cuts in his skin, red and swollen, some covered in gauze, looked at odds with his attire. But he was alive, tended. As Eva reached out for him, her connection to her magic slipped, like a novice rider off from a saddle, and she fell back into her body.

"Why couldn't I find him on my own?" Eva asked once she was in command of her senses once more. She was back on the bluff with Attin. Her feet hurt as if she had just jumped from a height onto hard rock.

"You are weak, and he is a long way away." Attin fixed his liquid-gold eyes on her. "If you practice, finding him might come easier. But tell me, what good will it do? You cannot help him. There is no magic that can bring him home."

Eva bit her lip against her tears. She wanted to tell Attin he was wrong, but that would have been a lie.

"Tell me about your son, your firstborn," Attin said.

"Rhyl killed a host of men with his magic. Then he brought Talo back from the brink of death," Eva told him without emotion. "How can it be possible?"

"The *simul rami* runs within every living thing, but when a *sanarii* connects to the magic, like with the cendari tree, for instance, they can take more—"

"But Rhyl did not have a cendari tree," Eva interrupted.

"Rhyl is special. His magic does not just come from you. It does not just come from the *simul rami*."

"The *varing*," Eva stated.

"Yes."

"It's from Illiah—from Crea. Who—or what—is Crea? Who was she?"

"Yes, it is from Crea's bloodline. But others can take the *varing* and control it. I am a Guardian now; I do not remember the time when Crea and I walked the earth together." Attin remarked. Some help he was. "You and I are descended from the *rauna*, the Allmakers, who are almost as old as the sun," Attin said. "Crea descends from something else …Something other …"

"What?"

"I am not sure."

"I thought Allati got their magic from the *velidar*?"

"Yes, that is part of it too. It is in the mixing of blood that the magic takes a more potent form."

"Like Rhyl," Eva murmured. "So he saved Talo not just with the *simul rami* but also with the *varing*?"

"Yes. For him, the line between light and dark, between good and ill, is different."

"His magic is not like mine. Who will teach him?" Eva asked, her heart aching for the journey her son, her sweet little boy, would one day be forced to make.

"You still do not trust us, do you? Us Guardians?" Attin asked.

Eva shook her head slowly. She didn't. She couldn't. Tayeh's betrayal had wounded her and taken her ability to trust in the deities. Yes, Stone was back in Kitarra. And Rhyl was as safe as she could make him. Safe as life. Not a comfortable thought.

"And yes, Rhyl's magic is different," Attin continued. "You can teach him a little, but in the end, his learning will be different from yours."

"Attin, please teach me all you can."

Attin smiled. "So … Fire. And Air. The reason why your powers can be so potent. Fire and Air are kin elements."

He held out his hand, palm toward the sky, and a flame appeared, small and dainty, but harmless. At least to him. Eva reached a finger toward it and felt its heat.

"The *simul rami* is a river of magic," he said. "A river of energy, to be tapped like a well of clear water. It is like a river, but also like a tapestry. The threads connect to everything—root, tree, wind, earth, person, animal, each grain of sand. Infinite threads that shift as one creature, plant, or person dies. Energy that flows, and breaks, and stops, and dies, only to return and circle, and regrow and meld into something new. Fire is taking one thread and adding it to another—Air. Come, sit with me," Attin suggested, reaching out his hand for hers. She took it—it felt strange, insubstantial yet sturdy, like he wouldn't let her fall. It felt like comfort. They sat, facing one another, on the bluff looking down on the Queen's Keep, Kilev, and the Great River winding out to the sea.

"Will we be disturbed here?" Attin asked.

"No. No one knows I am out here."

Attin lifted a disapproving brow. Eva ignored it.

Attin once more made a fire, cupped in his hands, and held it before Eva.

"Connect," he commanded, but his voice was gentle.

Once, it had taken a gold bowl, water from the hot creek, and a Guardian's touch to find the *simul rami*. Now it was waiting, just below Eva's consciousness. She held out her hands in an identical fashion.

"You have done this already, without thinking about it. Take the two elements and meld them using your own energy. Almost like healing, but instead of clearing out ills, you are building." Attin's voice was more distant in her mind. "Feel the essence of Fire; feel its energy. Take it. Feed it."

A tiny flame appeared in her hand.

"Why can't I feel its heat?"

"You are its creator; your energies are one. Very good," Attin purred. "Now fan it, just a little. And then quench it."

Nothing happened. The flame swayed in the breeze but grew no larger. Then she remembered the air. Fire needed air to grow. Eva called the air, and the fire grew, licking her face, her hair, up toward the tree branches. Eva doused it instinctively, taking away its energy. Her heart pounded in her chest.

"Well done," Attin told her, laughter on the edge of his voice. "But you must not lose control. You may be immune to its heat, but no one else will be. Now, this time, make the fire and send it to that rock over there. I don't want you to burn down the forest."

"No, I don't want to do that."

Eva recreated the little flame in her hand. It *was* like building. She took a little thread of magic to make the fire, and she took another thread of magic from the air, and the fire grew. Next, she sent the flame to settle on the top of the rock, burning through her own energy, like she was the candle. Eva moved the flame this way and that, made it stretch tall into the air, then as small as a torch. Then she extinguished it.

"Tayeh said you were intuitive. He was right." And with that, the Guardian disappeared. Eva would have expected more of a show, a flight of feathers and gold-white hair streaming in the wind.

Eva stared at the space Attin had just vacated, caught in the illusion that she had been dreaming. She looked at her palm and created a little fire there to assure herself that it had been real. She was caught between horror and delight.

# CHAPTER 42

# COTOCH

RODAN STUNK. There were too many people. There were too many poor people. Why did the poor and downtrodden not care about basic hygiene? Oh right, the lack of fresh water meant no baths. And most of the residents of Kara, being slaves, were not allowed in the ocean to bathe. Cotoch wasn't sure why; if it stopped the smell, then wasn't it worth it?

Maybe they couldn't smell themselves. But Imal could. The emperor noted it every time he set foot outside his palace. Granted, that wasn't often. Cotoch didn't understand why his cousin, who was so fond of exuberant rules, didn't force everyone to bathe and clean up their shit.

Cotoch couldn't wait to go home.

Imal in the flesh unnerved Cotoch a hundred times—no, a thousand times—more than Imal in the gold basin of *candarii* magic. Imal was clever, Cotoch observed. But he was edgy, given to rash choices, and he was a masochist, a sadist. Cotoch had known that. But knowing it and seeing it were two different things.

Cotoch was infinitely uncomfortable around his cousin. And he didn't even want to start on the crazy bitch that was Imal's sister—and Cotoch knew crazy—or his cousin's assassin, the man known as the Wolf. Cotoch had yet to see the man actually transform into a wolf. It sounded ludicrous. But he believed it. The man was too eerie, too other, not to believe it. Cotoch could almost feel Aiyan's glowing amber eyes piercing his skin and reach into his mind. And Aiyan was so still. Like a statue. Then Cotoch would blink, and he would be gone without movement or sound. He was probably a damned good assassin.

Cotoch didn't have the courage to ask Imal where he had found the man and how he had made him so loyal. The Wolf was not *daeum*; he was under no magical enslavement—versus non-magical enslavement—Imal was a curator of both.

Kara writhed with pain and despair. The *varing* wafted through the streets like the stench. Cotoch could feel the dark magic's restless spirit, its roving ambition, and he was reminded of how it had abandoned him in the crypt that day he killed his wife. The *varing* was not what Imal thought it was. It was not merely a tool—it felt dangerous.

Imal had allowed Cotoch to join him in what he called the ascension, to show him how to make an army of invincible men. (Cotoch didn't bother to point out that Illiah's army had defeated the *daeum*. One did not go around poking venomous snakes and expect to live.) Imal took poor weakling boys and turned them into monsters. Granted, some boys became monsters all on their own, but this was a quicker process. It was not something Imal allowed people to watch—only Cotoch and that wolf-man, and his guards. Always the *daeum* followed Imal like a shadow.

Cotoch had asked if the process was reversible. Imal looked at him like he was a child asking if the moon would fall on the earth.

"No," was Imal's answer, full of mocking venom.

Some of the ascensions went wrong, and the boys died. Cotoch wasn't sure how he felt about that.

"The ascension doesn't work on Kitarrans. Or the *heera*." Imal glanced at his wolf-man in the corner.

"Not at all?"

"No," Imal said with a sigh. "Which is why my father had the *heera* culled. Well, most of them. That was the reason they fought, your father and mine."

"Over the *heera*?"

"Your father thought killing them was unnecessary. Obviously, he lost that fight."

"Obviously," Cotoch mumbled. He glanced to where the Wolf stood, silent, at attention. *Heera.* The people of the mountains. A wild, magical people who had waged war with Imal's father, Cotoch's uncle, and lost.

"But not all *heera* are dead." Cotoch looked at the man in the corner. He could only meet those blazing amber eyes for a heartbeat.

"No. My father was wrong to have them all killed. But there were too many. Now I control the last of them; there is no chance they will rise against me."

Imal's sister came to Cotoch's mind. Imal's mother had been *heera.*

"Your turn, cousin," Imal said, gesturing to the next boy placed on the chair. Imal instructed Cotoch how to take over a boy's will with the *varing.* Cotoch practiced under Imal's careful eye. None of the boys died. But neither were they as crazed and battle-ready as Imal's. They were limpid husks. But Cotoch could feel a faint pull from his mind to theirs, linking them, letting him control them. It was vaguely similar to how he had controlled Eva, but much less satisfying.

Imal inspected them and shook his head, redoing the ascension. Any connection Cotoch felt dropped away as Imal took them over with his own magic.

"Better luck next time, cousin," Imal said, preceding Cotoch out of the dank pit of a room where Imal performed his magic. At least the wretched room was cool.

"You fail because you care too much," said the Wolf. He slipped out of the shadows to stand beside Cotoch. The gold embroidery of his silken jacket glinted like treasure in the torchlight. Cotoch tried to hide his unease, but it was poorly done because he had jerked when Aiyan spoke, even though the man's voice was quiet—maybe because his voice was quiet. "You must mean it." The Wolf spoke with what might have been encouragement or sympathy; Cotoch couldn't tell.

It was time to go home.

Imal threw Cotoch a farewell party. Cotoch may have gotten a little drunk, because when Imal announced he had a special presentation for Cotoch, Cotoch may have muttered "get me out of here" out loud. Cotoch held his breath, but Imal had not heard; he was distracted by watching the next slew of slaves enter the room, one of which was dressed like a performer.

"May I present Killor, a great teller of tales, from Kitarra. He knows many old legends, all the legends of the *candarii*. He has one to present to you, Cotoch." Imal grinned and gestured for the skinny little man to stand in the center of the gathered nobles,

Imal's rodaeri, and their companions. Cotoch was not the only one more than a little drunk. One of the rodaeri gave a high, girlish laugh as the slave stepped up, as if something about him was exceedingly funny. Imal glared and silence ensued.

"Once, there was a spirit named Tsuga," the little man began. "She was a spirit of the earth, and the air, the wind, and all growing things. She was nourished by the sun, by the day, and the seasons. But she was lonely because there were no other spirits like her. No others that she could speak to. She loved the otter, the pine, and the fawn, but they could not speak to her, not really.

"On a winter day, a great storm cascaded across the sky turning day into night, turning the wind mad and the rain violent. Lightning struck the earth so hard it shook. Tsuga heard a cry in that strike, a cry of pain and longing, and when the storm subsided, a great rift had been opened in her forest by the storm. There, in the bare patch of land, lay a man, another spirit. He was black where she was white. He was soft where she was hard. He was not of the wind or the rain or the forest, but she could speak to him. He did not remember his name, or his home, or why he had come down in a storm to her world, but she did not care.

"The two spirits loved each other more than the stars love the moon. More than the leaves love the rain. More than the bee loves the flower.

"But over time, Tsuga grew jealous of her lover's favors to the human folk. She grew envious of his ability to call on the dark river of magic. So she crafted a spear from the branch of her heart tree, a rare and powerful thing. She struck it through the heart of her lover, trapping his power. Then she broke the spear into nine pieces and spread them throughout the realms of Praedan so that not one person could wield her lover's power.

"They are lost still, the nine pieces of the spear, until one finds them and is powerful enough to combine them back into the Stormspear, then the person will have the power of the dark one, the first *candarii*, and the entire dark river at their command."

The story came to an end just as Cotoch came to the bottom of his wine glass.

"What do you think, Cotoch?" Imal asked him.

"Of what?"

"The story," Imal grated.

"I'm not really fond of bedtime stories."

"Fool. Every story holds a shred of truth."

"You believe there are nine artifacts that together will form an item of power?" See, he was paying attention.

"I do." Imal smiled. "And I want you to find them for me."

Cotoch's wine-induced fog slipped from his eyes as something unsettling took over instead. "And how am I supposed to do that?"

"You are a clever man. Tell him." Imal turned once more to the story teller. Cotoch could see the whites of the little man's eyes as clearly as if Imal held a knife to his throat.

"The Allati know about the artifacts," the desperate man said. "It is said the Shadow Guard collected them under the Guardian Attin's direction and hid them in the Wanderling Mountains."

Imal opened his arms wide in triumph. "See?"

"That's hardly a map," Cotoch remarked.

Imal's eyes darkened. "Cotoch, you will be king of Allati—I know your ambition. And when you are, you will find me those items and bring them to Rodan."

*And why wouldn't I keep them for myself?* Cotoch mused inside his head, thankful he had not said them out loud. Those words, spoken before Imal, would likely end his life.

"And if you keep them, know that I have the final piece. The rest are useless without it." Imal held a small dagger in his hand. It was carved from wood, faded in places, shining in others, the wood grain swirled gold and red, like a jewel. The amulet against Cotoch's chest warmed where it was hidden beneath his tunic. The amulet pulsed, as if it called to the dagger in Imal's hand.

He waited for Imal to sense it, for the emperor to pounce, to demand Cotoch's treasure, for surely it was kin to the piece Imal held. Imal's story was true, then. Imal did not seem to notice Cotoch's discomfort or feel the pull of magic between the two items.

"Where did you find it?" Cotoch asked, amazed at how steady his voice sounded.

"It was in Jullayah, looted from one of their temples. I've had it for years, sensing its magic, looking for answers as to what it was. Finally, I heard of a slave from Kitarra who knew many old tales, and he had one that explained this little trinket." Imal looked at Killor, then back to Cotoch. "Bring me the other eight pieces, or I will raze Mahlas to the ground."

The bars of Cotoch's cage tightened, lined with spikes and prods.

"Your wish is my command," he said, his tongue thick.

Imal smiled. "That's the spirit."

# CHAPTER 43

# MILA

FIVE DAYS PASSED. Five days Mila spent being paraded around the city with Nulla or Dart, wearing thin, revealing clothes, adorned with makeup and jewels like a foreign princess. Her heaviest adornment was her slave earring.

On the fifth day, the day Mila's "virginity" was to be sold, Nulla was flush with excitement. She already had several offers but assured Mila she would sell her only to the highest bidder. Nulla's eyes glistened with greed as she spouted numbers that meant nothing to Mila.

"You will bring even more than Cresa!" Nulla exclaimed with a peel of laughter. "But if you don't make your patron happy, he will come complaining, and I swear to you, I will sell you." She threatened to sell Mila daily.

All Mila could do was wad up her disgust and reach for her courage. She had to reach far.

Mila was bathed in sweet oils and dressed, her hair plaited and twisted into designs to match the finest craftsmen. She sat in the brothel common room, smiling at the men who were gathered to bid on her body. Their faces were blurs, their words dust. She would play her role, and she would survive.

After an hour, Nulla came to her, smiling, her golden hair dancing in the candlelight. She took Mila's hand and simpered to the waiting men, pulling Mila out of their midst. As they left, a dozen beautiful women descended to placate the men.

"Time to prepare," Nulla said in Mila's ear.

Mila's nerves tingled with apprehension. Somewhere deep down was a longing she had not felt in years. She wanted the culla. Her body longed desperately for the drug that would numb her soul and her heart and give her the strength to survive what would come next. This time, she had no choice but to survive on her own accord. She must.

Nulla's slaves helped Mila change into a nightdress that looked like it was sewn from moonlight. Mila wondered if she would be able to untangle herself from it. Nulla muttered in her accented voice, but Mila couldn't make out most of what she said.

The thrum of voices and laughter and music from below permeated through the thin walls along with other sounds less muted and conspicuous. A concert of footsteps on the stairs, down the hall. Light, prancing steps of women and girls, heavier steps of their patrons. Mila heard laughter and other more guttural sounds that she would not in a lifetime hear and not be reminded of sex.

Memories floated through her mind. She harvested what she could from them, things that would help her through this night. Survive.

She thought back to Illiah's lessons, the ones she had overheard. Know your enemy. Don't underestimate. Prepare. Practice. Mila felt like she was preparing for combat, and she would not lose. Not this time.

"Come," Nulla said, shoving Mila toward a door. "Do not disappoint him."

Mila observed her hand unlatch the door. Her fingers looked foreign, like they belonged to a stranger. She forced her feet, her hips, to enter.

Mila had known many handsome men in the years since Serac. The Keep abounded in handsome, strong, kind men. And some had tempted her, just enough to feel at home in a body that had once felt alien. But none of Mila's past patrons or lovers could compare in looks to the man before her.

She had not seen him downstairs. She would have remembered. His long, black hair was loose, falling below his shoulders, glinting like mica in the lantern light. His eyes burned amber in a face that was both beautiful and masculine. His skin was dark and warm like the earth. His perfect form, his face, was a drug many a woman would willingly take.

So then why was he in a brothel paying for companionship?

Serac had been beautiful, too, a monster in disguise.

Mila swallowed her fear with a smile. She was a survivor.

# CHAPTER 44

# AIYAN

THE BROTHEL smelled deceptively wonderful. Aiyan took a moment to admire the dainty jasmine growing around the windows, hugging the wall like a whore's bodice. The flowers were small, delicate, but they looked lost; they clung to the wall with desperation.

The fragrance of the jasmine followed Aiyan inside. The main room was beautiful. Gold and white filled the space, reminding Aiyan of the moon. The windows were draped with airy curtains. Plush cushions littered the couches. Candles flickered and swayed all over the room, adding a warm glow. Nulla's patrons paid exceedingly to bed the most desirable whores in Rodan, and the brothel reflected that wealth. Every patron of Nulla's had a slew of personal bed-slaves, and yet they still came to Nulla's and paid her high prices. Nulla had made her master a rich man. Oh, how effectively humans ignored the depravity of their souls.

The room was full of people. Men smiling, women laughing. Music played softly from a few musicians in the corner, the sound not entirely covering the soft footsteps of a couple headed to the darker recesses of the building.

The women and men who worked Nulla's establishment were all uniquely beautiful specimens of the human physique. The women were supple and elegant, some fair as a spring day, others dark as the richest wine. The men were lean and muscular, or slim and feminine. But men and women both wore masks that most could not detect, and fewer could dissemble. Nulla's whores were masters of their art.

Aiyan saw her almost instantly, the woman, swarmed by a group of rodaeri. She smiled shyly, like a maiden princess being courted by rodaeri, not a young slave being leered at by a group of men who saw her only as a way to satiate their carnal lusts. Her dress was thin, gauzy, and left just enough to the imagination. Aiyan's tongue felt thick. He swallowed. The man closest to her traced her collarbone with a finger.

Something inside Aiyan roared. He wanted to lunge and bite, to feel the flesh under his claws and taste the unique scent of fear that came just before death. The intensity of his anger was so unusual and consuming, Aiyan did nothing at all. He rooted himself, forcing the emotion to pass, hoping for some instinct to kick in and tell him how to act. The feeling of possession was new to him. He owned slaves, people who were his property, people who were his to command, and his to kill—his power over them was absolute. But this was different.

Aiyan sensed Nulla's proximity an instant before she looped her arm in his. Her perfume surrounded him like a fog. The heat of her body reached his heightened senses. Her touch made him feel cornered. Aiyan fought the impulse to push her aside.

"Ro Aiyan." Her voice was velvet and honey. She pressed her body against his. It made him uncomfortable, and she knew it.

"You did not return my messages," Aiyan stated. A threat crept into his voice—occupational habit.

"Oh, Aiyan! It is just business," Nulla crooned. "And, as you can see, you are not the only one interested in the girl." Nulla gestured to her crowded room. "Mystery adds suspense, and suspense is good for business. And when all the cocks are in the same room, they will pay more for their time with the hen. But honestly, I am surprised you are here," she said with a little laugh that did not hide her displeasure.

*That makes two of us.* "It was smart, parading her around the city," Aiyan remarked, nodding to the throng gathered around the woman. Nulla preened.

"I know. I will get three times what I would for any other bedding. That woman is going to make me rich. It was exceedingly fortunate Porthos put her up for auction. I am surprised he didn't keep her for himself."

"Porthos likes money. And his tastes are less … exquisite," Aiyan commented.

"*I* like money."

"You are already rich, Nulla."

Nulla shrugged, but Aiyan could sense her agony. No matter how much money Nulla had, she would still be a slave. A slave with more freedom than most, surely, but a slave nonetheless. She could never buy her freedom. A slave could only be freed by the emperor himself.

"But as flattered as I am to have you in my establishment, you should not be here," Nulla whispered in Aiyan's ear so quietly, only his magic unfolded the soft sounds into words. "You are bad for business." Aiyan did not need to scan the room to feel the eyes following him. "They are afraid to bid against you, thinking you will come into their beds at night and eat them."

"I don't eat people."

Nulla raised her brows. "That cannot be proved."

Aiyan didn't bother defending himself. They would believe the worst, regardless. "I am here for the woman," he told Nulla. "Only her."

Nulla dropped his arm and put on a smile; fake expressions were like breathing to Nulla. "Thirty thousand. For one night."

Aiyan sucked in air between his teeth.

"That is ridiculous, Nulla, and you know it."

Nulla grinned, then shrugged. "Presdian offered twenty. And tomorrow, he can have your leftovers for half of that."

Aiyan had not considered that. He could feel the growl in his throat. "Only one night is not going to work for me."

"No?"

"No. I will give you fifty thousand for her. All of her—no one else touches her."

Nulla frowned. "I cannot say no to that price. But why don't you give it a go and see how you like it first? I didn't even know you liked women." Nulla's voice had teeth.

"All of her. Fifty thousand."

Nulla swallowed, reaching for his hand. "Done," she said, sealing the deal with the trade's gesture. "Follow me, patron." Her voice was honey once more. Her hips swayed like gale winds as she led Aiyan up the stairs. "Cresa," Nulla said, halting the whore with a touch on the arm. "Make sure you give those rodaeri some extra attention—they are going to be very disappointed." The girl, Cresa, smiled, glancing uneasily at Aiyan. Aiyan could read her thoughts in her face. *Aren't you going to warn her?* her eyes said. *Aren't you going to tell her she is bedding a monster?*

"Enjoy," Nulla said at the top of the stairs, opening a door for Aiyan.

The room was dim, the windows shielded by dark, gauzy curtains shifting gently in the evening breeze. The sun was setting, but the room faced east. Twilight had already descended.

Aiyan wondered how long he would have to wait. He wondered what he was supposed to do while he waited. Aiyan did not like waiting. Ever. He was beginning to think he had made a terrible mistake. What was he thinking, buying a woman he had never met, never spoken to? A woman taken from her own land, forced into slavery—forced into prostitution. She would be terrified, despite her sweet smile downstairs. And that was without knowing who— or what—he was. Aiyan could almost hear the other whores educating her as she prepared.

*He is a little—odd, that one.*

*Strange.*

*Deranged is more like it.*

*If you don't please him …*

*He is a monster …*

Aiyan had not even asked her name.

He moved to the window and contemplated the jump to the street below. He could do it, especially if he shifted to his wolf form. But before he could decide between fleeing or facing his own mistake, the door opened, and the woman slipped inside with surprising speed. Aiyan's chance of escape was lost.

The trace of the woman's unusual dicidium was a distracting twinkle. Her pale skin was almost luminescent, a rare quality in

Rodan where the old spirits had long ago gifted the humans with darker skin to counteract the pounding sun. Her cloud of dark hair tumbled around her face, framing her features. She had freckles; Aiyan hadn't noticed them before. Her dark blue eyes blazed at him. His eyes trailed down the lines of her neck, the curve of her shoulders, lingering on her nipples, outlined by the lace of her dress. With difficulty, he tore his eyes from her breasts to see that she was watching him. She looked … assessing. There was nothing meek and timid and fearful about her. She raised an eyebrow at him.

"Are you afraid of me?" she asked, her voice almost playful. Aiyan did not reply, which was itself an answer.

She was the one who was supposed to be afraid. Timid. Aiyan had not been prepared for her strength. He had not been prepared for this at all. Gods, what was he going to say to her? For the second time that evening, his instincts were useless. He stood still, his body taut and embarrassingly interested.

She walked over to him, standing so close, her finger a hair's-breadth from his jaw. Her hips, her breasts, were the sharp point of a hook, and he was the fish.

"Don't touch me," Aiyan managed, but it came out in a rasp. The girl paused, looked confused, but recovered quickly.

"You speak Jullayan?" she asked, withdrawing her hand.

Aiyan nodded, his tongue like paste in his mouth. A smile appeared on her lips as she poured two glasses of white wine. A smile that would have convinced anyone except a *heera* wolf. Aiyan inhaled. He could smell her magic. He could see her dicidium without shifting his perception. She suppressed her magic well, but he could sense it. It was a reflection of his *heera* magic. It paced, anxious to be free, to run, to live. But she was no more a *heera* than he was a Kitarran.

"So you are the one who bought my virtue," she stated. She took a sip of her wine, set it on the table and returned to him, standing close, her eyes just below his. She reached out and placed her hand against his chest. Aiyan's heart thumped harder for it. "What is your name?"

"Aiyan."

"Why are you afraid, Ro Aiyan?"

He could feel the heat of her skin through the thin shift of his shirt as she slid her hand down the length of his chest, gripping his betraying protuberance lightly. Aiyan moved away as if he had been stung. He met her eyes and read them; she was easy to read for a man versed in lies. She was bold, but it cost her. Anger, not fear, drove her actions. He could see the hate seething behind her false smile and her swaying hips and honeyed touch. Aiyan knew what it took to pretend when one's heart, one's soul, was dying.

"You have been a whore before," Aiyan stated.

She paused, her mind flexing in her eyes. "Yes," she answered slowly. "This is not my first time enslaved in a brothel."

Aiyan felt like she had punched him in his gut. Or perhaps lower. He was a fool. He couldn't save her; she was already broken. Why had he not seen it? But her diciduim was clear, beautiful. There was no taint about her. Nothing that spoke of wounds to the soul. Only anger. Not like Allia, whose dicidium was rotting and putrid. It didn't make sense.

"You were hoping for a virgin? Are you a virgin? That would explain why you are afraid to be touched." Her derision leaked out in her voice. For some reason, his first instinct toward her insult was to smile. He preferred honesty in any form.

"I am not a virgin," he replied.

"Could have fooled me. I would ask if you don't like women, but you betray yourself." Her glance toward his now cowardly member made his cheeks burn. Instinctively, he covered the region with his hands, only realizing too late that it must make him look like a fool.

"Are you trying to insult me? I paid a small fortune for you, you know."

She shrugged. "Men have done so before. But I am not sure the fates are in your favor. The last man who paid a fortune to own me is dead."

She talked fast, and Aiyan had to concentrate to decipher her words underneath her accent. He could speak Praedan well … but—dead?

"How did he die?"

"I killed him."

"Is that supposed to arouse me?"

"That is my job, isn't it?"

Aiyan shook his head, smiling again. She took it as a victory, stuck out her hip, and leaned toward him again. He put up his hand to stop her again. She looked confused.

"I thought there were no slaves in Praedan," he stated.

"Not openly. And I was a no one. I had no family. I was prey."

"But?" Aiyan could hear it in her words.

Her eyes narrowed at him for an instant before she said, "Some-one rescued me."

"And now you are once more a slave."

She sat down on the edge of the bed, crossed her arms over her chest, and pulled her feet under her. Gone was any trace of sensuality, of desire. "You are not going to fuck me, are you?"

"No."

She narrowed her eyes at him again. "Then why did you buy me for a fortune?"

*Because you have magic. Because I have magic. You and I are the same.* But Aiyan's words stuck in his throat.

He held up a finger, begging for her patience. He slipped off his boots and unbuttoned his tunic. He unfastened his pants and let them fall, standing naked before her. He cursed. Usually, nudity did not bother him, but her eyes on his body made his face burn. He should have just changed, destroying his expensive clothes as his shape became too unaccommodating. It would have been worth it. Too late now.

He changed.

The wolf form came over him like a warm summer breeze, welcoming him home to the most familiar place he had ever known. It was like shedding his mask and wearing his heart, making him feel almost whole.

She didn't scream, and with her pale skin, Aiyan didn't know if she was about to faint.

"That is a nice ... trick," she said slowly, her voice trembling slightly.

*Thank you.* Aiyan did not know if his *heera* magic would fully work on her; she obviously could not be *heera*. But she heard him. Her face blanched. She leaped to her feet.

"What are you? What do you want?" she asked. Fear permeated from her skin into Aiyan's wolf nose.

*Change,* Aiyan whispered in her mind.

She shook her head. "I can't. I won't. I can't," she hissed as she backed up to the wall-end of the bed, looking around for something to use as a weapon. Aiyan realized his mistake. She was terrified. He was a monster. Why did he think she would see him as anything else?

He changed back into a man. He felt defeated. He was a failure.

"I did not mean to frighten you," he told her, sitting down, pulling his pants with him, dressing slowly, stiffly.

The woman eyed him silently, wary. He had only wanted to show her, to befriend her, and he had botched it. Of course, he had. What kind of friend would he make? Aiyan did not have friends. Gods, Aiyan didn't even know her real name—had not even asked her real name. That would have been a good place to start, instead of turning into a monster and assaulting her mind with his magic. He wanted to vomit.

He couldn't meet her staring eyes. She said something, but his pounding heart made it impossible to translate. He escaped into the hall. Aiyan was not used to feeling so disoriented. He ignored the brothel patrons and Nulla's questioning gaze as he streaked by. He focused on the door, on the darkness beyond that would hide him and let him disappear.

Loud whispers from the patrons followed him into the night.

"She really did a number on him, didn't she?"

"Who would have thought it?"

"I didn't even think the Wolf liked women."

Of course, they didn't think he could hear them. He wished his wolf senses would shut out the noise instead of amplifying it. He felt raw. Like a boy all over again. Nyamish appeared in his mind, leering, his cheeks red and his forehead beaded with sweat. Aiyan could almost smell him and feel his hands pressing down on his shoulders.

Aiyan retched violently into the corner of the alley.

Some wolf. Some assassin. Maybe the woman was right. Maybe she would be the death of him.

# CHAPTER 45

# AIYAN

AFTER AIYAN'S disastrous venture to Nulla's brothel and his coinciding failure with the strange woman, he had fallen onto his bed consumed by regret and shame and some other emotions he tried not to acknowledge. And eventually, he must have slept. It was his wolf instinct that woke him, whispering warnings that were so abstract Aiyan's human half could not decipher them. He strained, lying still, listening for any sound that was unusual in his slumbering house. There. Downstairs. A footstep. Then another.

An intruder.

Someone was trying—and failing—to walk through his marble halls with the utmost stealth.

Aiyan could pick out the characteristic footsteps of all his slaves. Tilley walked with almost no sound at all; her Kitarran instincts and padded feet made her the least detectable. Day walked with more weight on his left leg, his uneven gait the result of a shattered knee that never healed properly. The smell of soup hovered around Wani persistently, announcing her presence before the sound of her shuffling gait. Cliff moved like a mouse, in quick gestures.

These footsteps were hesitant, thoughtful, and most certainly did not belong to any of his house-slaves.

Aiyan slipped his hand beneath his silk pillow, his fingers closing around the curved handle of his dagger. He took another dagger from his nightstand. A third lay close by, but he didn't think he would need three. Even the second was just a precaution. Well, if he was honest with himself, all three daggers were precautions. Aiyan was the real weapon.

What kind of idiot would break into his house? He thought he had weeded Rodan of stupidity.

Aiyan slipped down the hallway like smoke. It was his house; he knew every shadow, every secret. The intruders were in the main hallway, making their way toward the staircase.

"What do you want?" Aiyan asked the silence.

The man before him froze. Tall, wide, thick, all the usual features of a slave sent to solve conflicts between rodaeri with the subtlety of a blacksmith's hammer. Not a *daeum* soldier, of course, but the next available thing. The man's small eyes leered at him stupidly—only a fool would trap themselves in a small space with a wild creature.

A second man swung at Aiyan from the darkness, a dagger narrowly missing Aiyan's throat. Ah, assassins. A second assailant explained the first's confidence. A ploy, a distraction meant to weasel Aiyan out of the shadows. Well, Aiyan was a wolf, and a weasel was a morsel, a snack. Aiyan deflected the dagger point, slamming the man's elbow against the marble wall in the process, using his own dagger and ramming it into the man's thick neck. Aiyan threw his second dagger. A soft thunk and a groan let him know it hit something fleshy.

Aiyan's eyes adjusted to the darker passage. His dagger had hit the man, but not brought him down. Aiyan pounced, incapacitating him with a blow to his back. There was a snap. Aiyan slit the man's throat for good measure. The last thing he wanted to do was spend the next half hour listening to a man die a slow, painful death. And he needed silence to search the resounding quiet for sounds of more intruders.

He narrowed his eyes and relaxed his sight, looking for flickering energy in the space between his consciousness and the walls of reality that signaled another person, another soul. There was one, but one Aiyan knew. He released his magic.

"Really?" Cliff appeared out of the shadows, his mouth twitching slightly. "Who would dare? Here? In the house? What a mess. Gods, Ro Aiyan, what a mess."

Aiyan crouched, tilting the dead man's head to get a good look at his slave earring. Brass. No gemstone. A League Man, hired by whoever had the coin to pay the League Master. Grendal kept his business anonymous. Everyone knew and accepted that—even Imal.

"Clean it up," Aiyan told his slave. "Someone is trying to be bold, or stupid, to send League Men here."

Cliff nodded, his bulging eyes darting from one body to the other. He pulled a rag from his waist belt. Aiyan was fairly sure Cliff would need a bigger rag; already the blood was pooling. The marble would need sanding to get it all out. Cliff would complain about it for weeks.

"I'll wake Day to help you with this," Aiyan said, patting Cliff on the shoulder as he walked by.

"My thanks, Ro Aiyan. We will have this cleaned up by morning."

Aiyan's servants slept on the main floor of his house, not far from the kitchen. It was an unusual arrangement; most rodaeri preferred their slaves out of sight unless requested. But Aiyan liked to keep his slaves close; he only had a handful, after all.

Day was sleeping like a babe, a young room-slave next to him. Aiyan had not met her before; she looked awfully young.

"Day!" Aiyan's sharp voice made the sleeping man jerk. The girl did the same before cowering behind Day's larger form.

"Master?" Day peered at Aiyan, then glanced at the girl beside him as if she had materialized there without his knowledge. He looked back at Aiyan. "What is it?"

"Intruders. League Men. I killed them in the downstairs hallway."

Day hissed. "Who would try such a thing? Imal?" Fear laced through Day's brilliant green eyes like lightning.

"If it were Imal, we would be dead. This was a message. I am not overly concerned—League Men I can manage. Go help Cliff clean up the mess, please."

"Aye! Aye, I will," Day assured him.

"That girl is too young for you, Day."

"Which girl?"

"The one in your bed."

"Oh, that one." Day looked crestfallen.

"How old is she?"

"Eighteen."

"Right, and I am the bastard son of Imal."

Day looked applicably guilty.

"Nulla gave her to me," Day replied.

"Send her back—with money. And tell Nulla the girl is too young."

"Yes, Ro Aiyan." Day nodded, his shoulders slumped. He would do as he was told. Day was a degenerate, but a loyal, obedient degenerate.

"Good," Aiyan snapped, leaving Day to dress and get about his business.

Tilley and Wani had mercifully slept through the incident and Cliff's loud mutterings as he cleaned up. Aiyan was thankful for that. The young Kitarran had seen enough bloodshed, and Wani was prone to worrying. Aiyan didn't want to listen to her roam the halls at night, too afraid to sleep, finding assassins in the drapes and cupboards.

Aiyan went back to bed, wondering who he would need to kill next.

"A message for you," Tilley reported the next morning while Aiyan was watering his plants. After many weeks of careful monitoring, the fawn lilies were nearly in bloom. The delicate flowers were not comfortable in the hot region of Kara. They grew in the mountains, under the protective canopy of cedar trees surrounded by moss. Aiyan needed the seeds for a poison he was working on, but he couldn't keep the flower healthy to fruition. Frustrating.

The low morning sun streamed in through the tall windows, making the gray stripes in Tilley's fur dance. Early morning was Aiyan's favorite part of the day, when the sun was weak enough that he could feel it on his skin like a kiss rather than a flame. All too soon, it would be too hot, and the windows would be drawn, and the sun would become the enemy once more. By the Spirits, he missed the mountains.

Tilley handed him an innocuous paper. "I believe it is from Ro Beric."

"I believe you are correct," Aiyan said, eyeing the rodaeri's mark. "Thank you, Tilley." Aiyan ripped open the delicate envelope that smelled like spices, another calling-card of the aristocratic rodaeri.

*Dear Aiyan,*
*Please meet with me.*
*- Ro Beric*

It was—short. Beric was always one to drawl; he enjoyed the sound of his own voice. What could he want? Another offer, no doubt. But Aiyan had no interest in Beric as a lover, or an ally, or anything. But, if it had been Beric who sent the assassins into Aiyan's house, he might send more. And if Aiyan had not been home ... he shuddered to think of what might have happened to his slaves. If Beric touched his people, he would be a dead man.

Perhaps they should talk. Aiyan really didn't like ruining his marble.

"Send Beric a reply. Tell him I will meet him at noon," Aiyan grumbled to Tilley, who was waiting.

"Very well," Tilley replied, but Aiyan hardly heard her.

Maybe he could stop by Nulla's on his way to Beric's. Sleep had been elusive; his mind had been consumed by the fear on the woman's face, fear that he had caused by his rash display of magic. He was not used to making mistakes. It was uncomfortable. But he didn't know if he had the courage to face her again after last night. What would he say to her?

He forced his thoughts away from the Praedan woman and

back to the matter at hand. Aiyan hoped Beric was not going to proposition him for sex. Again. Aiyan took a moment to plan in his head how he would dissuade Beric this time. Teeth? Claws? Beric loved to remind Aiyan how he fit Beric's preferred mold for young, dark-haired, slim, pretty-as-a-wench (Beric's words, not his) men. He also loved to remind Aiyan that if Aiyan were still a slave, he would pay a fortune for a night with him. Aiyan had growled and Beric had just laughed—Aiyan was not accustomed to being laughed at. Aiyan couldn't tell if Beric was bold, or just stupid.

Luckily for Beric and his habits, he was rich and well liked by Imal. Beric owned more than half the farms taken from the *heera*, and ran them so efficiently, even Imal could see Beric's value. Homosexuality was not often tolerated, but the emperor did make exceptions if it suited him.

Aiyan decided to take Tilley with him to Beric's so he would not be tempted to deviate and visit Nulla's brothel along the way.

Beric spent a great deal of his time away from Kara, overseeing his farms to the north, but he also had a house in the city. It was a grand villa, probably the most beautiful property in Kara, though Aiyan would never admit his envy to Beric. A wall surrounded the house, and inside the wall was a garden, complete with trees and vines and hundreds of flowers, an oasis in a city of dust and heat. Beric's gardens were fed by a rare cistern, keeping the house cool even in the Rodan summer. It was a secretive place and rivaled Imal's palace for beauty, if on a smaller scale.

Tilley's eyes lit up when Aiyan told her she was coming with him. Tilley, like Aiyan, envied Beric his lush paradise. She was from a land of green forests, tall mountains, and deep lakes. There was nothing of that in Kara. Kara's streets were ash, its buildings dry old bones, its people, rotting flesh. Kara was a parasite.

Tilley was adept at anticipating Aiyan's needs, like any valued slave. Besides being clever, subservient, and young, she could speak Rodan almost fluently. She had cost him more than he cared to admit.

Aiyan watched Tilley breathe in the smells of Beric's garden. Her eyes were pools of longing as the shade of Beric's small forest shrouded them.

The main door of Beric's house was a cascade of blue violas. Tilley reached down and plucked one, slipping it into the pocket of Aiyan's tunic, so just the petals peered out. She was smiling. Beric himself opened the door to greet them, his silk jacket and slippers the same shade as his flowers.

"Ro Aiyan, greetings," he said, but there was an edge behind his smile. Something was different. Gone was Beric's usual air of gentility, his friendly, harmless flirting. His eyes glinted with anger. "Come in, come in. Tilley, lovely to see you as usual." The greeting to the Kitarran was not a lie; Beric liked Tilley, and Tilley liked Beric.

The door closed behind them, and two guards materialized from the shadows. League Men. Two more were beyond the windows in the garden. Aiyan had not seen them because he had not looked. Betrayal caught in Aiyan's throat. Beric *had* sent the assassins. Tilley loved to recount tales of legendary Kitarran warriors, but she was not a fighter. Aiyan was fairly sure Beric wouldn't hurt Tilley, and likely Aiyan could handle anyone Beric could throw at him.

Aiyan exchanged a look with Beric, trying to understand what he had done to earn Beric's anger. Beric guided them into his house, through the beautiful arched hallway and into a bright, airy sitting area complete with table, chairs, a platter of fruit and cheese, and chilled drinks.

"Ro Aiyan," Beric said, smiling toothily, his round face becoming rounder with it. But the coldness in his smile was disconcerting. "Come sit, eat." He looked meaningfully at his slaves, and the guards disappeared. So it was not an ambush. Not yet. Tilley eyed Aiyan, asking without asking, for direction. Aiyan nodded, and she left, leaving him alone with Beric.

Beric poured Aiyan a glass of fruit juice.

"What, no wine?" Aiyan asked.

"Too early."

"Here I thought you were immune to toxins."

"Har har. Wine and I only get along after dinner."

"You sent the men to my house last night, didn't you? What do you want, Beric?"

"That was a mistake. See, wine and I do not always get along. I was angry. I am still angry, but I know you are not entirely to blame."

"Who did I kill?" Aiyan asked, wondering which of Imal's recent victims would stir such rage in Beric.

Beric did not answer. Could not answer. Aiyan could smell the anger—and grief—washing over the man. Aiyan numbed himself to it.

"I want to kill Imal," Beric said instead of answering Aiyan's question.

Aiyan almost choked on his harmless fruit juice. "You are not serious."

"Oh, but I am." And he was.

"You know I should kill you for saying that. Right now. Right here."

"I do. But you won't."

"And why not?"

"Because you hate Imal. Because you hate us all."

Aiyan said nothing.

"You hate us. You are *heera*. We killed your people. Enslaved and raped your wisewomen before we killed them. We tortured and killed your warriors. You want revenge."

"Imal raised me from a slave. I owe him everything," Aiyan said. Maybe Imal was testing him through Beric. The emperor was canny and prone to sudden bouts of distrust. Everything was a test. What could be given could be taken away. How many times had Aiyan learned that? It was a lesson a slave never forgets.

"How often do you think about killing him?" Beric asked.

Aiyan was silent. He felt the trap closing in. He should kill Beric for his treason. Now. Any moment Imal could step out of the shadows with his *daeum* guards, and Aiyan would be a dead man. And his death at Imal's hands would not be quick. Oh no, Imal would take Aiyan's *heera* magic to feed his *varing*, piece by piece, until Aiyan was nothing but a husk of pain, and his soul was flayed into so many tiny pieces, the Muro would never find them all.

But Beric was right; not a day went by when he didn't think about plunging a dagger into Imal's back.

Neither Imal nor the *daeum* appeared.

Aiyan breathed again.

"You want me to kill Imal?" Aiyan asked quietly.

"He trusts you."

"Imal trusts no one," corrected Aiyan.

"You can get close to him."

"You put a great deal of faith in me."

"Faith? No. My life, yes." Beric's eyes bored into Aiyan. How many times had the man teased and nagged him? Aiyan realized it had been an act. A misdirection. There was more behind Beric's eyes than a lusty, albeit intelligent, rodaeri. Aiyan had not seen it, but he saw it now.

"Miyamoto is dead," Beric stated. "Miyamoto, and his rebellion, was my hope. But he is dead. And all I have left is you." Beric's smile disappeared under his anguished voice. Hatred made his eyes hard. "You dragged him through the streets. You treated him like—like vermin." Beric waved his hand. "No, don't say anything. I know it was Imal's idea."

Aiyan's voice wasn't fit for speaking at the moment anyway.

Beric looked mournfully at his fruit juice. "I wish I had ordered wine. This is … harder than I envisioned." He paused. "Tranio was my lover. He had been for nearly five years. I loved him."

Aiyan felt his heart fall into his feet in a shapeless lump. In his mind flashed the picture of the man he had killed, ravaged and bloody, his corpse left on the front steps of Imal's palace. The tear trickling unchecked down Beric's face made something twist like a knife in Aiyan's chest.

Beric seemed to notice Aiyan's discomfort, and his eyes softened. He wiped the tear from his cheek.

"Tranio was Miyamoto. But Kara can still be saved," Beric continued. "I was right about you. You do want revenge. You feel remorse for Tranio's death." Pity, not hatred, filled Beric's eyes. "I want you to kill Imal."

"If Imal dies, chaos will ensue. With their master dead, the *daeum* will be unchecked. Everyone knows this." Aiyan did not need to illustrate the horror that would be. It had happened once, when Imal's father died, and his *daeum* army nearly destroyed Kara. Imal had stopped them. Only he could control them now. And his *daeum* army was larger than his father's. Kara, the city, its slaves, it people, would fall under the madness of Imal's beasts.

"Yes, but—"

"There is no 'but.' The *daeum* will destroy Kara without Imal's control."

"What if there was another who could control them?"

"You mean Allia?"

Beric nodded.

"Allia does not have that kind of power, and she is not well in the head. Imal keeps her on a short leash. And she has no love for anyone," Aiyan said. "Imal has taken that ability from her."

"She loves you."

Beric *was* well informed. Aiyan leaned toward Beric. "Beric, you do not understand the darkness in Imal's soul. His poison has spread through all of Rodan. Allia has been infected with it, not unlike the *daeum*. Her soul is poisoned, she is dying, and she cannot recover. She does not know what love is."

"She is Imal's sister—she is *heera*."

"But she is not like me. She is not a shifter."

"You are truly the last?"

Aiyan nodded. But his thoughts traveled back to the woman from Praedan.

"There was a story about a *heera* woman who took a *daeum* man for a husband. A *daeum* man who had escaped his entrapment of dark magic," Beric said pointedly.

Fuck, Beric was well informed. What else did he know? Not that Aiyan had anything to hide. Not anymore.

"That was one man, not hundreds."

Beric nodded. "But it is a start. Listen, Imal is a fool. He runs Rodan poorly. In ten years, there will be no food. People will starve. The fires burned half my farms last summer. And this summer will be just as scorching. Imal ignores this and chooses instead to punish the slaves. Do you know how many slaves I have lost to this madness? Pay the slaves well, treat them well, and they work well. Give them a life, a purpose, freedom even, and they flourish. Imal won't allow that. Either Imal dies, or the rest of us die. And the way Imal runs the slave market is insane, wasteful," Beric said, spitting out his disgust with each syllable. "The man is deranged. He has no head for business. His need for control will destroy us all. Imal needs to create and feed his *daeum*. To do that, he needs somewhere to harvest dark magic—"

"What do you know of magic?" Aiyan interrupted.

"Enough to know that Imal uses it. Takes it, feeds it to his *daeum*. It makes him stronger. If it makes him stronger, perhaps it is his weakness as well. What if you kill the *daeum*? Poison them?"

They spoke in whispers.

"Poison hundreds of men? *Daeum* don't take ill like other men. I don't think I have a poison strong enough to make it past their magic. And ..." Aiyan had killed many men, bad men for the most part—there were not many good men in Kara—but the *daeum* were different. Sure, their crimes were heinous, but did a person destroy a dog merely because its master forced it to bite, took its will, starved it, tortured it, gave it no other choice? What if there was a way for the ascension to fall from the eyes of those poor men? They might regain some of their souls, their minds. Aiyan wasn't sure he could take that chance from them. "I will not poison them."

Beric frowned. "Slavery does not have to be done in such a cruel manner. Freedom can be bought. The rodaeri can still get rich. Servants can have a voice." Beric's words were infused with an honest passion Aiyan had never met. Beric believed in a better world, a better Rodan, and was putting his life on the line to make it happen. It was ... admirable. "I need you to kill Imal."

Aiyan stood, tweaking the folds of his coat, smoothing the hem. "I will consider your suggestion, but I can't make any promises."

Beric's face was unreadable.

"And I am sorry about Tranio," Aiyan said, for what it was worth. Words did not make sorrow softer. "Good day, Ro Beric."

"Good day, Wolf."

# CHAPTER 46

# MILA

THE MAN had turned into a wolf.

And he had known she could turn into a wolf.

Mila had never told anyone about her magic, her secret. Not Eva. Not even Murryn.

Mila could still feel the residue of his magic in her head. His touch on her mind, his magic, had felt similar to Eva's, but loud, invasive. Mila shivered. She wasn't frightened, she realized. Shocked, yes, but not afraid. She pulled the blanket over her and curled into a ball, trying to sort the tangle in her heart.

She could not deny he had been beautiful—as a wolf and as a man. His skin marked by tattoos she would have loved to put on fabric. Black whorls and knots that slipped over his neatly made muscles like the most intricate embroidery. And the way he had shifted in his other form had been so fast and elegant, like water slipping over rocks. Mila wanted to see it again so she could try to pinpoint the exact moment the magic shifted his form from man to animal.

For the first time since she could remember, she felt something akin to longing. For the first time, she saw the possibility of her magic as something beautiful instead of a curse.

Mila closed her eyes and reached into herself, in the deepest recesses of her body, looking for the place where she had pushed her magic down, deeper and deeper, over and over until after many years, it was almost nonexistent. Almost. She touched it. She begged it to come. She willed herself to change, to shift.

Nothing happened. She could not change.

The disappointment she felt was … surprising. How many times had she longed for her magic to be just a figment of her imagination? How many times had she suppressed it, convincing herself it was not real and therefore not a danger?

She wanted to know who the wolf-man was. She wanted to know about his magic, so like hers, yet a sea apart. She wanted to know, know, know.

Serac had been handsome too. Serac had been kind, at first. Mila would not make that mistake again, however pretty the wolf-man had been, however contrite and unusual. She would not let herself be distracted by his bright eyes and enigmatic magic.

Maybe she would never see him again. Maybe she would be given to another patron. Maybe Nulla would sell her. Maybe she would be sent to the Pit. Those thoughts didn't scare her as much as she expected. Never knowing Tarran's and Murryn's fates— never knowing what it would feel like to run as a wolf—those were the possibilities that turned restlessly in her mind.

Hot tears dripped down her cheeks. Her tears were not just for her inability to call her magic, they were for Murryn and Tarran, for her friends left behind, friends who were dead or taken, she didn't know—would never know. For a home she would never see again. For the memory of blood on her hands. For the little girl she had been when her mother had been taken because of magic.

And her father—she didn't even know what had happened to him. Magic was the reason Mila and Murryn had become orphans. Magic was the reason Mila was still alive.

The dawn came, bright and early and warm. Mila had only dozed, her fragmented dreams full of cliffs and edges. Would ever sleep deeply again? Already the sounds of the city rose like a tide. Mila could smell the sea.

She rose and crept into the washing room she shared with Cresa. The adjoining curtain was closed. Mila washed in the cool water and combed her long, curling hair. When she turned, young Letti watched with round eyes. She was a pretty child; in a few years, she would be put to another use. Mila knew how it worked.

"Would you like me to dress your hair?" Letti asked in a sweet voice.

"Thank you, but I can manage it myself."

"Would you like some breakfast?"

"I would. Thank you, Letti," Mila said, smiling. The girl smiled shyly back before she trotted off.

Mila opened the wardrobe, pulling out the only plain dress in her collection. She wasn't sure if the fashion in Rodan was less chaste than Jullayah, due to the hot sun and dry air, or if it was the wardrobe of a sex slave, meant to appeal to the lusty nature of men, but all the dresses were gauzy, light, and far from modest. At least the dresses were loose, unlike Jullayah where fashion was an exemplified prison for the womanly figure.

Cresa came in with a swish of white and gold fabric and lay with relish on Mila's recently abandoned bed. Every morning Cresa had come to wish Mila a good morning and share gossip. Cresa was a human from Kitarra and only too happy to have someone to chat with who spoke her native tongue. She taught Mila some words in Rodan, but beyond the brothel, Mila didn't think they would be helpful. How often would she need to describe a man's member in Rodan? But then, perhaps she would never leave the brothel. Her finger brushed her slave earring.

"Good morning, Mila," Cresa sang in her sweet voice with a mischievous sparkle in her morning-blue eyes. Cresa seemed well suited to being a rent girl; she liked the attention. She liked the men, mostly. And she was expensive enough that she had some autonomy in her choice of patrons—an enviable position for a slave. Cresa had told Mila about her capture in Kitarra by the *daeum*, her luck at having a pretty face, too valuable to rape and beat. It was the ugly and plain girls who had suffered.

Two years she had been a rent girl, and she was one of the lucky ones. The Kitarrans had not fared so well, Cresa explained. For warriors, they were a sensitive race. They did not endure death and pain well. Not anymore. Mila was not sure what that meant. But hearing Cresa's tales, even after what the Kitarrans had done to Illiah, Rhyl, and Eva, Mila pitied them.

"So, I heard you were bought by Ro Aiyan. *Ro Aiyan,* Mila! The whole house is dying of curiosity to know all about it."

"Why?"

"Ro Aiyan is not a patron of Nulla's house. It is well known that he does not go to brothels. He has no room-slave—only a few manservants—a Kitarran and a gnarled old cook. And he is *heera.*"

Did that mean everyone knew he turned into a wolf? Mila didn't want to mention it, regardless.

"What does that mean, '*heera*'?" The word was strange, and it made Mila's tongue twist to say it.

"The *heera* are a people. They used to live in the mountains, from what I understand. They fought against the emperor, not the one now, the one before. The emperor had them all killed because of their shifter magic. Except the woman he took as his wife. And Aiyan, I guess."

"So this Aiyan is the last one? The last ... *heera?*"

"Other than the half-*heera* emperor and his sister, I believe."

"So why wasn't Aiyan killed?"

"I have no idea why he is alive when all of his people are dead." Cresa shrugged. "And I don't want to know. There are some things my patrons don't like to discuss with me. Ro Aiyan is one of those things. No one talks about him—much. They are too afraid."

Mila could understand the fear surrounding this Aiyan. Watching him turn into a wolf had been unnerving. And afterward, his manner was so intense that she had forgotten how to speak.

"So, what was the Wolf like?" Cresa asked again, her hand on her chin, eyes glinting eagerly.

"He was strange," Mila told her, knowing Cresa would not relent without *something.*

"Of course, he was strange—the man can change into a wolf, for goodness' sake. Details!"

Mila felt uncomfortable recounting her encounter experience with the shifter. He had shown her something vulnerable. By the Names of the Old Ones, he had blushed; even with his darker skin, it had been noticeable. It felt wrong to share.

"It was quick."

Cresa would make her own assumptions about what "it" was.

Cresa shrugged. "Well, you should feel flattered. Apparently, the Wolf doesn't even like women. At least that's what Presdian told me last night. He wouldn't shut up about him. I mean really, it was ridiculous when you are trying to …" Cresa went on with a little too much detail about Presdian and his fixation for Aiyan.

Letti came in with a tray of food, followed by Cresa's young slave carrying an almost identical tray for Cresa. Cresa shook her long blond hair from her shoulder and sat down at the table, letting her slave pour her tea and spoon honey into her hot cereal. Cresa enjoyed her servant; Mila tried not to resent her for it. Cresa had told Mila how in Kitarra, she had been the daughter of a fisherman, forced to spend days mending nets and smoking fish until her hands were calloused, and her hair always smelled fishy. Here in Rodan, she could do almost as she liked and dress in fine clothes and bathe every day with sweet-smelling soap. She grieved for her family, but she did not miss the fish. Cresa had not seen her family since she had been taken.

Mila and Cresa exchanged curious glances as Dart appeared in the doorway with his pretty smile.

"A visitor to see Mila," he said, bowing, but there was a hint of mockery in his poise as he stepped aside to let the visitor enter. The visitor was slim and tall and furred—a Kitarran woman. Her short, dark gray fur was mottled with brown stripes fading to a sandy brown on her hands and feet and tail. Her eyes were light green. Mila had never seen a Kitarran close up before. Her first thought was that she was an exotic beauty; her second was that these were the people who killed Illiah and Rhyl.

"You are Mila?" the Kitarran asked in a sweet voice. A young voice.

"That's me," Mila said, rising, holding out her hand to the Kitarran in greeting. The longer Mila studied her, the younger she appeared. The Kitarran took her hand gently, her mouth curling in a small smile. A few sharp teeth appeared.

"I am Tilley. Ro Aiyan sent me to fetch you."

"Fetch me?"

"Yes. He wishes for you to accompany him to the palace as his consort."

"I see," Mila said, even if she didn't.

"The palace!" Cresa exclaimed, enchanted. Mila looked at her in surprise, noticing the Kitarran did the same. "But you cannot wear that, Mila, not to the palace! Give us a few minutes, Mistress Tilley." Cresa ushered Aiyan's envoy out the door. "Letti, keep the lovely Kitarran company downstairs for a few minutes."

No sooner had Tilley and Letti disappeared into the hallway than Cresa was digging through Mila's wardrobe to choose the most appropriate attire. She insisted on applying makeup to Mila's eyes, just a little, to add mystery, Cresa said with a hush. She rebraided Mila's hair, entwined with dark red ribbons, wrapping it around Mila's head like a dainty red crown.

"Perfect. Blood-red to enchant the Wolf." Cresa grinned. "Off you go."

Mila felt far from enchanted. But something softened inside her when she walked downstairs to see Letti grinning up at the Kitarran as they played a clapping game with their hands, like two little girls. The innocence of it made Mila's eyes sting.

Tilley gave Letti one last farewell clap, but her eyes were sad. Mila remembered Cresa mentioning that Kitarrans in Rodan had particularly difficult lives. Tilley looked cared for; her fur was glossy, her eyes bright. She did not wear a collar. But she did look lonely.

Outside, just under the shade of the awning was a slave-pulled contraption that Mila knew was called a golla. Two large wheels sat under a seat for one or two people, and a slave lifted the handles and pulled, like a donkey. Tilley gestured for Mila to hop in, and she took the seat next to her. The awning over the seat kept the hot sun from their faces. The slave wore a broad-brimmed hat, but by the look of his leathery skin, it did not keep the effects of the sun from his face.

It was not long before the palace loomed before them. The main gates were tall and arching, carved with leaves and images Mila would not have associated with this hot land. As they drew close, Mila's stomach dropped. A man stood beside palace entrance, slouched and drooping. What she thought were clothes, were long rents and gashes in his yellow skin. His face was marred and unrecognizable. It was a corpse. It looked like he had been killed by an animal—something large. A bear or … a wolf.

Mila realized the golla had come to a stop and that her hands had forged onto the rail. She ordered her fingers to release, her legs to move, her stomach to settle. Her body obeyed, but it was only because she had mastered mind over body long ago.

Aiyan appeared from the shadows of the gate. The Wolf. He had killed that man, Mila was sure of it.

Aiyan wore a white tunic and dark trousers. There was no embroidery or embellishments, and he still looked regal and beautiful. Powerful. And yet, the night before, he had scurried away—from her—like a frightened fox, not a killer wolf.

"Thank you, Tilley," he said to the Kitarran. Tilley waved as the golla took her back into the city, leaving Mila alone with her patron. "I am sorry about last night," Aiyan said to Mila in accented Praedan. "I didn't even ask your name."

"Mila."

"I am Aiyan."

"The Wolf," Mila stated warily, unable to keep from glancing at the rotting corpse.

"Yes. They call me that." He sounded—resolved. He held his arm out for her like a perfect court gentleman, if there were such a thing. She looped her arm in his, feeling his lean muscles under the thin fabric of his tunic.

"So everyone knows you turn into a wolf?"

Aiyan nodded.

"And you are a murderer."

His muscles tensed with just a hint of a missed step. His silence was an admission.

"How did you know about me?" she asked. "No one knows about me. No one. I never even told my own sister," she whispered fiercely.

Aiyan fixed his amber eyes on her and leaned closer. He spoke quietly, "I shouldn't have asked you to change. It was foolish. And dangerous. Unlike mine, your magic should stay a secret."

"You don't seem like a man who makes mistakes." Mila felt the rightness of her statement bone deep.

"I don't—often," Aiyan agreed. "I have been invited to dine with the emperor. It is customary for me to bring a slave or a few from my household."

"I am not from your household."

"You are. I bought you from Nulla." He glanced at her earring. "I am just waiting for Nulla to finalize the paperwork with her master."

"Oh," Mila said. "Why did you do that?"

His amber eyes blazed. He did not look like the kind of man who explained himself.

"Please know that many here can speak your tongue, so do not use it loosely," he told her without answering her question.

"You think I have a loose tongue?"

"You seem uninhibited in speaking your mind."

"Elegantly put. Yes, perhaps I have given up being cautious."

"Guard your words in the palace. And your expression," Aiyan instructed.

"And if I can't?"

"Then you will find yourself under the interest of the emperor. I don't recommend it."

"All right, I will take your advice," Mila conceded.

The guards did not speak a word to Aiyan; they merely opened the tall, metal doors and allowed them access to the emperor's private domain. And a beautiful domain it was. Airy, intricate columns framed halls with bright tiled floors, lined with lush green plants. The sun poured down into courtyards of white stone, dotted with pockets of benches and lounges. Music drifted in the air around the stone. Birdsong greeted Mila's ears. She looked around and saw a huge cage of colorful finches flitting between branch and metal.

Mila glanced at Aiyan's profile. He belonged here, in the beautiful palace of the emperor. He had the same chiseled beauty, the same elegance.

The thought lasted only until Mila saw the emperor. He was surrounded by three of the most beautiful women Mila had ever seen and a handful of colorfully dressed men. They were not slaves; they wore no earrings. Mila knew he was the emperor because he was the one striking a slave across the face with a hard fist. The slave was barely more than a boy. Mila could not imagine what he could have done to earn such a punishment.

Aiyan squeezed her arm and she remembered to school her face.

The man struck the slave one last time. The poor boy fell to the hard floor. Two more slaves materialized quickly to drag the faltering body away. The whole scene dissolved into the shadows. Only the outrage in Mila's mind remained.

The emperor then turned toward them, his face changing from annoyed to welcoming. He reached out to Aiyan, clasping him by the shoulder with affection, like friends.

The emperor turned to her, his eyes raking up and down her body. He spoke to Aiyan in Rodan. Mila could only decipher tone and cadence. Perhaps it was better she not know what they discussed. She could not imagine anything the emperor could say, a man who could beat a boy like a dusty rag, that would not enrage her and make it hard to control her expression. She might be a bit rusty, but she did have years of practice pretending. She laughed inwardly. Never trust a whore; they were always lying.

Mila stayed close to Aiyan. Close enough to hear when he asked for something, and she, being his slave, fetched it. A glass of wine. A plate of food she thought might be bite-sized meat pies. She took one for herself at Aiyan's insistence, and it tasted good enough, but Rodan spices were not what she was used to.

Mila ignored Aiyan's companions and the furtive glances filled with lust and longing that they hoped the Wolf did not see. She recognized Ro Presdian, Cresa's patron. She looked him straight in the eye, daring him to say something. But he looked away—he looked at Aiyan, as if to make sure he had not been caught staring at the Wolf's property. It was almost satisfying.

There were two people Mila caught looking at her with blatant interest. One was a woman with long, black hair, similar to Aiyan's, with the same dark skin and a proud face. Her eyes were a shade darker than Aiyan's, and bright with an emotion Mila could not name. It was not a comfortable gaze. The woman was pregnant, but only the slight swelling of her belly betrayed her state; the rest of her body was lean. Two large *daeum* guards trailed her.

Mila was distracted from the intense woman by the second person watching her, man dressed in an audacious shade of green. He had short, curling hair and a beard, a round, almost-boyish face. He winked at her. He rose from his seat and came over to sit beside Mila on the long, cushioned bench.

"My name is Beric," he said, holding out his hand to her. Mila put hers in his, and he brought it to his lips, kissing the back of it neatly. As he did, he glanced at Aiyan, who was watching the exchange. Aiyan frowned but turned back to his conversation with the emperor and another rodaeri.

"I'm Mila," Mila told him. "You speak my tongue."

"I do. I am a great lover of learning new things," he said with a wide smile. "Languages. Skills. History. People."

"You speak it well."

"Thank you," he said, feigning bashfulness. "The rumors regarding Aiyan and Nulla's new whore—begging your pardon—seem to be true. I must admit, I am shocked."

"Why does everyone say that?" Mila mused out loud, making him laugh.

"Because our mutual friend does not keep companions. Without reason," Beric added.

So, Beric was probing her for information. Mila smiled at him like she knew a secret, leaning toward him, just a little. It had the effect she wanted; Beric's eyes glinted hungrily.

"And what reason are you hoping to discover?"

Beric shrugged, glancing at Aiyan out of the corner of his eye, but not out of fear. He was hoping that Aiyan was listening.

Mila ran a finger up Beric's leg. "Why, are you jealous?"

"You are not going to tell me, are you?" Beric said with an exaggerated sigh.

If she had anything to tell, would she? Mila shook her head apologetically but was still smiling.

"Good," he surprised her by saying.

A test. Interesting.

"Just do yourself a favor: stay away from Allia." Beric nodded his chin in the direction of the pregnant woman. The woman was still watching with hawklike intensity.

"Why?"

Beric raised his brows at her impertinence. "Because hurt animals often bite the hand that would tend their wounds." He sounded sad. He leaned into Mila's neck to whisper in her ear. "And be good to Aiyan. The Gods know he could use a good lay." He grinned wickedly as he moved aside for Aiyan, who was approaching them with purpose. The smile Beric flashed at Aiyan was pure mischief.

Aiyan sat in the seat vacated by Beric, leaning back into the cushions. The emperor followed him. Slowly. Deliberately. As if knowing every step he took brought fear and pain, and he relished it.

"You are quite taken with this woman of yours," the emperor drawled in Praedan, obviously so Mila would understand. But why? Why bother if she was merely a slave? There was an edge to his voice. Jealousy? That didn't seem right. He sat beside Mila and ran his finger down her neck. His touch was a brand of ownership, as if to remind Aiyan he could take whatever he wanted.

"You may have her if you want, my friend," Aiyan said, taking a sip of his wine.

Mila felt ill. She had almost believed Aiyan wanted something else from her, something because of her magic. She was wrong. She was just another slave to him, another thing to own, to use—and to sell.

"Maybe when you are bored with her. She is very beautiful," the emperor said, tugging on a wayward strand of Mila's curly hair. "Such fine skin, like porcelain. I could make such pretty patterns in your skin, my dear." And, like magic, in his hand was a small knife made of bright, sharp steel. He held it lovingly, twisting it expertly around his fingers. Sitting still beside him, with his knife close and his threats closer, tested Mila as nothing else had. In her mind, she could feel the knife along her skin, cutting into her flesh, blood blistering along the delicate cut.

In her mind, it was Serac shushing her cries of pain, his dark eyes glinting with pleasure. The memory was pulling her back into the dark hole she thought she had escaped when she had killed the bastard.

And then Aiyan was in her head, calm and wordless, but somehow twisting through her memories, brushing away the bits that stole her breath, giving her air, giving her light. She knew it was him because he smelled like wolf and magic. His hand was hot on her arm. The physical touch nearly jolted her, but it brought her back and anchored her into the present. The emperor put away his knife, smiling at the effect it had on her.

"Are you sure she is strong enough for you, Aiyan?" the emperor said with a laugh. He stood and moved back toward the others, leaving them alone. Aiyan's hand was still on her arm.

*Are you all right?* His voice in her head was like the moon after a night storm.

*Yes,* Mila answered forcefully, unsure if he would hear her. She felt Aiyan's gaze on her and looked up, catching his eye. His amber eyes were soft, filled with something that might have been compassion. But perhaps that was her wishful thinking, looking for kindness and caring and hope.

Something flitted into her mind. Trees. Green. An old woman's face. Images, calming dreamscapes filled with peace and courage. Aiyan relinquished his touch on her arm, and the feeling, the images, vanished.

*I will send you home.* Aiyan waved to one of the slaves in the corner, a tall man with long legs and arms and a dour expression. "Day, take Mila back to Nulla's. And give this to Nulla as well," Aiyan said in Mila's language, reaching into his pocket for a little satchel.

"Very well, Master," the manservant said with a Jullayan accent. He bowed and reached his hand out to Mila. She stood, feeling more eyes on her back. The woman was watching her again. Mila's back itched under the unsettling attention as she followed Day out of the courtyard.

The slave Day was silent, but it was not an uncomfortable silence. Mila put her hand on her chest, to encourage her lungs to work. Day looked at her with curiosity but said nothing until they arrived back at the brothel where he wished her a good day, giving her another bow. His slave earring caught the light, flickering blue and green with veins of black—azurite. Mila remembered seeing a small hole in Aiyan's ear, in the place a slave earring would have been. She had not thought anything of it at the time.

"Day, was Ro Aiyan a slave?" she asked as Day turned to leave.

Day smiled faintly, but there was no humor in it. "We are all slaves, miss. Except the emperor. He is a monster."

CHAPTER 47

# MILA

AIYAN DID NOT return to the brothel in the evening. Not that he said he would. Not that Mila wanted him to. And Nulla did not send Mila to seek a different patron. For whatever reason, Aiyan seemed reluctant to bed her. She was not going to complain.

Nulla came to Mila's room wearing an ugly expression. She paced around the room as if trying to decide how to best unleash her anger.

"What is it, Nulla?" Mila asked.

"Aiyan has purchased you. Exclusively. I am trying to decide how to punish you."

Mila folded her arms across her chest. "If you touch me, Aiyan will destroy you." Mila had no way to know if that was true, but fear flashed in Nulla's eyes and Mila guessed she had hit a mark.

"Bitch." Nulla flung up her hands and stomped out of Mila's room.

No, Mila would not complain.

Yes, Nulla complained and muttered insults and snide remarks whenever she saw Mila. Mila did not bother asking why Nulla had agreed to Aiyan's contract in the first place. Everyone, sparing the emperor, seemed terrified of the Wolf. So why had Aiyan bothered to pay for Mila at all? Why had he not just taken her, claimed her as his own? After all, Aiyan was rodaeri, a friend to the emperor, and Nulla was just an old whore.

Aiyan had purchased her, so why was Mila still living in the brothel? Would she move to his house? Did he even own a house? Maybe he lived in the palace. Mila wished she had someone to ask. Nulla would know, but Mila did not want to speak to her more than necessary.

"Oh. It's you. The useless whore," Nulla said, waltzing into the brothel kitchen looking for Dart but finding Mila instead. "Someday, Aiyan will grow bored with you, he will sell you back to me, and I will make you work every night all night until what is left between your legs is—"

Mila interrupted. "Yes, yes, until my cunt is as dry and stretched and scarred like an old woman's. You have told me this before."

Nulla glared. Mila held the other woman's gaze easily. Nulla barked at the cook and then left in a flutter of lace and gauzy fabric.

The cook did not speak Praedan, but the older woman understood, sighed, and gave Mila an apologetic smile. The cook had stiff hips, and she walked over to Mila with a slow waddle and placed a small box into Mila's hand. Mila opened it and smiled in delight. An assortment of brightly colored thread lay in neat rows, a selection of needles beside, and a tiny knife for cutting thread.

"Thank you. How did you know I love to embroider?" Mila asked, hoping the woman could understand her. The woman's eyes became slits behind her nearly toothless smile, but she didn't answer with words. Mila fingered the threads. They already whispered pictures and designs to Mila, making her fingers itch with the desire to create. It had been so long.

Mila took the box up to her room and sat in her window, gazing out into the city bathed in descending night. She asked Letti to fetch her a tunic, a scarf, anything that she would like embellished. Letti brought her a gray sheath dress, one that the serving girl wore often. Letti watched with fascination as Mila began a design, the thread and needle moving up and over, and in its wake unfolded a story of bees and flowers and little green leaves.

The brothel's carnal heartbeat was loud in Mila's sensitive ears. She tried her best to ignore the off-tune sounds that permeated the walls. Questions circled in her mind in rhythm to her fingers, pulling the thread through the fabric. Murryn and Tarran. Out and in. By the Guardians, Mila prayed they were alive. Over and under. With hands like knives and a tongue like a war drum, Murryn would not make an obedient slave. Would they kill Murryn for her spirit? Or rejoice in breaking it?

If Mila wanted to stay sane, she needed to barricade her heart from the worry of the unknown. She was safe. She was unharmed. Perhaps Tarran and Murryn were as well. Hope. She tied her thread and started another.

Chimes tinkled down the hall of the brothel, announcing dinner. Letti tore her eyes from Mila's creation and went to fetch food.

Mila had good ears. She could pick out sounds easily, a skill she'd had since childhood. She could hear the faint scratching of the rat—or perhaps three—in the wall by the door. She could hear Cresa laughing in the next room and the answering voice of a man. She could hear footsteps patter down the hall. Quick footsteps. Hurried footsteps. Mila's door opened like a gust of wind as Letti burst in, her eyes wide.

"They are coming! They are coming!" she squealed.

Mila looked down the hall and several—no three—*daeum* appeared at the top of the stairs. Their scarred faces were grim, their shoulders squared. They were not looking for pleasurable company.

"They are looking for you, Mila!" Letti pushed Mila with all her small might back into the room.

Mila closed the door and locked it. The heavy footsteps of the men stopped outside her door. With a loud crack, the door burst open, the lock splintered. Shouts of outrage, then fear ricocheted in the hallway. Mila pulled Letti behind her, backing toward the window. It was not that far to the ground if she could reach the awning and then jump. She was good at things like that. Agile. Strong. But she couldn't leave Letti.

The *daeum* fixed their eyes on Mila. Slow, ugly smiles pulled their scarred lips into jagged lines. She could feel Letti shivering in fear behind her.

The *daeum* were the emperor's guards. What did Imal want with her? Mila swallowed the lump of fear in her throat. Aiyan had warned her about the emperor's attention.

"Come with us," one of the guards said, then spat on the floor. His accent was the same as Mila's. He was Jullayan. The knowledge made Mila ill.

"I will come. Just leave the girl alone," Mila told them.

The guard made a noise and jerked his head at Letti. The little girl understood the unspoken gesture, slithered from behind Mila, and ran out through the open door. It was a relief to hear the quick footsteps of Letti fade down the hall.

The guards took a step toward Mila, making the room shrink. She remembered Imal's cold eyes and his colder blade, how both had lingered hungrily on her skin. She would rather die on the streets, or in the Pit, than become that man's plaything.

She turned and slipped out the window, one foot finding purchase on a small ledge. She twisted and leaped for the window ledge next to hers. She hoped the *daeum* were not stupid enough to come after her. She couldn't turn to look; she had to keep her eyes on the infinitesimal handholds that kept her from falling two stories and potentially breaking something. She couldn't run with a broken foot. She swung from the ledge, hoping the awning of the street stall was sturdy enough that if she landed on it, it would slow her fall, at least a little. It was her only chance, and she took it.

The proprietor of the stall was gone for the night, his wares with him. Mila tumbled through the canvas onto the ground, feeling pain in her hip, but she could still move and move she did. She ran toward the darkness at the end of the alley. She could see better in the dark than most. She hoped that included the *daeum*.

Mila did not know Rodan at all. She ran blindly from alley to alley, careful to choose a path that might hide her trail. Would the *daeum* be able to track her? She had no idea. She ducked inside a building that looked abandoned, but once inside, she recognized it as a warehouse filled with spices and pottery. She was no warrior, but she could move silently and knew the importance of paying attention to her surroundings.

Mila squeezed behind a large crate in the dust. From there, she could see into the cavernous building. She could see the entrance, the windows. She tried to breathe as quietly as possible, but her breath came ragged and desperate.

The *daeum* burst through the door like a battering ram. Mila crawled as quickly and silently as she could toward the back door, expecting at any moment for them to see her and give chase.

"Come here, little mouse," they heckled. But they had not seen her—yet.

Mila gained the alley once more, but it was a trap. There were three more guards on the street. They saw her, calling out in their rough voices, their scars stretching across their grinning, anticipatory faces.

Mila's heart clenched tight in her chest. Her knees threatened to give up as the *daeum* approached, slowly, with a swagger, assured she was about to be their captive. She stood up straighter, preparing to dart from the hounds' teeth.

A shadow dropped down between her and the guards. A man, his frame almost feminine, his waist slimmed to narrow hips, his long, black hair loosed from its braid, tangling down his back well below his shoulder blades like some living thing.

"What is the meaning of this?" the man asked, his accent thick, but he spoke Praedan. Something slid over Mila's fear as she recognized the voice. "What do you want with this woman?"

The *daeum* paused. Their grins vanished like smoke in the breeze.

"I asked, what do you want with this woman?" Aiyan's voice was like a thunderclap, strong and undeniable. Power rippled through him. No, not power—magic. Mila could almost see it. *Damn*, she thought. *I want to do that.*

"What does Imal want with her?" Aiyan stepped forward. Two long daggers made for death appeared in Aiyan's hands.

"Not the emperor, the princess," said the *daeum* with long, brown plaited hair and lips like a nightmare.

Mila didn't see any change in Aiyan's posture, but she knew, somehow, that his anger had shifted into surprise—and fear. She blinked. She flexed her fingers. She could feel the magic in them. They tingled, singing to her, alive and real.

"We need the woman," the *daeum* said. Mila searched the *daeum*'s eyes and saw a chain. A mask. And behind it was fear and pain and hatred.

Aiyan moved like an invisible wind. The first *daeum* did not even see the blade before he was down and bleeding out. Aiyan moved to the next. He looked small and thin beside the huge guard, but he leaped and buried his knife deep into the man's neck. The next fell in similar fashion. Mila watched, horrified, yet unwilling to tear her eyes from the fight, or more aptly, the slaughter. There was a sickening crack. The last man fell. Silence followed. Aiyan was no contender; he was a master.

Aiyan offered Mila his arm, and she took it. She hadn't even realized she had stumbled and fallen in the dirt. Aiyan pulled her to her feet gracefully but did not relinquish her hand.

"Are you all right?" Aiyan murmured, his face a cresting wave of anger.

Mila nodded. "How did you know—how did you know I needed you?" Mila asked after a few deep breaths.

Aiyan raised his brows. "Did you need me? I watched you for a few minutes to see what would you do."

"Why would you do that? They were chasing me!"

"I thought maybe your magic would save you."

"Well, it didn't."

"Maybe I should have waited longer," he said with a ghost of— yes, it was a smile. This was nothing to him. He wasn't even breathing hard. What *was* he?

"No, your timing was good," Mila assured him. "Why would the princess send *daeum* men after me?"

"The question is, *how* did she send *daeum* men after you? Only Imal can control the *daeum*—or so I believed. And *daeum* can't lie unless ordered to by their master."

"Imal controls them fully? Like puppets?"

Aiyan nodded. Mila shivered. Slaves. Their minds, not just their bodies. Their souls.

"Thankfully, there were only the three—more and I would have had trouble. Come. I will take you to my house. You will be safer there, I think." Aiyan sounded like a hundred years had passed with slow agony.

"You *think*?"

Aiyan fixed his amber eyes on hers. He waited, but she didn't drop her gaze.

"With me, there is no place safer." And he flashed a wolfish grin.

CHAPTER 48

# MILA

MILA GLANCED AT AIYAN as he walked beside her, leading her down the streets of Kara to his house. Even as a man, he walked like a wolf—with calculated movements and a lithe gait. Gods, he was exquisite. Why did he have to look like a summer sunset? He even smelled alluring, like sharp spices and something earthy. She wanted to run her fingers through his long, shining black hair.

He was a murderer. She had just watched him kill three men. Thinking there was anything tame and touchable about him was delusional. What was it that drew her to him?

She had felt the power of his magic. She wanted that power for herself.

"You see well in the dark?" Aiyan asked. They had walked without talking for long enough for Mila to find Aiyan's voice soothing against the harsh song of the surrounding city. The sun had set; dusk had settled over the streets.

"I do."

"No one has ever commented on it?"

"I never mentioned it."

"No one knows about your magic?" His accent spiced his words.

"No. I never told anyone. Not my sister. Not my dearest friends."

"Is magic so feared in Praedan?"

"Yes," Mila said without hesitation. In her mind, she saw her mother. Her black hair haloed by the bright green of the spring forest, her eyes blue like a twilight sky, her smile wild and precious like a glimpse of a forest creature. Then arms grabbed Mila's mother, and her mouth curved into a snarl, her eyes stretched wide with fear. The men in black took her mother away, and all that was left in Mila's memory was green leaves. She didn't know if the memory was real or a dream. It didn't matter. Her mother was dead and gone.

"My mother was taken too," Aiyan whispered, as if he had seen the pictures in her mind.

"But you don't talk of it to anyone, do you? You and I are alike, Ro Aiyan. We keep our secrets close, but not from each other, it seems." Mila let her irritation grate her voice. She had no wish to share this man's thoughts. And little desire for him to know hers.

"This is my house," Aiyan said softly.

"It's very close to the Tower," Mila remarked, looking at the square thumb of a building that housed the *daeum*.

"Do not worry. You are as safe here as anywhere."

Mila shrugged. It was the best she could hope for, really.

Aiyan opened the door and gestured for her to precede him.

"Your house is very grand," Mila said, turning around, her gaze swallowed by the tall ceilings and intricate moldings and stonework. The floor was like a lake on a still night, smooth, reflecting every little twist of the candles in their lanterns.

"It belonged to my former master. It is what it is."

"Day told me you were a slave."

"I was."

Mila looked at Aiyan more clearly. She could see the hole in his ear that had once held a slave earring, a small, tiny scar never to heal over entirely.

"Ah, Master." Day stepped out of the shadows, bending at the middle. He resembled a willow tree almost more than a man with the grayness of his skin and hair, his narrow face and bright green eyes. His movements most of all, slow and smooth. "Should I find our guest a room?"

"I will show her myself. Thank you, Day," Aiyan said, leading Mila up a wide, curving stairway.

Mila ran her fingers along the wood of the banister. The wood was smooth, almost liquid-like, making Mila's fingers tingle with delight.

"How did a slave become a master?" Mila asked.

"My master died, and Imal granted me his estate."

"Ah. Imal is your friend."

"Men like Imal and me don't have friends," Aiyan quipped. "Here, this is your room. Cliff will bring water for bathing."

"Aren't you going to show me the rest of the house?"

"There is not much to see. It is a big house with very few people. Most of the rooms are empty."

"I see."

"Wani or Tilley will fetch you for a late dinner."

"Thank you, Aiyan." She wanted to ask him more. She wanted to ask him how to change, how to use her magic. But she found her tongue tied, and Aiyan left before she could gather her courage to ask him.

Cliff was a big man who did not speak any Praedan. He came

carrying two large buckets of hot water, muttering words Mila did not understand. He filled the basin, managing to meet her eyes only once before leaving her alone. She stripped off her dusty dress, noticing it was torn from her escape out the window. She rubbed her sore hip; dark bruises were blossoming on her skin. She bathed. She wondered if there was anything to wear, or if she would have to dress again in her dusty, torn clothes. She should have asked Aiyan.

A knock came at the door as she was brushing the grit out of her hair. The door opened to reveal two large gray-green orbs in the dim hall light. Tilley's eyes.

"Dinner," the Kitarran said softly with a smile in her voice. "And here, I thought you might need something to wear. This might fit you." She held a swath of fabric in blues and reds. A dress, simply cut and sewn. It looked comfortable.

"Thank you, Tilley."

"Hurry up, we are all hungry," Tilley said, gesturing for Mila to put on the dress. "I will take your dress and see if we can get the worst dirt out." Tilley picked up Mila's discarded clothing.

Aiyan's house was all tall hallways, blue shadows, and floral smells. It was a labyrinth. Tilley led Mila down and through the house to a wide room with a wide table. Mila's stomach groaned with hunger to see the food and wine laid ready to eat.

"This is Day, Cliff, and Wani," Tilley said, introducing the others who sat around the table. Then she said something in Rodan, and the little old woman, Wani, grinned and gestured for them to sit and then began serving.

"Where is Ro Aiyan?" Mila asked.

"Ro Aiyan? Oh, he likes his space. He is often alone," Tilley told her.

A lone wolf. Wolves lived in packs. Mila could vaguely remember stories from childhood about the local wolf packs hunting deer and taking out lambs in spring, how the fearsome predators denned and hunted together. The village where Mila had been a child had been close to the Great Forest. The villagers had been superstitious about killing the wolves, afraid the Forest Folk would seek revenge. They had been stories, but, as Tarran would say, all stories held a touch of truth.

Mila finished eating quickly and forwent Day's offer of wine. She told them she was exhausted and excused herself from the table, thanking Wani as she did so. The woman did not speak her tongue, but Mila had a feeling she could understand quite a bit.

Mila was tired, ready to fall into her bed and sleep. But she wanted to find Aiyan.

It was a big house. Mila didn't have the slightest idea of where he might be. Since it was night, the only light was from the torches set in lanterns of colorful glass that added to the mystery of the large house.

Mila closed her eyes in the dark hallway and listened. She could hear the rest of the household still at the dinner table. She could hear a hush of noise beyond that was the city. She could not hear Aiyan. She reached for her magic, her wild senses, rusty and buried. When Aiyan had touched her magic with his mind, he had awoken them, just a little. Mila reached for that place, and when she opened his eyes, she knew where to find him.

She went up a flight of stairs. At the top was a red door. She opened it slowly, wondering if Aiyan would sense her approaching. It was never smart to startle something that had sharp teeth.

The red door opened into a room lined with shelves brimming

and overflowing with books and jars and specimens and plants. Lanterns and candles lit the space, a small fortune spent to work at night. But Aiyan was nowhere to be seen.

Mila moved through the room into another chamber that held a bed crammed between more shelves and more things—more plants hanging from the ceiling in baskets, vines crawling up walls and over sills. He was not there either. She moved through the bedroom and opened a third door. It led out into the night, onto a balcony thick with yet more vines, arching branches of small trees, and lush ferns and shrubs. The night washed out the colors, leaving only shades of gray. Aiyan was sitting there, looking up at the sky.

"You aren't really allowed here," he said in a huff, still looking up at the night.

That annoyed Mila. He was the one who had pushed himself into her vulnerable self, and now she was not allowed to do the same?

"You didn't tell me the rules."

"I didn't change your earring either." Aiyan stood with a liquid motion that was more wolf than human. He reached for her ear and plucked Nulla's earring from it. "Hold on." He went into his room and came back with another earring. "A slave without an earring is sent to the Pit," Aiyan said quietly. He pushed the new earring through the now-vacant hole in her ear, folding the clasp around so it wouldn't come loose. The closeness of him made Mila realize Aiyan was hardly taller than she; what was it about him that made him seem so big and fearsome? He was a slight man, slim, but also hard, muscular.

Mila eyed his ear and the vacant hole. "I was told you are the last *heera.*"

"I am."

"What does that mean? Who were the *heera*?"

Aiyan ran his fingers through his long hair. "My people. My family." There was pain in his voice. Grief. Longing. Mila knew what that longing might feel like. "Some *heera* were shape-shifters—warriors that could change into the shape of a wolf. They were stronger and faster than anyone. They could see the magic of the world. They could see the light from the dark and help those in need."

"But, they were destroyed."

"They were hunted mercilessly."

"By Imal."

"By Imal's father."

"But you were left alive."

"Yes."

"Why?"

"Greed. Don't touch that."

Mila snapped her hand away from the long white petals of a flower she had been about to touch.

"It's poisonous. It will give your hand a nasty rash."

"Oh."

"The *heera* wisewomen were herbalists. They knew which plants were used to heal, and which were used to kill."

"You are not a wisewoman," Mila stated, folding her hands in her lap.

"My mother and grandmother were. They taught me what they could, knowing the dauem were hunting our people."

"How old were you when—when you were taken?"

"Fourteen."

So young. Mila's heart hurt for the boy he had once been. She tried to imagine what he would have been like at that age. She remembered when Tarran was fourteen, growing like a weed, his voice changing, noticing Murryn for the first time with a man's perception, not a boy's.

"Stop," Aiyan whispered. "Your magic is in my head. You are more powerful than you think."

She couldn't help herself. She smiled. "Teach me."

"I ... I am not sure how. I don't want to scare you."

"You were too abrupt. Try now."

Aiyan bit his lip. The gesture made him look much younger. He looked at her directly, his amber eyes prying.

*Can you hear me?*

Mila nodded.

*I can touch your magic, but it is weak. Tenuous.* "We should try tomorrow. You are exhausted," he said out loud.

Mila felt her fatigue crash against her at his words. He was right. "Promise? Tomorrow?"

Aiyan nodded, his eyes bright.

She stood, turning to go, careful not to touch the plants around her. Then she paused. "Aiyan, why did you buy me? What do you want from me?"

"Nothing. Yet."

But Mila could sense the lie in his voice.

# CHAPTER 49

# AIYAN

DARKNESS was an effective tool. Aiyan had made use of it time and time again, and it never failed him. It had allowed him to creep along the inner palace halls and infiltrate the lavish chambers of Rodan's princess. Allia's chambers were the last place he wanted to be, but he felt he had no choice but to confront her. And better in the dark, in the dead of night, instead of somewhere Imal or Imal's slaves could see.

"Allia."

Imal's sister stirred and stretched like a cat. The sleeping form next to her did not. Allia's lover was deep in his substance—rum or wine or culla. The drug from Rodan was gaining popularity in Kara. The man was inconsequential. He would wake in the morning and have no memory of a midnight visitor.

Allia sat slowly, letting the blankets fall from her swollen breasts and rounded tummy. Aiyan glanced at the table beside her bed where an empty bottle had tipped its last dregs onto the floor. Two dirty cups attracted flies.

"You should not drink so much. You are going to lose this baby too," Aiyan murmured.

Allia tossed her head, her face devoid of emotion. "And here I thought you didn't care."

"Why did the *daeum* come after Mila?" Aiyan asked with a hiss. "How did you do it?"

"The girl?" Allia cocked her head, the resemblance between her and her brother impossible to miss. "You think it was me?"

"Was it?"

"Come and find out," Allia said, reclining back on her cushioned bed.

"I would rather you just told me."

"But I won't. And I am not afraid of you, Wolf." Her smile looked wrong on her perpetually sad face.

Aiyan gritted his teeth and put his hand on her leg, gently, with as little contact as possible.

Images. Memories. Mila's was not the only mind Aiyan could read. Allia with her lover. Allia putting her hand on the *daeum* and coaxing dark magic into them, just as Imal did during the ascension.

Aiyan let go, feeling breathless and sweaty. Allia's eyes were dark with pleasure.

"I killed your *daeum* before they could kill her," Aiyan said, watching as Allia's smile died, replaced by rage, a familial trait. Allia had always been a jealous creature, another familial trait. "Where did you get so much *varing*, Allia?"

Allia startled Aiyan by laughing, loud and sharp. She sounded crazed and trapped.

"My brother! He is such a fool. But he won't listen to me. Never has. The *varing* is everywhere—here, there, growing like a pernicious weed across this city. But it leaks from below this palace with a vengeance. It was easy to gather up enough to take control of a few *daeum*."

The idea of dark magic leaking through the city was uncomfortable. Sure, there was plenty of *varing* in Kara; it fed on the city's misery and pain. But there had never been enough for anyone but Imal. What was the emperor doing to release so much *varing*? Aiyan would wager it had something to do with his "gift" from Cotoch. Aiyan could feel his hackles rise even in his human form. What was Imal playing with?

"What did Cotoch bring for Imal from Praedan?"

Allia pouted at the mention of her cousin from across the sea. "Cotoch was such a boring bastard! I am so glad he went back home. I am surprised Imal has the patience to deal with him—don't you mean *who* Cotoch brought from Praedan?" Allia's thoughts and words jumped like a headless chicken. "I am shocked—shocked!— that Imal hasn't shown you his prize. You are his favorite, after all." Her words were thick with jealousy and loathing. She hated her brother, but she yearned for his approval above all else, a state of contradiction Imal had manipulated into her since she was a young girl.

"Did he show you?"

"My brother? Of course not. What I know is from rumors." She jerked her chin at her lover, who was still oblivious to the world around him. "If you spent more time at the palace, you would hear things too."

"What do you think Imal will do if he discovers you can manipulate his *daeum*?"

Allia shrugged. "What can he do that he hasn't done already? Kill me? I don't fear death, Wolf."

Aiyan didn't have to use his magic to know she spoke the truth.

"I know you don't care about your life, Allia, or that of your unborn baby, but I promise you, if you hurt my people, or use the *daeum*, I will make you suffer like you haven't before. You will die a thousand deaths before I give you release."

"You are a monster." Allia spat in his face. "What happened to you, Aiyan?"

Aiyan grinned, baring his teeth. "Nothing you don't already know, Allia."

He turned to leave.

"Come here, Aiyan. Come into my bed, and I will give you the *daeum*. I will give you Kara. I will be empress, and you will stand beside me as we rule this land."

Aiyan nearly retched. He hid it well, a practiced skill. She would be a leader as fair and just as her brother. It was an impossible choice.

"No, Allia."

"Aiyan …" Allia's voice was small, childlike. Soft. Aiyan closed his eyes, remembering Allia as a girl, innocent and hopeful—before Imal had turned her into a bitter, broken woman. "Why her, Aiyan? Why her and not me?" Her voice was a plea that broke Aiyan's heart all over again. But the question was a trap. Allia's momentary sweetness would dissolve as quickly as rain on a Rodan summer day.

"Answer me, Aiyan!" And there it was. Allia screamed as she picked up a cup from her table and threw it with all her might at Aiyan. He ducked it easily; it smashed against the wall and broke into a thousand tiny pieces, just like Allia's soul.

Aiyan left the princess to her misery.

# CHAPTER 50

# STONE

IT WAS ALMOST as if Stone had never left Kitarra. He moved through the Queen's Keep, and it felt like the home he had always known. The stone corridors. The lanterns. The tapestries. The nooks and crannies and sentry holes and barricades and portcullises. The wide window sills where he spent many childhood days reading and daydreaming.

And then he would come across Emri's favorite haunts, the nook where she liked to sit and meditate, or the window with her favorite view of the city, and it was almost as if the last seven years had not happened, and he would come around the corner, eager to surprise her. But she was not there. She was dead.

He had not visited her grave. He could not tolerate seeing Arrain's grave marker placed beside his wife and their little daughter. The man Emri had loved was dead.

Kitarra had a hard time accepting that, naturally. Being hailed as Prince Arrain was a jolt to Stone's nerves. Every. Time. He hated it. But he had already caused his people more grief and pain than they deserved; he couldn't deny them their faith. If the people of Kitarra needed to call him Arrain and Prince, he would not correct them.

Eva continued to call him Stone, as did young Rhyl. A small bit of satisfaction. And Talo called him Da. And that was a name Stone would spend what time he had trying to live up to.

Illiah's absence was a crater. From the Peace Guards, the new army, to the queen's high council, and the peasants of Kilev, they mourned him. Stone had vastly underestimated the reach of one man, the hope Illiah had brought to the realm. Was it Kitarra's vulnerability that had led them to place their hope in the hands of a foreigner? Or was it Illiah's gifts and charisma that had brought him into the folds of Kitarra's ample bosom? Stone did not know. He hadn't known Illiah.

Eva gave him back his journal. He flipped through its pages, instantly taken back years by its contents. The disturbing findings. The strange happenings. He remembered clearly the cold dread that filled him at the thatcher's cabin outside Withe, how the intangible emotion had swept over him like smoke, choking his hope and joy. His terror had weighed his legs down like boulders. It had taken significant willpower to flee.

The *revenant* on the beach he had killed with his vercuri a year ago had felt the same. By the Guardians, he had not realized it until re-reading the pages of his journal. He had lost so many memories to grief and addiction.

The *revenant* had formed the essence of a man from Jullayah, but the emanating fear had felt the same. Intangible. The kind of fear that did not respond to logic. The *revenant* had taken over Illiah right down to his heroic soul. And it had taken Eva as well. She told him how she felt like she'd been drowning in a river of magic, and that thing was the dark taint, the oil in the water. He still did not understand what drove him to strike it with the vercuri. Instinct?

Luck? It didn't matter. What mattered was that it had worked. He had defeated a thing made of magic.

Magic.

Why did it have to be magic? Magic was for legends and stories from a time forgotten. A man, an army, that was something Stone felt capable of tackling. But magic with the ability to take shape, to form into something real? No wonder they needed a prophecy—as long as Kitarra could survive until Rhyl could grow into a man.

Rhyl was the child of a prophecy taken from a dream of a seer shepherded by a Guardian. Stone had not thought of the seer Mags for years. She had been an old woman years ago. Maybe she was dead. She had been the first to mention a prophecy. Stone wondered if she had any more clues or answers.

Eva had been silent about the contents of Arrain's journal. She had read the journal with the ferocity of a hound after a rabbit. She knew it had been Arrain who had planned the kidnapping of her son. Sure, he had abandoned his people before the actual plan was put into action, but it was undeniable that Arrain—and therefore Stone—was the fulcrum of Eva's unhappiness.

Stone looked at the vial in his hand and the pinch of gray powder inside. His fingers shook, just a little. The thirst at the back of his throat traveled down to his soul, urging him to take the entire vial, but he didn't. He took a third and put the vial back in his locked box under the bed. The familiar surge of energy flowed through him as the culla worked its own kind of magic.

"Stone!" Eva's voice made him start. "What are you doing?"

"You know what I am doing," he growled. He did not keep

his addiction from Eva, but still, he didn't want her to see him in thrall to the culla.

"Look at me." She reached her hand up to cup his cheek, pulling his gaze to hers. "Let me help you."

After everything, she wanted to help him. She should hate him for his failure.

"You cannot help me."

Eva bit her lip and dropped her hand. "I will not give up on you."

"Even after everything I have done?"

"Everyone deserves a second chance."

"I would have killed Illiah. I would have. Without hesitation."

Rage flashed across Eva's face. It satisfied him, greatly. He needed her anger. Her hate. It was so much easier than her pity.

"For the children," she stated.

"For the children."

"I'm so tired of this, Stone," Eva said, her anger gone. She linked her arm in his, resting her head on his shoulder. The weight of her was an iron rod grounding his heart to his home.

"Of what?" he asked. "Life?"

"This life. Why can't I just have a family, raise my children without all this?" If her broken heart had been an object, she would have gestured to it.

"Privilege brings responsibility. You and Illiah will suffer because you make a difference. You cannot have one without the other."

"When did you get so wise?"

Stone smiled but did not feel pride in it. "Must be the price for losing so many lives."

Eva huffed in response.

"I have done things I cannot speak, Eva. I have paid my price. We all pay the price."

"Is it worth it? Making something good from our lives when the cost is so high?"

"Do nothing, then. Let your husband die. Leave your children to fate. Ignore the pleas of Kitarra's people. Stop being a leader, an inspiration. Do something else."

Eva turned to the window.

"Feeling sorry for yourself won't help anyone either," Stone muttered.

Eva ignored him, bless her heart.

# CHAPTER 51

# MILA

"READY?"

Aiyan appeared at Mila's elbow just as she took the last bite of her breakfast. Her stomach instantly writhed with uncertainty. Her boldness from the day before, asking Aiyan to teach her about her magic, was gone, leaving only nerves and doubts. There was something wild and magical and strange within her; she wasn't sure what would happen if she let it out. Breakfast may have been a mistake.

Tilley looked up from the stack of ledgers she'd been working on, pen in hand. "Ready for what?" she asked.

Feeling slightly recovered, Mila didn't miss the opportunity. "Aiyan wants to show me something." Mila flourished her voice with innuendo. Just as Mila had hoped, Aiyan blushed. It made him look like a little boy.

"Oh," Tilley said, looking back at her work. If her fur hadn't been so thick, Mila would have been positive the girl was blushing too.

"Where are we going to do this?" Mila asked when they were alone in the hallway.

Aiyan sighed. "I wish we could go into the hills, to the forest. But it is too far, and I am going to the palace this afternoon. Maybe in a few days. So today, we will use my garden," Aiyan told her. Mila smiled, remembering the lush little oasis bathed in starlight. It felt like years since she had seen anything green and living.

"So long as you tell me which plants might bite," she said.

To her surprise, Aiyan laughed, a rich, warm sound that made something inside her purr.

The plants of the garden filled the stony space, cascading up the walls, creeping onto the little path. The flowers that had been dark and dull the night before were bright purples and pinks and reds. The garden was only ten paces wide and perhaps twice as many long, too small for a wolf to stretch his legs, but in a city hot like Kara, it was a small miracle the garden existed at all.

Aiyan sat on the ground covered by a carpet of creeping plants that smelled minty. He gestured for her to sit likewise.

"Are you going to shift?" Mila asked, wondering if he was going to start taking his clothes off.

"I don't think so. I have never done this before—helped someone else learn to change," Aiyan said. "Although I have seen it done when I was a child."

"Because you are the last one," Mila stated. Aiyan flinched, just a little.

"Imal and Allia's mother was *heera*. There is a chance a child of theirs could be like me."

"How many children does Imal have?" Mila asked, thinking a man such as him would have many natural children, but Mila had never heard mention of a wife.

"Imal has plenty of children. Most, he keeps close. He sent one of his daughters to Praedan. But none of them are shifters like you and me."

"Why would he send his daughter to Praedan?"

"He has kin in Praedan—his cousin. He sent her to Cotoch a few years ago," Aiyan said. "Cotoch is like Imal, a sorcerer."

There was a whole world Mila did not know. She knew nothing about Kitarra, or Allati, or Rodan. She did not even know about herself.

"Anyway, I thought you were going to teach me."

"You are the one changing the subject." Aiyan's lip almost twitched into a smile.

"Right." Mila flexed her nervous fingers.

"We close our eyes," Aiyan said, closing his. Mila did the same. Immediately, her other senses took over. The breeze tickled her skin. The smell of the garden filled her nose. She could perceive Aiyan's proximity without physically touching him.

*Can you hear me?* Aiyan's voice was in her mind.

*I can.*

*Good. I am going to reach out for your wolf form, your magic. I am going to try to pull it from you, show it to you.*

Mila drew a long breath and released a longer exhale. Then she felt it, small and subtle at first, like a hair tickling her nose, only it was inside her, tugging at her magic from the deep recesses of her soul. It felt uncomfortable. Like Aiyan was taking her clothes off, bit by bit, exposing her body and then shaming her for her nakedness.

*He doesn't want to hurt me,* Mila told herself. But she wasn't sure it was true. She didn't know what Aiyan wanted from her. Flickers of memories rose inside her, stirred by Aiyan's touch. Being tied and gagged. A knife running down her arm. Pain. The smell of her blood.

Mila yelped. Her face was drenched with tears, her throat choked by them. It was not Serac before her, just Aiyan. Serac was dead. Serac was dead.

Aiyan too had tears on his cheeks. That surprised her more than anything.

"I am so sorry," he said in a whisper, slumping forward. "Your magic is wrapped up in dark things." Mila could sense that he didn't know how to break it free.

Mila rubbed her dripping nose on the back of her hand. "The past is done, Aiyan."

"Yes. But it leaves scars. And sometimes those scars bleed. Sometimes those scars are a cage."

A few more tears escaped and dripped down her nose.

"We can try again. But not now, not today," Aiyan said, rising, offering her his hand. She didn't take it. She couldn't touch a man, not with her past hemorrhaging inside her.

"I will leave you alone. Please stay in the garden as long as you need to. Here …" He plucked a white flower from the vine growing beside the door and rubbed it between two fingers. He placed the small, bruised blossom in her palm. "It will bring you some peace."

Aiyan left. Mila opened her hand to see the crushed flower. Its mangled petals gave off a delicate fragrance that filled Mila's head, helping her mind to calm. Mila looked at the flower and wondered why some things had to be broken before they could fulfill their purpose.

# AIYAN

As Aiyan made his way to the palace, his mind was filled with Mila's memories. Someone had tortured and raped her. And yet she was so strong. Her dicidium was so vibrant. How? But her magic was still caged, nearly impossible to reach. He needed to take her to the mountains.

At the top of a hill, Aiyan paused and gazed past the tallest buildings of Kara to the faint smudge in the distance that were the Heera Mountains. He yearned for the crunch of sticks and leaves beneath his feet. For the flickering, filtered sunlight through the leafy canopies. For the little creeks filled with crystal-clear water.

He couldn't let his thoughts linger on what once was or what could be. Dangerous, precious things had crawled into his thoughts of late.

He forced his mind to his task at hand. He needed to keep on his toes around Imal.

"I have decided to share something with you," Imal said to Aiyan as they convened, as they often did, in the latter part of the day. "Come with me."

Imal preceded Aiyan through a small door reserved for slaves that led to a maze of twisting, arched corridors leading down, and down. Aiyan categorized the path in his mind. The stale air smelled of dust and damp and fear. Something constricted Aiyan's heart—what if Imal knew the truth? What if he was being led to a long, slow demise under Imal's knife?

It took all his will to keep his feet moving. As he watched the broad back of Imal ahead, Aiyan realized the implications of being alone with Imal—they were never alone. Aiyan had inhuman speed. He could thrust a dagger into Imal's back in the space between one heartbeat and the next. But Imal was a sorcerer. Aiyan didn't know if speed would be enough. And if Aiyan failed, it was all for nothing. He would die slowly and painfully, and his body would be left to rot on the palace steps. Beric's rebellion would never see the light of day. Kara would suffer and die the same torturous death.

And could he do it? Could he really kill the man who had bought his freedom? Without Imal, Aiyan would be dead.

Imal led him around one final torch-lit corner. They had arrived at the end of the passage. Five *daeum* stood in front of a metal door—too many for him to take on in the small space. The moment was gone. Aiyan had lost his chance. Imal took a key from some inner pocket and unlocked the door.

They entered a large underground prison. Light danced off the roughly hewn walls from the ocean lapping at the foot of the single window. A form lay on the rock floor, limp, roughly man-shaped.

"This is my prize." Imal walked over to the man. Imal crouched and tipped back the man's head with a finger. The man was alive, but his gaze was tired, empty—a broken man. Imal's eyes danced. He looked as crazed as his sister. "Tell me what your *heera* eyes see."

Aiyan looked from Imal to the prisoner. The man's dicidium

screamed at him with so much potency, there was no need to shift his vision into the space between reality and energy and substance. The man's dicidium writhed with dark shapes, shifting into corporeal hands and faces, caressing the limp man like beggars picking over the dead, then back into tendrils of smoke. The dark vapor smelled like Imal's sorcerer magic, but it was stronger, virulent. A disease. Aiyan lurched from it.

With difficulty, he trained his eyes on Imal's. He had expected to find the *varing* pouring from Imal's "prize," but he had not expected the sheer immensity of it—the awareness in it—the force of its longing.

"I see the *varing*," Aiyan told his emperor.

Imal smiled a smile meant for kings and sadists. And Aiyan was no king.

Aiyan managed to nod and smile a little, trying to find some semblance of pleasure in his friend's acquisition, as Imal expected. But his insides screamed with dread. He flexed his restless fingers. Imal did not have a prize, he had a weapon that could destroy a city, a world. Imal had no idea what he was playing with.

But neither did Aiyan, not really. *Heera* legends spoke of dark things from a dark time, but Aiyan had not heard the histories of his people since he was a boy.

He forced his eyes to ignore the dicidium and took in the man's physical features instead. He could have been considered handsome once. Strong. A warrior? It would explain his dark dicidium, but not the copious volume of his dark magic.

"He came from Praedan." Imal crouched beside his captive with a strange, doting expression. "Rest, Prince of Kitarra," he said in Praedan, patting the man on the head. The man did not move, he looked asleep; drugged perhaps.

"A prince?" Aiyan asked when they were back in the cool marble halls of the palace. Aiyan thought putting distance between himself and Imal's prisoner would be a relief, but it wasn't. He could sense the *varing* following him like a stench. *Heera* magic had always attracted the other, more foul energies of the world. But Aiyan didn't think even the magic of the ancients could fight the filth that Imal had brought to Rodan. No wonder Cotoch had been jumpy.

"Yes. Sort of. A man of great influence, at any rate." Then Imal laughed, loud and full of self-assurance. "Not so much anymore though."

The poor soul would rot in that room. Aiyan hoped death would come quickly to the poor bastard. Maybe he deserved it—how else did one get such a thick black diciduim? Aiyan knew that after a particularly successful torture, Imal's halos were black and thick as lifeblood. But it didn't last. Imal needed to recharge, to harvest more *varing* to feed his sorcery. This man must have the *varing* hovering around him, ready and alive. Waiting.

"I need you to contest Valint," Imal said as they stepped into the world of light once more.

"Of course," Aiyan answered. Another knot tightened over the others in the pit of his stomach. "What did he do?"

"Valint was responsible for the well-being of my prisoner, but he came to me much bedraggled," Imal growled. "That is why I had to wait so long to show you. He was quite a mess."

Aiyan swallowed his disgust. "Only a fool would not abide your orders," Aiyan said, speaking the absolute truth.

Imal grunted in appreciation. "I don't like it when a *daeum* makes their own decisions. I sometimes wonder if the ascension slips, especially the further they are away from me," Imal mused, fingering the slight stubble on his face.

"You worry unnecessarily. Have the *daeum* in Praedan not done exactly as you asked?"

Imal clapped Aiyan on the shoulder. "You are right, Aiyan. I am overthinking it. However, I still need to make an example of Valint. And, anyway, it has been awhile since a contest was held. The people always enjoy it. The day after tomorrow, the rodaeri will gather at the Chalice."

Aiyan nodded. "Is that all, my lord?"

Imal waved his hand deliberately, dismissing Aiyan.

Away from Imal, Aiyan let his guard slip. He let his hands shake. He pinched his eyes shut. His legs quivered; he paused in a hidden corner of the palace to press his back against the cool stone, quenching his desire to run, to flee.

There were not many things his wolf feared, but it was afraid now. Something was watching him, reaching for him. He looked down the hall. Empty. Not even a slave. Yet Aiyan's *heera* senses were tingling; his wolf form lurked just beneath his skin, warning him of—something.

Aiyan scanned the empty corridor. He moved forward, rolling his shoulders to release the tension in his body, the screaming nerves that itched in warning.

A cool draft tickled his neck, and a growl rose involuntarily in his throat. He spun, and behind him was something from Gran's old stories. Dark as midnight, thick as mud, it hovered in the air between two doors, watching him from a featureless face. It moved like smoke, and as Aiyan stared, it swirled and dissolved into nothing.

A *vivus*. That was what Gran had called them.

The walls of the hallway seemed to sway, pressing against him. The sounds of the city roared in his ears. He heard a crying woman somewhere on the streets. Kara could not be saved … the people would die … Imal's prisoner, his prize, would destroy them all.

# CHAPTER 53

# MILA

"WHY DOES AIYAN HAVE TO FIGHT THIS MAN?" Mila asked for the third time.

"Like I said, it's a display of power. Think of Aiyan as a blade, and this is how Imal sharpens his edge," Tilley told her, taking Mila's arm in hers as they slowly walked down the cascading steps of the oval amphitheater known as the Chalice.

The Chalice was a sprawling affair; the circle of seats surrounded the arena like rings of a tree. The seats and aisles swarmed with rich rodaeri, the aristocrats of Kara. Mila marveled at the colors and textures of their silks, of their gowns and robes. Their slaves dressed in finery to match, carrying parasols and awnings for their masters to keep the hot Rodan sun from their delicate skins.

Everyone was moving, talking, laughing. Slave children poured wine, flitting around the crowd like little birds. One rodaeri complained that his wine was too warm and struck the child with the back of his hand with enough force that the young, scrawny slave fell into a heap. The crowd moved, blocking the scene from Mila's view.

She turned to the arena where dancing slaves wove an intricate display, though hardly anyone was watching. Petals fell from their hands onto the sand, making it look like a bed of wildflowers. Beauty and death. The city of Kara wove the two together like a tapestry.

Most of Kara's elite had come to witness the battle between Aiyan and Imal's captain. Mila could see the bets exchanged between men, slaves jotting down the transactions in well-worn notebooks. Mila supposed that was to avoid any arguments later.

Mila did not know what the captain had done to earn Imal's discourse; she had not asked, and Aiyan had not volunteered to tell her. Perhaps Aiyan was the one Imal meant to punish. The thought made Mila's hands tighten into fists.

"Here are our seats, Mila," Tilley said, steering Mila toward a large white awning.

"Ah, my lady Mila," came Beric's warm voice. Mila turned and curtsied. Beric was dressed in red and gold. The young, pretty man beside him was dressed in gold and red. "Sit with us, my dear. Get away from the pestering sun. Your pale Praedan skin cannot handle it."

Mila wanted to tell Beric she could handle it just fine, but his awning was not held up at the expense of a slave, it was built with its own supports of wood, so she didn't mind the shade. Though, no doubt, it had been slaves who made the structure.

"Thank you, Ro Beric," Mila said, sitting beside him on the slightly cooler bench.

"Are you worried? You look at the arena like it wants to eat you," Beric noted.

"I am. A little."

"Can it be that you are fond of the Wolf?" Beric said with one of his charming smiles. Mila did not meet his eyes. "No one expects Valint to win. Only the risk-takers will bet against Aiyan." Beric spoke as if it settled the matter. "Ah, there is Imal and his entourage. It will begin very soon."

Mila looked across the oval, open-air theater to where Imal stood under the pink shade of his awning. Allia, the pregnant princess, was with him, along with several pretty slaves and some men Mila guessed were his advisers, though Imal struck her as a man who lived only by his own counsel. *Daeum* guards flanked Imal, but they kept well back.

Imal's entrance signified to the assembled to find their seats, which they did with more speed than Mila would have expected of the tangled mass of people.

"That is Valint?" Mila asked as a man walked into the center of the arena. Beric nodded. Valint was *daeum,* of course. His thickly knotted muscles were blotched and marred by his scars—raised lines that circled his arms to his shoulders, up his neck, curving along his strong cheekbones. His matted hair was pinned upon his head. He wore a sword on his back and held another in his hand. He had knives in his belt and a shield tied to his other arm. The arsenal of iron didn't look like it weighed him down at all.

"He is huge."

Compared to him, Aiyan would look like a boy.

Beric patted her thigh companionably. "Don't fret."

"I am not fretting. I have seen Aiyan fight." Aiyan had taken down three *daeum* in the space of a few heartbeats. This was one man. One huge man.

Then the crowd erupted in cheers as Aiyan stepped into the arena.

"Beric? He is not going to fight him like that, is he?" Mila asked fiercely, looking at the small, lone wolf that was Aiyan.

"Don't you have faith in the man—err—wolf?"

Mila looked at Aiyan in his wolf form. Claws and teeth and speed were his only weapons. Not much compared to the arsenal of the madman before him.

They circled each other, Valint weighing his weapon in his hand, waiting for the attack, Aiyan, head low, shoulders tight, ready to spring. Aiyan was a blur as he darted in at Valint's heels, then away from Valint's slow counterattack. The crowd cheered. Valint tried not to let Aiyan circle around to his back, but in the wide-open arena, it was impossible. Aiyan went for Valint's leg again and dragged him down. Aiyan lunged away, then pounced, bit, and lunged away again. Bright points of blood showed on the *daeum*'s skin. A wounded beast was still a beast, and Valint was no prey animal ready to give itself to death. And Aiyan couldn't keep up the rapid pace, could he?

The crowd hissed, in surprise or displeasure, Mila couldn't tell. Valint had struck Aiyan. Aiyan went low, his ears plastered against his skull, teeth bared. Tilley grabbed Mila's hand and held it tight.

Mila looked at Beric for reassurance, but his focus was on the fight, his expression hard. Not at all reassuring.

As the fight wore on, becoming more of a battle between wild things bent on survival, it was harder and harder to watch. Each bite Aiyan landed was brutal but not fatal. One wolf against a tall, thickly muscled man wielding two very solid weapons. It was madness. If Aiyan could fight armed with daggers or a sword, there would be no contest. But as a wolf, it dragged on and on.

Valint left a streak of blood on the sand as he dragged one foot, his leg bleeding at the knee. He was faltering, finally. It was with morbid relief that Aiyan circled and leaped on Valint's back and pushed him into the dirt. Aiyan's teeth sunk into Valint's neck and shook him hard. The man lay limp. Finished.

Mila, filled with disgust, wanted to look away but found it impossible. Aiyan stalked off the arena, tail limp, head low, fur dingy and mussed. The crowd erupted into a thunderous cacophony of cheers and shouts—praise for Imal's wolf.

Mila looked to the emperor and noticed his almost-bored expression. It infuriated her.

A touch on her arm pulled Mila back to herself. Beric had his searching eyes all over her.

"Nothing to worry about, see?" he said, but his words fell flat and acrid like the hot sand scattered with blood.

"Where is Aiyan going?" Mila asked Tilley.

"He will be on his way home unless Imal requires his presence. I don't think he is too hurt." Something in her voice quivered. Tilley was worried about Aiyan. Mila knew that if something happened to Aiyan, his slaves would be sold. But she didn't think that was the reason Tilley worried for her master.

"I'm going to find Aiyan," Mila declared.

The crowd was thick. She reached for her magic, just a little. It would show her where Aiyan was. She followed it through the crowds into the city—Aiyan was on his way back to his house, alone. Mila picked up her feet to catch up to him.

Something caught her eye from an alleyway—not so much her eye, but rather her senses heightened by magic. She halted and turned.

"Aiyan?" she called out.

The alley was empty but for a pile of broken pottery. Then she saw it, a black vapor that poured from the air, from the seams of the buildings. It massed into a form that became more animal-like, more alive every second that passed until two long arms reached out for her, fingers blindly searching.

Mila turned and ran, from what, she had no idea. She could feel its menace, its yearning. She could sense it following her. The smell of iron filled her nose. Her mind became clouded, and anger and rage seethed through her fear. She wanted to hurt something—someone. For everything that had happened to her, Serac, Eva, Illiah, Rhyl—for Tarran and Murryn—she wanted someone to die, to bleed and break and become nothing.

"Mila, stop." A voice broke through her anger. "Fight it. Block it. It does not control you."

The chill of Aiyan's hand through the thin fabric of her gown cleared her mind. Instinctively, she put her hand over his.

With the contact of his skin came her magic, not a flood or cascade, but a gentle nudge. In her mind, she saw Valint's death from the eyes of a wolf. She saw the death of a man while he slept. She saw a man's body, mauled and beaten, dragged along the streets of Kara, and dumped at Imal's feet. She saw the forest speed by, tall trees encompassing the twisting path, full of green shadows. She saw a house in the trees surrounded by a garden of flowers with design around the door. She could smell pine needles and wood burning from a fireplace.

Aiyan removed his hand from under hers.

She opened her eyes. The menace—the black thing—was gone. Aiyan stood before her, naked, his tattoos stark against his skin. The design that curled up his torso to his neck and face reminded Mila of the design on the house.

Mila blinked.

"What happened?"

"Dark magic. You blocked it," he said with relief.

"I wanted to kill you." Her voice was as brittle as a skeleton leaf.

"I know." He lowered his arms. The lines and scratches on his skin were not from his fight with Valint.

"I did that to you?"

"Don't think about it. That thing was a *vivus*, materialized from dark magic. Something is changing in this city, growing." Fear laced his words.

Aiyan was Imal's blade in the dark and Imal's monster during the day. What did he have to fear? Aiyan was death disguised as a beautiful man. But Mila could not shake the image of that wolf, downcast and bedraggled, exiting the arena after the fight.

CHAPTER 54

# MILA

"DO YOU want to come out into the city with me?"

Mila looked up from her unmotivated work, a small piece of embroidery, to see Tilley standing with her notebook clasped in her hand. The list. Tilley's precious document that tracked the whereabouts of Kitarrans taken as slaves.

"Are we allowed?" Mila asked, thinking of the dark magic that had felt like her worst nightmares.

"Of course. Who would bother us? We belong to Ro Aiyan." Tilley rolled her eyes like this was so obvious, Mila should know better.

Mila put down her work and stood. She was aching to stretch her legs. She had always been a woman of industry and doing embroidery all day wasn't enough to keep her mind and body satiated. Both Wani and Day refused to let her help around the house.

"Where are we going?" Mila asked, wrapping her bare shoulders in a thin shawl to protect her skin from the hot sun.

"Across town. I heard a rumor I would like to corroborate."

"What are you looking for?" Mila asked as they stepped out of Aiyan's house into the busy street.

"I am looking for a Kitarran. There are rumors that one came on the same ship that brought you."

"I didn't see a Kitarran on our ship. But then I didn't see much at all. The ship was dark and crammed full of boxes and stalls of people. I could hear other prisoners, but I could not see them."

Tilley looked undeterred. "Aiyan told me the *daeum* have given up attacking Kitarra, that Kitarra has abandoned the Long Isles and the settlements along the ocean, retreating to the safety of the inland."

Mila didn't know what that implied. All she knew about Kitarra was from that fateful day when the Kitarrans stormed the Keep, stealing away a father and his child, only to murder them later. Unless Eva had been right and Illiah and Rhyl were still alive.

"Tilley. I know you are from the Isles, but did you ever hear anything about Lord Illiah and his son Rhyl, of Jullayah?"

To Mila's great surprise, Tilley grinned. "Yes, of course! Everyone knows of the wee prince and his father. Before I was taken, I couldn't go a week without hearing some news about what the princes have been up to."

"What do you mean?"

"Everyone in Kitarra despises the necessity of their kidnapping, but it was the queen's command, and everyone trusts Queen Arrah's judgment. And it's not as if Arrah could just go up to the king of Jullayah and say, 'Your nephew is going to bring peace and balance to the realms, how about you let us bring him to Kitarra?' And Lord Illiah and Prince Rhyl seem happy enough, from what I had heard ... before."

"Happy? Kidnapped? They are alive?"

Tilley blanched. "Of course, they are—Queen Arrah would protect the child of the prophecy with her life."

"Prophecy! Tilley, Illiah and Rhyl—dear little Rhyl—they are my friends. Dear, dear friends. Tell me everything, please." Tears made Mila's cheeks itch. Again.

Tilley told her about a prophecy, a child who would save Kitarra from the evils to come. She could not remember all the words, something about a "starlit child" born from "two thrones." Their Guardian Tayeh had proclaimed that Rhyl was the child they needed, and the only way to get him to Kitarra was to bring him there. Tilley assured Mila that even though she had never been to Kilev and seen them herself, her aunt had—before—and she knew the truth of it. But Tilley didn't know anything about Eva.

"What's wrong?" Tilley asked, her voice full of concern.

Mila wiped her nose on her hand, pushing tears from the corner of her eyes. She took a deep breath to calm the sobs inside her.

"You have given me a gift, Tilley, knowing Illiah and Rhyl are safe."

Tilley wrapped her furry arms around Mila.

"Damn it," Mila said as she wiped away more tears. But she was smiling. "Tilley, in the boat with me was my sister and brother—a girl with short red hair, the color of that awning over there. And my brother is an expert fighter. Have you heard anything that might be about them?"

Tilley's furry brows convened in the middle of her head as she thought hard, or maybe it was just pity leaking out of her expression.

"If your brother is a fighter, then there is a good chance Waffa would have bought him. That is where we are headed."

Hope rose in Mila's heart despite her mental dialogue about chance and luck.

The building Tilley brought her to was built like a fortress with crude square battlements along the roofline and tiny slits for windows. The door was thick, studded with metal. Tilley knocked three times. A hatch in the door opened. The face of a man—an ugly man—appeared. It was not his face that was so unpleasant as his sneer and the smell that accompanied him.

"What do you want this time, kitten?" he snarled in a voice thick with mucus. He spoke Praedan. Mila was continually surprised how many in Rodan could speak her language.

"I want to see Ro Waffa's lineup for tonight. Ro Aiyan is interested in placing a bet—if the fight is right," Tilley told the horrid little man.

The man grunted and shut the hatch. A moment later, the door swung open to admit them. Inside, everything was dim. And it stunk. Sweat and blood and urine—like how a battlefield might smell after the fight when despair and death settled in.

The man was round and squat and smelled worse than the hallway. His slave earring was so covered in grime, Mila couldn't discern what kind of stone it was. He had one blind eye, and a scar that told its history, but he looked Mila over with his good eye. She suppressed a cringe.

"Tilley, what is this place?" Mila hissed in the Kitarran's ear as they followed the man.

"Shhh."

"Here they are: Jago, Toren, Killous." The man pointed to the men lined up along the wall. The chains around their wrists and ankles clanged and chimed as the men shuffled a little to see their prospectors. They were big men, fierce, reminding Mila of the *daeum*. But they lacked the maniacal facial expressions, the telltale etched scars, and the dangerous, gleeful glint that lusted for death and blood. These men were broken. Resolute. One cradled a man-gled arm, the skin torn and bloody.

"These are all of them?"

"For tonight, yes," the man told Tilley.

"I heard Waffa has a Kitarran."

The man cleared his throat noisily, at length. It was disgusting.

"Who told you that?"

"Rumors," Tilley replied with an indifferent shrug, glancing at the men along the hall, her face blank. "Is it true?"

"These are the men. Take them or leave them," the man said with a wild gesture, huffing off back down the hall the way they came.

"You are hiding something," Tilley said with an air of disdain. "Ro Aiyan will hear about it." She penetrated the man with her serene Kitarran gaze. He flinched but did not tell her anything else.

They left as quickly as they could without looking like bolt-ing hares. Outside in the hot sun, with the warm stone buildings around them, Tilley sighed.

"I hate that place," she told Mila. "I hate Waffa, and I hate what he does."

"He hosts fights?"

"Yes. Takes bets, makes the contestants fight to the death. Usu-ally. He has a few champions that he keeps around for a while. Imal's contests at the Chalice are polite in comparison."

"There was a man in Jullayah who did that, only not with people—with dogs," Mila said, disgusted.

"Just as bad. Maybe worse because dogs are so trusting."

Mila wrapped her arm around Tilley's to comfort her, pulling her close.

"Maybe Aiyan will speak to him for us," Tilley stated. "No one will lie to the Wolf. We cannot give up hope, not ever, Mila. Then, we might as well give up our lives."

# CHAPTER 55

# AIYAN

AIYAN CAREFULLY MEASURED the bacara root he had spent the last hour meticulously grinding into a fine powder. It was essential he only disrupt the powder a small amount; its poison was potent. He had seen how the culla, the drug from Rodan, could take over the body of a regular person; could another drug do the same for the *daeum*? Was there something similar that could leach the magic from their bodies while leaving the flesh intact?

A knock came at his door. He growled, "Who is it?"

He could use his *heera* senses to find out, but his focus was on the poison before him.

"It's Tilley and me," came Mila's sweet voice. If it had been anyone else, Aiyan would have sent them away, but the truth was, his mind was too often focused on Mila.

"Come in," he said, putting the powder aside with utmost care.

Tilley and Mila entered with identical expressions that made Aiyan curious about what they had been up to. Cliff had informed him the two women had gone into the city, but he had not known where. After the *vivus* the night before, Mila being out in the city was an uncomfortable thought, but Aiyan was not willing to chain her down.

"Ro Aiyan."

Aiyan recognized Tilley's demeanor. It was preemptive to her asking for a favor.

"Mila and I went to Waffa's this morning—"

"Tilley, you really should not do that to yourself," Aiyan interrupted, horrified. "That man is scum."

Tilley waved an arm in dismissal, but it was a shallow gesture. Aiyan could see the grief behind her eyes. If the culture of Kara, germinated by Imal and his forefathers, was horrifying, the subculture was more so. And Waffa was the mold that grew between the dead spaces of the rotting city.

During the plunder of Kitarra, only a few mature Kitarran warriors had been captured alive by the *daeum*. Most had died protecting their people. Waffa had almost gone broke purchasing them for his fights. They had not lasted long. They refused to fight and were cut down by Waffa's less scrupulous fighters. But their deaths had still earned Waffa enough to make his money back and then some. His business glorifying death and violence had made him a rich man.

"I heard from Feros that Waffa had a Kitarran who came in the same shipment as Mila. I think he does, but his little imp would not tell me." There was something different about this Kitarran, something that made Tilley's mouth a serious line and her eyes glisten with feverish desperation.

"You want me to pay him a visit?"

"Yes!" Tilley pounced on his offer.

"What did Feros tell you about this Kitarran?" Aiyan asked.

"That he was young. And an outstanding fighter."

"And?" Aiyan could sense something else.

"The description of him sounded like someone I knew. A boy. I know the chances of it being the same boy I knew are slim to none … but …"

Aiyan was both horrified and delighted that Tilley was in a fuss over a boy. "I will try to find him, Tilley."

"Thank you, Ro Aiyan. I knew you would," Tilley said, looking at Mila pointedly. Mila cleared her throat, her hands in a tangle.

"I am worried there may be someone else at Waffa's—two others, actually," Mila said. "My kin. They are fighters too, you see, taken alongside me. Perhaps they were sold to Waffa along with the Kitarran."

Aiyan would not tell her that if it were true, they could already be dead. "What do they look like? What are their names?"

"My sister, Murryn, has short red hair and looks like me, but skinny like a boy."

Aiyan's eyes flitted to Mila's generous curves despite himself. Unfortunately, she noticed. And unfortunately, Aiyan felt his cheeks redden.

"She is only sixteen," Mila added. Aiyan could see the well of worry and pain in her eyes. Why hadn't she mentioned it earlier? He would have helped her.

"And the other?" he asked.

"My brother. Well, he is not my brother by blood. He is my sister's partner, lover. He is the same age as Murryn. He has longish, curling brown hair, skin a shade lighter than yours, eyes a bit darker. Oh, and he is from Rodan."

Aiyan blinked. "He is from Rodan?"

"Yes."

"How is that possible?"

"It's a long story."

"Sit, tell me." Aiyan's heart was pounding. Stupid hope. All these years, he had been chasing his ghosts, or they had been chasing him—he wasn't sure. Her description could fit a hundred young men.

"The *daeum* attacked Jullayah—I think it was seven, no, maybe eight years ago. Anyway, they attacked and were eventually defeated and killed. Tarran was a slave to the *daeum*, just a boy. My friend's husband took pity on him and adopted Tarran as his ward," Mila told him. Tarran was not the name Aiyan knew. "It was before when I was a whore, so of course, I didn't know Illiah then, and neither did my friend, the woman who would become his wife. The woman who saved me, Eva." Aiyan had noticed Mila sometimes prattled when nervous. Tilley's glance shot at Mila, her eyes full of recognition. Mila noticed and bit her lip.

Something nagged at Aiyan. Why did the name Illiah sound so familiar?

"Tarran served Illiah until—" Mila faltered, looking at Tilley. "This gets complicated."

"I have time," Aiyan assured her.

He was soon lost in the tale Mila told of her life in Praedan. How she lived in a place called the Keep, as the Head Stewardess—no wonder she chafed at being idle—a friend to the lord and lady, who were royalty. A fanciful tale about magic, prophecies, and the realm of Kitarra. The way Mila spoke of the lord and lady made it clear they were very dear to her.

Aiyan wondered if he had slipped into one of Gran's tales. He could almost hear her tinkling laughter in his head as she waited for him to sort out the meaning, the learning, for all tales, good or bad, sad or joyful, held some essence of learning.

"Tarran believed Illiah and Rhyl were alive and wanted to find them. We had to leave the Keep because I killed the king's cousin—"

Aiyan shook his head. "The man you killed was a"—he searched for the word in Praedan—"nobleman?"

"That story is for another time. We were on our way to Kitarra when the *daeum* captured our ship," Mila finished. She still looked sad. And it wasn't just that she was worried for her missing kin; Aiyan could sense there was something else. But she didn't say anymore.

"Will you look for them?" Mila asked.

Aiyan nodded. "I will look for a Praedan girl with red hair, and her young lover."

"Thank you, Aiyan," Mila said. Aiyan looked away, feeling a rush of something warm yet unsettling. He didn't like emotions. Emotions got in the way of his instincts. He didn't like how Mila made him feel, but why then did he let her close again and again? Why did her proximity feel like the first day of spring in the mountains? He had no answer for himself.

# CHAPTER 56

# AIYAN

WAFFA HAD BEEN A FRIEND of Aiyan's dead master. So, naturally, he didn't like Aiyan. If there came a day when Imal asked Aiyan to kill Waffa, Aiyan would do so gladly. Waffa was a bastard.

But Imal liked Waffa. And Waffa was not clever enough to be a threat or raise even Imal's paranoid suspicions. The fights hosted by Waffa in his fortress of a house were enjoyed well enough by the rodaeri. They enjoyed watching the carnage in the same way they enjoyed watching a wolf fight a man to the death. It was sickening.

"Ah, Ro Aiyan." Waffa greeted him like a friend. He could do no less, even if they despised each other. Appearances were worth something when you were speaking to Imal's assassin.

"I heard rumors that you have a Kitarran," Aiyan stated.

Waffa's eyes glinted bright and greedy. "I heard your little Kitarran wench was here snooping about this afternoon. You will just have to come tonight—find out for yourself."

That was the last thing Aiyan wanted to do, and Waffa knew it.

"Ten gold coins and you tell me now," Aiyan offered. It was no small pittance. He pulled out his pouch and put the ten heavy gold coins on his palm.

Waffa's greedy eyes grew. If there was one thing Waffa loved more than carnage, it was gold.

"Fine. You can have a quick look at the Kitarran." Waffa gestured for Aiyan to follow him. "But don't tell anyone what you see. I sent Padra away when he came snooping—though he didn't offer me anything quite as pretty as these coins." He bit down on the gold before pocketing them with a satisfied grunt.

The thickening of the air, and subsequently the stench, told Aiyan they were close to the contenders' quarters. Waffa didn't expect his fighters to last long, so what was the point of hygiene?

Waffa led Aiyan through a room with four men tied by chains to the wall. None of them matched Mila's description of her kin. They were all human.

"I heard of a young wench who is supposed to be a good fighter. Red hair, looks like a boy?"

Waffa was not a particularly clever creature. His blank expression was not feigned—the man could not create a facade to save his life. "Never heard of such a thing," he grunted at the same time he yanked his pants closer to his middle.

Waffa led him down another hallway, into another room with several more men tied in chains. Aiyan almost missed the Kitarran completely; he was lying in the corner, hunched, bound hand and foot. But he surveyed the room with dark eyes. Eyes of a warrior. Kitarrans were inordinately strong, their stamina legendary. It must have taken some wrangling to make this youth succumb to the chains.

Aiyan crouched beside the poor cur. The Kitarran glared at him. His gray eyes seethed with fury and outrage. *This one will fight, and fight hard,* Aiyan thought, his gut churning.

"I have a proposition for you," Aiyan said, turning his attention to Waffa, who looked like a bear holding a honeycomb. "You know my young Kitarran female—a good, chaste, pretty creature. This Kitarran looks young, healthy enough. Let me have him, and their first offspring is yours."

Waffa rubbed his fingers together thoughtfully. Most of the Kitarran children brought to Rodan had died, but not before being sold for exorbitant prices.

"Tempting. Very tempting. Your Kitarran is very pretty, for one of their kind. But how do you know she is a good breeder?"

"I don't. But the best deals always have an aspect of risk."

"The kit would be mine to raise as I see fit?"

"Of course," Aiyan assured the man. There would be no child; Kitarrans did not breed as prolifically as humans. There was something curious in the way their mating worked. Tilley had blushed too hard to explain it. Aiyan hadn't pressed her; he was not that cruel.

Waffa considered the offer, or pretended to. Then he shook his head. "I want him to fight. Tonight's fight will be something special. That Kitarran took out three of my guards just wrestling him from the boat to my house. I have been waiting too long to toss him into the arena. How about, if he doesn't die in the fight tonight, I will sell him to you for twenty gold pieces—and their firstborn."

"Done."

Waffa grinned. "But, I give no guarantee to his condition."

"Fine," Aiyan said, shaking the man's gritty hand. "I will wait for your message in the morning."

"You are not coming to the fight?"

"I have other engagements."

"Pity. It'll be a good one."

Aiyan crouched down at the Kitarran's level. The young man had been watching their exchange, but of course, he would not be able to understand Rodan.

*Don't die, Kitarran. Tilley would be very sad.*

The Kitarran blanched and jerked backward like he had been branded. "What did you say?" he hissed. "Where is Tilley?"

Aiyan was too dumbfounded to reply. How was it possible the Kitarran heard him? Could it be that Kitarrans had similar magic to *heera*? To Mila?

Waffa kicked the Kitarran in the gut, knocking the wind and any other questions out of him.

"Come, Ro Aiyan, let's prepare that paperwork." Waffa laughed like he had discovered the most amusing joke. Like Aiyan was the joke.

Aiyan gave the Kitarran a backward glance. The Kitarran coughed and gagged. He could barely move. He wasn't going to make it through a fight.

Aiyan needed a better plan.

Aiyan wished he had a little more time; then he could walk to Beric's house as a man, fully dressed. He needed to get to Beric's quickly, and Kara was a big city, which meant shifting into a wolf so he could run through the streets. It meant he would have to shift back into a man to speak to Beric. And that meant he would be naked.

"Ah, Aiyan, how nice to see you so soon," Beric said.

Aiyan shifted. He ignored how Beric looked at him. All of him.

"Beric, I need a favor."

A grin stretched across Beric's face. He took a moment to sit with relish on his cushioned chair before answering. "And I need someone dead, remember?"

Aiyan growled. "It's for Tilley."

As Aiyan had hoped, something softened in Beric's expression.

"There is a Kitarran boy at Waffa's, a friend of Tilley's from Kitarra. He is going to die in the fight tonight," Aiyan explained, hoping Beric's romantic heart would be swayed for the poor girl.

"Waffa is a son of a bitch," Beric hissed. "But what do you want me to do?"

"Ask Miyamoto's men to take Waffa's. Before the fight. Save the Kitarran."

"And you think I know how to contact them."

"I am betting that you do."

"I will consider your suggestion, but I can't make any promises," Beric said.

It was not lost on Aiyan that Beric was repeating his words back to him. And it was not lost on Aiyan that he couldn't say anything about it.

It was near midnight. A sliver moon hung low in the sky. Aiyan watched it, and it watched him. The night air was still and thick. Summer had arrived in Rodan, and with it came heavy, suffocating nights.

The moon offered no answers for him. Aiyan listened to the city beyond his house, but nothing sounded untoward. Nothing made his pulse race, nothing spoke of rebel attacks and *daeum* in the streets. Perhaps Beric did not care enough to act. Maybe Aiyan had read him wrong.

*Help me.*

The force of the cry ripped through Aiyan's head. It was not Mila. It felt different—masculine energy, a different kind of magic.

He let his *heera* eyes show him the world in shades of magic that were the dicidiums. He tried to pinpoint the owner of the plea, and found him, a small spark of light, like Tilley's dicidium, but it was surrounded by dark, writhing magic.

"Tilley! Mila! Cliff!" Aiyan shouted through his door, running down the stairs, hopping the last three entirely.

"Master?" Cliff appeared almost immediately.

Tilley's eyes were wide as she came up behind Cliff. Mila appeared at Aiyan's elbow, embroidery in hand. She had been working on the design—leaves, little animals. Her skill astounded Aiyan.

"Something is wrong. We need to get to Waffa's. Cliff, Tilley— follow with the wagon. Mila, will you come with me?"

Mila nodded. She didn't even question him. Mila was the sturdiest, most practical person he knew. And if the Kitarran were dead before they got to him, Tilley would need Mila's support.

Aiyan shifted into a wolf and led Mila out into the street. They ran. Fortunately, Waffa's wasn't too far from Aiyan's. And Mila was fast.

They approached Waffa's building, and everything was dark. The street lanterns were extinguished. Every light from every window on the street was black. But Aiyan and Mila could see in the dark. The heavy door was open, unguarded. Aiyan could smell something smoky and acrid.

A figure lurched out of the open door and fell into the street.

It was the Kitarran. He slumped, as if barely conscious. Aiyan shifted and held the Kitarran's face above the dirt. The Kitarran's thoughts flooded into Aiyan's mind:

Waffa never had the fight. Something had happened. The men started to scream and weep. Then the killing began. Prisoner against prisoner, guard against guard. The Kitarran had watched everyone inside devolve into madness. Someone had cut his bonds, but then they too, had gone mad, lashing out at him with the same blade they had used to free him. He could hardly move, but everyone was already dead. Then, in desperation, he had called for Aiyan.

"Tilley," the Kitarran said before falling, his eyes rolling back into his head.

"Fuck," Aiyan whispered. The Kitarran was all legs and elbows, tail, and blood. Aiyan shifted his vision and looked with his *heera* sight for the young man's dicidium. He could see the light pulse from his heart, the little bit of magic every Kitarran had. It was strong. He had a chance.

"There's Cliff! We need to get him into the wagon," Mila said.

Tilley hopped down from the wagon and ran to them, her hands over her mouth and her heart in her eyes.

"Cliff, help me," Aiyan said.

"Tilley, hold the lantern." Mila handed her the light. Tilley stifled a sob as she took it.

The ride back to Aiyan's house felt like an eternity. Aiyan spent the time categorizing his plants and potions so when they arrived, he knew which to apply first. Tilley sat with the Kitarran's head her in her lap, stroking his matted fur. Mila was quiet.

Between Day and Cliff, they carried the Kitarran inside on a slab of wood and brought him into one of the unused rooms. They placed him gently on a clean bed.

"Tilley, get hot water from Wani," Mila ordered before Aiyan could.

Mila crouched beside Aiyan, taking the Kitarran's head in her hands with such care and kindness it broke Aiyan's heart. "What can I do?" she asked.

"Talk to him. You have a very soothing voice," Aiyan told her.

"Thank you," Mila said.

"I need to fetch my herbs," Aiyan said, touching Mila's shoulder. She spoke to the Kitarran.

"Don't give up," she told him. "You are with friends." Her voice followed Aiyan upstairs.

He grabbed his herbs and his grinding stones and returned to the injured boy.

With Mila's help, they stripped the Kitarran of his remaining clothes. He was tall, all stretched out on the bed, feet nearly dangling off. The move had caused his wounds to open and bleed onto the clean floor.

Tilley came in with an armful of clean cloths. Wani was behind her with a basin of water and a kettle. Tilley made a sound— Aiyan did not know what it meant—but at least she did not drop the clean bandages.

"I am not good with wounds," Tilley said. Wani patted her shoulder. Mila took the clean linens from her. Wani didn't like blood either. Mila looked unconcerned and poured the water from the kettle into the basin. Aiyan took a cloth and pressed it to the worst of the boy's contusions. Mila did the same.

"Tilley, if you cannot help, I need you to wait outside," Mila said with a touch of exasperation. "Do you think you can help?"

Tilley's gray lips looked pale. She ran from the room, and Aiyan heard her retch.

"Poor girl," Mila said, wringing out a cloth, steam coming off her hands.

They worked in silence, Day and Wani bringing fresh water and taking away soiled clothes and rags. Eventually, the worse of the boy's injuries were clean. Aiyan felt Mila's eyes following the movements of his hands as he divided the different plants and crushed them in his mortar. He made a poultice and applied it to the wounds that were still bleeding. He put the crushed valisha leaves on the Kitarran's tongue.

"I did not know you were a healer," Mila stated.

"When you learn which plants kill, you also learn which plants bring life, which heal," he told her. "Before …" But he could not speak of the day when they came to his family's home and took everything he held dear.

"Oh," Mila said quietly. Aiyan wondered if she had seen his thoughts, but she didn't press him.

They bandaged the Kitarran's wounds. Mila put pressure where needed, lifting a damaged arm gently so Aiyan could circumference the bandage properly. They worked effortlessly together. Aiyan wondered if it was because Mila could sense his thoughts or if it was just her practical nature.

Wani brought in a few blankets. When they finished bandaging their patient, Mila tucked a blanket around the Kitarran like an oversized child.

"Will he live?" Mila asked finally.

"I think so. Kitarrans heal remarkably fast. If he hasn't died yet,

I think he will pull through," Aiyan said, standing and stretching. He was stiff and sore. Even after washing his hands periodically in the basin, his skin was itchy from the blood.

Tilley was back with more color in her face. "I do know him. His name is Aisha. He visited my family the summer before I was taken." Something in her voice made Aiyan think there was more to it than just a visit. But then what did Aiyan know about reading emotional youths? "His father is Lord Susor of Withe." Tilley said the title as if it was notable. Unfortunately, it was lost on the rest of them.

"He should live, Tilley," Aiyan told her. "But we will know in a few hours."

"Thank you, Aiyan. Thank you," Tilley said, wrapping her arms unexpectedly around Aiyan's neck. He froze under her embrace, but she released him to kneel beside Aisha. "His body is in rejuvenation. He won't wake up until he is mostly healed," she told them sagely.

# CHAPTER 57

# COTOCH

COTOCH WAS NEVER setting foot on a boat for as long as he lived. The return voyage from Rodan had been … tolerable. Enough said. He was never going back to Rodan, even if Imal threatened him with a long, painful death.

He should have sent Selene back to Rodan to try to beg her father for Illiah's life. Should have. It had been a mistake to leave a lovesick girl in charge of his precious hostages. Regrets were like farts, everyone had them; but no one wanted to acknowledge them.

What a fuckup.

"Tell me what happened." Cotoch leaned back in his chair, letting the cushions support his tired body as he basked in the feeling of being home.

His serving girl poured wine and smiled prettily, genuinely pleased to see him. *A slave would never smile in devotion,* he mused. Cotoch smiled back, knowing she would come to his bed later, not as a slave, just as a mistress, a woman looking for a good time. It was one small rush of pleasure in the nasty business before him.

He turned to Geral before him.

Geral straightened under Cotoch's attention. "Stone and another man, Irri, stole the children just after you left for Rodan."

"Who is this Irri? Where is he from?"

"He was from Jullayah."

"With no connection to Kitarra?"

"Not that we are aware."

"What happened?"

"They slipped away in the night—"

"The guards?"

"Killed."

"Stone did it?" The Kitarran had style.

"Yes."

Cotoch swallowed another wave of betrayal. By the Old Ones, he should have just killed the damned Kitarran the day he'd slunk back with his tail between his legs. Cotoch had believed the culla would secure him a second time. Well, Cotoch had been wrong. Cotoch hated being wrong. He hated facing his own failings. Who didn't? Damned Kitarran turncoat.

"But your men caught up with them in the Tarm?"

"Yes, Stone was heavily outnumbered."

"But still, all the men died."

"Yes."

"With no wounds."

Geral nodded reluctantly.

"And now the children—and Stone—are back in Kitarra."

"We believe so, yes."

Stone had stolen Cotoch's main store of culla from his study. It would last the turncoat a few months, but then what? Stone hadn't died the last time his body had gone through withdrawal. Would he survive a second time? Cotoch fervently hoped not.

"How are Mahlas's defenses?"

"Strong."

"Our stores?"

"We have enough to last a three-year siege, if it came to that."

"Very good." Cotoch idly fingered his amulet. "I plan to go to Allati, Geral. I want to leave you here as regent in my stead."

"My lord, such an honor. Thank you," Geral said, his hand over his heart.

Besides the failure with the princes and Stone, Cotoch had arrived home to find a message from Selene awaiting him that contained all the things Cotoch had hoped. Selene was doing well in Allati. Already, she had formed strong alliances with many of the favorite wives. She was invited to dine with the king and his closest family. She expected proposals of marriage any day. In case the message was intercepted, she didn't mention anything about using her *candarii* gifts. The Allati were fools, but still, if they knew Selene was *candarii*, they would kill her, and their plans would be in ruin.

Cotoch briefly daydreamed about storming Allati with his army, plundering, conquering the great city, establishing himself as emperor. The *varing* would flow and Cotoch would reap it, growing stronger and stronger until even Kitarra would fall beneath his strength.

But—and there was usually a but.

Something niggled in the back of his mind. A thought, a realization he could not yet bring into the light or rational thought. It was instinctual, like knowing he would drown if he stayed underwater. It whispered that if he did those things—if there was war and blood and widespread massacre, something worse would happen … Something would … he almost had it—awaken? The thought slipped through his mind and was gone.

No, his plans for Allati were better achieved slowly, with *candarii* stealth and cleverness. He was not like his cousin. He did not want to create another city like Kara. The Allati's religion was dying. As a people, they were ready for someone to come along and feed them the assurances they needed. They were sheep without a shepherd, ambling and careless, and their pastures were drying up—the wolves were coming.

Imal was wrong. It was so much simpler to build loyalty with sentiment rather than fear. For all the riches of Imal's palace, his fearsome *daeum*, and all his beautiful bed-slaves, Cotoch preferred the wink of a serving girl and the gratitude of a man who had worked to earn his place at Cotoch's side.

He wondered if there were any beautiful Allati princesses with fair hair and blue eyes.

"You are leaving." Crea had appeared from thin air.

"Fuck."

His sleeping chamber was too small for both Cotoch and a spirit woman with the wingspan the size of a fishing boat.

"I am going to Allati," he spat.

"Pity. You know I can't visit you there."

"I'm counting on it."

Crea clicked her tongue. "Are you going there to look for the Stormspear?"

"No." It was almost a lie. Cotoch had not forgotten about the Stormspear. But he still hadn't even begun to fathom how he was going to find all the pieces. Would Imal fulfill his promise to destroy Mahlas if Cotoch failed to get him the last eight pieces? Was he prepared to risk Imal's bluff? He fingered his amulet, feeling it pulse under his hand with the *varing* encapsulated within its essence. Once it had been a comfort; now it felt like a chain. But if he was king of Allati …

And if he really feared Imal, he would have handed over the amulet.

"Your mother would want you to find the Stormspear."

Cotoch swore. He had forgotten about the token Crea had given him. Now that he remembered, it was an itch he couldn't reach. Crea was a monster for stirring old emotions Cotoch had thought were long gone.

"Goodbye, Crea. Leave me alone, for good," Cotoch told her. Maybe this time, it would stick.

"Cotoch, if you don't help me, I will find another who will," Crea warned.

"Do your worst," Cotoch growled. He was tired of the spirit woman's wan threats. "I have work to do." He returned to his packing. He didn't see Crea leave, or hear a flush of feathers, but when he looked up, she was gone. He hoped it was for good.

Once his chests were packed, and his servants saw them to the wagons, he went below to the crypts for one last farewell.

He took a torch. He peered into the empty cell where he had kept Illiah. There were still dark stains on the floor from his blood. They looked black, and Cotoch shivered, remembering the magic on the boat that had come alive when he had taken his wrath out on Illiah. It had taken his father's shape, the shape of Cotoch's nightmares. When he had killed Sandra, the *varing* had fled, but with Illiah, it grew, breeding.

Heart pounding, he walked on, his hand on his amulet, calling his last prisoner to him. He placed the torch in the bracket so he could have both his hands free.

She was there, waiting, hunched and faded. She put out her wrists in submission to his knife. She didn't raise her head or look at him. She never did. The creature hummed, an inhuman whine. Cotoch could feel her fear in his bones before he even laid steel to the spirit's flesh—if its bark-like skin could be considered flesh.

The *varing* waited, close. The spirit's pain would make the magic flow. He could almost smell the magic and feel it in his body, thick and powerful. But … he couldn't do it. He couldn't bring the knife down. He lowered his hand. The spirit looked up. Her gaze flickered over the knife at his belt, his empty hands, before returning to the floor.

"What are you doing?" she asked.

Cotoch shook his head. He honestly didn't know.

"The *varing* is ready." She jutted her wrists out for him. She wanted him to hurt her. "Take it," she whispered, cringing, waiting.

"I don't want to," he said, feeling sick.

Her eyes bored into him, round, yellow and green and brown, swirling like a fire. It was not comfortable to be under her gaze. "Take it," she said again.

"No."

"Take it!" Her shriek echoed off the walls.

Cotoch took a faltering step back. The creature lunged at him. He took another step, tripped and fell to the stone floor, his leg twisting, his butt aching. The spirit was crying now, a high, birdlike noise. Cotoch stood and grabbed his torch, turning to escape the monster he had created.

## CHAPTER 58

# EVA

THE AIR SMELLED HOT AND BURNED. The shadows crawled as if alive, reaching out long, black hands toward Eva, eager to caress her mind, her soul. She had felt the hard stone beneath her head, and her back ached in a hundred different places.

A dream.

In the dream, Illiah's eyes had been her eyes. His hurts had been hers. But he was still alive, and that gave her courage.

Eva shivered. The night had turned cold. Where had summer gone?

Eva rose from her bed and tossed a robe around her. She slipped out into the courtyard, unheard, unseen. The moon was a waxing sliver; soon it would be the new moon, the darkest night of the month. But Eva knew her way across the familiar garden. The cendari tree's gray bark was bright in the night; shadows did not linger by it easily. The dry leaves rasped and crackled in the breeze.

Eva slipped out of her robe and stepped into the water of the pool. The splash echoed across the empty courtyard. The hot water tingled her cool skin. She relished the feeling of the water cascading around her, holding her in its embrace. Too long, she had forgone the hottest pools knowing the heat was unhealthy for her unborn babes.

She swam to where the roots of the cendari tree dipped and twisted into the water. She settled there, amongst the tangle, and closed her eyes. She had to find Illiah. If she could see him in her dreams, she should be able to find him with the simul rami, even without Attin to guide her.

The first time, Attin had led her across the sea to Illiah. The second time was easier. The distance sped by, miles and days, in a heartbeat. She followed the same path Attin had shown her.

Illiah's prison was a tall chamber of rough-hewn rock and arching columns. A single window latticed with heavy, pitted metal bars looked out on the lapping waves of a high tide. The ocean. The corners of the room felt thick with shadows.

Illiah lay on the smooth rock floor. This time, his injuries were more numerous and more profound; raw cuts crisscrossed old scars. Someone was torturing him, over and over.

Eva strained, pulling the threads of the *simul rami* tight so she could reach him. A dark, rotten knot was tied around the source of his pain and anguish. It hurt to touch him. She poured everything she could into him, desperate to heal him, to bring him relief from the pain of his butchered body.

"Let me die." Illiah's words were weak and desolate.

The *varing* pushed Eva away from Illiah and his prison, away from the sea and the dusty land, back into her body. Her chest heaved. She couldn't breathe. She was caught in a box of dark magic, her mind held captive by it. She couldn't open her eyes. It was surrounding her, holding her. But this time, it wasn't Cotoch assaulting her.

Illiah was drowning her with *candarii* magic.

A cold blast of air hit her face. Unyielding stone pressed into her body. She was shivering, wet, lying on the ground. The cendari tree's branches were invisible against the night sky, but Eva heard the rustling of the leaves. The same breeze caressed her wet body with winter's touch. A form loomed over her.

"Eva." Stone's voice was grating.

Eva tried to reply, but she could only cough. Her nose hurt. Her lungs hurt. She had been drowning, not in the *varing*, but in the pool. Stone had pulled her out of the water.

"You would be dead if I hadn't followed you."

Eva had never heard so much anger in her amourii's voice.

She lay on the rocks, weak from coughing, and looked up at the tree. Armeria shoved her nose into Eva's face.

Stone sighed and wrapped her in her robe.

"They are torturing him," Eva rasped. "They torture him and then tend his wounds. They will not kill him. He wants to die."

The grim set of Stone's mouth was easy to see with his light fur. Light like cendari bark, Eva thought absently.

"That is both a blessing—he is still alive—and a terrible curse," Stone said eventually, just outside the door to Eva's chambers.

"I need to see the babies," Eva said, overcome with a sudden need to see her children, to see them well and alive. Stone nodded, looking uneasy.

A new room had been made for the twins, adjoining Eva's chambers. A nursemaid slept there, alongside the babes, to feed them if they woke at night. Eva's milk had dried up. Her inability to feed her children was just one more grief atop the teetering pile. She looked at the sleeping twins and felt—nothing. The babes were darling, she knew that, with their dark hair and dark eyes, their round faces and snub noses. They took after their father. She knew somewhere was joy, pride, warmth. But all she could find was an echo. Her emotions had been robbed from her, and she did not know which thief, which villain, to hunt down to retrieve them.

"I am so lost, Stone," Eva said. She could feel his presence in the doorway. She spoke softly, careful not to wake the children or the poor nurse. But Stone was a Kitarran, and he had excellent hearing. "I can't help Illiah. I don't know how to help Rhyl … his magic … those men he killed. By the Spirits, he is just a child … Rhyl. My poor boy."

"You need to be lost to be found," Stone muttered.

Aralis squirmed in his swaddling, one of his arms escaping. He stilled when it impacted his sleeping brother. Eva silently backed out of the room.

"Wine?" Stone asked, holding a bottle in one hand, two glasses in the other. Eva nodded, even if she wasn't sure it was a good idea. "Prince Arrain's favorite—blackberry."

A smile stretched her lips briefly. It was good wine, but it hit her stomach hard, and there was an odd aftertaste she didn't fancy. Suddenly everything spun, her head felt heavy, and her eyes closed.

"You … put … something … in … the wine," she stumbled out.

"You need to sleep. Now you will. Good night, Eva."

CHAPTER 59

# ILLIAH

EVERY TIME ILLIAH HEARD FOOTSTEPS, his body convulsed. The whisper of Imal's blade taken from its sheath made sweat break across his body. His gut was ice. The world was gray. The shadows grew and became living things around him. They started to whisper to him.

In the dark of the night, when there was no light but the moon shining off the waves, he yearned for Eva. For his life. For his children.

But pain was a cruel enforcer. And what it wanted was his hope, his light.

Imal would come, and Illiah eyed his knife and wanted it. He wanted the pain to take him. He wanted Imal to take him away from his misery. But Imal wanted his pain, not his life.

"Kill me," Illiah hissed.

Imal laughed. "And what good would you be to me then?" He leaned over and patted Illiah's cheek. "You make me strong. You are a gift. If you were a woman, I would fuck you and take your *varing* that way. But you don't inspire me like that. This"—he held up the bloody knife—"this works better. I can fuck a woman later."

After, in the quiet dark, Illiah lay on the stone floor, his body burning from the wounds. His mind was numb. He struggled to not think of his future. What future? How long would his heart last when his body was wrecked and broken over and over?

Then he felt a hum, a tingle, a touch of magic. Illiah recognized it, and it made his heart lurch with longing … and despair.

"No, Eva. No. Don't," he whispered into the darkness. But Eva's magic knotted around his broken flesh as she healed his wounds, lending him strength, life. Perhaps she didn't hear him. Perhaps she didn't care.

"Let me die," he begged.

But Illiah knew his wife. She would not let him die. She would not give him up. But her love for him would only prolong his suffering, his nightmare—how could she not see that? She was a fool—a cruel fool. Illiah was as good as dead to her. Why keep him alive when he would never see her again? Never see his son and Talo? Never see his babes or know their names?

"Let me die," Illiah repeated, putting intent into his thoughts. He pushed her away with all the strength he could muster.

The shadows hummed. The room was not dark. Not really. Light flickered from the grate, reflecting off the vibrant blue ocean water. Illiah had long given up the idea that the blue water and flickering sunlight were comforting. The glimpse of freedom was cruel, just another form of torture. There was no escape from his prison. There was no hope.

The acceptance came with relief.

The walls were damp from the mists that rose in the night. The stone was cold. But where there was light, there was shadow. And the shadows of Illiah's prison moved. They were alive. They were ghosts. Not his ghosts, but he recognized them. They were there through every fight, every battle, every drop of blood spilled at his command. When he smelled blood upon his hands and reveled in it, they were there.

Hate coursed through him. The shadows flickered with it, echoing it. He hated the sun, the glittering water, the blue. He hated Imal and his knife. He hated Eva most of all for keeping him alive, for letting him become a man who had nothing left but his hate.

"Kill me," Illiah whispered to the shadows. Then louder, he said, "I told you to kill me."

Then the shadows were gone, and in their place was a man. The shadow man stood against the stone wall, farthest from the prison door. No, not quite a man. The shape was a bit wrong, the skin twisting and knotted, like roots, but maybe it was just the dark, and the pain, that distorted Illiah's reality. The shadows were too dense for him to make out a face or eyes, but Illiah could feel its awareness focused on him like an archer's arrow.

The shadow man moved, coming close to Illiah without apparent footsteps. The pale light from the grated window pushed the shadow back, bit by bit, turning twisted roots into skin, shadow into a face, transforming the monster into a man.

Illiah gasped, feeling something akin to despair. The man was him. Is this what death looks like? A mirror?

The shadow version of Illiah walked out of the dark and crouched beside him, his eyes dark pools of starless night. He cocked his head in a way that was more reptilian than human, his face inches from Illiah's. The face changed from human, from a mirror, to something else. Black, rotten roots twisted where nose and eyes had been. The stench of rotten earth and iron filled Illiah's nose, making his throat burn, but he couldn't move, not even to release the tightness in his chest.

The writhing wormlike roots formed into a human mouth, curved in a predator's smile. With two long dark, twisting fingers, it opened Illiah's chest, and Illiah felt it climb inside him, pushing him, shoving him into a space of darkness.

Death had come for Illiah at last.

CHAPTER 60

# AIYAN

IMAL STRUCK HIM, hard. Aiyan fell to the floor, tasting blood in his mouth. Aiyan's wolf instincts snarled and twisted in response, yearning to attack, to defend. Aiyan ordered his inner wolf to stand down, but the chain was tight.

Imal grabbed Aiyan by the hair, pushing his face into the floor, his knee on Aiyan's back. Aiyan's heart raced. Sweat beaded on his forehead. For a moment, it was not Imal on top of him, but Nyamish. No. Nyamish was dead. Aiyan had killed him. Killing his master was a capital offense, but instead of execution, Imal had raised Aiyan from a slave and gave him his master's estate. Aiyan owed Imal everything. Aiyan's life was Imal's to use as he saw fit.

But, no, that was Aiyan's abuse muttering in his mind. He was *heera*. He was not a slave. He owed Imal nothing.

"What did I do, Emperor?" Aiyan asked as Imal released him.

"Waffa is dead. The place is destroyed. I need you to find out who is responsible. Kill them. Bring me their bodies to place on my wall. Better yet, bring them to me alive and I will nail them to my wall myself and let the birds do the rest."

Aiyan nodded, pretending he had not just received a beating.

"Good. Go. Or do you need an incentive?"

"Of course not, Emperor. Your word is my command." Aiyan had not considered Imal's rage when he had asked Beric to intervene on the Kitarran's behalf. But then he hadn't expected everyone at Waffa's to die.

Imal did not smile. His hawk eyes glinted. Aiyan was dismissed.

In the hall, he brushed down his clothes and rubbed the blood from the corner of his mouth. He readjusted his long hair, smoothing it into a braid, his fingers shaking.

"Beric."

"Aiyan."

Aiyan faced Beric over a table littered with empty bottles and plates. No slave had come to clear the dirty dishes. No slave stood at the door, ready to do his master's bidding. No ears to hear, no tongues to repeat. It was just Aiyan and Beric.

"What happened at Waffa's?" Aiyan asked. "Imal wants the men responsible. And he wants them alive." He sat down in a chair opposite Beric and leaned back. The chair gave a slight squeak in protest, making Aiyan's heart jump. Beric noticed and smirked.

"And? You should have expected this," Beric pointed out.

"I didn't expect it to be a massacre."

"That was not the plan. I don't know what happened, Aiyan." Beric rubbed his face with his hand. "They are all dead."

"I am sorry." Aiyan closed his eyes. "When I got there, only the Kitarran was alive, and just barely. It was like ..."

"Like what?" Beric's asked tiredly.

"Like their minds were poisoned by dark magic."

Beric was silent a moment. "Is that possible?"

"Yes. No. Maybe." Aiyan stared up at the ceiling. "I don't know what to do," he admitted.

"You are losing your edge, Wolf," Beric said, taking a sip from a dirty glass. "Maybe it's that woman of yours—love does silly things to us all."

"Love?" Aiyan said before thinking better of it.

Beric merely raised his brows, his frown tired and heavy.

"If you don't kill Imal soon, the rodaeri I have recruited will get cold feet. I need them when I take control of the city. The longer we wait, the more time for Imal's suspicions to breed, and if he orders you to kill them, what then? If you disobey Imal, or the men go missing instead of dumped at his feet, Imal will suspect you. And then everything will go to shit. Shit, Aiyan."

Beric was a little bit drunk. Aiyan hadn't noticed at first. Maybe he was losing his edge. Maybe it was already turning to shit.

"Are you afraid?" Beric asked.

"I am not afraid to die," Aiyan said without hesitation. "I am no coward. But Imal has grown strong. He has found a way to tap into the very essence of dark magic. I think if I kill him, we will unleash it, and it will destroy all of Rodan. The destruction at Waffa's will be just the beginning."

"You think? Or you know? Two very different things."

Aiyan shook his head. "Imal has a prisoner from Praedan. No ordinary man. This man has a power I have not seen before, and Imal is feeding off it."

Beric twirled the stem of his wine glass between two delicate fingers. "Then we kill this man. A sorcerer is crippled if the source of his magic is dead."

"I can't get to him."

"There must be a way."

"I will consider it."

"So, you kill this man, and then kill Imal, and then … what of the *daeum*?"

"I will have to poison them. I see no other option." It felt like a betrayal. What would Aiyan's father say?

"Will that work?"

"In a perfect world, maybe."

"No sense going for less than perfection. That would be a waste of time."

"I just wish I knew more about the *heera* legends. I feel like there is a connection between them and this man," Aiyan said, catching Beric's eyes. A silence fell between them, an acknowledgment that they had moved from enemies to something softer. Friends, maybe.

"You are not the last," Beric said thoughtfully.

"Allia doesn't count. She was born into captivity. She knows nothing about what it is to be *heera*."

"I wasn't talking about Allia, the lovely girl." Beric set his wine glass down on the table. "Brental!" He hollered for his slave. Young Brental poked his head in the door. "Bring him," Beric commanded.

If Beric thought he had another *heera*, he was likely mistaken. Aiyan knew all the secrets of Kara; if there were a *heera* hiding, he would have known about it. He was the last.

But still, doubt settled over him, gnawing at his vitals. His hope, so long extinguished, rose like a deluge. Not long ago, Aiyan would have considered himself in control of his emotions, master of his countenance, but something had changed. His acquaintance with Mila, perhaps. He would not say love.

The door opened and in came Brental followed by another young man. This man had curling brown hair and amber eyes that raged hot enough to melt stone. His hands were bound.

Aiyan could not breathe. The tight threads in his chest held him captive. The young man saw him and mimicked his statuesque stance. Beric, on the other hand, was smiling wickedly.

"See, dear Aiyan?" Beric purred.

"Ben." Aiyan's tongue stumbled over the name. His brother was a man grown, but Aiyan could still see the child he had been behind his features.

"Brother." Ben's voice was sharp. How could he blame his brother, his little brother, for hating him? Ben raked Aiyan over with his eyes, lastly lingering on his ear, his naked ear. "You are no longer a slave."

"I was freed when my master died," Aiyan said, knowing how insufficient it sounded.

"Fortunate," Ben drawled.

A ruckus came from down the hall—shouts, shrieks, curses followed by a soft thud that might have been a sack tossed about, or a body. Aiyan knew the sounds of a melee. A small person forced his way into the room like a tempest; his flame-red hair might have actually been on fire for all the ferocity in the stance.

"Murryn!" Ben shouted, aghast.

Murryn? Had Aiyan heard correct?

"They didn't tell me where they were taking you. I needed to make sure you were all right." It was not a boy, but a young woman. Her flaming-red hair was cut like a boy's, but she had a pretty face.

A very pretty, familiar face. She could be Mila's sister. Damn, she *was* Mila's sister.

A contingent of Beric's guards poured into the room, making it feel small. The girl put up her fists expertly and stuck out her feet and her chin, ready to take them all. Ben put a hand on her shoulder. Beric watched them like they were the best entertainment he had seen in years. He held up a hand to stop his guards, who looked tussled and angry. Beaten by a wisp of a girl could do that to a man.

"Murryn, do you have a sister?" Aiyan spoke Praedan.

The young woman turned to Aiyan, giving him a look that made him feel as important as a beetle under her boot. But she nodded.

"Her name is Mila?" Aiyan continued.

The girl nodded, her arms dropping to her sides, and her entire body softened. She looked like she might cry.

"You know her? Is she all right?" Murryn squeaked. Ben also appeared anxious about what Aiyan had to say. Aiyan suddenly had so many questions for his brother.

"I do. She is well—under my care." It was the wrong thing to say. Ben's face darkened. Murryn put her hands over her mouth to keep her tears in check. Ben looped his bound hands over Murryn, pulling her to him, but still glaring at Aiyan.

"Have you had him all this time?" Aiyan demanded, turning to Beric.

Beric took an unapologetic sip of his wine. "Yes."

"Knowing he was my brother?" Aiyan spoke in Praedan so Murryn could understand.

"Yes," Beric admitted.

"So you could bring him out as leverage." Aiyan paced. He needed to chase something. A good chase always calmed him.

"Again, yes."

"You don't trust me," Aiyan stated. The truth in Beric's eyes sunk into Aiyan's skin like thorns.

Beric took a moment to reply. Clever man.

"I want to trust you, Aiyan."

"You can trust me, Beric," Aiyan said.

"When a man begs you to trust him, chances are you can't," Murryn chimed in.

Aiyan felt a growl in his throat and stifled it. "You have no choice but to trust me," Aiyan said, giving each of them a look in turn.

"I know. That is why I am turning Tarran and Murryn over to your care instead of keeping them as leverage. Tarran is a smart lad, maybe he can help you," Beric said.

"Help with what?" Ben—Tarran—asked.

"Killing Imal," Beric crooned.

# CHAPTER 61

# MILA

MILA COULD NOT BANISH the image of Aiyan up to his elbows in blood as he worked desperately to save the Kitarran. How was it that the Wolf, under all his masks of violence and terror, had the heart of a healer? He worked to save the Kitarran—a stranger, a slave—with his heart on his sleeve.

Fate was cruel to force him into the life of an assassin—a murderer. What kind of life would he have lived if he had not been taken as a slave? What kind of man would he have grown to be? It hurt to think of Aiyan as something more, so much more, than the Wolf. She thought of his rare smile. She imagined how happiness might transform him. She hoped, someday, she might see it.

Working with her hands helped soothe her ragged thoughts. Mila looked down at the piece of embroidery she had just finished, a little sun shawl filled with butterflies, to match the dress Mila had already made for Letti during Mila's short time at the brothel. Little Letti would adore it. Mila hadn't seen the girl since escaping the brothel, but she had thought about Letti every time she passed a little girl on the street.

She wrapped up the finished garment in a bundle of scrap fabric and tied it with a ribbon.

"Day, I am going to drop something off at Nulla's brothel. I won't be gone long," she told the house slave. Day looked up from his ledger and nodded.

Mila didn't want to see Nulla, or even Dart. But maybe Cresa was around. Or the old cook, Lis, who had shown Mila kindness. But mostly, she just wanted to see Letti, to remind the little girl that someone cared.

The low afternoon sun was hot on her neck as she walked. The breeze gusting through the streets pulled at her dress, blowing sand around her feet. She ignored the merchants calling for her to test their wares, trying to entice her into a purchase. She couldn't ignore how their expressions changed when they saw her slave earring. She belonged to the Wolf, which meant no one could touch her. And no one wanted to.

Mila knocked on the back door of the brothel. Usually, it was locked, but the door moved under the force of her hand. Mila pushed it open further. The kitchen was dark. There was no fire in the grate—no food cooking. The room was empty. Then Mila smelled it. Ashy and sour. Iron and heat. Blood and fear.

She almost tripped over the cook. Old Lis lay on the floor, her eyes pinched in death, staring up at nothing. Poor Lis. Perhaps her heart had given out.

"Nulla? Dart?" Mila called, hoping someone would answer. Silence and mystery replied.

Mila pushed through the kitchen, down the hall, into the common room. Bodies lay strewn across the room. Smears of blood marred the furniture. Limbs dangled. Mouths hung open. A cold breeze touched her neck. She turned, her magic rising. Mila blinked, and the room became alive with dark, writhing shapes.

Mila almost choked on the dark magic that was only visible with the help of her magic. She had blocked the magic before, with Aiyan's help. She had done it then, she could do it now. She could see and smell the dark magic, but it did not consume her.

"Letti!" she called out. "Letti!" Some instinct within her urged her to change. But nothing happened. She could feel her magic. She did not shift, but what magic she had was enough to protect her. "Letti!"

Mila heard a voice. She rushed toward it. Cresa lay in a crumpled pile on the stairs, her pale hair splayed and dotted with blood, her eyes sightless. Mila bent down and reached to find a heartbeat. There was none. Cresa was dead. Beautiful, cheery Cresa.

Mila heard the voice again, calling. She bounded up the remaining stairs, following the sound

"My baby, my baby." The voice solidified as Mila neared. Nulla sat hunched in the hallway, rocking on her heels, her arms painted red up to her elbows. Not paint—blood. A dagger lay on the floor beside her. "They took my baby. They took her. They took her. They took her. My baby. My baby."

Mila crouched next to Nulla, but Nulla did not see her. She saw only her nightmares.

"Nulla," Mila whispered, gently touching Nulla's shoulder.

Nulla screamed and lashed out at Mila, catching her around the ankle. Mila kicked her, hard, shoving her off. Then she ran. She ran through the house. Nulla chased her, limping, her dagger in her hand like she wanted to flay Mila's skin. Mila was fast, but so was Nulla. Too fast. Mila ran into the street. And ran. And ran.

In her mind, she called out for Aiyan.

CHAPTER 62

# AIYAN

"HOW IS IT POSSIBLE THAT MILA IS HERE?" Murryn stated, her eyes bright as she inspected the door of Aiyan's house, as if her beloved sister was about to materialize from the wood.

Aiyan didn't have a proper answer for her. Sure, he had told her somewhat awkwardly how he bought Mila from a brothel. He left out details about the daeum and Allia's involvement. He didn't want to go into the epic story in the middle of the street. But Murryn didn't mean that; she meant what were the chances of Tarran having a brother, and that brother rescuing her sister?

It sounded like a fucking miracle. But Aiyan didn't believe in fucking miracles.

Ben—Tarran—was quiet. Aiyan didn't know what to say to him. He wished with every sinew of his heart that he knew the right words to bridge the silence and years between them. He didn't have them. Perhaps the words didn't exist. His little brother had always been the one gifted with words.

Aiyan opened the door, and Murryn hopped inside like an eager puppy.

"This house is different than I remember," Tarran said as they walked into the cool entry hall.

"I had most of the house changed," Aiyan said. Because if he was going to live there, it couldn't remind Aiyan of his former master. Still, Aiyan could not walk into his master's old room without seeing blood smeared on the floor. Aiyan's blood.

"Mila?" Murryn called. But no Mila appeared. Instead, Tilley greeted them from the top of the grand staircase.

"She is out," Tilley said. Murryn's lip quivered. Tarran put his arm around her, whispering something in her ear.

"Tilley, this is Tarran and Murryn," Aiyan explained. "Murryn is—"

"Mila's sister! You look just like her," Tilley exclaimed. She grinned and flitted down the steps, her tail bouncing. "Welcome! I'm Tilley," Tilley said at her bubbliest, ready to throw her arms around the newcomers—but she stopped herself. Murryn was polite, but Tarran looked like he had seen a ghost.

"And Tarran … is my brother." Aiyan forced out the words. Tilley deserved to know. They all did. There was no point keeping it a secret.

Tilley's eyes widened, but she said nothing. Without remarking on the hostile silence emanating from Tarran, she offered to see Tarran and Murryn to their rooms and to show them the house.

"Room," Tarran corrected her. "Murryn and I share a room."

"Right. Of course." And if Tilley had been a human girl, her cheeks would have blossomed. Aiyan felt a keen disappointment that Mila was not here to see it; she was endlessly teasing the poor girl.

Tarran turned to Aiyan. "You let Mila go off alone into the city?"

"No one will hurt her. She is marked as Aiyan's slave," Tilley said. Aiyan wished she hadn't. Murryn blanched.

"It seems not much has changed," Tarran remarked. "You still see people as property."

Tilley glowered at Tarran, then at Aiyan, as if daring him to reprimand him. Aiyan shook his head for her to stand down.

"Tilley, I will show them to their room, then I will come check on your Kitarran," Aiyan said in Rodan. Tilley nodded and rushed off up the stairs, no doubt back to the bedside of the Kitarran boy. That made Aiyan smile.

He led Tarran and Murryn upstairs.

"This room is yours. Mila's is just down the hall, there. I will fetch you slave earrings. But don't antagonize my people," Aiyan warned. "Tilley doesn't deserve your anger. And she is right—if you wear my colors, you are safe anywhere in the city."

"Why is that?" Murryn asked, clearly appalled by the idea of being marked as property.

"Because no one touches my things," Aiyan told her.

"How is he?" Aiyan asked from the doorway. Tilley readjusted the blanket around the sick Kitarran, her long fingers careful not to disturb his wounds or bruises.

"Better. He is still in rejuvenation. He should wake later. Right now, his body is healing, see?" Tilley pointed to Aisha's arm, where the wounds were visibly better. Aiyan walked over to inspect them, and to place his fingers on the Kitarran's heartbeat. It was slow but steady.

"Remarkable."

"Yes," Tilley said proudly. "So. You have a brother."

Aiyan sighed. "I do. I thought he was—gone forever. I sent him away to Praedan when he was younger than you. He hates me for it."

"I am sure you had your reasons."

Oh, sweet Tilley and her kind heart. "It doesn't matter."

"And your brother just happens to be Mila's sister's lover? Basically, her kin? That means that they knew Lord Illiah and Prince Rhyl as well. No wonder he looks at me like he wants to eat me. Actually makes me see the resemblance between you two. But I just can't believe you have a brother. I can't."

Aiyan left Tilley to her disbelief and went to find Day to inform him about their new acquisitions, and the need for slave earrings. Day sighed but had nothing to say about the sudden appearance of Aiyan's long-lost kin; all he uttered were complaints that Wani would send him to the market for extra food. Aiyan rolled his eyes.

He went to his study to work but found himself sitting restlessly instead. He had dreamed of Gran's house the night before, a vivid dream filled with impossible promises. He had walked through the ornately painted door into the kitchen, which always smelled of Gran's baking, even in his dream. He moved through the house, to the little room at the back where he and Tarran had often stayed. Gran had painted it full of ferns and flowers, but Aiyan could not remember the pattern; the memory of it had slipped away, never to be regained. Gran was waiting in that little room. Like the painted wall, her face blurred in his mind, leaving only her voice. "It's time to leave this place, my little wolf."

Then he woke up.

He would never see the house again. Gran was dead. The house had been burned.

Aiyan thought of his brother with a new name and a new life and a beautiful, fierce woman he loved. But Ben—Tarran—had been dragged back to Rodan. Back into slavery. A fighter, Mila had said. Despite his grim thoughts, Aiyan smiled, remembering the stolen bits of time he had managed to find to teach young Ben to fight, just like their father had taught Aiyan. Looking back, those were the only memories of his life in Kara when Aiyan could recall anything comparable to happiness.

And then he had sent Ben away.

Aiyan took out his bacara root and valisha, and began crushing the valisha into a soft powder. The Kitarran would need more to help him recover. Aiyan had learned to fight from his father, but he had learned herb lore from his mother and grandmother. *Heera* women knew the world revolved around balance, and to heal, one also needs to acknowledge death. *Heera* women once were legendary for their abilities to create healing draughts—and poisons. Imal used Aiyan's poisons to coat the daeum's blades.

Usually, the knowledge was passed down from mother to daughter, as Aiyan's grandmother had taught his mother, but Aiyan was an exception. The emperor's cull of the *heera* people had already begun when Aiyan was a child, and hiding places were scarce; it was only a matter of time before they were found. So Aiyan's mother taught him what she knew, in the hope that he would survive and pass on the knowledge.

Aiyan wondered if the legends were true, if his ancestors were watching over him. Did they watch as he turned his ancestral knowledge into a weapon for a monster? Were they weeping for the death of their culture? Would his mother and grandmother understand why he had forced Ben away so long ago? Would they understand what he had to do to survive?

The dinner bell rang, shaking Aiyan from his thoughts.

"Where is Mila?" Aiyan asked when he reached the dining room.

"She went out to Nulla's brothel to give one of her designs to her friend there. She is not back yet," Wani told him with a cluck.

Mila's designs and pictures in stitches and knots held Aiyan secretly in awe. Aiyan wondered what it would feel like to receive one of her creations she had labored and poured her love into. He shook the thought away. He wondered how long Mila had been gone. He was not worried. Was he?

Aiyan introduced Tarran and Murryn to his gathered household. He introduced Murryn as Mila's sister and Tarran as his brother. No one in his house had served Aiyan's old master Nyamish; no one would remember Tarran as Ben, his little brother. Their surprise and delight were genuine.

"You never told me you had a brother," Cliff huffed for the fourth time.

Wani pinched Tarran's cheek. "He doesn't look *heera* to me."

"I take after our father," Tarran said, his voice bitter, but his eyes softened under the old cook's smile.

"And you, dear, you look just like your sister!" Wani said to Murryn in Rodan.

Aiyan translated for Murryn, who smiled.

"I wish she were here," Murryn pouted.

"Soon enough. She will kick herself to have been gone so long," Wani said, still in Rodan. She could understand Praedan better than she could speak it, even with Tilley's tutoring.

"Tilley, you just missed the big news!" Wani said as Tilley came in, walking slowly. The Kitarran was with her, looking like a rake, his gray eyes wide and slightly disbelieving.

"I know, Wani. I met them earlier," Tilley told the cook, helping the Kitarran into a chair.

"Oh, look at the poor waif. Here, Tilley, feed him up," Wani said, passing a bowl of cooked root vegetables toward them.

"This is Aisha," Tilley announced proudly. "Aisha, this is Day, Wani, Tarran, and Murryn, and this is Ro Aiyan, who saved your life."

Aisha looked at each of them in turn and politely nodded. He had nice manners, especially for a man just off his death bed and fresh from horrible captivity.

"Tilley saved your life, Aisha, not me," Aiyan told him. Aisha looked at Tilley the same way a drowning man would look at a raft. Tilley smiled shyly.

"Ro Aiyan, I still can't believe you have a brother," Tilley said, looking sideways at Tarran.

"No one knew!" Wani exclaimed. "Not surprising, really, the master being such a secretive sort."

"It is a long story," Tarran grumbled in a voice that made it clear it was a story he didn't want to tell. He didn't look like he wanted to eat either. He eyed the Kitarrans uneasily. Aisha didn't seem to see anything beyond the food before him and Tilley beside him. Tilley made sure her Kitarran ate—mostly broth, she instructed. Too much rich food would make his stomach sick. She fed him while glancing at Tarran and Murryn, a question in her eyes. Aiyan wondered how long it would take her to spit it out.

"Tarran, Mila talked about you often. She told me you served a man named Illiah," Tilley said.

Aisha looked up sharply at the name. As did Tarran. The two young men looked at each other. The tension in the room rose.

"Lord Illiah, Prince of Jullayah," Murryn spoke before Tarran could. "He was our friend. Our mentor. He was taken by Kitarrans." She glared at Tilley and Aisha.

"Lord Illiah," Aisha groaned.

Tarran's eyes narrowed. "You know of him?"

"Of him? I *know* him," but his tone was anguished.

"Your people took him. And Rhyl. They kidnapped them," Tarran stood, his body rigid with anger. "Tell me he is alive, or I will kill you right here."

"Tarran," Murryn warned before Aiyan could open his mouth.

"My lord is not dead. Or at least he wasn't. He was captured several months ago by our enemy and sent here," Aisha said sadly.

"*Your* lord?" Tarran spat.

"Lord Illiah, Prince of Jullayah, First Defender of Kitarra. Beloved by all. Our leader. Our hero. Husband to Lady Eva and father to Prince Rhyl and adopted father to Prince Talo. Yes, *my* lord."

Tarran sat, and a tear slipped down his cheek. Murryn hugged his arm. Aiyan could see the demons eating away at his brother's heart.

"What happened to Illiah?" Aiyan asked Aisha.

"I am not sure," Aisha replied. "We were captured by Cotoch and put on a boat. We were separated. But before, I heard Cotoch say Illiah was bound for a fate worse than death." Aisha pushed his bowl of broth away. Tarran's eyes snapped back to Aisha.

"Illiah was captured? And Eva is alive, in Kitarra?" Murryn confirmed.

"Yes," replied Aisha.

"Eva left Jullayah—we all thought she had gone mad and was surely dead," Murryn said, looking at Tarran.

"She came to Kitarra a year ago," Aisha said. "She and Illiah are expecting twins. They might even be born by now."

"Mila will be so happy to hear that. She often talks about her friend Eva," Tilley said.

"She does not know?"

"How could she? Aisha just woke up a half hour ago," Tilley explained.

"Which is why he needs food. Eat, Aisha," Aiyan commanded. To Murryn, he said, "Tilley was taken by the daeum over a year ago. She is from the Isles. She knew little about what went on in Kitarra, and nothing about Eva."

Murryn looked at Tilley, and Aiyan saw recognition dawn on her face. Recognition of what Tilley must have gone through.

Aiyan! I need you.

The voice was a whisper on the edge of Aiyan's distracted mind. It repeated, louder, more desperate. Mila.

There was no time and no use explaining. He left the room and shed his clothes, changing to a wolf in an instant. He could find her easier as a wolf than as a man.

Sure enough, following her trail was easy. She had been wearing the jasmine oil he'd left in her room for her. The delicate, sweet smell mixed with hers was impossible to miss.

# CHAPTER 63

# MILA

AIYAN WOULD FIND HER. He would come.

Mila paused. She could no longer hear Nulla chasing her. Mila waited, but nothing happened. The street was silent. Mila could hear her heartbeat pounding in her chest. It was too quiet. Like a shroud had covered the city.

"Mila!"

Mila spun and tripped. Aiyan caught her. She clung to him, his naked body warm against hers. She sobbed into his chest. He cupped her face in his hands, lifting her eyes to meet his.

"What happened, Mila?"

"I—I don't know."

"Show me what you saw."

And she did. She opened her mind and let him take it all. Cresa. The dark magic. Nulla, crazed and murderous.

"The *vivus*," Aiyan said through his teeth.

Mila stood straight, disentangling herself from Aiyan. "We have to go back. We have to find Letti."

"Who is Letti?"

"She is only a little girl," Mila sobbed. Aiyan clenched his jaw and nodded.

"Are you all right?" Aiyan asked. "Maybe—"

"No. I am coming with you. I need to find Letti."

Again, Aiyan nodded. He did not shift back into a wolf but stayed at her side as a man.

The sun was setting. The streets were empty—barren. Maybe the people sensed the poisonous evil and kept away.

As they neared the brothel, they found Nulla's body in the dust. Dead.

"Don't touch her," Aiyan warned. "Can you see it?" He looked up at the brothel.

Mila followed his gaze letting her magic show her. The building was covered in vaporous nightmare creatures crawling from windows and doorways, moving, climbing, searching.

And Letti was in there. Mila took a step toward the building. Aiyan put his hand out to stop her.

"Wait," he whispered. He closed his eyes and drew a long breath. On his exhale, a sound rose from his throat, melodious, deep, and calming. The tone in his throat changed pitch and took the form of another, a chant. Or a song. It was not in any language Mila had heard. But as the sound lifted, sonorous and thick into the air, it filled her with peace. And sadness. In the song was love and beauty, family and mountains, stars on a clear night. She closed her eyes, and when Mila looked again, the sky was lighter, the air clearer. With her magic, she could see Aiyan's words as thin lines of light that struck the dark shapes, burning them, sending them away.

It was beautiful. Like a flash of lightning in a thunderstorm.

The evil retreated before Aiyan's magic. Aiyan began another song. There was something wolfish in the sound, something Mila thought might be a howl. Something that called and commanded—something final.

They went inside. It was the same as before, not some illusion as Mila might have wished. It was bodies, blood, and death.

Aiyan's song faltered. "It looks as if …"

"As if they killed one another," Mila finished for him.

"Yes."

Aiyan crouched to put his hand on a dead man's face. He opened his mouth to say something, but nothing came out. He looked sad.

Mila searched among the dead for Letti. She called out the girl's name. She searched cupboard and corner, under beds and in closets. Aiyan followed her.

Mila found Letti in the little room she shared with the other servants. She was dead. All the slave children were. Mila dropped to her knees. Aiyan put his hand on her shoulder.

"Sometimes I wonder … sometimes I think it is a kindness to stay a child forever," he said softly.

Mila sensed his eyes on her and looked up at him. Under his amber gaze, her shoulders softened. She wanted to reach for him. But she didn't. Of course, she didn't. Aiyan was a strong man, but not that strong. He couldn't take this grief from her. It was hers to carry.

"Come, Mila," Aiyan said, holding out his hand. She took it, and he pulled her to her feet.

She let Aiyan lead her back onto the street, away from the awfulness, away from Letti. The world was gray in the twilight. The sounds of the city returned. A loud cacophony of shouts and rattles and creaks descended upon Mila's senses.

"When I found Nulla, she was crying for her child," Mila said absently.

"There were rumors that Nulla had a baby, and it was taken to the Pit. She would have been an easy target for the *vivus*."

"The *vivus* …"

"The *vivus* in *heera* legend is a thing birthed from violence and dark magic, capable of twisting the mind. The *vivus* must have destroyed Waffa's as well. This feels the same."

Aiyan lifted Nulla's body gently in his arms and carried it toward the building.

"What are you doing?"

"I am going to burn it," he told her.

Mila didn't argue. Her mouth hurt. She must have bitten her lip. Her skin was cracked and dry and her tears left spots on the back of her dusty hands. She felt scrubbed out and raw. Like every color had been taken from her.

When Aiyan returned, smoke already crept out of a window. The building was stone, but there was plenty inside that would burn.

They stood and watched the fire lick out through the windows, consuming. It spread and grew quickly, sending thick black smoke curling into the air. The air smelled foul, but not as foul as the dark magic. Somehow, it felt cleaner. It felt like relief.

She had not noticed how close she was to Aiyan until she felt the heat of his body contrasting with the air. His bare skin was so close, so potent. He turned to see her watching him. "Mila, I found them. I found Tarran and Murryn."

Mila reached to wrap her arms around Aiyan's neck and kiss his cheek, but he had already shifted back into a wolf. She put her hand on his back, letting his fur tickle her skin. He dipped his head. His ears twitched.

"Let's go home," Mila sighed.

# CHAPTER 64

# COTOCH

IT HAD TAKEN some subtle use of his *candarii* skills and some not-so-subtle coins to find his way, along with Selene, into the private circle of the Allati king. Selene was well liked by the wives, as was to be expected. Cotoch thanked Kitarra's eel-like relationship with Allati; no one knew Selene had spent years at Queen Arrah's side. The Allati had never visited Kitarra's court.

Cotoch was, however, displeased to find that all the pretty Allati women were married. Cotoch liked women, and he liked power, but he did not understand the desire to own so many women. King Ottela had thirty wives. Cotoch could only imagine the bickering that went on behind the palace doors. And why not just have mistresses? All the benefit, without the commitment and responsibility. Cotoch cringed, imagining his dear Sandra left to manage a complement of wives. A twinge of guilt and grief followed the thought of his dead wife.

"Legitimacy," Selene reminded him. "If a mistress birthed a bastard with pure blood, what then? He couldn't inherit. Legally, anyhow."

A good point, Cotoch noted.

Like the greatest craftsman, Cotoch had perfected the art of weaving through the high court of Allati. It was no small feat. The sheer number of women and names and traits was astounding, but he knew them all. Befriending the lords had been a simple task; it was the ladies who were the challenge.

The wives of the king took the most effort. Cotoch had assumed they were more ornaments than political pieces, but he had been wrong. Lady Talia, the king's oldest and most favored wife, was a force. Cotoch suspected she controlled more of the realm than her husband, the ailing king, was aware. But she was old, a great-grandmother, though she hardly looked it with her chiseled eyes and proud posture. She was "Of the Blood," as the Allati called it, with her pale silver hair.

"Lord Cotoch, how are you this evening?"

Lady Talia enjoyed seeking his company after the evening meals. Cotoch smiled at her, knowing full well that behind it lurked a bitch in heat. He didn't fear Talia; she would play nicely into his plans. She had a strong will, but Cotoch knew he could break it with his *candarii* magic if needed.

"Lady Talia, as radiant as ever this evening. How is the king?"

King Ottella was an elderly fellow. The wasting sickness slowly claiming his life was blamed on old age. No one had realized he had worsened around the same time Selene had arrived in Attingard. But the process for selecting a new king was more complicated than Cotoch had planned on.

"Not well, I am afraid." A shadow passed over Talia's face that could be grief or regret. Cotoch did not know if her emotions were genuine; Lady Talia's emotions seemed subject to the outcome she desired.

"I am sorry to hear that," Cotoch said.

"Are you?"

"How can I do business with a sick man?"

Talia shrugged. Clearly, the subject bored her. "My nephew is quite entranced with your niece."

"Yes, I daresay he is." Cotoch followed Talia's glance across the room to where Selene sat with Lord Rollis. Selene looked beautiful, desirable; many of the Allati men admired her. She had none of the pale beauty that the Allati coveted, but her auburn hair and curvaceous figure were enough. Selene's *candarii* magic was hardly necessary. Just a little, she had told Cotoch, was all it took to make them love her. Selene adored their attentions.

Lady Tersia came over to hand her mother a full glass of wine, her expression void, like all the other times Cotoch had seen her. Cotoch knew that expression. Once, he had discovered a group of his men had taken a wench, using her most unkindly. When Cotoch found out, he took the girl away. He had chastised the men and found a place for the girl, but unfortunately, she took her own life not long after—poor thing. Lady Tersia had the same look, but evidently, she had never been brave enough to escape.

Tersia sat beside her mother, silent. The candle light caught her profile, and a memory of another woman, another face, flashed into Cotoch's mind. The resemblance was strong.

"Is Lady Tersia your only daughter, Lady Talia?" Cotoch asked.

Talia took a sip of wine and looked at Cotoch with a little less softness.

"I had two daughters. The other went mad and ran away. Lord Vagar's mother."

Ah. Lord Vagar was due at court at any time. Cotoch was

expecting to use a fair amount of *candarii* magic on the man who had a reputation as difficult, arrogant, smart-mouthed. Cotoch could almost imagine liking the man.

"She ran away to Jullayah," Tersia spoke quietly.

"Yes. But we don't speak of it." Talia wore her disapproval like a crown.

Cotoch wanted to know more. Desperately. He used his amulet and pushed on Talia gently. Tersia required only a passing thought of magic, but her mother was strong.

"A year ago, my granddaughter arrived in Allati, looking for an inheritance, a husband. But she lied. She was on her way to Kitarra," Talia told Cotoch.

"What was her name?"

"Eva."

"Tell me." Cotoch pushed a little harder.

Talia rambled on about Eva arriving in Attingard mortally wounded. How the Guardian Attin healed her, saving her life. How her guard, a Kitarran, helped her leave the city. They killed a Shadow Guard in their wake, a terrible crime, Talia assured him.

"You are sure the Guardian healed her?" Cotoch asked.

"Yes. She would certainly have died. The Master Healers had no hope for her, and then suddenly, overnight, she was cured."

"Amazing," Cotoch whispered, in genuine awe. Why would a Guardian heal Eva? Cotoch had never given Attin much thought. It made him uncomfortable. Like he was being watched. The Shadow Guards were said to be Attin's men. But if Attin were really a power, he would have destroyed Cotoch the moment he first manipulated Lord Eldin with *candarii* magic years ago. Regardless, Cotoch pushed down the niggling doubt where he could no longer feel it.

So, Stone and Eva had come to Attingard. And Lord Vagar was Eva's half brother. Eva must have learned that—they must have spoken.

"My Lord." Lord Pruit ambled up before them, his pudgy cheeks rosy from the wine Cotoch could smell on his breath. "I have a gift for you."

"A gift? I require no gifts, my good man," Cotoch assured the fat lord.

"Nonsense. We Allati are generous people."

*Were they?* Cotoch needed to button down his thoughts lest they come out of his mouth.

Pruit brought a girl before Cotoch. She was tall for her age, but she couldn't have been older than eleven or twelve. She wore a long, lavish gown, her hair dressed upon her head in a fashion that reminded Cotoch of Lady Talia. It made her look a tad older. Cotoch felt uncomfortable inspecting the child dressed to look like a mature woman. The poor girl didn't even have proper breasts, just tiny budding blossoms.

"This is one of my daughters, Lady Gemma. I offer her as a wife," Pruit said, beaming proudly. Little Gemma curtsied with the air of much practice.

"My lord, your own daughter," Cotoch began, making a pretense of inspecting the girl.

"She is a virgin."

*Really? Shocking.* Cotoch pinched his lips into a line.

"Her mother had eight children for me—a good breeder. We heard your wife passed away not long ago. You must be a lonely man."

*She is a fucking child.*

"Thank you, Pruit." Cotoch had foreseen this occasion. The Allati loved their wives—loved them as possessions. And he knew he would likely be offered one as a gift. He just didn't expect her to be so young. She probably hadn't even bled once.

He reminded himself it was his prerogative to be inducted into Allati culture. And here he was, gifted with his first wife, a great honor by Allati standards, a mark that he had succeeded in earning their trust. How many young Allati men were exiled just for being competition? How many did Cotoch have in Mahlas, under his employ? It was a moment of triumph, but Cotoch could not wash the taste of disgust from his mouth.

"I am honored," Cotoch replied, as was required by courtesy.

"Excellent. I will have her sent to your room. The marriage documents are prepared. I just need you sign," Pruit told him, presenting the document.

Pruit signed his daughter's soul away with one swift pen stroke.

"What are you going to do with her?" Selene demanded in a quick, breathless whisper. "You can't fuck her—she is a child!"

"Calm down. Of course not. I agree that is perverse, even for me."

"So?"

"I will give her to Redi. He deserves a reward."

"Redi? He is barely older than a child himself," Selene hissed.

"Yes, that is why it works. And he is a good boy. He would never force her. He will be her friend, they will fall in love, it will all be very sweet and romantic," Cotoch said, knowing it to be true.

Maybe in a year or so, the two would wed. Redi was a good boy, an Allati runaway. He had no love of his people, but he pitied the women.

"Ugh. I had no idea you were so idealistic. Won't that offend Pruit?"

"I will have to work on that."

"The king is still alive."

"I am aware."

Selene waited. "And?"

"Patience, my dear. I am hoping Lord Vagar will come. He is the wobbly block in our barricade."

"I could ask Rollis to send him a message."

"Do that."

"You think Vagar is the most likely to ascend to kingship?"

"I do. So do most of the Allati, resentful as they are. He has the clearest bloodline to the king and to their Guardian. He is also Eva's half brother," Cotoch added, watching Selene's face darken at the news.

"It might be hard to use the *varing* on him. Eva did a good job of breaking through yours." Selene was still resentful of Eva. In many ways, she was still such a child.

"Get over it," Cotoch replied, nonplussed. "We may need to kill him."

"That might be harder. They say he is a good fighter, and paranoid."

"Sounds like a real charmer," Cotoch drawled.

"Just like his sister. I wouldn't mind killing him. Or seducing him. I like a challenge."

Cotoch raised his brow at his niece. "Rollis wouldn't like it."

"Rollis is weak. Easy."

"Right."

"I am done with love," Selene spat into the darkness of the hall.

"We all say that, at least once or twice," Cotoch warned her.

"Go fuck yourself."

Women. Cotoch wondered why the Allati hoarded them like treasures.

# CHAPTER 65

# EVA

EVA COULD NOT BREATHE. She could not *breathe*.

She couldn't find Illiah. The wind would not take her to him. The water would not part with its secrets. Fire caressed her hand, whispering dangerous promises. Eva sat down on the rocky cliff, far enough from the edge to be safe, close enough to feel the wind around her.

Her chest released, and air rushed into her lungs. But it was a struggle. Her tears were drowning her. Her nose burned.

She closed her eyes and listened to the forest. The branches swaying and scratching, trees moaning, leaves shivering. The smell of the earth, the moss, the dew. She let it envelop her. She let it ground her and leach the sadness and despair from her body.

When she opened her eyes, she was not alone. Her stomach lurched.

"Crea," Eva spat.

Crea, the Guardian of Jullayah, gave a smirk and a curtsy. "At your service," she answered in her strange, androgynous voice.

Year ago, when Eva had been a prisoner in the Goddess's temple in Caer Andri, Crea had been full of arrogance. Now, Crea looked—less. With no temple surrounding her, no minions to assert her power, she was nothing. A spirit, a ghost. But still …

"Why are you here? *How* are you here?" Eva asked.

"Tayeh is distracted these days. I have a few minutes before he senses my presence and shoos me from his realm—so don't make me waste my time. I have noticed your little lessons with Attin."

"How—?"

"Time, Eva. Time is short. Tayeh and Attin don't trust you. They refrain from teaching you your true nature—the true power of the *sanarii*. Or the true nature of your son. Yes. I know what he did. The power he wields."

"Attin is teaching me—"

"Attin is teaching you enough to make you useful—but not a threat."

"What do you mean?" Eva couldn't ignore the shock of anxiety when Crea mentioned Rhyl.

"You have more power than you realize. You can help Rhyl. And you can bring Illiah home."

"How?"

Crea grinned. "You need another vercuri. Go to Withe."

"*Sanarii* can't use the vercuri."

"That is what Tayeh wants you to believe."

Eva's heart pounded like a war drum.

"Go to Withe," Crea repeated. Then with the sound of wings in the wind, she vanished.

Eva looked out at the expanse of air the Guardian had disappeared into. She waited, but neither Tayeh nor Attin appeared.

Eva did not trust the Guardian of Jullayah. But still, her hope flared, and she knew she would go to Withe. For Rhyl. For Illiah.

C H A P T E R  66

# STONE

"STONE, are you my amourii or are you the Prince of Kitarra?"

Without hesitation, Stone answered, "Your amourii."

"Good. I need to go to Withe," Eva declared.

Stone digested her words. "Why? What's in Withe?"

"I need to find the vercuri there."

"I feel a 'but' coming on."

"But I don't want the queen to know about it."

"Why do you need it?"

"I don't want to tell you."

Stone nodded, as if her mistrust in him did not make his gut squirm like a corpse covered in maggots. "Where is there a vercuri in Withe?"

"I was hoping you might know."

"Maybe Susor knows," he mused.

"We will ask him."

Stone pulled out his vercuri dagger that he always kept close. They had decided, he and Eva, not to reunite it with the other two vercuri currently in his mother's care. In fact, they had decided not to tell the queen about his vercuri at all. It had been an instinctual decision that both Stone and Eva agreed on. Stone's vercuri needed to stay in his possession, and if his mother knew about it, she would insist it join the other two in the guarded vault of Kitarran treasures.

"You should stay here," Stone said. "I can go to Withe to retrieve it."

"No. I need to go."

"You would leave your children behind? Now? The babes—"

"Don't. Stone, if I stay here, I will go mad. Mad with grief and longing and doubt and hopelessness. I need to do this."

Stone bit his lip. "This has something to do with Illiah?"

"Maybe."

Stone could hardly blame her. If he'd been in her position, and Emri was alive but beyond his reach, he would have razed kingdoms to get her back.

"How long does it take to get to Withe?" she asked.

"A week. We might be able to do it in less. I know a shortcut through the Deep Pass."

Eva's eyes brightened. "Then we won't be gone long."

"What if we don't find it?"

"Then we come back regardless. I won't hunt aimlessly. I promise, if we don't find the vercuri in Withe, we will come home."

Stone nodded. It sounded sensible.

"I can keep watch on the children from afar. If I sense anything, we come right back."

"What do we tell Arrah?"

"We tell her we need to go to Withe, but we don't tell her why."

"She will not like that."

"No, she doesn't like secrets any more than you do. But she can't force us to stay. She can't force us to tell her. I can handle her anger."

Stone laughed. "As can I. By the Allmakers, she has had reason enough to be angry with me over the years."

"What, you weren't the perfect son? Stone, I am shocked to hear it."

Stone was grinning. He was looking forward to this. A journey, getting out of the palace, out of Kilev, traveling with just Eva through the Kitarran mountains. Roasting tubers and herbs on the fire. Sleeping under a summer starlit sky. Waking to dew on his face. It would be just like old times, without the brigands and tyrants. It might even be a bit fun.

# CHAPTER 67

# MILA

THE REST OF AIYAN'S HOUSE SLEPT, but the knotted threads of fate kept Mila awake. She would close her eyes and see blood and bodies and dark, twisting shadows. Then, she would remind herself that Murryn and Tarran were safe and whole, and the images of death would retreat. But she was afraid to fall asleep.

A day had passed. A day of tales and explanations. Of fear transformed into gratitude. Of unknowns becoming certainties. Of lost being found.

Beric, the cur, had had Murryn and Tarran all along. Beric had bought Tarran before he landed in Rodan. Murryn had put up such a fuss that Beric bought her as well. He had kept them at his house under lock and key but treated as well as any exalted guest. Murryn spoke of Beric like he was her eccentric uncle. And Tarran …

"Mila, Tarran is my brother," Aiyan had told her.

Mila couldn't decide if the knowledge hurt her head more than her heart. What an impossible reality. But Tarran and Aiyan's reunion was not one for fond embraces. Tarran treated his older brother with a cool distance bordering on hate. There was much amiss between the brothers.

Tilley and Aisha, on the other hand, had become inseparable. Mila learned the two young Kitarrans had known each other, a little, from Kitarra. And they were of an age. Mila could see by the way the two looked at each other, it would not take long for their young love to blossom.

Aisha shared news about Kitarra. About Eva. And Rhyl. And Illiah. Illiah's fate was more fuel for Mila's nightmares.

Oh, how her heart ached to be with Eva, to be at her side, to make her laugh, to share silly and serious confidences. And twins! Mila had kissed Aisha's furry cheek in happiness to hear news of her friend. Eva was a wonderful mother. Mila would never have children of her own—that future had been taken from her when she had been forced to take culla. To know Eva and Illiah's children would have been a gift. But that was impossible. Kitarra was an impossible dream.

No, she couldn't sleep.

She closed her eyes and let the memory of Aiyan's song flow through her mind. The hair on her arm stood on end, remembering the vibrations of his voice. Never in all her years had she imagined the kind of magic that he had uttered.

Was her magic the same?

*You must never do that again, Mila. Never. Never. Do you hear me?*

Her mother's voice was loud in her memories. She had not known as a child how her mother's anger was just desperation and fear, fear for her little daughter, who, at eight years old, used magic to shift into the form of a wolf. No wonder Mila couldn't shift; she had conditioned herself to drown her magic since she was little.

Mila slipped out of her bed, pulling on her thin night-cloak.

She crept through Aiyan's house. The night had always been a kindred spirit. Now, the dark felt like a void with eyes. Her steps quickened.

She knocked on Aiyan's door.

"Aiyan?" Mila opened the door, peering into the dim room.

"Mila?" Aiyan appeared from the shadows before her. Something whisked across Aiyan's face—something that brought a smile to Mila's lips and sent a rush through her to her toes.

"What you did yesterday—the *vivus*, your magic …" Her words were failing miserably to describe the awe and envy she'd felt with his voice, his magic, in her bones. "I want to try again," her intent stumbled out, clumsy as a drunk at dawn.

But Aiyan knew what she meant—what she wanted. "All right," he said, a slow smile spreading across his lips. "Right now?"

Mila answered by stepping inside his room.

"I want to take you to the forest," Aiyan said. "My forest. A wolf needs the wild."

"Then, let's go."

Aiyan smiled. It was the middle of the night, but he didn't seem to care. "We can be there by dawn."

Mila grinned.

"Meet me on the street in a few minutes."

Mila nodded. She felt ten years old, like she was running off into the forest to play dragons and heroes. She went to her room and changed quickly into something more suited to adventures in the night than lounging around Aiyan's grand house.

Aiyan was waiting for her in the street with a cart pulled by a thin yet spry-looking mule. Mila climbed up and settled beside Aiyan. She could think of a hundred reasons why they should not leave Kara for the mountains, but she didn't want to admit any of them. She wanted the forest. She thirsted for the forest.

Her enthusiasm died after an hour. She leaned her head on Aiyan's shoulder and dozed, the rhythm of the cart, the mule, lulling.

"Mila, wake up. We are here." Aiyan's soft voice woke her.

Mila looked around. The dust and dry of Kara were gone. The air was sweet and warm. Insects buzzed. The dawn was fast approaching. Dew glistened on the dry grass. The rush of a creek was close by. The wind held the promise of the wild. Before them stretched a line of gray trees, and beyond, the hills reached toward the mountains covered with great swaths of forest.

Aiyan held his hand out for her. She took it, stepping off the wagon. The mule was already feasting on dry grass.

"Follow me," Aiyan said.

Mila noticed that the forest was—hurting. Many of the trees were brown and burned. Even the saplings seemed stunted, struggling to grow in the arid ground. Mila paused to smell them. Aiyan caught her glance, his eyes sad.

As they continued, the trees grew taller and slightly greener. They paused at a creek to drink; the little ripples gleamed in the pale light of the approaching dawn. Rodan did not have an abundance of water, and the stream bubbled up from the ground only for a few meters before disappearing once more.

After drinking her fill, Mila looked around. Remains of buildings circled the forest around the spring. Like the trees, they were burned, husks of a former life—remnants of something gone.

A smell caught Mila's nose. Something sweet and wonderful, a memory she hadn't recalled for so long, it may have just been a dream.

She followed the scent into the forest. She could smell the dry grass turn to moss before she could see it and feel it under her feet. White flowers dotted the moss, first here and there, and then as clumps. Soon the forest was carpeted with the small, fragrant flowers, bright points in the last lingering shadows. Mila sensed Aiyan following her, but slowly.

"What is this place?" Mila asked, feeling a sense of other. She had lived close to the Great Forest long enough to know what it felt like to be close to magic. That was the smell—Forest magic.

Aiyan didn't answer immediately. Mila followed his gaze to a clearing. In the center was a black, charred circle. Mila could read his sadness, his grief. She walked over to the edge of the ruins that looked like it might have been a house, not a big house, but just the right size for a small family.

*It was my home.*

Aiyan's voice in her head was so faint, she almost missed it. Yes, she could see it. She could see Aiyan in the forest, a young boy chasing after bugs and picking flowers. Aiyan the boy was always shadowed by a little brother who was constantly making trouble. But Aiyan didn't care. Aiyan was patient with his brother, showing him the best places to find berries and which spiders should not be kept as pets. He taught his brother how to defend himself against an enemy or a wild cat.

*But Aiyan, there are no more wild cats.*

*Ah, little Ben, it is good to be prepared, isn't that what Father always says?*

And they would spar and fight, and sometimes little Ben would get too rough, even angry with his big brother. Then they would pause and take a break and watch the clouds.

Then a day came when they had to hide. And hide fast. Ben was so small and scared, but he stayed as quiet as the dead. Aiyan led Ben out of the house into the forest with the ease any wildcat would be jealous of. Behind them, the house erupted in shouts and screams. Men were everywhere, searching. But Aiyan and Ben could not turn back, not for their mother or grandmother. They had their instructions; they had been told to run, and run they did.

Mila wavered. "Aiyan," she whispered.

"I'm sorry. I didn't mean to put my memories in your head."

"You had to leave your family behind."

"It was what Gran told me to do. To take Ben—Tarran—to safety. We had a place … but Ben and I were caught before we got there."

"And sold as slaves," Mila finished. "Why? I thought all the *heera* were hunted and killed."

"Nyamish found us. Yes, the emperor offered coin for *heera* heads, but Nyamish's greed was not just for riches." Aiyan said the name of his former master like a knife had pierced him.

Aiyan plucked a little flower, spinning it in his fingers.

"After a year of being slaves to Nyamish, I smuggled Ben away. When I was sure Ben was on a boat headed for Praedan, I ran." Aiyan's fingers minced the petals of the flower in his hand. "Nyamish's men followed me. Back then, I couldn't shift into a wolf, or I might have been able to outrun them," Aiyan said, looking at Mila directly.

"Why couldn't you turn into a wolf?" Mila asked. Aiyan nodded— that was the question he was waiting for.

"The same reason you can't. Because my magic was so caught up in darkness and pain."

"How did you get out of it?"

"Murder. Revenge. Anger."

Mila knew he was a murderer. She knew the blood on his hands was thick and deep.

"That didn't work for me," Mila huffed. "I killed my rapist. I slit his throat."

Aiyan turned to her, standing close. He tucked one of her stray hairs behind her ear, his palm brushing her skin like a kiss.

"You should take your clothes off," he suggested.

"Excuse me?" Mila's cheeks burned.

"So you don't destroy them when you shift," Aiyan said in a rush, as if he suddenly realized the implications of his suggestion.

"Oh. Right."

"You don't have to if you don't want to."

"No. It's fine." Mila peeled her dress over her shoulder, then her small clothes. She stood naked, surrounded by forest, the breeze tickling her skin. The shadows warmed as the first glimmer of sun peered through the trees. Aiyan kept his eyes on hers.

"Let the forest help you," he said.

Mila smiled and closed her eyes.

Something loosened within her as she listened to the forest. As if the trees, the air, were a thread pulling her magic from deep within, releasing it from its cage. Her magic flexed, breaking free of the bonds she had created. She closed her eyes, concentrating, pulling it from its hidden cave. Magic came around her like a wind. Her skin prickled and warmed.

She opened her eyes and felt the world tilt. She was falling. Then she wasn't. The world was straight once again; it was her perspective that was different. She was looking up at Aiyan from below. He was smiling—no, he was grinning wickedly. His handsome features were dazzling, like the sun shining through on the darkest of days bringing color to where there had been none. She twisted and turned, all legs and paws and tail and nose. She twirled on four legs, leaping into the air. It felt so natural. It felt right—it felt like home.

*You did it!* The happiness in Aiyan's voice made Mila's heart jump. He reached down and ruffled her fur with both hands.

*Your turn,* she told him.

By the Old Ones, Aiyan was beautiful when he was happy. He stripped off his clothes; Mila sat and watched him. Usually, Aiyan changed without hesitation. His nudity did not bother him or the rest of the household.

"You are making me blush," he said, pulling off his small clothes off and shifting into a wolf so quickly, Mila had no chance to view his indiscretion.

*Time to run!* he insisted, tongue out, amber eyes dancing.

Mila nipped at his long heels. She had never felt so alive. Her insides were bursting with energy. Aiyan gave a playful yelp. She wanted him to chase her. She ran, her heart pumping with life, over logs, between trees, over rocks, Aiyan trying to catch her.

Mila lay, panting. Aiyan collapsed beside her in the same state. Mila shifted back to human, laughter bubbling from her very core. She had never been so happy.

Aiyan shifted back. He was grinning. His laughter joined hers. It was musical. It was perfection. It tore her heart because she knew she could not live in a world without his laughter.

She kissed him.

When their lips parted, Aiyan's laughter was gone.

"Mila ..."

She liked the way her name sounded with his accent.

"*Heera* magic gives me the ability to read other's thoughts and memories through touch. But it also allows me to share my thoughts …"

He took her hand in his. The way his fingers brushed hers begged for her to understand. They were an invitation. Mila closed her eyes and used her magic to touch his, to see what it was he wanted her to see.

What she saw was—horrible. Aiyan's memories cascaded over her. Tears streamed down her cheeks for what Aiyan had gone through, the pain of rape, the ugliness of abuse. Years. He had succumbed to his master's abuse for years.

She reached out and traced her finger down his arm. She spread her palm across his shoulder toward his chest, wishing her touch could wash away the residue left from Aiyan's past. She desperately wanted him to know how love felt.

Aiyan took her hand and held it away from his body. "Mila, I am not a good man. You deserve more than I have to offer. I gave up my own brother. I kill at the command of a tyrant. I am a murderer. I live because others die."

"You are a man who loves his brother and mourns those gone forever. You survive because you know, in your heart, you are fighting for what is right. You are a man willing to die for those he loves. But are you willing to live for them, Aiyan?" Mila said, pushing her words into his mind, flooding him with the moments she had seen. The kindness he showed Tilley. Aisha. Day and Cliff and Wani. And—herself.

Aiyan said nothing.

"Aiyan, look at me." Mila rubbed away his tear with her thumb. His skin was warm against her hand. She leaned into him and kissed his lips, a brush, a taste. When she pulled back, he was smiling, just a little.

"How do my tears taste?"

"Like truth."

Aiyan brought his hands up to her face, his fingers curling into her hair. His lips, his hands, his skin spoke the words his tongue could never utter, words of hurt and peace, of tearing and mending, of pain and beauty, of wanting and giving. Mila had never wanted anything—anyone—the way she wanted Aiyan.

Mila traced the black designs on Aiyan's skin, the mark of a *heera* warrior, he told her. He ran his hand up her back, between her shoulder blades, cradling her against him, moving her against him. He found secret places to lay his lips, his tongue.

The dawn blurred into a timeless knot of embraces and sensations. The wild forest was warm and forgiving, cradling their naked bodies, coaxing their bruised hearts.

The sun rose, playing in the trees above them. Mila smiled against the warm skin of Aiyan's chest, his strong arms around her, the waves of his long hair tickling her nose.

Mila felt the energy of the forest, of the tall, quiet trees, of the small birds calling. Her eyes drank the sight of the white flowers and the green ferns like water. The energy wrapped around her, held her, embraced her.

She realized she had been brought to the forest, to Aiyan, by every pain, every grief she had endured.

Not a curse, but a gift.

She sighed and her magic danced on the edges of her mind, because now she could see it. Now she could be who she was meant to be. Now the line between her life and her heart was nonexistent.

She was a creature of magic. She was other. Magic flowed through her as vital as life-blood. She had not known that pain could be transformed into peace.

"Aiyan, look," Mila said, sitting up.

Illuminated by the light of morning, the forest moved and rippled. Something green moved like a snake through their meadow of white flowers. It rose, transforming into arching branches—a tree where a moment ago, there had been none. Impossible.

"The Muro." Aiyan sounded breathless, awed.

"The Muro?"

"Our mother. Our goddess."

Mila stood and stepped toward the tree. She reached her fingers to brush the delicate branches adorned with tiny leaves that looked like the first breeze would take them. Her fingers touched them. It did not feel real—it was like touching sunlight. The tree shuddered. Mila worried it would shake itself apart. Then the tree dissolved. It was like the sun going behind a cloud.

Where the tree had stood, there was a small person the size of a child. But it was not a child. It was an old, frail woman. Her skin was green, tinged with brown, and crackled and dry, blistering. Sick. Rotting. The Muro stumbled. The sound of a tree groaning in the wind filled the meadow. Aiyan reached out and gathered the tree spirit in his arms.

Aiyan tried to soothe the dying spirit with words—for that was what was happening. Mila knew the little woman was dying. The spirit stroked Aiyan's face with her small hand, her mouth moving, but Mila could not hear her words. Only a moment later, the spirit closed her eyes, and her body vanished into a few white petals on the breeze. The cascade of white flowers of the forest glen wilted.

Their blossoms, just moments before bright and fragrant, were withered and brown.

Aiyan held something in his hand left behind by the spirit. He turned it over in his hands. A weapon. No, it looked like wood, but it was the shape of a small dagger. Like a child's plaything. Aiyan showed it to Mila, his eyes more thoughtful and less sad.

"What is that? What did she say to you?"

Aiyan's amber eyes were bright, electric. "She said that we are stronger together. She said we would need this." He held up the odd dagger.

"What does that mean?"

Aiyan shrugged. He reached out his hand, and she took it in hers, clasping tightly. "This. Maybe it means this."

# CHAPTER 68

# AIYAN

THERE WERE TALES from the eastern swamps of giant snakes that constricted their prey in monstrous coils, slowly squeezing tighter and tighter until their prey suffocated. Aiyan could guess what that prey felt like—his dreams were choking him.

Aiyan and Mila had traded forest and green for dust and despair. They had returned with the afternoon sun. And everything was the same as before. But it was nothing like before. Dangerous thoughts slipped into his head. Mila was close, but she wasn't his. In the forest, he had been just Aiyan. He had loved a woman, and earned her love in return. But in Kara, he was the Wolf. He was a murderer. A monster on a chain.

Aiyan could hardly admit to himself that it had been real. But the dagger in his hands and the burning heat of his skin where Mila had touched him told him that it must have been real. Mila, her body, her embrace was a sequence of perfect moments that made life unbearable. His body felt more alive, more vibrant, than he could remember, and yet he had never felt so desperate and lost.

He should have told Mila everything the Muro had said, but

how could he? There was only one way forward, and that was through blood and violence and death.

The dagger … Imal's dagger. How the Muro had spirited it away and given it to Aiyan defied belief. Most of the *heera* legends and lore had died with the *heera* people; magic had become a thing of mystery, not fact.

"Tarran, thank you for meeting me," Aiyan said. He had had no expectations that his brother would come, but Aiyan was thankful he had. Now, at the end of things, he wanted his brother to know the truth.

Tarran prowled around the room, looking over Aiyan's shelves and peering at Aiyan's plants.

"This was our old room, but I hardly recognize it," Tarran mused. "Why didn't you take the rodaeri's rooms?" Tarran stood in front of Aiyan, and suddenly a knife—Aiyan's knife that he could have sworn was in his pocket—was pointed at Aiyan's throat. "I should kill you. You are a traitor to our people."

"I did what I had to to keep you alive," Aiyan said, his voice washed out by his emotions. He didn't blame Ben for his hatred. Ben's—Tarran's—eyes jittered like his insides were being pulled apart. "If killing me would bring you peace, then I lay my life gladly at your feet." Aiyan meant it. Tarran didn't drop the blade. Aiyan released his held exhale. Now was the moment. "I need to tell you why I sold you to Captain Jagu—why I sent you away." The words stuck in his throat. He could do this. He needed to do this. For Ben—for Tarran. "Nyamish was a pederast. He liked boys—young men."

Tarran lowered the knife.

"He raped me, Tarran. I tried to fight him, but he always won.

He had slaves to help him. And when I fought him—" Aiyan swallowed hard. "It only … it only made him—" Gods, he would never forget the crushing weight of Nyamish.

"Aiyan," Tarran's voice was soft.

"I knew it was only a matter of time before—before Nyamish came for you. I sold you to get you away from here, away from him. And I hoped that in Praedan, you might find freedom."

"You made me think you didn't want me around. You were so distant … I thought you hated me."

Aiyan shook his head. Hot tears made his voice a rasp. "No, dear brother. I hated myself for what Nyamish turned me into."

Tarran took a step back. "Gods, Aiyan." He bent double, breathing hard. "Fuck." There were tears in his eyes. He took a few long strides and wrapped Aiyan in his arms, tight. "I'm sorry. I am sorry for hating you."

Aiyan closed his eyes and let the embrace seep under his skin. "Don't be. I am a man worthy of your hate. I am a murderer," Aiyan said, his voice muffled by Tarran's arms. Tarran released him.

"Beric said you are close to Imal," Tarran said. "His friend."

"Imal does not have friends. But yes, I have played my role."

"To stay alive."

"To stay alive," Aiyan repeated. The understanding in Tarran's eyes unraveled one of the hard knots in Aiyan's heart.

"Aiyan, the *vivus* …" The tenderness in Tarran's eyes was usurped by fear. "Mila told me what happened at the brothel and how you stopped it."

The ancient *heera* chant was one Aiyan hadn't heard since he was a young child. He had never uttered it himself, yet it had come to him in his desire to help Mila. The chant had appeared on his lips and in his memory. Mila's presence rearranged many things inside his mind.

"Do you remember the *heera* tales?" Tarran asked.

"You were the one who always loved tales," Aiyan said, trying to keep the longing out of his voice. Memories of stories told around fires crept up behind him, reminding him of a life that could have belonged to someone else, it was so distant.

"Yes. Do you remember the tale of the *vivus*?"

"A little. But I never liked that one."

"No one did. Some tales are not meant to be comfortable."

Tarran sat, his shoulders hunched. He rubbed his wrists as if remembering binds. Then his voice came, slow and melodious, the perfect storyteller's voice. It was a gift to Aiyan to know his brother had never lost his childhood love of telling tales. It was a gift to hear his brother's voice begin the tale. Aiyan closed his eyes and listened.

"When the world was younger, there were the *rauna*, the wise and wondrous creatures who used the *simul rami* to create life and beauty. But it came with a cost. As they took from the *simul rami*, the dark river, the *varing*, leaked through and into the world. But there was balance. There was life and death. There was night and day. There was rain and there was sun.

"One day, the earth shook, causing a great rift in the *simul rami*. The *varing* poured out into the land, feeding off the pain and sadness and despair. Whole forests died. Nightmares became real. The *vivus* crept into the day and into the hearts of men and women and children. And some it took as its kin—the sorcerers who gathered the *varing* through death and pain.

"So, the *rauna* held a great meeting to decide what needed to be done. Most decided to flee the land for another, leaving the humans to their fate. But the Muro stayed and gave her gifts to her people. The *heera*, the people of the light, were created to fight the *varing*—the *vivus*, the soldiers of the dark river. The *vivus* grew, feeding on the souls of people. Invisible, toxic, they spread violence and hate through the lands like a disease. Only the *heera* warriors could defeat them."

Tarran paused and rolled up his sleeves, showing Aiyan long-healed scars that looked like claw marks. "When I was twelve, I was attacked by—by something—I don't remember what it looked like. But Murryn, who was there with me, she said it was a monster. Part animal. Part person. Not unlike a *vivus*, but more real. Tangible. I would have died there in the forest except for Eva. Her magic showed her a vision of me, bleeding and dying. She found and healed me. She is a *sanarii*."

"What happened to the creature?" To be caught between animal and human, stuck between forms, was one of Aiyan's greatest fears. The creature in Tarran's tale sounded horrific.

"It was killed by the Forest Folk."

"Forest Folk?"

"The shifters of the Great Forest. Shape-shifters, like yourself."

Mila had mentioned them.

"Can your friend Eva shift form?"

"No."

"Are you sure?" Mila had kept her secret close; perhaps this woman had too.

"Eva and Illiah had no secrets from me."

"Everyone has secrets," Aiyan muttered.

Tarran frowned.

"What is a san-ar-ii?" Aiyan asked.

"Healers. Vision-finders. Here in Rodan, there are the *candarii*. *Sanarii* are their counterparts. The *candarii* were hunted in Praedan and killed long ago."

"But there are *candarii* in Praedan. I know of at least two." An idea formed in Aiyan's mind, one that was unpleasant and made his heart ache. "This man Illiah, did he have magic? Is he a *sanarii* or a *candarii*?"

"Illiah is not *sanarii*. They are marked by their unusual starlit hair."

"Rodan has been dying for a long time under the hand of sorcerers. But it is only recently the *vivus* have come."

Tarran's eyes narrowed. "Why would you ask if Illiah had magic?"

"I think Illiah is Imal's prisoner."

"Aiyan. I—we need to know—have you seen him?"

"I have seen Imal's prisoner. A man from Praedan—tall, dark hair, green eyes, lean. A prince, Imal said."

Tarran's face brightened with hope, the most dangerous weapon of all. Aiyan didn't need to ask whether the description matched.

Aiyan grated through his next words, knowing that Tarran's hope was doomed. "What would happen if a *candarii* used another *candarii*? What happens when you add fuel to a fire?"

"The *varing* would surge and feed and grow." Tarran's face darkened like an eclipse. "You think that Imal is using Illiah to gather the *varing*? That is why the *vivus* is growing, feeding? That means Illiah ..."

"Is being tortured. Yes." Aiyan's stomach clenched and roiled. "Did you tell Beric about Illiah?"

"Murryn did. She trusts him."

"Beric is trustworthy, never fear, but he is devious. Illiah is a prisoner in the palace." Beric knew this—Aiyan was sure of it. That was why Beric handed over Tarran and Murryn. It was not out of kindness, or to prove his trust; it was a clever part of his plan. Damn him. He knew Tarran would not rest until Illiah was rescued. And to rescue Illiah would mean destroying Imal.

"If Illiah is a *candarii*"—Tarran choked on his words—"if he is, he doesn't know. He wouldn't ..." Tarran's face fell. "Illiah had a weapon. A wooden dagger. He kept it on him, always. I asked him about it once—only once. He told me it was called a vercuri." Tarran faltered a little, watching Aiyan's face.

Aiyan wondered what Tarran saw in his eyes. Could he see his heart pounding? Illiah had had a vercuri. Imal was looking for the vercuri. Imal had told Cotoch there were nine. And one was now in Aiyan's possession through magical means.

Tarran continued, "Illiah didn't tell me what the vercuri did. I only saw him use it once, years ago, to kill a *daeum* captain. It was just after he found me. I wondered why he would use a wooden knife, but if it were an object of power—of magic—it would make sense."

Aiyan's heart sunk further. It was damning evidence that Illiah was a *candarii*.

"Illiah had uncanny skills and speed," Tarran said. "But I will not in a thousand years believe that Illiah is capable of doing what a sorcerer must do to gather magic."

"True—being a *candarii* is a choice," Aiyan said with care.

"We can't let Illiah die here," Tarran begged.

Aiyan didn't have the heart to tell Tarran that Imal would not kill Illiah, that he would keep him alive, to torture him again and again and again. And so long as Illiah was alive, the *varing*, the *vivus* would spread through the city.

"Aiyan, please help me."

Aiyan knew he couldn't offer his brother impossible promises. "It may already be too late to save your friend."

"But you are a *heera* warrior, blessed by the Muro—destroying the *vivus* is what you are meant to do!"

"To truly defeat the *vivus*, Illiah has to die," Aiyan answered quietly. "I am a wolf. The Muro designed me to kill and destroy—there is no other way."

The silence was thick as oil—Aiyan knew a single spark would ignite it. And Tarran's face was a whole fucking wildfire.

# CHAPTER 69

# MILA

WITH THE DUST and despair of Kara in Mila's nose, the feeling of Aiyan's lips on her skin was almost impossible to imagine. In the forest, Aiyan had been *heera*, a man. In Kara, he was only the Wolf. Distant. Like he wanted to forget what had happened in the forest. But Mila would never forget.

Mila told Murryn everything. Everything, except Aiyan. That dream was too precious to share.

"I always knew, Mila," Murryn told Mila.

Mila stared at her sister, her mouth open.

Murryn smiled. "As a child, I remember seeing you turn into a wolf—you were so beautiful with your black fur and long legs and tail. And then Mother raged and raged at you. I was very little, but I remember that clearly."

"And here I thought you couldn't keep a secret," Mila said. Then she started laughing. Relief pulsed like wine through her veins making her giddy. Murryn laughed too. Their laughter was loud enough that Tarran came to investigate.

"Murryn told me a few years ago. I told her about the *heera*," Tarran admitted.

"So, you can't keep a secret after all!" Mila flicked Murryn lightly on the nose with her finger. But she was still laughing. Then she noticed there was something off about Tarran's face.

"What is it, Tarran?" Mila asked.

"Aiyan knows where Illiah is."

"Illiah is alive?"

"Where?"

"He is a prisoner of the emperor. Aiyan thinks Imal is torturing Illiah to feed his magic."

Mila sat. Her legs shook. Murryn shouted in anger or grief—it was hard to tell.

"Aiyan thinks Illiah is the reason the *vivus* is spreading through the city," Tarran went on.

Mila wanted to weep, but her tears did not come. Nothing. She almost vomited.

"Where is Aiyan?" she asked.

Tarran shrugged. "He went out, I think. I don't know if Aiyan will help. We can't let Illiah die here." Murryn put her arms around Tarran.

Mila needed to find Aiyan. She shifted. She didn't bother to look back to see their reactions or heed their exclamations.

Her wolf nose could smell Aiyan, but it took her a few minutes of pacing around the house to find the freshest trace. He had left the house. She followed his trace into the city, down dusty paths. Mila slunk between shadow and wall, hoping to move unnoticed.

"You mangy cur!" a slave yelled at her, mistaking her for a dog when she slunk behind his stall, knocking over a few bottles. She growled at him, and he shrunk back, but his hand reached for a stick or knife—Mila didn't stay around to find out which.

She only had one other moment of panic when she thought she had lost Aiyan's scent. But she picked it up again and hurried along.

Aiyan's trace led her to a large estate surrounded by green gardens. And a wall. There were guards at the entrance, but they were slouched in front of their posts, like they had fallen asleep. Mila crept close. The guards weren't dead. Mila could smell something on them, something familiar. She had smelled it in Aiyan's room. One of his poisons.

She nosed the gate open and crept through, keeping low, ready to dart back into the street.

Her wolf ears heard Aiyan's voice from the back of the huge house. He was shouting. Mila had never heard him lose his temper. She slunk closer.

"Aiyan, what did you do to my guards?" Beric's face was flat.

So it was Beric's house. That made sense. Beric loved the color green. Mila sneaked closer and kept low. She could see Aiyan pacing around the small patio. Beric sat, watching him with both fear and amusement. Mila crouched behind a pillar.

"I poisoned them—don't worry. They are not dead," Aiyan snapped at Beric. "They will be fine—eventually. Why, do you think I am a monster who kills everything that moves?" Aiyan showed Beric his teeth. Mila saw Beric swallow his retort along with his nerve. "You knew!" Aiyan continued. "You knew Imal's prisoner is Illiah, a man you knew Tarran would do anything— anything—to rescue. And you knew the only way to rescue him would be over Imal's dead body."

"I must say, this raw anger is not like you, the controlled wolf—"

Aiyan growled. The sound was not human. Beric clamped his mouth shut.

"You cur ..." Aiyan muttered.

"I must say, it was a brilliant plan. It was well known that you had a brother, a brother whom you managed to sell and send to Praedan. It was an epic story—how you ran away and Nyamish, the slug, had to chase you down." Beric's eyes were piercing. "You only attend the Market when shipments are brought from Praedan. I knew you were looking for your brother. And I knew if I could get him before you, then I thought I could use him as leverage. But then I learned Imal's prisoner is none other than Tarran's hero. I knew it was only a matter of time before he asked you for help.

"And now you can kill Imal, rescue your brother's hero, and Kara will be free. Your Praedan friends will be free to return home—I will make boats available. Everyone wins. I don't understand why you are so angry."

Aiyan laughed, loud and mirthless. It sounded wrong, far from the light, magical laughter that had enchanted Mila. "Beric, this Illiah—this *hero*—is feeding Imal's sorcery! The man is a *candarii*. He carries a taint unlike any I have seen. There is something inside him, that if it is released, will destroy us all. I can't rescue him. I need to kill him."

"Same difference. So long as Imal is dead."

Mila heard Beric's reply, but her heart was pounding. She took a step around the pillar.

*Aiyan, is this true?* she asked.

Aiyan spun toward her. His amber eyes flashed with rage and pain and anguish, filling her beating heart with pity. She saw his impossible choice. Kill Illiah and save the city, but lose his brother forever.

Beric saw her and stiffened.

"Another wolf?" Beric whispered.

Aiyan put his hand up to shush him.

*Why didn't you tell me?* Mila asked.

"How could I?" he said out loud.

*Don't you trust me?*

*I didn't want to hurt you,* Aiyan replied.

Mila shifted into her human form so she could be at Aiyan's eye level. Beric breathed through his teeth in surprise.

"Let me tell you a story." Aiyan reached for her hand. When she didn't take his, he dropped it like an afterthought. "The *heera* had many stories. Though Ben—Tarran—was the one gifted for storytelling,"

"Fine. Tell me," she said.

"Do you want some—ahem—clothes?" Beric managed, his voice still tight.

Mila glared at him. "I didn't think you, of all people, would be bothered," she snapped. If she wanted clothes, she would ask. She turned back to Aiyan expectantly.

Aiyan cleared his throat. He began. At first, his words were slow and awkward, but then his story unfolded. A story about the old world and the old spirits. And the *vivus*. And the duty of the *heera* warriors to defeat it.

"And Illiah is the catalyst for the *vivus*?" Mila asked.

"I am certain."

"But how? Eva is the one with magic, not Illiah."

"Perhaps he doesn't know. Or perhaps he kept it hidden, as you did."

Mila pressed her mouth into a thin line. Could it be true? Could Illiah have kept this secret from them for all those years?

"What do we do? There has to be a way," she said. This time, she reached out for Aiyan's hand. Beric's jaw gaped. Aiyan wrapped her hand in his, and something settled inside her. "There has to be a way to save Illiah."

Aiyan's expression was hard. His mind was silent. But his hand grasped hers like he was falling.

"So, are we going to talk about the other wolf in the room?" Beric asked with a sideways grin.

CHAPTER 70

# MUTE

THE RIVER HOVERED just below his consciousness, like a rain cloud lingering over the mountains. He was always aware of it. It was always there, waiting to trap him if he moved. But for once, it could not reach him. He was free of the swirling waters and currents that were the *simul rami*. He could see again. He could feel. By the black dust of the Maker, he could breathe.

While trapped in the river, his senses had been lost to him. Time. Touch. Awareness. But now, free, he knew where he was, even though the world had changed. The humans had spread like a forest, but it was not strange to him. He felt at home among the mortals.

But his mortal body was weak. He could hardly move for the pain it caused. The glorious pain. The glorious taste of iron in his mouth. The hard stone beneath him. The smell of the ocean. He could see it. His mortal eyes were undamaged, and he could see the blue and the sparkle of the sun. Not the *simul rami*. No, this was real water, real ocean.

He stumbled on hands and knees to the grated window with its iron bars. He rattled the bars with his hands, but the iron was too strong for his human body. The memories of his human body were his as well. Taken across that beautiful, betraying sea to a land not his own. He knew that tale well. The human had a home, a family, a lover. Children. A realm that beckoned to his pride. Illiah. His name was Illiah. But he was Illiah no longer.

Illiah had been weak, beaten and caged, but now he, Mute, was free. He reached out to the surrounding shadows, gathering them, coaxing them, commanding them to make him strong once again.

CHAPTER 71

# COTOCH

COTOCH WAS IN THE MIDDLE of a lovely dream. Pale hands and pale hair and a mouth wet and warm. But someone kept interrupting, calling his name, softly at first, then loud enough that he pushed away the lovely woman in his dream to concentrate.

*Wake up.* It was her. His prisoner. From her lair in the crypts of Mahlas, she called to him. *He is coming for you.*

Cotoch woke, his heart pounding, his eyes open, his senses straining in the darkness. Clarity came instantly. Cotoch had no time to think; he could only react. He grabbed the dagger under his pillow and slashed up at the figure looming above him. The figure moved to the side, blocking Cotoch's defense with an arm. Cotoch came to his feet, striking with his other hand, hitting his attacker's jaw. The hit did little. The assailant kept coming. His short knife aimed for Cotoch's heart.

Cotoch took from his amulet and used his *candarii* powers, pushing against the man. The man faltered, took a step back, eyes trained on Cotoch's amulet where it hung on his bare chest, hot against his skin.

"Impossible," the man whispered. He wore white. White tunic.

White cloak. Bald head. A Shadow Guard. A warrior trained to seek out and defeat *candarii*. Cotoch had expected they would come; he just hadn't expected them to be so sneaky.

The Shadow Guard held his dagger in front of his face like a shield. A dagger made of wood. What a strange implement to use as an assassin's weapon … The magic of the room became thick. It was another artifact, another piece of the spear. What a foolish sod. He had brought it right into Cotoch's hands.

Cotoch lunged with *candarii* speed at the bewildered warrior, knocking the dagger to the floor and twisting his knife into the man's shoulder. The man cried out, immobilized by pain.

"Tell me, where are the other pieces of the Stormspear?" Cotoch hissed, twisting deeper.

The man spoke in ragged gasps. "I don't know."

"Where are the other pieces!" Cotoch demanded, pulling what little *varing* he could from the man's fear and pain, and pushing it into the man's consciousness, forcing him to answer. He wasn't sure if it would work, but there was no reason he shouldn't try.

"Gone. I swear it."

"Gone where?"

"Gone. Taken. Stolen. The Guard does not have them. This is the last."

"Are there any more coming for me?"

The man shook his head, pale now, from fear or pain, Cotoch didn't care.

Cotoch believed him so he sliced his weapon across the man's throat and let the body fall slowly to the carpeted floor. It wouldn't take long for the Guard to bleed out and soak the carpet.

He had to get rid of the body. A Shadow Guard attacking him at night was the same as putting a sign on his chest announcing his *candarii* magic.

Cotoch's guard in the hall was dead. Cotoch had a moment of panic, thinking of Selene. If the Shadow Guard had known about him, maybe he had known about Selene and she was already dead.

Locking his door behind him, he went down the hall to Selene's room. He knocked softly, and after a moment, she answered.

"What is it?" she asked, pulling her robe over her bare shoulder. Cotoch could see a dark form shifting in his sleep on her bed. Did the woman ever sleep alone?

"A Shadow Guard tried to kill me in my sleep, so I thought I would make sure he hadn't killed you first," Cotoch whispered.

Selene's eyes were wide in the dim light. "Too kind of you. Do you think there are more?" Her voice caught.

Cotoch shrugged. "I don't think so. Go back to bed. We will talk in the morning."

He went in search of his captain and found him in a pool of ale.

"Get up, Easra. Get several men. Kullin is dead."

"What? Dead?"

"An assassin. I killed him. We need to get rid of the bodies. Now."

"An assassin? Didn't know the Allati had it in them." Easra blinked hard.

"We need to control this. Now."

Easra impressed Cotoch by sobering instantly. Cotoch didn't mind his men drinking, so long as they were able to do what was needed of them at any given moment.

Cotoch inspected the body under candlelight while waiting for

Easra's team. The man was roughly the same age as Cotoch, but more sinewy, like he had lived a lean, uncompromising life. His face was tattooed, a mark of the Shadow Guard, Cotoch assumed. Why were elite groups always tattooing themselves? The *heera* had a similar tradition. The *daeum* loved to mark their flesh, branding themselves as warriors unafraid of pain and death. Was it boredom that drove them to mar their skin?

Cotoch would hunt the last of the Shadow Guards and kill them. There would be no more sneaking into his chambers with a dagger to kill him in his sleep. The dagger. Cotoch picked it up from where it had fallen.

It was not so much a dagger as a pointy piece of wood; there was no delineation between blade and handle. It didn't look strong enough to be used as an assassin's weapon. Cotoch pulled his amulet from beneath his shirt and looked at it beside the strange dagger. They were made of the same wood. Cotoch picked up the dagger and held it, closing his eyes, searching it. Yes, it was the same as the amulet. It reeked of magic, but subtly different.

Cotoch's heart pounded in his chest. Why would the Shadow Guard use a magical dagger to kill him? Why not use a blade of steel?

Cotoch put the dagger down beside his amulet. The instant they touched, something shifted. The two objects became fluid, melding before Cotoch's eyes into something else, something new. Cotoch reached for his amulet, but it was too late. The amulet was gone. The dagger was gone. In their stead lay a long weapon— broader, almost oar-like, with a long, slender curved handle ending in a curved blade.

Cotoch picked it up. The magic was so sharp and potent, it

was like being stung. He dropped the wooden blade on the bed, unable to hold it, grieving the loss of his amulet. His mind could not comprehend how this would affect his bargain with Imal.

"My lord?" Easra punctuated Cotoch's wonder. Behind him were three of Cotoch's men, faces puffy from sleep.

"Get it done, Easra."

His men worked silently, efficiently. They hoisted the bodies and cleared the mess. Cotoch kept a watch for any Allati that might be out for a midnight walk, his magic poised in case he needed to influence anyone or get their attention away from the dead Shadow Guard being carried down the hall.

Cotoch's men were efficient. Cotoch was soon alone once more, two guards posted at his door. He felt vulnerable without the amulet. Naked. He had worn it always, since he was a boy, its magical presence constant and comforting. The knife—small sword?—was alien to him, and it did not look friendly. It was not small enough to carry concealed.

He laid a fingertip on the magic weapon. This time, the feeling was less intense; just a trace of the *varing* pulsed inside the weapon. He gripped it in his fist and closed his eyes. It was not so different from his amulet, after all. He could still reach out and connect to his prisoner in Mahlas. He could see her. Her shape and form were more real than he had ever seen her. Her face was odd, almost birdlike. Plumes of feathers rose from her black skin, shifting into leaves and branches that might have been hair.

*You warned me. Why?* Cotoch asked.

The creature did not speak. Cotoch could feel her wrath, her disgust, and something else—something more human. Lust? Longing? Cotoch suddenly did not trust her. He did not trust the wooden weapon. He did not trust magic. There was something sinister and alive within the artifact. And he did not think that it liked him. Not at all.

# CHAPTER 72

# EVA

THE CITY OF WITHE was in the mountains. Eva rode Sasha. She hadn't ridden since before her body grew awkward carrying the twins. Riding once again felt like a kind of freedom. But it was also bittersweet. With Penn, the loyal warhorse dead, Stone was on foot. There were no horse in Kitarra that matched his height, and besides, Kitarrans were fast and had more stamina than humans. Yes, poor, loyal, brave Penn was dead, but his legacy would live on. Illiah had bred the stallion to every mare in season along the Ilba River. Eva told Stone he could have his pick of the foals.

The mountain road took them past the tree line, up and up, until the hills were bare but for a few scraggly trees and the endless green meadows dotted with alpine ponds and creeks. The air smelled like honey, and the breeze was cool.

The beauty, at another time, would have been breathtaking. The green rolling hills tipped with gray rocks were dotted with flowers of every hue. Between tumbled moss-covered rocks. Butterflies danced everywhere she looked. Eva saw it and knew it was beautiful, but it did not move her heart. It did not warm her.

Stone's shortcut to Withe was through the Deep Pass, which was more high than deep. It would be impossible in winter, Stone told her, with the snow deep as a house and the winds sharp and constant. Even the main road that ran through less narrow, dangerous passes from Kilev to Withe was prone to dense layers of snow.

"What is that?" Eva's eye caught something across the valley that did not belong in the alpine landscape. A small, black speck moved, covering ground with the speed of a bird diving from a great height. It was bipedal, like a man, not four-legged like a deer or bear, but not obviously Kitarran, who were capable of great speed.

"I don't know." But Stone's words were edged with ice; a chill spread down her spine. Her hand tightened on her sword handle. She drew it as Stone drew his latha. The meadow around them was silent. Sasha snorted and shifted. Eva had to check his reins to keep him still, which was unusual for the placid horse.

Like an arrow, the creature, man or other, came straight for them. As it neared, they could hear it breathing, a rasping, dying sound. It was a man, legs pumping, arms pulling it across the rolling ground. Eva had never seen a human move with such speed. She did not believe for a second it did not mean them harm.

It hurtled up the small hill, right toward Eva. It didn't even glance at Stone. Eva saw the man's eyes for an instant—for it was a man, a human, crazed and wild and rippling with the fiery *varing*. Stone pounced with equal speed, slashing his latha through the air. His blade came down on the man's neck, immobilizing him with a swift death. It happened in a blur—a blink.

"He was infected with the *varing*," Eva whispered, sliding off Sasha's tall back to inspect the dead man. "Look at his feet."

"He ran them raw."

"He was crazed."

"And so fast."

"The *varing* gave him strength."

"Strength in madness."

"This is why the Allmakers created the Kitarrans. No human could have stopped that man," Eva whispered. "I think he would have run Sasha down." Eva smoothed the hair on Sasha's neck.

Stone agreed, nudging the body with his clawed toe. "Who was he, do you think?"

"Does it matter?" Eva stated.

"I think so. We will reach Withe tomorrow. We can send someone back to get the body. I don't fancy carrying it with us, do you?"

"Not one bit. Will animals get it?"

"There are only mountain cats and alra up here—neither are scavengers. We can't do anything about the birds."

"Stone, in your journal, you mentioned dark spots—is there one close to here?"

"By the Guardians, I think there might be. I had forgotten about that."

"Should we check it out?"

"That is the last thing I want to do—but yes, perhaps we should."

"You have your vercuri," Eva stated.

Stone nodded.

Not long after, they left the narrow road and headed farther up into the hills, to the Valley of Pines, as Stone called it. There were pine trees, sure, but they were small and slender things, like everything that grew up on the mountain slopes. A few small herds of wild alra watched them from a wary distance.

The narrow path disappeared beneath the green scrub and wildflower carpets. They passed over little creeks and brooks filled with the clearest, coldest, sweetest water Eva had ever tasted. She found it impossible to believe in anything evil touching and marring the tranquil landscape.

"We should make camp here, then walk on without our gear. I don't want to stay close to the dark spot after nightfall," Stone suggested.

They made camp. Tied and fed Sasha. Prepared the tent against the morning dew that fell like rain over the mountain meadows. Then, with just weapons and canteens, they made their way forward once more.

"Do you sense that?" Eva asked Stone an hour later.

Stone shook his head. "Your human nature is more susceptible to the *varing*. It would make sense that you would sense it before I do."

"I can sense it. But it is not what I expected." What Eva had expected was a clenching in her gut, a tingling at the edge of her mind, fear lancing down her back like a blade. But this was less menacing, more—lamenting. Lonely. They walked on, and the longing in Eva's chest grew and stretched until she was almost hunched over from it.

"There—look." Stone gestured to the hill beside them. Bones. Alra bones littered the hillside, white with age. Around the bones, nothing grew, the ground was dry and cracked.

"Stone! Look at that tree!" Eva exclaimed. She was not sure why the dead tree upset her—it was just a tree. Its limbs were black and sagging. It was a big tree for the area, where most were short. The growing season in the mountains was brief.

"A dead cendari sapling," Stone said.

Eva climbed the hill where the tree stood and touched her hand to its ashen bark. She closed her eyes and reached with the *simul rami* to find the tree's link to the magic river. It was gone, severed, and in its place, the *varing* lay waiting like a trap.

Eva took her hand away.

"The *varing* is in the tree," Eva said. Stone had moved off a few paces, looking at something beyond the crest of the hill. She joined him, looking down on a small valley filled with abandoned houses and buildings. Almost abandoned. A small tendril of smoke curled into the air from one of the houses.

"Is that it?"

Stone nodded.

"Who would live in a place like this?" she asked.

The buildings looked like the tree. Infected. Eva knew without looking that behind the black, lifeless windows would be the dusty remains of the folk who used to live in the village. A graveyard. A tomb. Covered in a layer of dark magic.

Eva gripped her sword handle. The feeling of loneliness and desperation intensified. She pushed down the sob that threatened to rob her of breath.

"Let's find out what kind of person lives in a hole of dark magic," Stone said, unlatching his latha.

They moved through the buildings carefully. The streets were barren. Not even weeds grew. It smelled like wet ash, but Eva could see no sign of a raging fire.

The house with the smoke was in the center of the village. The shutters of the two small windows were closed tight. Stone knocked on the door.

The door creaked to life, and Eva braced herself against an attack, sword raised. The door opened slowly, revealing a place lit by the sun. Water rippled, bright blue and golden, behind a layer of black pitted bars. A prison. She was not in a little mountain house, she was somewhere else, and Stone was not beside her. A person lay on the ground. Eva stepped over to him, taking in the high ceilings, the warm air.

The man on the floor stirred, groaning as a door opened into the prison. His face turned in profile. It was Illiah, lying on the floor, gazing up at something on the ceiling.

"This will be the end of you," Illiah spoke. Eva thought he was talking to her, but she was wrong. Another man stood gazing down at her husband, a man wearing an evil smile and carrying a long, sharp knife.

The man crouched beside Illiah and ran his blade down Illiah's arm. Drops of blood followed the steel tip. The man snatched one on the end of his finger, put it to his lips. "Why are you not afraid?"

"I don't fear pain."

"You will. Oh, you will."

And Eva watched, helpless, as the man fulfilled his promise to Illiah. Her rage and helplessness was a white fire within her heart, burning her flesh, consuming her voice.

*Eva.*

Eva heard a shout in her mind.

"I am here, Illiah. I am here! Stay with me!" Eva shouted through her tears.

*Eva!*

"Eva!"

Eva opened her eyes. Her head was pressed against Stone's shoulder; his arms were underneath her, carrying her. The night air chilled his fur. The sky above him was darkening. A few stars peered down at her.

"I can walk," Eva told him. Stone put her down gingerly. "What happened?"

"Nothing I didn't expect. You went mad. Screaming about Illiah and torture, begging someone to stop." Stone's voice shook.

She shivered. But it came back to her. The burned tree. The ashen village. The house with the smoke.

"Who was in the house?"

Stone shivered. "A *revenant* in the body of a man."

"There is more," Eva stated, hearing it in his voice.

"Yes. But let's not speak of it. Better to wait until the dark has passed."

Back at their camp, they built a fire and brewed tea and ate a warm meal. They sat close together. The night mountain air was cold at their backs.

"What I saw was not a concoction of dark magic, Stone. What I saw was real."

Stone's eyes were wells of pity. "We should not speak of it now. I will take first watch."

Eva didn't argue. She crept into the tent and curled up in her fur blanket. But it was a fitful sleep. When Stone woke her for her watch, it was a relief.

The day came with birdsong and humming insects. The morning sun reflected off the thousands of tiny beads of dew. The air was thick with the smell of flowers. The sun warmed Eva's face. She stoked the fire back to life. Sasha stirred, making soft, horsey sounds. Eva assured the horse he was a good boy. Stone crawled out of the tent, a blanket wrapped around him.

"We should talk now," he said.

The darkness of the village the day before was almost hard to imagine surrounded by bees and flowers and morning sunlight. And yet, the shadow in Eva's thoughts was all too eager to turn those things gray.

"What was in the house?" Eva asked.

"A man. A murderer. A monster. He attacked me. I killed him. There were dead and dying things as well—things that had once been creatures."

Eva was sorry she'd asked. "What happened to me?"

"The door opened, and you went a bit mad. Fell to the ground sobbing, rocking. I was concerned, but the man came at me with a knife. I had to deal with him first."

"Just one man?"

"Yes." Stone looked haunted. There were ghosts in his eyes.

"What I saw was real, Stone. I know it was."

"These places—these dark spots—they make your worst thoughts turn real. They take your fears and amplify them and put evil thoughts into your head."

"Stone, I know this was real. He is alive. Illiah is alive. But they are torturing him—for fun, Stone, for fun!"

"Eva. It is not real. You must believe that."

"I can't."

They said no more. They packed up in silence. Eva climbed back into the saddle. They backtracked until they found the little road through the mountain valleys to Withe.

Withe was nestled in a long valley cupped between several great mountains. At the center of the valley was a small lake, and at its edge was the city. The buildings were tall with sharply slanted roofs to keep off the snow in winter. It was not a large city, but it was grand.

The lord's hall was located at the city center, right along the edge of the lake. It was there that they headed to seek Lord Susor.

"Can you sense anything?" Stone asked as they walked through the narrow, cobbled streets.

Eva shook her head. "You're the one carrying the vercuri," she muttered.

"Maybe I should give it to you." Stone handed Eva the wooden dagger. It was not as heavy as a metal blade. Eva slipped it into the inner pocket of her cloak.

"Still nothing."

"Well, let's not get discouraged. Susor is a helpful soul—if I remember correctly."

The people of Withe greeted them with friendly smiles, but no one recognized them. Stone didn't resemble Arrain with his lightened fur, and Eva wore a cap over her short, star-gold hair.

"Lord Susor is at the hall," they were told when they inquired. But that was all. Withe was a city that saw many travelers in the summer months come to purchase ore and jewels, mined from the highest peaks of the mountains. Jade was its most abundant resource. The green stone was loved by all for its beauty and hardness. It shone on fingers and around necks and in doorways and windows.

The door of Withe Hall was framed with jade columns, its door intricately carved and inlaid with more of the green stone. A guard appeared, and once they told him who they were, they were shown inside immediately with great fuss and hustle. When Susor found them, they were sipping chilled wine and sampling a variety of alra cheeses. The older Kitarran's ears were heavily stripped with gray. Eva had seen him only a few months earlier, and he had not looked so old then. Aisha's capture had aged him.

"Arrain," Susor exclaimed softly.

"Susor," Stone said, grasping Susor's arm. Eva knew Susor had been like an uncle to Arrain. Something passed between them. Stone softened ever so slightly.

"Eva," Susor said, releasing Stone. He kissed her hand in the Kitarran fashion before his long Kitarran arms enveloped her in a hug. "What brings you to Withe?" There was a glint of hope in his eyes, but Eva had none to offer him.

"A delicate nature," Eva told Susor as they all took seats at the table. This was a conversation for sitting, not standing at awkward attention.

Susor's long, furred brows peaked.

Eva glanced at Stone. Knowing Susor was a man who appreciated truth and brevity, she said, "We are looking for another vercuri. We are under the impression there is one in Withe."

Susor poured a glass of wine. "I assume the queen did not send you for it?"

"Not exactly," Eva said, hoping the truth would be better than a lie.

"And let me assume you have not asked her?"

"Our quest is not known to the queen," Eva admitted.

"You are too late. The vercuri is gone." Susor shook his head. "I don't know where—one minute it was in our vault, the next it was gone. Stolen? I don't know."

For some reason, a memory flashed in Eva's mind. She was a child, and Tayeh held out a gift for her, a pendant in the shape of a cendari leaf, a real thing gifted from a spirit. Of course, she hadn't known it was a vercuri then. She had never considered where Tayeh had gotten it. Had it gone missing from someone else's treasure vault? And if a Guardian could take a vercuri, why had Tayeh asked her to look for them all those years ago? What game had he been playing?

"I am sorry," Susor said. "I would have given it to you if I could. With or without Arrah's permission."

"Thank you, Susor. That means a lot."

"How long are you planning to stay in Withe?" Susor asked.

"We will leave tomorrow. I made a promise."

"Arrain, it does my heart good to see you come back to us. It gives me hope that so will my son, and your man, Eva." Susor's smile was kind.

Eva swallowed the lump in her throat with some wine. "Time will tell."

Susor reached over to squeeze her hand. "My lady, it will be all right in the end. Tell me, how are the little princes?"

# EVA

"Milady, are you awake?" Stone's voice was quiet.

"I am." Eva sat up in her bed. She had not been sleeping; she was too afraid to dream. Stone closed the door behind him and crept across the dark room. He settled on her bed, cross-legged, his eyes yellow slivers in the dark.

"I think there is someone we should visit before we leave the mountains."

"Who?"

"Magda."

"The witch?"

Stone made an unusual sound in his throat. "I wouldn't call Mags a witch, but she is … not like the rest of us."

"She is the one from your journal. I know she was the one who gave you the prophecy." Eva failed to keep the bitterness from her voice. She could almost see Stone cringe in the darkness.

"She is. If I had told my mother that the prophecy came from the lips of a seer, a queer one at that, she would never have believed me. You are the only one alive who knows."

"Or anyone else who has read your journal."

"No one else has read it."

Eva dismissed how he could know that. But she was inclined to agree.

"Magda gave you the prophecy, but Tayeh must have given it to her, somehow," Eva mused. "He has always had his hands in this. Tayeh told me about the prophecy even before I fell in love with Illiah. And Tayeh instructed Arrah to bring Illiah and Rhyl to Kitarra, but not me. Tayeh told me it was for you. I was meant to save you."

"And you did."

Eva didn't know what to say.

"Magda lives close to Withe?" Eva asked, addressing the subject at hand.

"She used to. She lived up in the hills. We will have to go on foot. But we should make it there and back to Withe before dark. Handy are these long summer days."

"Odd, I would have thought you would be a skeptic on things like seers."

There was a flash of pointed teeth in the darkness. "I was. Until I met Magda, and she pried my secrets open as easy as a wax seal. Only a fool would think she was a fake."

"Are you calling your mother, the queen of Kitarra, a fool?"

"My mother is a great woman, but she has a blind spot when it comes to mystics. Or at least she used to."

Eva shook her head. "In a world where a Guardian protects Kitarra, she would not believe a seer?"

"I think my mother was prejudiced because Magda is human— and—well, you will see when you meet her. Mags is not like anyone else I have ever met."

"I look forward to meeting her, this woman who birthed my family's torment."

Silence fell between them. But it was not an easy silence; it was a held breath. Eva waited. Stone had something else; she could sense it.

"Do you forgive me?" It was Arrain asking, not Stone.

Eva searched within her heart for an answer. "You are my friend, Stone—Arrain—always and forever."

"Thank you," he said, as if her answer meant everything to him.

CHAPTER 74

# STONE

STONE HAD FORGOTTEN how wretched the dark spots were. And to hear Eva cry and weep as her mind paraphrased all her worst fears had been almost too much. He should have never brought Eva to that place. And that man … And those poor creatures … Stone took a deep breath to wash away the hopeless feeling crawling up his throat. Eva's son was Kitarra's hope. But at what cost? How could a person face that kind of darkness and come away unscathed? That was not hope, it was torture.

"This place doesn't feel alive, Stone," Eva muttered, coming to a halt in front of him, pulling him from his thoughts.

Stone followed her gaze to the little house on the hill before them. He had to agree. The garden was full of weeds, the quaint pastures empty. There was no smoke from the chimney. Besides selling fortunes, Magda had sold gems and alra wool. She had been an excellent rock hound; her crystals had been much sought after.

How many years had it been since Stone had last visited the seer? He rolled the years around in his mind and could not come up with a good answer. It had been after the death of his daughter. With his daughter's death, Arrain had been intent on finding answers.

And his questions had led him to Magda. But after that, the years blended into a coalition of pain and grief.

The first time he had met the seer, he had been a weedy youth, driven by a desire to know everything. To know the histories, his ancestors. He learned to read the ancient script of the record keepers. He spent far too many hours in the archives. It had been shortly after his father had died, so his mother allowed him the passion of neglecting his princely duties to pursue more useless pastimes. He had been a spoiled child.

Magda had been at the market, her stall bedazzled with mysterious stones and runes. Stone still wasn't sure if they had been part of the allure to bring in customers, or just if it was her nature to share the things that brought her joy.

"Ah, Prince of Kitarra—tell me, how does your search go?" And with those few words, she had snagged him.

Young Arrain had spun, pinpointing the strange voice to a strange person dressed in pinks and reds, draped in long, shimmering fabrics, makeup heavily applied. But there was something other about the woman—it wouldn't be until much later that Arrain would figure out what.

"My search?"

"Yes. You search for the darkness, do you not?"

"Don't we all?"

She had smiled at his wit. So had he.

"Your father warned you of it."

That was when Arrain first felt the tingling of something more. His father had warned him of the unbalance—it had been his last conversation with Arrain, a conversation Arrain had not repeated to another soul, not even his mother. The words of his dying father had filled him with dread and he hadn't known at his young age, how to put that dread into words.

"How did you know that?" He had been stupid too.

"I am a seer, boy," Magda said, as if it was apparent and as if Arrain was trying her patience. "I could tell you your fortune?"

"No, thank you. I don't want to know."

"Wise. I wouldn't want to know either … unless …"

"Unless what?"

"Unless it could save those I care about most."

"You are trying to trick me," Arrain scorned. "You are just trying to goad me for my coin."

The seer cocked her head at him. "We will meet again, young prince. Maybe then I will tell you what you need to know."

And she had. She gave him the prophecy on a piece of paper and told him it was from a dream. That was after Arrain had already found the areas of death and evil that sprung like poisoned springs across Kitarra. But Arrain had still been unsure. The only soul he told about the witch woman's prophecy was Emri. She didn't laugh at his foolish ideas; she merely told him to be logical, to look for proof.

But it was Emri who brought proof when she came back from Jullayah speaking of a young woman of royal Allati blood who was about to wed the Jullayan prince. Only then did Arrain believe the prophecy. Then after the death of his daughter, he knew Kitarra needed the child. He sent spies to Jullayah, to watch Eva and Illiah from a distance, never imagining how his life would become entwined with theirs.

By the time Rhyl was born, Arrain was dead. Arrah took over his mission, determined to save her people, as she was unable to save her son.

Stone wasn't sure how much of this history Eva knew. If she had read his journal fully, then she knew enough.

"Let's have a look inside," Stone said, swatting a fly from his ear.

Magda's house was a sturdy, small building in the typical mountain style with a steep roof to shed snow, built over top of a stone barn where the animals would live, their warmth below adding to the warmth above.

"Stone, look." Eva stooped to inspect something on the ground.

"Bones."

"Not human. These are from an animal."

"But no predator came to rip them apart. This is the whole skeleton."

"It doesn't feel like the other place," Eva said, referring to the dark spot. "But it doesn't feel—good."

Stone left the bones behind and went inside. The door was tight from disuse but not locked. No one locked their doors in the mountains. In a storm or bad weather, anyone's home could be a refuge.

The house was dark. Stone left the door open and threw back the shutters to get a better look. It was dusty, like no one had been there for years. But other than dust, it was clean. There was no corpse, for which Stone was grateful. He half expected to see signs of violence.

Magda's herbs were arranged in dusty jars or hanging, draped in cobwebs, from the beams, stale and forgotten. It looked as if her belongings were all accounted for. A pang of concern made Stone grit his teeth. Perhaps she had wandered off into the hills looking for crystals and gotten lost, or fallen. Being her hermit self, no one would have come looking for her. The thought made Stone sad. To die, forgotten. But no, Magda did have family and loved ones. She lived alone, but they would have come looking for her eventually.

Stone examined Magda's jars of herbs, rubbing the dust away from the labels. She had kept an extensive collection. Stone saw what he was looking for and opened the jar, his heart pounding. Ragwood. He glanced at Eva, but she was inspecting the bedroom and the little washing room.

He opened the jar. The sweet smell of the herb made something in the back of his throat desperate. The smell was the only vestige of the contents; all that was inside was a piece of paper, thin and scrawled full of Magda's tiny, flowing script.

*Stone—that is what she calls you now, isn't it? A fine name, to be sure. I knew you would look here. Sadly, my ragwood has been gone these past few years and I have not been to the coast to find more. But if you go to the coast, look for the cordoza trees. At their roots grow ragwood. You will not find one without the other.*

*But that is not the real reason you are here. It is hidden away, in Kilev. The vercuri. By the cendari tree, there is a rock shaped like a tooth. It is there, in a box, buried in the moss. When we meet again, maybe I will tell you how I found it. Tell your friend to use it well. Its magic is in revealing things, which is not the same as finding. Good luck, my friend.*

*Magda*

*Also: I didn't give you the whole prophecy before—you didn't need it. The last bit may not be all that useful anyway.*

Stone turned the paper over, hoping to find more words, but there was nothing. More to the prophecy?

"Find anything?" Eva called from the other side of the house.

Stone wanted to crumple up the useless wisdom on the paper and rub it into the floorboard with his toe, but he couldn't. He handed Eva the paper.

She took a long time to read it.

"The vercuri was in Kilev all along. Why did Crea think it was in Withe?"

"Crea? What are you talking about?" Alarm bells rang in Stone's mind. "Eva, when did you see the Guardian of Jullayah?"

"She came to me and told me to go to Withe to find the vercuri that could help me find Illiah," Eva admitted.

"And you didn't think it might be a bad idea to follow the advice of a deity that once tried to keep you captive? Why didn't you tell me?"

Eva's chin was set like a battle ax. "Don't get mad at me. We found this, didn't we?" She held up the note. "We will find the vercuri. We will go to the coast to collect ragwood—we will make this right," she growled. "We will find the other half of this fucking prophecy."

Stone stood still and silent, knowing he should do something, say something, but all he could feel was his pounding heart.

"Swearing really doesn't suit you," was what he did say. Damn him. But she smiled through her tears and swatted his shoulder, and Stone knew that for the moment, they were still friends.

# CHAPTER 75

# COTOCH

COTOCH'S GOLD BASIN glared at him like the hot Rodan sun while he berated himself for letting Crea get under his skin. In his hand, the token Crea had given him cut against his skin. For weeks, he had tried to ignore his curiosity. After all, his mother was dead. So why did he care? He cared. Even though Crea was full of shit, he cared enough to bring the token with him from Mahlas to Attingard.

So here he was, searching for a vision about a mother he had never known on the word of a Guardian he did not trust.

He dropped the strange token, his gift from Crea, into his gold basin.

Cotoch was a silent observer in the vision. He could feel the *varing* lick his mind; he could feel the brightness of the gold seeing bowl, and the darkness of the trinket settled at the bottom, but all he could *see* was the past.

*Two men faced each other. Brothers. The relation was evident by their shared features. A woman stood, hunched and fearful, hiding behind the man who Cotoch recognized as a younger version of his father. They stood in an airy and elegant room. They were in Rodan, in Kara, in Imal's palace. Cotoch had been in that room.*

*"You took a* heera *for a bride? You know it is forbidden," said the man who must be—or had been—Imal's father, Cotoch's uncle.*

*"You took a* heera *woman for your mate," Cotoch's father argued.*

*"I am the emperor." The other man's sneer grew. "And besides, bedding a woman does not make her a bride, brother. Your woman has to die. All* heera *have to die, you know this."*

*"Not your woman."*

*"She serves another purpose. And when her purpose is done ..." The emperor spread his hands.*

*"I will not let you take Pena."*

Pena. Until that moment, Cotoch had never known the name of the woman who birthed him. Why had he never known? Oh right, because his father was a sadist who never talked about the mother of his only child.

*"You can not keep her," the emperor snarled. With a flick of his wrist, two men appeared and grabbed Cotoch's mother. She whimpered but did not call out.*

*"NO!" Cotoch's father roared. "You can't. She carries my child. Please, brother. Please." He was on his knees.*

*The emperor drew a long breath. "Fine. If you take your wench and leave Rodan, she will be spared. Go to Praedan—if you can find it."*

*"You wanted this all along. You wanted me to leave," Cotoch's father raged.*

*The emperor smiled. "Leaving is your only chance to save your* heera *woman—and your* heera *child."*

*"I will take Pena and leave. You can keep Kara—and Rodan. May you rot here." Cotoch's father spat at his brother's feet.*

The vision shifted to gold, and Cotoch blinked it away. The hot-metal smell of the *varing* surrounded him.

Everything Cotoch knew about his father threatened to rewrite itself. How was this the same man who abused his own child? How was this the same man who tortured and killed to harvest the *varing*?

His father had left Rodan because of a woman, Cotoch's mother. And to save his unborn child. Cotoch sat up straighter. His father had known how to love. Cotoch stood. And somehow, somewhere, his father had lost that love. Had his love perished with Pena? Or before? Had Cotoch's father murdered his wife like Cotoch had murdered his Sandra?

Cotoch sat again, looking into the bowl. At the bottom was the little trinket that had belonged to his mother, that connected his magic to her existence. *Heera.* She had been *heera*.

He kept the word in his mind as he connected to the magic that it held—the magic of his mother's life.

*A forest. Tall pine trees held the autumn light. The floor of the forest was a golden carpet of dry grass. A group of people sat around a crackling fire, drinking and eating, a simple gathering. There was a look about them that spoke of knowing, of the wild. The* heera. *The people looked like part of the forest.*

*A woman stood and spoke, and they all listened. Her face was young and beautiful. Her hair was black and almost to her knees, and woven into her braid was a selection of ribbons and trinkets.*

Cotoch recognized the token from Crea, but it was shiny and

new. Cotoch's mother, but this time younger, happier, obviously before she had become a slave.

*"Pena, sing us the ballad of the Stormspear," a young man piped up.*

*"Yes, it is my favorite," said a little girl with large, luminous eyes. Pena smiled; no one could win against such a sweet adversary.*

She had a beautiful smile, did Cotoch's mother. Had she smiled at his father like that? Had she smiled at him like that, her son? Something deep and buried clawed at Cotoch's chest.

*"All right, Stara. But you must promise not to interrupt this time," Pena said.*

*Little Stara nodded solemnly.*

*Pena paused, and when she sang, it was obvious it was something she excelled at. Her eyes were bright, and her mouth twisted as if it couldn't wait to create the notes. The tune was slow and lamenting.*

*"The turning of leaf and moon were Tsuga's kin,*
*Earth and rain nourished Tsuga's skin.*
*She loved the forest and critters tall and small,*
*But could not speak their tongue at all.*

*For she was Old and Other*
*Nam hei tull a dor*
*Nam hei tull a dor*

*A great stone fell from the sky,*
*A rift from forest edge to mountain high,*

*Trembling thunder shook her throne,*
*And tore her heart down to the bone.*
*From the dark chasm came,*
*Someone who could speak her name.*

*For she was Old and Other*
*Nam hei tull a dor*
*Nam hei tull a dor*

*She saw his eyes of glowing dark,*
*And knew they had hit their mark.*
*She took his hand and two became one,*
*And together they walked with the sun.*

*For she was Old and Other*
*Nam hei tull a dor*
*Nam hei tull a dor*

*But the night does not fast,*
*And the day does not last.*
*The magic of her world crept into his heart,*
*And tore his soul right apart.*

*"Kill me now, my love," he cried,*
*Knowing magic took him as its prize.*
*He told her how, and she agreed,*
*Tearing a limb from her heart tree.*

*For she was Old and Other*
*Nam hei tull a dor*
*Nam hei tull a dor*

*She watched her tree turn black and dead,*

*She watched the varing share her lover's bed.*
*She carved a spear with a tip like ice,*
*And plunged it through his heart but thrice.*
*Her love for him was strong as wrath,*
*And she could not destroy his path.*

*For she was Old and Other*
*Nam hei tull a dor*
*Nam hei tull a dor*

*Trapped in a cage of dark,*
*The spear she took and spliced apart.*
*And time past and slumbers on,*
*The pieces lost 'til magic's dawn.*

*But some say her lover lives,*
*Trapped like her, where no light gives.*
*And in time, he will break and burn,*
*Through her betrayal of his turn.*

*For she was Old and Other*
*Nam hei tull a dor*
*Nam hei tull a dor"*

"What happened to the pieces of the spear, Pena?"
"I told you not to interrupt, Stara!" Pena exclaimed, rolling her eyes.
"How could she destroy the spear if her lover was inside of it?"
"It's just a legend, Stara. And it does not say that he was inside it."
"Would magic ever change us?"
Pena sighed. "The *varing* can change us all if we let it."
"That is why we have the warriors."
"Yes, Stara."

"*So they can get rid of the* varing."

"*Something like that.*"

"*But Yala was saying that the* varing *is getting stronger. The sorcerers are getting stronger. They are killing the* heera."

*All eyes around the fire looked at Pena. A cold, nervous energy swept among them. They all knew the girl spoke the truth, but none wanted to acknowledge it, giving wings to the girl's fears. The people, the fire, the smoke that smelled of pine-cones and stories, the forest, faded.*

Cotoch stepped from the vision feeling cold and sick.

His mother had been *heera.*

He was *heera.*

Cotoch felt like he had glimpsed his face for the first time—and saw a stranger.

CHAPTER 76

# IMAL

"WELL? HOW IS OUR GUEST?" Imal asked the young woman. She was slender and pretty, with light golden hair and pale skin. She would tempt any man, especially a man who had been without female comfort for as long as Lord Illiah. And Illiah deserved a woman.

The girl did not meet his eyes. "I think he was happy with me."

"You think?" Imal demanded with less patience. "Did he take you or not?"

"Yes, my lord."

Good. A man needed a good fuck to be truly well. And he was worried that he had pushed Illiah too far. Aiyan had told him once that a man could die from lack of spirit. And Imal could not let Illiah die. There was too much power in him. It was proving difficult to abstain from torturing Illiah. A week had passed, and Imal felt the *varing* calling to him, begging him to indulge. If Illiah was fit enough to fuck a woman, he was healthy enough to resume their partnership. Excellent.

"Good girl. Here." Imal gave her a handful of coins. Her face glowed, and she thanked him.

Imal went into his chambers and opened the drawer to his long cabinet. Arranged on velvet were his knives, their metal shining bright in the shadow. Imal selected two to bring with him to the prison.

"You would think *I* fucked the girl by the bounce in my step, aye, Herta?" Imal said while the guard unlocked the prison door. The guard grinned at him as he stepped aside.

Imal stepped into the prison and paused. The air still smelled of the sea, but it also smelled like the sharp tang of heated metal. Imal shivered but didn't know why. Illiah sat, straight-backed, staring out the window to the rippling blue of the sea.

"I see you are much rested, Lord Illiah," Imal began. He paused again as he approached. Illiah was naked, but Imal could not see a trace of scar or wound on his body. True, Illiah was a fast healer, but something about Illiah's poise suggested strength and agility. A week without torture and a night with a beautiful woman could not account for it.

"Herta, come," Imal said, circling Illiah like a wolf. Imal was an adept fighter, but he knew Illiah was too. And this Illiah before him was not the same man who had arrived weak and nearly dead. He was not the same man Imal had tortured relentlessly. Imal's nerves hurt as they screamed out in warning.

"Imal." As Illiah spoke, he turned to Imal.

*So this is what fear feels like,* Imal pondered.

Illiah's eyes were black as pitch and far from human. And he smiled, but the smile was so wrong on his princely face that Imal expected a forked tongue and fangs to appear.

"I have you to thank for this body. For this … opportunity," Illiah said.

Imal found his throat had constricted. His tongue was mush in his mouth. Herta had come at his call and stood beside him, equally transfixed. The thing that was Illiah snapped his eyes to the *daeum* guard. Imal could almost see the *varing* flicker through Illiah into Herta. Imal's fear crashed into his gut. He nearly wet himself.

"I have you to thank. So, I won't kill you … yet," Illiah addressed Imal, stepping forward, slowly, like a cat stretching in the sun, his movements deliberate, focused, pleasing.

*What is this thing?*

"Bring me clothes. Nice clothes. Red clothes," Illiah ordered Herta. The guard nodded, turning on his heel and out of the prison without a glance at Imal. A *daeum* guard. Imal's guard.

"Who *are* you?" Imal asked, but all that came out was a harsh whisper.

Illiah cocked his head. "I am Lord Illiah." Then he laughed. And at the edge of his laughter was something sharp and inhuman and not altogether sane.

# CHAPTER 77

# AIYAN

*"You … cannot let him live … He will block out the light … This dagger will … destroy him and the … vivus. Remember, you are stronger together."*

The Muro's last words rang in Aiyan's mind. He could not forget them. Oh, how he wanted to forget them.

Tarran would never forgive him. But what choice did Aiyan have? Illiah had to die, or the *vivus* would destroy Rodan. That was why the Muro gave him the dagger. Why would she sacrifice herself if there was no hope?

And Mila … Aiyan was about to betray the woman he loved by murdering her friend, her hero. For he did love her, desperately. Completely. But if he did nothing, if he ignored his duty to peace and goodness, what was the point of love? Aiyan had no choice. Illiah had to die.

The dagger had a dicidium made of *varing.* But it was not meant for *heera* magic.

Imal had talked about the vercuri. Nine magical artifacts from a tale about love and betrayal. If Aiyan had not been *heera,* he would have scoffed. But the *heera* believed in stories and legends and learning. Stories were histories. Stories were truth.

Aiyan greeted Imal with a smile, but inside he was a writhing mess. The desperate nature of his task triggered memories of Nyamish, of being struck on the head and the subsequent daze. Nyamish's heavy hands immobilizing him. The frequency of the events etched the memories into his mind.

Imal had saved him from Nyamish. Imal had freed Aiyan from his nightmare. Imal, who he was about to murder.

In his pocket was the wooden dagger. He felt the weight of it against his hip. The dagger could be the key to his cage or the ax that would sever his neck.

"Wine?" Imal offered, oblivious to Aiyan's discomfort. Or so Aiyan hoped.

"Of course."

A slave placed a goblet in Aiyan's hands. At least his hands didn't shake as he took it.

"Allia lost her child," Imal told him with no trace of remorse.

Aiyan was unsurprised to hear it. Allia had been self-destructing for a long time.

"My sister is useless," Imal continued. "Maybe I should give her to the *daeum*. I should have given her to you all those years ago when you asked me. Do you remember that?"

It had been the one time Aiyan had wanted something enough to risk asking Imal for it. Even then, as a young woman, Allia had been addled. Aiyan had thought he could save her … had wanted to save her. Back then, he'd thought he loved her, and that love would be enough. Now he knew what love was, and he could see that his relationship with Allia had never been more than hope. His heartstrings tightened. Love was not for him.

"I remember," Aiyan said.

"You were brave. I should have killed you for it."

"I was a fool," Aiyan admitted.

"Now I am the fool." Imal took a long drink, turning his back to Aiyan. It was Aiyan's perfect moment. His skin vibrated with the pounding of his heart. He pulled the dagger from his pocket and used every ounce of his strength to propel it toward Imal's throat. It would not be an honorable kill, but Imal did not deserve honor.

Cold, hard fingers seized Aiyan's wrist. The vercuri dropped to the floor with a soft thud, the sound of Aiyan's hope dying. His other hand was thrust behind his back, immobilizing him between one heartbeat and the next.

Aiyan twisted his head. Illiah held him. Illiah had saved Imal's life. Aiyan was *heera*-strong, but his hands ached where Illiah held him in his viselike grasp. The smell of hot metal crawled down Aiyan's nose into his throat, making his stomach churn.

"Aiyan. You cur," Imal seethed. He picked up the wooden weapon. "Where did you get this? Thief! How *dare* you? After *everything* I have done for you."

Aiyan was not about to explain how he got the dagger through uncanny means.

Aiyan's hands burned as his blood moved through his fingers once Illiah released him. Aiyan watched black roots crawl from Illiah's pupils into the whites of his eyes. Aiyan blinked and staggered, using his *heera* sight. There was no dicidium around Illiah, only black vapor and dark tendrils that reached like hands, touching, licking, taking. Illiah's dark magic enveloped the room. With effort, Aiyan locked away his *heera* sight.

"Give it to me," Illiah demanded. Imal obeyed. Without

hesitation. Imal, emperor and sorcerer, handed the dagger over to a man who had once been his captive. Aiyan's head spun.

Illiah took the wooden weapon and laid it in his palm, running his long fingers over the smooth wood, following the lines of the grain.

"Where did you find this, Wolf?" Illiah asked.

"You wouldn't believe me," Aiyan replied through gritted teeth.

"Try me."

"A tree gave it to me."

Imal looked ready to snarl a response, but Illiah held up one finger to silence him.

"Yes, yes, that would make sense. One of the Old Ones … the"—he searched for a word—"Allmakers. Yes, one of their kind would be able to take a vercuri." He tapped the side of his head. "This mind knows quite a lot."

The words of the Muro came back to Aiyan. He had made a grave mistake.

This was not Illiah. This was the *varing* wearing Illiah's skin. Illiah was already dead. He was too late.

The thing made of dark magic slipped the weapon inside his tunic. "You are an interesting creature, Wolf," it said. "But, this weapon is not meant for you."

CHAPTER 78

# MILA

"WHERE IS AIYAN?" Mila asked at breakfast. She had fallen asleep waiting, hoping that Aiyan would come to her room. She had fallen asleep asking herself over and over why she didn't just get up and knock on his door. But she hadn't. Her body wanted his; her mind wanted to touch his; her wolf wanted to run with his. She wanted all of Aiyan, but perhaps he didn't want all of her.

Her disappointment made her question sharp. She felt the eyes of everyone in the room.

"What?" she asked. She was missing something. They were all there—Tarran, Murryn, Wani, Day, Cliff, Tilley, and Aisha.

"We are leaving," Murryn said.

"What do you mean?"

"There is a boat in the harbor waiting to take us to Kitarra," Murryn said softly.

"All of us?"

"Wani and Cliff are going north to the farms with Beric. Day will go with you."

"What about you and Tarran?" Mila demanded.

"We are waiting for Aiyan's signal, and then we will find Illiah."

"Where is Aiyan?" Mila growled.

"He has gone to kill Imal."

Mila hissed through her teeth. Aiyan was trading his life for Illiah's.

"Aiyan doesn't expect to come back," Mila stated.

"Aiyan is a murderer. Illiah is our friend," Tarran said.

"Fuck you. Aiyan is a good man—your brother!" Gods, her eyes were rivers of tears.

"But so is Illiah," Murryn said, a tear falling down her cheek.

"I am going after him," Mila said.

"Mila, no, you can't! It's too late."

"I am not getting on that boat, not until I know Aiyan is alive."

"But Mila." Murryn's voice broke with a sob.

Mila placed her hand on her sister's wet cheek. "What time is the boat leaving?"

"Last quarter—Mila!" Murryn exclaimed as Mila turned into a wolf, her clothes falling to pieces around her, floating like feathers. Mila put her wet nose on Murryn's hand before bounding out into the street.

How long would Imal keep Aiyan alive if he failed? Mila reached for the place where Aiyan was in her mind; she felt him, faintly. Mila pushed herself faster, her claws digging into the dusty dirt of the street. Imal's palace came closer and closer. She stepped cautiously from the shadows, but no one noticed her.

The streets of Kara were busy, bright, and colorful, but the alleys were dark and narrow and perfect for a wolf to slip through. Following Aiyan's scent through the city as a wolf gave Mila a route that would otherwise be unknown to her. Her wolf ears picked up the footsteps of people; her wolf nose told her where the danger lay ahead.

*Where are you?* Mila asked, waiting, hoping for an answer. She did not get one, but she could follow her nose and hope her instincts were accurate.

Aiyan's scent led her down into the near darkness of the tunnel. It was cold. She could smell damp and rocks and beyond, the sea. And more organic smells. Rot. Excrement.

A single guard stood outside a locked door. It could only mean that Aiyan had failed, and he had been imprisoned. At least he was not dead.

Mila needed to get past the guard. She went back up the tunnel, out of sight from the guard. She howled. The sound reverberated through the stone halls. Moments later, the guard came up the tunnel, short sword brandished, his face glowering with confusion and alarm. Could the *daeum* feel fear? Mila had thought not, but the *daeum* looked like he had seen a ghost.

Mila gathered her courage for what she had to do. She waited until the man's back was toward her, then she leaped at his neck, her teeth finding purchase on his vertebrae. But his muscles clenched as soon as he felt her teeth; his arms grabbed for her. Mila held on, crushing his neck in her jaws, using all her strength to shake the meat under her. She felt and heard a crack, and the man fell, dead.

The door was locked by a large latch, not a key. There was no way she could open it as a wolf. She shifted. The iron bit into her hands as she released the latch and pulled the heavy door open.

Aiyan was waiting for her.

"Mila ..." Her name was like music on his lips.

"Come on, quickly," Mila said. Aiyan's arms came around her and gave her life. His eyes burned brighter; his fingers twisted into her hair. With his hands against her skin, she wanted to linger, but there was no time.

"Mila—it is not what we thought."

"Oh dear, what have we here?" a voice said behind Mila. She recognized it. Relief washed over her. She met Illiah's gaze. Her relief died. Something was wrong. The man before her looked like Illiah, but his eyes were pitch-black and piercing. He smiled. But it was not Illiah's smile.

"Run," Aiyan whispered.

CHAPTER 79

# AIYAN

AIYAN HAD URGED MILA TO RUN, though he had no intention of running himself. But she did not run. She shifted back into a wolf and gave a low, almost inaudible growl.

Illiah was not alone. Imal was with him, and behind them flowed a host of *daeum*. The prison of towering rock felt small and loud with the press of large men.

Mila lowered her head, her tail tall, pressing her body against Aiyan's leg. She was not backing down. His heart ached with pride, even as his hands shook with fear.

"Aiyan, you did not tell me you had a mate." Imal's voice might have been light with amusement if it weren't for the tone of anger—and unease. Illiah, not Imal, was the predator in the room, and everyone else was just a meal. Including Imal. And Imal knew it.

"Interesting," Illiah remarked, looking between Aiyan and Mila. "Take the woman, but don't hurt her," he commanded the *daeum*. "Leave the other wolf here. I have a plan for them."

The *daeum* rushed at them. Mila growled and lunged, her teeth finding flesh and bone. Aiyan begged her to comply. There were too many of them for her to fight. She conceded, her ears plastered, her tail down. The *daeum* grabbed her by the scruff and took her away.

"Love is grand, is it not?" Illiah said, turning to Aiyan. "I was in love once. I would have done anything for her. Moved oceans. Razed mountains. She was everything to me. But in the end, she betrayed me. Is your love true, Wolf? Can you save her? Or will you betray her with your weakness like my love betrayed me?"

Aiyan said not a word. But it seemed Illiah did not expect a reply.

"We will find out," Illiah said. With a wave of his hand, the rest of the *daeum* followed him out the door. Imal trailed behind without a backward glance.

Aiyan's heart screamed for Mila. He reached for her in his mind. He had felt her call before and blocked her from his mind hoping she would not come for him. Now it didn't matter. He reached and touched her, anchoring her in his mind. She was not hurt, but Aiyan could feel her despair.

The night was long. No one came to torment him. He lay on the hard rock listening to Mila whispering in his mind. Her rage that he would leave to kill Imal, her utter relief when she had found him, and her confusion over her friend Illiah. In return, Aiyan told her about Illiah's dicidium, how he believed the *varing* had taken over him. He didn't tell her that the Illiah she had known was likely dead; he could not add to her despair.

Aiyan did not know what would happen to them, but he was afraid. Mila reminded him of their time in the forest. That day had been Aiyan's greatest gift. Aiyan wept with longing for her, longing for a life where he could hold her in his arms. A life where they could run free in the forest.

In the morning, a host of *daeum* guards came for him. He had no choice but to follow. As he walked, trapped in the press of huge, dangerous men, the path became familiar, and he knew where they were taking him.

The arena was crowded. The noise of the audience was deafening. The bystanders shouted in harsh, angry voices as he stepped onto the circular stage of sand. He was no longer Imal's Wolf, feared assassin, enforcer of the emperor. He was an outsider, a usurper, a betrayer.

They wanted to see his blood spill onto the sand.

They armed him with a sword—they still wanted a spectacle, after all. The portcullis dropped behind him with a soft, disproportionate thud, trapping him inside the arena with his fate.

He stepped forward. The noise of the crowd surged. Aiyan scanned the mass of people gathered to watch his death. He wondered if Beric had come. And his slaves. He couldn't bring himself to look for them. His gaze fell on Imal and Illiah. Illiah sat in the emperor's throne. Dressed in red and gold, his short, dark hair glistening, he looked like a prince. His dark eyes devoured the crowd's anger, its hate.

Another entrance opened, and an animal was shoved into the arena.

But it wasn't an animal; it was Mila.

*No, not this.*

Mila was not a warrior. She was strong because of her magic, but she did not have the strength and skill to survive the arena. Aiyan ran over to her. But he was too slow. The side entrance opened.

In winter, great waves would lash against the shoreline of Rodan, like great monsters roused from the deep. The force would shake the rocks. The sound would send even the brave for cover. Salt spray would turn the dusty streets to mud. The *daeum* poured into the arena like one of those great waves.

Aiyan bared his teeth and screamed his defiance and his desperation.

CHAPTER 80

# STONE

KITARRA PEAK'S rocky expanse gleamed in the setting summer sunlight. The peak could be seen from miles away, but now, almost at its base, Stone could feel its malice. How many foolish Kitarrans had died trying to summit it? There was a plaque somewhere. It was said the great Tayeh had mastered Kitarra Peak in his youth. Stone almost believed it.

The ferryman recognized them and hustled into action to take them across the river. They thanked him, offering him coin for his effort. He would not hear of it, for Muhala and her lost prince, he would do anything, he assured them.

Eva told Stone not to scowl so much.

The boys were overjoyed to see them. Rhyl flew into Eva's arms and Talo into Stone's. Stone held his son tight. His heart flipped and danced—he had not expected Talo to miss him. Anfru ordered them a late supper, his dark brown eyes gleaming with satisfaction to have all his wards under one roof. The wee twins were healthy and strong, and nursing well. Stone could tell Eva was torn between immersing herself with her children and running out into the garden to look for the hidden vercuri. The children won. Eva cuddled with the four of them on her wide bed. Armeria was still trying to lick Stone's ankles as he joined them.

Talo and Rhyl fell asleep, and Ashlin took the babes away to nurse. Eva's eyes became desperate and hard once again.

Eva put an extra blanket over the boys and turned to Stone. "Come," she said, leading the way into the courtyard.

The cendari tree rustled in the night breeze. The moon had risen. A warm breeze picked up around them. It was a glorious summer night, a night for dancing and laughter, for wine and tales. Not for magical artifacts and secrets.

"Here—does this rock look like a tooth?" Eva asked.

"I don't know. That one does more, I think," Stone said, pointing to a taller, mossier rock a little farther from the cendari tree's roots and closer to the forest.

Eva scowled. "I think you're right. Let's look there." She crouched behind the rock, and when he came around, she was up to her elbows in moss and dirt, prying at the earth with a stick.

"I think this may be it." Her voice rose half an octave in her excitement.

"Maybe we need a shovel," he suggested.

"No. Here. I feel it!" She smoothed the earth, and there was a flat surface beneath, like the lid of a box.

"By the tree spirits' good graces," Stone mumbled as he crouched to help her uncover the rest. It was a long box, and narrow. Eva wasted no time and opened the little latch, which amazingly had not rusted shut.

Inside was the vercuri. It was not a dagger, nor a pendant, but a small carven bird—maybe an eagle or a raven. Eva picked it up in her hand, a frown on her face.

"This is not what I expected," she stated. "But it feels right." She cradled it and moved to the cendari tree, settling herself among its roots, not unlike the object nestled in her hands.

Stone watched her. Part of him wanted to snatch the treasure, to stop her from using it. A warning bell rang in his mind, but there was no logic attached. Eva closed her eyes, her fingers tangled around the little wooden bird, her knuckles white.

What was she hoping for? How could a small wooden object give her the ability to rescue a man a world away?

She was still as a statue as she called magic around her. Stone could feel the power in it, prickling at the back of his neck.

Stone sat down on the ground and waited. When Eva came back from the *simul rami*, she would be filled with tears of helplessness, because what she hoped to accomplish, what she wanted with every beat of her heart, was the impossible.

# MUTE

MUTE SAT BACK WITH A SMILE. He watched the wolf-man lunge at the *daeum* like a mad thing. It was inspiring—really it was. The Wolf was a thin man, with hardly enough mass to walk upright, much less fight a man twice his breadth, much less twenty such men. But he was fast. And strong. His magic made him so. It was a pity he had to die. And his woman too.

The woman was fast. Her wolf form helped her keep out of the reach of the *daeum*. But for how long? The arena was a cage. Mute smiled. How long, indeed.

The wolf-man fought with a strength and skill that did him credit. But it was his heart that made him a true warrior.

Impressive. Most impressive.

Mute leaned forward. The sun touched his nose and made it tickle. He took a moment to think about the feeling. This human body—Illiah's body—was constantly surprising him. It had been so long since he had a body. So long since he could touch and smell and walk. He loved to walk, to feel the ground move beneath his feet, to feel his muscles working in his legs, his torso. He shook his head. He was easily distracted. He turned his attention back to the fight before him.

The wolf-man was crouching over his woman, protecting her. Mute watched the man's expression soften as he looked at his mate, his love. It was clear in that tiny gesture that the man would die protecting this woman. Was that love? The willingness to die and sacrifice oneself for another? He had believed it once.

A pain hit him in the heart. An ancient pain. An ancient hole. A betrayal. A longing. He had lost something, and he did not know where to find it. It was not here. It was not in this fight.

He stood and raised his hands. He pulled the *daeum* back, halting their attack on the wolves. Imal beside him did the same, in a vain attempt to wrest back some of his control. Fool. He eyed Imal, but the emperor only glowered, his mouth twisted in rage.

He shrugged. He pulled the long dagger from its sheath and drove it through Imal's chest. The slurping sound as he pulled the dagger out reverberated through the arena. Everyone, everything, went silent.

Their emperor was dead.

# CHAPTER 82

# MILA

THE DAEUM in the arena fell back, leaving a wide circle around Aiyan. Mila dared to tear her eyes from Aiyan to see Illiah pull a long dagger from Imal's chest. Imal fell to the ground with the smallest sound. The crowd gaped, then a wicked whisper began to rise from the audience.

Illiah wiped his blade on Imal's once-pristine tunic. The onlookers shifted uncomfortably. Someone's shout died a quick death under the penetrating gaze of their new emperor. Mila took advantage of the *daeum*'s pause to sprint to Aiyan's side. She pressed her slender wolf body against his leg, her ribs heaving. He put his hand on her head.

The *daeum*. They stood so still, like statues, it was eerie.

Illiah stood meditatively. But Mila could see the swarming cloud around him, emerging from his fingers, his eyes, framing him like a halo of darkness. The *vivus*.

Illiah hopped over the short wall, landing gently on the sand. He moved through the line of *daeum* toward them. Mila growled. She could feel her ribs vibrating against Aiyan's leg. The crowd began to shout. The *daeum* was a wall of warriors, the *varing* tying them to Illiah with invisible threads.

Magic filled Mila's nose. But it wasn't the sour ashy smell of the *varing*; this magic smelled like forest and wood smoke on a cold day. Mila blinked. A wall of fire rose, licking into the air, separating Illiah from the *daeum*.

Illiah saw the fire and roared. His *daeum* mirrored his anger, but they could not get through the flames.

The fire burned brighter, higher, with no apparent source. The *daeum* screamed in rage and made to move around it, but the fire blocked them, a living wall of heat and energy and death and magic.

Illiah drew his dagger. Aiyan shoved Mila away as Illiah closed the distance between them.

"Run," Aiyan said through gritted teeth.

*No,* Mila growled.

Illiah lunged with inhuman speed. Aiyan ducked, twisting out of Illiah's trajectory. Aiyan was going to lose. Illiah was too fast, too strong.

Mila lunged at Illiah's leg, biting and darting back. Her offense bought Aiyan a moment. He shifted to wolf, leaping out of his ripped clothes.

Illiah adjusted his strike and angle of attack. Aiyan snarled and howled in pain. But he managed to tear into Illiah's leg, aiming for his inner thigh. He hit muscle, ripping flesh, but did not spill Illiah's lifeblood. And it cost him. Illiah brought his blade down across Aiyan's back, and Aiyan fell. Illiah's dagger drove down into Aiyan's leg, pinning him to the ground.

Illiah loomed over him. "I am sorry, Wolf. I am sorry you could not save your lover. But then, love is an illusion, isn't it?"

Aiyan's blade glistened in the sand where he had dropped it. Mila shifted, grabbing the weapon. She used all her force and swung the short, heavy sword at Illiah, slashing at his side, just below his ribs, dragging the blade across his skin. Illiah roared with pain, and the *vivus* pulsed. Mila's arms were numb. She dropped the sword; she did not have the strength for another blow.

She draped herself across Aiyan's body. Aiyan's breathing was shallow. Rivulets of blood soaked the sand beneath from his wounds.

"Illiah. Stop," Mila said, her voice clear. She inhaled the scent of the forest magic. She pulled the magic into her chest, into her body, and exhaled it through her words. "Please, stop."

*"My name is not Illiah,"* the thing inside Illiah raged.

"Illiah. Please."

Illiah paused, but not because of Mila. His gaze went up into the stadium. Mila followed his line of sight with difficulty. The fire still raged, keeping the *daeum* away. Smoke rose around them in every direction. The flames spread, engulfing men and women, slave and *daeum*. The *daeum* raved. The crowd scattered with screams and shouts. Mila caught a whiff of burning flesh.

Illiah's expression changed as he watched the unearthly fire rage and pillage the stadium. Mila couldn't read it. Was it awe? Or fear? Or something else entirely?

"Illiah, please. I know you are in there," Mila continued. She stood, placing her body between Illiah's killing blow and Aiyan where he lay injured and pinned in his wolf form. She reached out her arms. "Illiah. Remember Eva. Little Rhyl. They want you to come home. They miss you." She took more of the magic in the air and pushed it toward Illiah with her words.

Illiah blinked. Hard. His black eyes reflected the fire. Then he turned to her, his eyes dark as night, filled with the *varing*, the life-blood of the *vivus*.

"Illiah. Please, come back to us," Mila begged. Her fingers tingled with magic. She reached out her hand and touched Illiah's arm. She had to keep Illiah distracted. She kept her eyes on his, fixing him with her gaze.

She could see Tarran coming up behind Illiah. How had he gotten past the fire? Tarran had no weapon. What was he thinking?

Mila wanted to shout, tell Tarran to leave, but she couldn't take her eyes off Illiah in case he sensed Tarran and turned.

"Eva loves you. Rhyl loves you," Mila said, taking a step closer to Illiah, her hand curling tighter around his arm. "Come back to us."

Illiah lowered his dagger. There was a flicker of green in the black depths of his eyes. Mila extinguished the spark of hope in her chest. It was too late for hope. Then Illiah's eyes blackened once again. That was when Tarran lunged.

"Too slow, boy," Illiah hissed. His hand grasped Tarran's wrist, twisting. Tarran grimaced in pain, but suddenly, as if by magic, Tarran had the vercuri in his hand, aimed at Illiah's neck. Tarran had pilfered it from Illiah's pocket.

But Mila knew Illiah had always been exceptional. In an eyeblink, he released Tarran and knocked the vercuri to the ground. Then he lifted Tarran by the neck, his feet dangling off the ground. Tarran clawed at Illiah's hands, desperate for air, for life. Aiyan growled, struggling toward Illiah.

"I know you, Tarran," Illiah said. Tarran's eyes bulged as he gasped for breath. "I wish I didn't have to kill you."

Mila didn't think. She reached for the fallen vercuri and leaped, plunging it into Illiah's back, just above his shoulder blade.

Illiah cried out.

He fell to the ground, hard, then lay still, the vercuri protruding from his flesh. His red tunic blackened as it absorbed his blood.

Mila drew a shaky breath. In her ears was the roar of the fire.

Tarran dropped to Illiah's side with a sob. Mila collapsed against Aiyan.

The fire rose and burned. The screaming intensified. The people in the stadium were trapped, burning. The fire moved like water, the sound of it like the rushing of a torrential river. And it wasn't just the fire—Mila could see the blur of the *daeum* through the fire, weapons raised, slashing, moving into the city. They had gone berserk. The fire could not contain them. There was no *candarii* to control the *varing* in their blood. There was only madness.

"We need to go," Tarran croaked, but he didn't move.

"No. Wait," Mila said, watching the flames. They ebbed and flowed; the screams subsided. The flames gutted and went out like a snuffed candle. Mila sneezed. The air was thick with magic. The smells of the forest engulfed her; her head felt light with it. She felt it on her skin, tingling, burning. It was Eva's healing magic, but how?

"No, Mila, don't!" Aiyan said, his voice rough, his eyes dulled.

"It's all right," Mila said, pulling the vercuri from Illiah's back. The texture of the blade leaving flesh almost made Mila lose her nerve.

Illiah coughed and rolled. He gasped and opened his eyes. They were green, the blackness was—not gone, but pushed back. He writhed in pain as if he were being stung by a hundred bees. Rivulets of tears washed the dust from Illiah's cheeks. Mila heard him speak a name.

"Eva ..."

# EVA

THE LITTLE WOODEN BIRD was cool and smooth in her hands. Eva could feel the *simul rami* course through it. Her heart soared. Crea was right; Eva *could* use the vercuri. She closed her eyes and followed its magic down, down.

The magic brought her to a meadow of tall, dry grass. She looked around, reminded for a moment of the Tarm, but this was not endless nor sprawling. Great trees circled the expanse of grass like a wall, tall and omnipotent.

At the center of the meadow was a pool of black water full of stars. If the *simul rami* was like a river, then this was its source. Eva knelt beside the pool and looked into the water.

A vision within a vision. Magic within magic.

She called to the magic, coaxing it to her. The magic that answered was not just the *simul rami*, it was the *varing*. The *varing* snaked around her, but it was not choking and terrible; it was pulling her down another path, another thread.

The vercuri and the *varing* took her to Illiah and *candarii* darkness.

A flash rippled across Eva's mind. One eye could see the *varing*, and the other the *simul rami*. Dark and light, and she was somewhere in between. There, like a dream, was a man made of rotten things, his hands holding something, someone, Illiah. The man made of *varing* held Illiah like a desperate lover.

"Let him go!" she cried into the vision.

She took more magic, and more, reaching for Illiah. The magic burned along her arms, her muscles and veins, into her heart. She opened her mouth, but all that came out was more magic.

Then, like the first evening star appearing in the sky, Eva perceived Illiah's thread in the *simul rami*. He was hurt. Dying. She paused. She could feel a third source of magic that was not from her or Illiah. She ignored it; Illiah was all that mattered.

She took more from *simul rami*, and more, manipulating it, twisting it. She could feel it strain—a chain pushed too far, like a bone ready to snap. But the fire was in her. She couldn't stop it any more than she could stop her own heart from beating. She burned and yet longed for the heat.

"Eva, you must stop …" Tayeh's yellow eyes hovered in her mind. His kind eyes, loving, like the rising sun. Calm as a spring dawn. "Eva, please. You must stop. You *must* let him go."

She couldn't. Not now. Not when she was so close to saving him. She ignored Tayeh and took more from the *simul rami*, giving it to Illiah, pushing it into his dying body.

"Illiah." His name tore from her soul.

She was the air in Illiah's lungs, the blood in his veins. She felt Illiah's wounds heal. She saw his death recede. But she couldn't stop. Her magic reached for another, then another and another. She could feel the *simul rami* stretch and tear and burn. She could feel the *varing* escape through the cracks.

A roar of pain and anguish ripped through the *simul rami*. Tayeh.

His face was enveloped in flame, his fur blackened, his skin peeling. But she couldn't stop. She could sooner hold back a waterfall than control the river of magic that flowed through her. The heat on her face blinded her, choked her. The flame consumed her. Her connection to Rodan had vanished. The *simul rami* was gone.

She opened her eyes. The cendari tree was burning. Its branches covered in thick, black flames of magic. Dark smoke rose into the air like a living thing. Something pulled at her arm painfully. Her hands were on fire. Fire and water. Death and glory.

Eva cried out, but water rushed into her mouth. It was an instant, and she was pulled out of the hot water, her lungs and hands burning. Flames danced above her, arching across the cendari tree, licking the leaves and turning everything to ash. Strong hands held her above the water. Yellow eyes tethered her to reality.

Tears streamed down her face. "Stone, I have done something terrible." Then everything blurred, and she fell into the dark abyss.

CHAPTER 84

# MILA

ILLIAH LAY LIMP ON THE SAND. But his breathing was even—his wound where she had stabbed him was red and angry but no longer life-threatening. Mila smiled. Somehow, Eva had found him and saved his life. And Aiyan's. Mila ran her hand across Aiyan's forehead, wiping the stray hairs from his face. A sheen of sweat was on his brow, but his wounds were closing, healing. His blood no longer turned the sand to mud.

Mila looked at the wooden dagger. The tendrils of *varing* absorbed and disappeared into its core. It had been hot in her hands when she pulled it from Illiah's back, but it was cool now. It looked harmless. Like a child's plaything.

The sounds returned to her. She could hear screams and shouts. She could hear death and anger and hate. The *daeum* were in the city, ravaging. The fire had died, leaving black smoke in its wake. There would be more destruction before the day was done, caused by less magical means. Imal was dead. The *vivus*—the thing inside Iliah—was dead. And soon, the city of Kara would follow. They had managed to rescue Illiah, but they had failed the city of Kara. The *daeum* would destroy everything, everyone.

"We have to get to the boat." Tarran's voice was rough. The bruises on his neck were healing too, Mila noticed.

"What chance do we have?" Murryn asked. Murryn had appeared just after Illiah had been healed and the fire subsided.

"What about Beric?"

"He has the League Men to defend him," Aiyan managed. He sat and slowly flexed his arms and legs.

"Can they win against the *daeum*?"

"I don't think so."

"Illiah defeated them, once," Tarran remarked.

"So, we just leave? Abandon the city?" Mila asked.

Silence.

"How can we?"

Mila shivered. The breeze smelled charred. The scent of magic had vanished.

Murryn put a scarf over Mila's bare shoulders. Aiyan retrieved his clothes that were not ripped to shreds from his shift.

"You two get Illiah inside. Get out of sight. Mila and I will scout the city and find a way to the docks," Aiyan said.

Mila had no clothes. She shifted back into a wolf and followed Aiyan warily across the open arena. Aiyan hoisted Mila up the wall; it was awkward, but it was too far for her to jump. He hoisted himself up after her. They walked past Imal's body but didn't linger. There were other bodies, some burned to the bone, some ravaged by the *daeum*'s blades.

The city streets were the same. The path of the *daeum* was evident by the carnage left in their wake. Mila and Aiyan walked the blood-soaked streets. At first, it was dead rodaeri and slaves, but soon they saw the whole host of *daeum* lying in the streets. Dead. Bodies upon bodies.

*What happened here?*

"They are dead. The *daeum* are dead …" Aiyan muttered.

*How …?*

Aiyan crouched over the nearest *daeum*—the man's eyes were open, his mouth slightly gaped. He looked young behind his scars and matted hair. Not much more than a boy. Mila could feel Aiyan's magic pulse through the air.

"How is this possible?"

*There are no wounds.*

"What killed them?"

*Or who?* Mila suggested.

"Who could have killed them like *this?*"

*Wait, this one is still alive,* Mila said. Aiyan was beside her in an instant.

The *daeum* man coughed, curling onto his side as if he had been drowning. Aiyan had a knife in his hand, but something stayed his attack.

The man turned and blinked at them. He started shivering. "What is happening to me?" he asked in Praedan; many of the *daeum* had been boys brought from Jullayah.

Mila looked at Aiyan.

"You are free," Aiyan told the *daeum*. "Free from your curse. Free from the darkness that has kept you chained."

The man looked confused. He sat up, unharmed. He looked at his hands, covered in blood not his own. He looked up and down the street. He looked back to Aiyan and Mila, his eyes wide.

"You are the Wolf," he said. "Where is … where is … the emperor?"

"Dead."

The man closed his eyes. Relief flooded his face. He hung his head under the weight of it. "What do I do now?"

"Come, there may be more," Aiyan suggested, holding out his hand. The man took it, staggering to his feet. The freed *daeum* crouched to inspect his dead comrades, looking for a pulse.

"How?" he kept asking.

"We don't know," Aiyan answered. "Mila, we need to get to Beric's house. If Kara is truly free, we need Beric to take control before another rodaeri does."

Mila nodded.

"What is your name?" Aiyan asked the *daeum*.

He looked blankly before answering, "Wynne—yes, my name was Wynne."

"You are in danger, Wynne. There are few people in this city who will leave you alive once they find out that Imal is dead—do you understand? We are those few people," Aiyan told him. "Can you run behind us?"

He nodded.

"Good. Let's go." Aiyan shifted back into a wolf. He touched his nose to Mila's. The man gave his head a shake and followed.

The wall around Beric's house was lined with League Men standing at attention. Beric was prepared for a siege. Aiyan shifted and told them to open the gate. They looked at Wynne, spear points out.

"He is with us," Aiyan snapped. The spears were lowered, slightly. "Imal is dead. We need to see Beric."

"He told us to watch for you," the guard said.

Stepping into Beric's oasis felt like stepping into a world without blood and pain and death and powerful magic. The green plants and trickling fountains spilled over into Mila's soul, helping her breathe.

"Aiyan, Mila," Beric said, rushing out to greet them. His robe was dirty, his boots scuffed, his hair tangled. He was almost unrecognizable. He tossed Aiyan a robe. "Here, cover your natural state, so we are not all distracted." His humor was still intact. "Are you all right, Mila, dear?"

Mila nodded but did not shift.

"Imal is dead. The *daeum* are defeated," Aiyan told him.

"What about this one?"

"He has been freed. You need to move now—take over Kara— send out the League Men, take the palace for your own. Call your allies."

Beric nodded. Then a smile stretched over his face, and he clapped his hands. "It is time!"

# CHAPTER 85

# COTOCH

COTOCH STUMBLED. His head swam. He retched onto the fine wool rug, but he managed not to upset the gold basin before him, a small victory. His vision swam with blood and violence. The smell of iron hurt his nostrils and burned his throat. But after the blood-bath in the vision, there had been peace. He had stopped the *daeum*. He had drained the *varing* from their minds, their bodies, robbing them of the magic that kept them alive.

Cotoch was a *candarii*, and *candarii* meant sorcerer. He was born to manipulate dark magic. He was born to a father who exercised both love and cruelty. Had the *varing* changed his father? Had the *varing* changed *him?*

But his mother had been *heera*. And that meant … what exactly? He didn't really know. But perhaps the part of him that was *heera* was the part of him that stopped the *daeum*—the part that *wanted* to stop them. The part that felt the wrongness of those men, and the warning in his heart.

Imal was dead. The *daeum* were dead. Kara—and Rodan—would live on.

A weight fell from his shoulders. If he reached for the stars, he might fly. He clutched his vercuri for strength.

"My lord." Cotoch's guard came in, his face pale. "We need you to see this."

"Not now."

"But, sir. It's very important."

Cotoch didn't like his guard's expression or the chill that spread through his too-weak body. He stood tall but walked slow.

His antechamber was filled with several Allati nobles, a scattering of their guards, Cotoch's men from Mahlas—and something else.

A person was gagged and tied but writhing and pushing at his bonds with unrequited desperation. Cotoch wondered that he had not yet attempted to chew through his own arm or leg to get free. But no, his mouth was gagged.

His eyes, though … his eyes were black with the *varing*. Cotoch wondered if anyone else could see or smell the iron that emanated from the prisoner.

"My lord, this man …," Lord Rollis said, his voice trembling. "This man is infected … with dark magic."

"How do you know?" Cotoch asked. He was *heera* and *candarii*; he could see the *varing*, but he didn't think anyone else had that curse.

The noble's lip quivered. "I can see it, my lord. My uncle was a Shadow Guard. I have the same gift to see magic in others."

*Curse. It is a curse.*

And then.

*But you haven't seen me?*

"But why are you bringing this to *my* attention?" Cotoch asked.

"Well … this is awkward, but—you have magic in you, my lord. I can see it. It is not *candarii*—"

Cotoch forced his face to remain calm, but his mind was screaming in confusion—and weeping in relief.

"It is not *sanarii* either, my lord. It is different. Other," he said. "I believe you can help us. The king is on his deathbed. The rest of the nobles are fools, not leaders—myself included. They can arrange marriages for their daughters and manage their households, but they are not warriors. And I am afraid that this man here is … just the beginning."

Cotoch straightened. "What about the *sanarii*?"

"There are none, my lord."

Cotoch took a deep breath. "There must be one …"

"There are none. And the Shadow Guard is gone—dead. A messenger was sent to their mountain stronghold and reported back that the Elder Torin is dead. Jani is missing. This is not the time for old traditions. This is the time for something else. Something new. We need you."

Cotoch could have leapt at the news, but he plastered a frown on his face. He looked at the poor, gagged man who was now a monster. Cotoch put his hand on the man's arm and felt the *varing*, strong and wild. A plague, an infection.

"If you have the same gift as the Shadow Guard, couldn't you can find a *sanarii*?" Cotoch stated. "Where is Vagar? His sister is a *sanarii*."

"He is on his way from WindeKeep." Rollis sounded less than assured.

"Make me king regent, and I will help you."

"You must marry one of the king's daughters," Rollis said. "And you must give Selene to me as my third wife." Even under dire circumstances, the Allati still had deals to make.

"Done."

Rollis grinned in relief. Cotoch wanted to roll his eyes, but he thought the action might make him lose his balance.

"Kill the poor cur. There is no other way," Cotoch instructed.

He needed the audience to be over. He needed to collapse on his bed. He needed to gather his strength for the task ahead. He needed to figure out when he had become the hero in the story instead of the villain.

CHAPTER 86

# EVA

"EVA, WAKE UP," the voice sang.

Eva opened her eyes and saw black wings and black hair and dark, greedy eyes.

"You."

"Oh, Eva. You were magnificent," Crea said, her strange voice full of glee.

Eva groaned. Her head felt like wood under an awl. "What have I done?" she whispered.

"Oh, plenty."

"You. You did this. You gave me hope."

"You should never have trusted me, Eva. You should never have listened. I lied to you. A *sanarii* cannot wield the vercuri. Or, they can, but it will fuck up everything. When you used the vercuri, it allowed the *varing* to poison the *simul rami*. It was glorious. The Guardians were supposed to keep the vercuri safe, but look how they have failed!" Crea gave a loud laugh.

"Tayeh!" Eva called, knowing he was the only one who could save her from the other Guardian.

Another laugh. "Tayeh is dead, darling. You killed him when he tried to stop you. Killed him dead when you set fire to the cendari tree! It too is burned and dead. I could not have done better myself!"

"Illiah ..."

"Ah, yes. *Dear* Illiah. I wanted him dead, did you know? I tried to kill him as a babe, as a man. I was a fool. But fate is kind. I didn't realize that he is much more useful to me alive." Her bark of laughter flayed Eva right down to her soul. "May your path be clear but ever winding. Ha!" The traditional Kitarran farewell sounded out of tune on Crea's lips. Her laughter faded. Eva opened her eyes.

Her room spun. She could not hear the usual chatter of children. Panic wrapped around her heart.

"Stone?" Eva called. Her voice was weak. "Stone?" she repeated. Where was he? Was he dead? Was he gone? Had he abandoned her after everything she had done?

"I am here." And he was. His yellow eyes were sunken, his fur dull. But he put his hand on her arm, and he felt warm and alive.

"What—what happened?" she asked.

Stone's face was a hundred years old. "You were asleep for three days ..."

"What did I do?"

"The tree is ... dead."

"I killed Tayeh," Eva wailed.

"Shhh. How can you say that?"

"I know it, Stone! I know it. I saw it. I felt. I did it! I killed him. I killed him."

Stone held her, and she sobbed and cried and raged. And with every ragged breath, his arms came tighter and stronger, until somehow the shards of her heart did not fall and shatter all around her.

# CHAPTER 87

# AIYAN

AIYAN WAS ALIVE because a woman from across the sea had used her *sanarii* magic to give him life. Or so Mila and Illiah believed. Aiyan was *heera*. His body was bestowed with magic from the earth goddess Muro, but it was a different kind of magic that had healed him. Magic that had smelled of the forest and burned through the fibre of his being, scrubbing him raw.

It was quiet in Aiyan's little garden. The sounds of the city had almost disappeared. The tall walls and foliage of his plants helped muffle the sounds, but it was more than that. It was the shroud of uncertainty that had fallen over the city with the death of Imal and the *daeum*. There could have been riots, violence, but Beric had a plan ready to put in place, and allies to help him achieve it, and so far, it appeared to be working. Beric did not ask Aiyan to stand at his side as the Wolf, and for that, Aiyan was thankful. Imal's Wolf was dead.

Imal was dead. The line of emperors who had murdered the *heera* were dead. Aiyan could not deny that part of him rejoiced even as his heart recoiled from the abundance of death that accompanied the victory.

"Aiyan, there you are!" Mila's soft voice filled the space of Aiyan's oasis.

"How is Illiah?" Aiyan asked.

"Good. Sleeping. Tarran is watching over him."

"Illiah seems worthy of the tales told of him, of the loyalty he has earned from Tarran and Aisha, and yourself." Aiyan turned to look at her. Her long, dark hair was pulled into a practical braid, but a handful of strands had escaped to frame her face. Her freckles were stark on her pale skin. Her dark blue eyes were tired, but peaceful. It physically hurt to look at her, to feel his body react to her presence. He wanted to gather her in his arms and never let her go. But how could he ask her to be his? Mila deserved so much more. She deserved a partner who was strong and whole.

"You have been avoiding me," Mila said, stepping forward, taking Aiyan's hand in hers.

Aiyan thought about lying but decided against it; Mila did not deserve his lies. He thought about dropping her hand, but he only clutched it harder. "I have."

"Why?"

"I—I am not good at this … Emotions. Words." He sighed into the silence between them. "You are going to Kitarra."

"I cannot stay here. My life is in Kitarra, with Murryn and Tarran and Illiah and Eva. They are my family."

"I know. I want you to go. I want you to be happy."

"How can I be happy without you?"

"Shh. Don't say that. I am a murderer. I used the knowledge of my ancestors to benefit Imal. I was just as much a pawn as the *daeum*. I don't deserve a second chance."

"You are wrong. You survived so you could stop Imal—and he

is dead. The Muro trusted you. I trust you. You were forced to do terrible things, but you have a good heart."

"The end does not justify the means," Aiyan muttered. Tears made his eyes itch.

"No. I guess not. Maybe death *is* easier. Life is complicated. It requires bravery. And hope." Mila sighed. "Tarran told me about your father. How he was a *daeum* soldier. That he broke free from his curse, and your mother fell in love with him. You do them an injustice believing you do not deserve to be loved. Accept the past and be who you were born to be."

Could it be that simple? An image of Gran flashed before his eyes. He could almost smell the crushed flowers on her hands, the scent of wood smoke on her cloak. The soft skin of her hand on his cheek.

"I—" What could he say? The truth? That he wanted to follow her to the ends of the earth? That he loved her? That she would be better off without him?

*Come with me,* Mila's voice whispered in Aiyan's mind.

Aiyan scrutinized Mila's expression. Mila's eyes dropped to her feet. "Never mind, forget I said that. I'm sorry. I could never ask you to come away from Rodan, for me. This is your home. Now you are free to go back to the mountains, the forest. I never took you as my lover thinking I could have you always. I knew I would have to give you up."

Her words contradicted the longing in her eyes. Aiyan forced his tongue to speak. "I have been avoiding you because you deserve someone better than me."

Mila's eyes flashed. "Who are you to tell me what I *deserve?*"

Aiyan's lip twitched. He imagined leaving Rodan, and the hot city of Kara, his forests, the land where his family had lived for generations. Many of the sacred, beloved places of the *heera* were not just gone, they were destroyed. The Muro, the goddess of his people, was dead. Why was he staying?

*Go.*

The voice was not Mila's.

*Go.*

Aiyan closed his eyes, wondering if the voice was his imagination, his conscience, the voice of his ancestors—or all of them. An image of tall, snow-crowned mountains and endless forests filled his mind. In the forest was a black wolf, her nose pointed to the wind, her blue eyes begging him to chase her, to run, to play, to *live*.

*Go.*

Something released inside his chest. A rope, knotted and strained, tore and broke and dissolved. Aiyan breathed in, and with his exhale went his shame and his guilt, but his longing remained. The longing to belong, to be part of a family, to be loved, to *love*. To choose love took courage, Mila was right. And he was *heera*. He could be brave.

"The *heera* are dead," Aiyan said, tilting Mila's chin so he could look into her eyes—eyes as blue as the deepest forest lake. He kissed her, his lips hard with urgency, not haste. She tasted like the wild. "Let me come with you, Mila. Please. Tarran would tell you its about the stories. And I ..." he faltered, "I would like to earn a place in your story."

"You would come with me? Across the ocean? To a strange land? Leave your mountains and your forest?"

"I am a wolf, and I will follow my mate wherever she might lead me," Aiyan said with a touch of a growl in his throat. "For as long as you will have me."

Mila grinned.

"I will have you. Always." She wrapped her arms around his neck and clung to him, and he to her, and Aiyan knew in his heart that magic was not just carved into their bones, but it danced between them, touched their skin, and their hearts.

The days passed quickly. The nights, quicker still, with Mila sharing Aiyan's bed. In fact, Mila was always close. Even if she wasn't physically close to him, Aiyan could always feel her presence in his mind. Aiyan had been alone so long. Before, the thought of someone being linked to him would have been terrifying, but he found it enchanting, and intoxicating.

Illiah was recovering, but still weak. There was something in the back of his eyes that looked sorrowful and guilty. But he was alive, which was no small victory. The wound from the vercuri alone should have killed him. Illiah had broken free of the *vivus* when Mila stabbed him with the vercuri, but the *vivus* inside him lingered, just a taint, just below the surface. Aiyan stayed close to Illiah, as did Mila, to watch for it, to help suppress it when it rose, in case it tried to take him over again. It was like an illness—treatable, but tenacious.

Illiah was anxious to get back to Kitarra. Aiyan couldn't blame him. Aiyan could see a desperate glint in Illiah's eyes when he spoke of his wife, his children, his home, his people.

Tilley studied her list of those taken from Kitarra. To the best of her abilities, she had kept track of their whereabouts in Kara. There were not many Kitarrans left, fewer than one hundred. The surviving Kitarrans would go free, but in return, Beric asked that Kitarra agree to a trade agreement with Rodan. Tilley could not speak for the queen, but Illiah could.

As part of the deal, Illiah wanted Beric to abolish slavery. Beric argued, telling Illiah of his plan to give the slaves rights, to make them more equal to their masters; it would be chaos to release the slaves all at once. Aiyan watched Illiah assess Beric with a shrewd eye, but he nodded and shook his hand. The agreement was made. Boats were prepared.

Beric also agreed to negotiate the release of any slaves taken from Praedan who wanted to go home. Ships would deliver them in time. Most of the captains had been *daeum* and were now dead. The vast seas between Praedan and Rodan were treacherous, and only two captains felt confident in their skills to make the crossing even during the fairest sailing months. It would take time, but those from Praedan would see their homes once again.

The day came. The boat was packed. Aiyan had never been on a ship before and opted to be in wolf form—at least until he became acquainted with the swaying motion of the waves. He sat with his back to the mast.

"Aiyan." Tarran sat beside him. It was a surprise Tarran put his hand on Aiyan's fur. Aiyan relished the touch. It felt like forgiveness. "Brother," Tarran called him, smiling until it reached his eyes. Their father's eyes. For a moment, all Aiyan could see was their father, a man much loved and adored by his two sons. His heart hurt through his joy.

Mila was speaking with Illiah on the ship's deck. Both had strong personalities. They appeared to be arguing—not heatedly, more like siblings, while around them, the crew prepared to make way.

Aiyan stored the image in his mind to cherish always: Mila arguing with one of the most powerful people in Praedan; Mila dressed in a silken red tunic with the sea breeze teasing her dark curls from her braid.

Mila threw up her hands and grinned. She caught Aiyan watching her, and her grin stretched. Illiah followed Mila's distracted gaze and saw Aiyan and Tarran. There was knowing and approval in his eyes. Damn the man for being so likable.

Tarran stood, likely to find Murryn. Aiyan gave his brother's fingers a lick.

"Ugh. Really?" Tarran wiped his hand on Aiyan's fur. Fair enough.

The ship groaned to life. The sails spread as the wind caught them. The boat surged forward through the surf. The stunted shore trees and rocky beaches sped past with surprising speed. Soon they were out of the bay and headed to the open ocean. The coastline disappeared into a thin line, and the Heera Mountains became a smudge in the distance. It was uncomfortable to watch the land of his forebears dwindle to nothing.

Tilley had told him about the Long Isles, now abandoned, but Aisha told him tales of the mountains and forests, thick and wild and wondrous. Aiyan wanted to run through those new mountains with Mila beside him.

"I hate sailing," Illiah said, sitting down beside Aiyan. "I can already feel it in my gut—don't mind me if I hurl over the edge."

Illiah did look a bit green.

"I am thankful you are coming with us, Aiyan," Illiah said, picking at the dirt under his fingernails. "Kitarra believes that my son Rhyl will be able to save them from the coming darkness—the thing that took over me. I need your help." Illiah paused, looking out at the horizon. His voice dropped as he continued, "Promise me that if I lose control, you will kill me."

Aiyan shifted back to a man. "How can I promise such a thing?" Aiyan owed Illiah so much; Illiah had been brother, father, and mentor to Tarran when life and circumstances had denied Aiyan that privilege. Tarran's life stretched ahead of him, filled with love and blessings because of Illiah.

"You are the only one strong enough to do it. Please," Illiah begged, glancing around at the deck to see if anyone could overhear their conversation.

"I promise that if you lose yourself, and we cannot reach you, I will do what needs to be done," Aiyan said through gritted teeth.

"Thank you."

# CHAPTER 88

# EVA

"ATTIN, WHERE ARE YOU?" Eva spoke into the wind. The ledge of mossy rock was the only thing between her and the air. Below, the turrets of the Queen's Keep and the twisting Ilba River, dotted with boats, stretched out before her. But Eva's attention was on the clouds, the wind. Kitarra Peak at her back was dusted with the first snow of the season. She glanced up at the peak; not a cloud marred its rugged, snow-crowned head. The blue sky stretched for an eternity. The deciduous trees tucked among the evergreens were golden. Winter was on its way, but the breeze still held the scent of summer.

It had taken her weeks to gather enough courage to seek out the Guardian of Allati. She did not know if he would come.

A rush of wings behind her made her turn. Attin was there, standing in all his timeless, immortal glory. Well, not quite immortal.

"Attin," Eva said his name as a sigh. Relief almost outweighed her nerves.

"My daughter." His eyes were iron.

"Cotoch has taken over the Allati monarchy with his *candarii* magic," she told him. Vagar had finally replied to her message. King Ottella was dead. Vagar was in Attingard, an adviser to Cotoch, who had been named king regent. Eva could taste the *candarii* magic in Vagar's letter, but there was nothing she could do to help her brother.

"I know."

"What can we do?"

"Nothing. I have failed my people. The Shadow Guard is gone. Perhaps the time of the Guardians is coming to an end."

Eva couldn't speak.

"You have something else to ask me, I can tell," Attin said.

Eva bit her lip. For most of her life, Eva had thought of her *sanarii* magic as something wondrous and special. Now she knew it was a curse. She was a murderer. How was she any different than a *candarii*? Tayeh had been right to hide the truth about the power of the *sanarii* from her. The truth had cost him his life. She had destroyed part of the *simul rami*, the very fabric of light that gave life to every living thing. And Tayeh …

Who was she to ask a favor from a Guardian? But she thought of Rhyl and plunged forward.

"The vercuri. Tayeh told me long ago that he needed them. They are part of this puzzle—what must Rhyl do?" Her dear little Rhyl, both *sanarii* and *candarii*. Her heart ached and ached. But she would destroy every cendari tree in all the realms to keep Rhyl safe. Did that make her a monster? She didn't know.

Attin rocked back on his heels, folding his fingers under his chin, regarding her. She couldn't stand the look in his eyes.

"Daughter, the vercuri are fickle things, not unlike their creator. I can not tell you where they are or how to find them, because I do not know. Only she knows, and she is not the creature she once was."

Eva sucked in her breath. "The spirit caged below Cotoch's house—does she have a name?"

"Tsuga, she was once called."

"Is she one of the Allmakers?"

"No. She is something older."

"She created the vercuri?" An image of the burned tree sitting on the hill above Mahlas flitted across Eva's memories. "She created the vercuri, but it destroyed the tree. Why?"

"To save us all."

"But the balance of magic is still tipping."

"Yes. But there is time. Time for Rhyl to grow into a man."

"And then what? His magic …"

"I know, child."

"I will never use my magic again, Attin. Never."

An expression tugged at Attin's lips. "Go now. I am not omnipresent, but I do see a ship has docked. It has traveled a very long way. Its passengers may interest you. Already they are making their way up to the palace."

Eva mumbled a hasty thanks, picked up her skirts, and ran down the tumbled path toward the palace.

A boat. Could it be Illiah? She cursed herself for not asking Attin. Her eager hope leapt and sang. She skipped past the dead cendari tree, over the damp cobbles of the courtyard, through the mist of the pools and into her chambers. She had to pause to catch her ragged breath. Her legs were shaking, her heart racing, and not from her run down the hill.

There were shouts in the hallway, exclamations of glee, laughter. Eva rushed out to see a crowd in the hall. Anfru was almost skipping. Talo was hopping up and down, and Rhyl was hoisted in the arms of a familiar face.

Illiah.

His dark hair was cut short. His beard trimmed neatly. The grin on his handsome face faltered as he saw her. The emotions in his green eyes cut her to her soul. Pain. Grief. Love. Eva drew a shaky breath, afraid she was dreaming, afraid that at any moment she would wake, crippled by longing and disappointment.

Eva didn't remember moving. His arms came around her, crushing her along with Rhyl and Talo. She closed her eyes. Real. Illiah was real. He was there. He was home.

He pressed his lips against hers and something sparked between them. Eva smelled earth and moss—and tangy iron—blood and darkness. Illiah drew back, his eyes searching hers. Fiery *varing* sparked across his eyes. Then Illiah blinked, and his eyes were green and just as she remembered. She wanted to lose herself in his eyes, his touch. *Illiah. Illiah. Illiah.*

But there were others gathering around them. A man came up beside Illiah. Eva was struck by his beauty, his features, his long, black hair, the dark pattern of whorls and lines on one side of his face. But mostly his amber, wild eyes. Eva felt something from him—something calming, and strange. Next to the wild man was Mila.

"Mila!" Eva shrieked, all else forgotten in her joy. She disentangled herself from Illiah to fling her arms around her friend. Then she noticed the faces of those around them. "Murryn!" She kissed the young woman's cheek. "Tarran!" She cupped the boy's face in her hands, feeling hot tears spill down her face. "Aisha!" The young Kitarran dropped the hand of the young Kitarran woman beside him to wrap his furry arms around her. Another piece of home fell into Eva's heart.

Stone appeared. His yellow eyes widened as he took in the scene. Then his face cracked into a grin, exposing every one of his long, sharp teeth. Illiah held out his hand. Stone took it, firmly, and pulled Illiah into a hug. Illiah looked swamped by Stone's embrace, but he clapped Stone on the back.

Mila introduced her wild man—for it was clear they belonged to each other—as Aiyan. Aiyan looked distracted, his amber eyes seeing, yet unseeing. He was watching Rhyl.

"Your son," Aiyan said to Eva in a voice thick with a strange accent. "He is—very special."

The charred branches of the cendari tree were barely discernible against the night sky. The cendari tree was dead, but it was not the fire that had killed it; cendari wood did not burn. Its leaves were ash, and its wood was black nonetheless. Eva had killed it with the *varing*. It took her weeks to work up her courage to touch its once-silver bark. Where once she could feel the light of the *simul rami* pulse within the tree, now there was nothing.

The twisting steam rose from the hot pools and mingled with the dead branches above before dissolving into the night sky. A memory flashed before Eva's eyes: another dead tree, this one overlooking the valley plain of the Tarm. Another flash, another memory, and the tree was from her dreams, but alive, its golden leaves rustling in the wind of the Tarm, stretching, watching every-thing. Eva blinked. The image vanished.

Beyond the courtyard, the night had turned the forest black. A dark shape shifted against the trees in front of her.

"Who's there?" Eva asked, even as the shape, outlined by the moonlight, morphed into someone familiar. Illiah walked out of the forest toward her. His inky eyes were a dream Eva had slipped into. The smell of flowers and dew surrounded her. She blinked, and when she opened her eyes the night sky brightened with green shadows. The stars stretched like a million jewels so vast, she felt she might fall into it. The wind in the evergreens was a hundred voices humming a lullaby. Kilev disappeared. She was in her dream.

"My love." The voice from Illiah's lips was not entirely Illiah's, but she had heard it whispered over a thousand summers; she had longed for it through a thousand winters.

Illiah was naked. His body thin, his muscles sinuous and tense. With Eva's bright dream-sight she could see the scars on his skin outlined like contours of tree bark. She could see the ripple of magic between them. She could see her heart reflected in his eyes.

"You came back to me," she whispered.

He came over to her, slowly. Trapped by his hungry gaze, she didn't move. Tears of relief dripped carelessly down her face. He reached out and caught one, holding it on the tip of his finger. It glowed green and alive.

Eva reached out her hand. Her skin rippled with green light. She touched Illiah and the green light rose and mingled with his dark, reflecting in his dark eyes, making them glow. He pulled her closer, wrapping her in his dark magic as she wrapped him in her magic of the living. Their lips met with fire; their bodies touched and fused like water. His skin was hot and delicious as they moved together, clinging, growing, creating.

It was the perfect dream. It was the perfect agony.

Eva woke. Dawn light filtered through the leaves of the forest above her. She lay in the moss and wondered why she didn't feel cold—it was almost winter. By the Guardians, she was naked and not alone. Her head spun with her dream remembered. Her body hummed. Not a dream after all. Illiah lay beside her, eyes closed. He stirred slowly, flinching as he opened his eyes. Black. He blinked. Green.

"Illiah?" Eva ventured, touching his arm lightly. His skin was a tapestry of fine scars that hurt to look at.

Illiah rose like he had woken from a very long and deep sleep.

"Eva?" He looked pale. "Last night? That really happened? I thought that was a dream."

"You look like you are going to throw up."

"Did I? Did I … what did we do?"

"Nothing I would not do again," Eva told him with a smile.

He blushed and smiled back at her. His smile warmed her more than fire or sunshine.

"But, I was not myself … I could feel him. I could feel you … but it was not you. Did I … did I use *candarii* magic?"

"No," Eva assured him. "No. That is not what *candarii* magic feels like. Last night felt like … like love."

He held out his arms for her, and she fell into them. "I feel like I have someone else living in my head."

Eva didn't know what to say. Aiyan and Tarran had told her what happened in Rodan, that the *varing* had taken over Illiah's body and mind.

"What do you remember?"

"More and more." He started to shake. "I can feel it—him—there, inside me. Things he—I—we did." He pushed her out of his arms as he sat up.

"That was not your fault, Illiah."

"Was it not? Over the years, I have done horrid things in the name of justice. This felt no different." He cradled his head in his hands.

Eva put her head on his shoulder, wishing she could take his grief from him and burn it to ash.

Illiah looked at her, his green eyes piercing. "What brought you to me last night?"

"I don't know. Something other. Something old. Something forgotten. I thought I was dreaming."

Illiah put his arm around her, pulling her against him once more. "You smell like magic," he murmured against her neck. "It—he— feels different. Somehow. With you here beside me."

"Illiah," Eva exhaled his name in her surprise. "The prophecy: *Two rivers join because two lovers rift*. The *varing* and the *simul rami*. Two lovers. You and I."

"Eva, that makes no sense."

Eva smiled. She had always appreciated Illiah's ability to cut to the truth without coddling her.

"It does … it doesn't. I can't explain it." Eva rubbed her palm on her forehead. It was close; the answer was close.

Illiah kissed her neck, her shoulders, her breasts, her ribs, her navel. "Maybe if I keep loving you, he will be calm. Maybe we can figure out how to get him out of my soul."

"We have help."

"Yes, we are not alone." Illiah kissed her forehead. And then her lips. And Eva knew that love was its own kind of magic. It could make miracles, it could destroy lives, it could bring joy and peace, and just maybe, restore the chasm in her heart.

# CALYPSO

CALYPSO looked up from the pool of water formed where the creek plunged between two, large mossy rocks. The vision followed the perpetual flow of the creek water and disappeared.

He sat, stretching his human legs which were cramped from crouching.

Mila and Murryn and Tarran, and Illiah and Eva and Rhyl—even Irri—were all in Kitarra. And he was left behind in the Great Forest.

Calypso had a job to do, but the knowledge didn't ease his heart.

"You are lonely." A voice startled Calypso. It was no simple thing to sneak up on Calypso Raven Boy. He turned and relaxed when he recognized his visitor. Yes, only a Guardian would be up to the task.

The woman standing close to him had pale skin and orange hair and bright eyes. There was something fox-like about her nose. Lulanan. Calypso hadn't seen her for a long time, and he had never spoken to her.

"You wish you could go to Kitarra. I see it in your eyes, child," she said kindly. "Is it not enough to know that your friends are safe?"

Calypso inspected the minute details of the moss and ground creepers. He plucked at their tiny swirling foliage with his fingers.

"I know I am needed here," he said to the moss. His gaze flickered up to meet the Guardian's. He saw only pity in her eyes.

"You can not leave the Great Forest, raven-child. Not ever. There is not enough magic to sustain a *velidar* outside the Forest for long. You would cease to be a *velidar*, and you would become just a raven."

"I know."

"But still you long for it."

Calypso shrugged.

Lulanan sighed. "The *varing* is spreading. I fear there isn't enough time."

"There is," Calypso said with certainty, earning him the narrow glare of the Guardian. "If Rhyl is the child of the prophecy, then there is time."

"I wish Tayeh were here …" This she said not to him at all. Perhaps he was not the only one who was lonely.

The Allmakers had felt the death of their own. The Great Forest had darkened and wept. Calypso mourned alongside them, but he mourned for Eva, for her sadness, the gravity of her mistake.

If he could leave the Great Forest, would he? It was a useless question. Calypso would never need to leave the Forest. Here, he would live and die. And death would come soon enough because death and darkness had already come to the Great Forest.

# LULANAN

LULANAN left the raven to his thoughts. He was still a child. A child in a world of monsters.

The Great Forest was silent. Of course, it was. The Great Forest was mourning.

Tayeh was gone. Dead. Taken. Lost.

It was coming. Maybe not for years or days or seasons, but it was coming.

Tayeh had made a mistake trusting Eva with his secrets. He should have concentrated on the child. He should have left Eva out of it.

Lula remembered the day, years ago, she took Eva deep into the Great Forest where a raven hatchling lay broken, dying, and abandoned. Eva had fallen in love with the feathered babe immediately and for the first time, used her magic to heal. Eva's love had saved a life then.

Now, Eva's love had destroyed a life.

Maybe there was only life and death and pain and joy. Maybe the Allmakers were wrong. Maybe the *varing* was part of them all.

# STONE

STONE LOOKED OUT AT THE OCEAN waves gnawing the rocky coastline. A cool wind came off the water making Stone's ears flatten against his head. The cliff was sharp where it dropped down to meet the shoreline. The void called to him. He had answered it, once. And he knew he would answer it again, someday, of his own volition or fate's, he didn't know.

He turned his back to the cliff, and the ocean.

The wagon behind him was loaded with as much ragwood as he could find. It would need to be dried and processed—Aiyan had offered to help him with that—but it would keep him alive.

Two wolves roamed the grassy hill with him—one black as night, and the other gray like stormy water.

The wolves were made of magic.

Stone was living in a legend. Stone was living in a prophecy.

Stone was an addict, and he was a prince.

Nothing in the world made any fucking sense.

# CHARACTER LIST



## GREAT FOREST

| | | |
|---|---|---|
| Lulanan or Lula | | Guardian of the Great Forest |
| Calypso | | Velidar, Eva's raven |
| Timur | | Velidar leader, mountain cat |

## KITARRA

| | | |
|---|---|---|
| Tayeh | tey-uh | Guardian of Kitarra |
| Eva or Evangeline | | Princess of Jullayah |
| Illiah | il-ee-uh | First Defender of Kitarra, Prince of Jullayah |
| Rhyl | ril | Eva and Illiah's son |
| Talo | tal-oh | Prince of Kitarra |
| Anfru | | Eva's servant |
| Arrah | ahr-uh | Queen of Kitarra |
| Arrain | ahr-reyn | Arrah's son |
| Aisha | ey-shah | Captain |
| Turk | | Illiah's Second |
| Kura | koo-ruh | Queen's Guard |
| Kuni | koo-nee | Peace Guard |
| Clari | klair-ee | Illiah's ward from the iudarii trial |

| | | |
|---|---|---|
| Diea | dee-uh | Peace Guard |
| Vayn | | Peace Guard |
| Juno | | Peace Guard |
| Fash | | Peace Guard |
| Grip | | Soldier |
| Antoli | | Soldier |
| Vox | | Soldier |
| Jasmin | | Captain |
| Susor | | Lord of Withe |
| Ashlin | | Wet nurse |
| Yolina | | Serving girl at the Queen's Keep |
| Uya | | Queen's Guard |
| Artesia | | Eva's midwife |
| Gregor | | Weaponsmith |
| Emri | em-ree | Deceased First Defender of Kitarra, wife of Prince Arrain |
| Irri | | Kitarran spy |
| Aralis | | Eva's son |
| Bren | | Eva's son |
| Selene | | Queen Arrah's handmaid |

## ALLATI

| | |
|---|---|
| Attin | Guardian of Allati |
| Lord Wilkim | Nobleman |

| King Ottella | King of Allati |
| Rollis | King Ottella's nephew |
| Pruit | Nobleman |
| Gemma | Lord Pruit's daughter |
| Vagar | Lord of WindeKeep, Eva's half brother |
| Talia | King Ottella's wife, Eva's grandmother |
| Tersia | Talia's daughter, Eva's aunt |

## JULLAYAH

| Crea | kree-uh | Guardian of Jullayah |
| Mila | | Head-stewardess of the Keep |
| Will | | Solider |
| Kaile | key-lee | War Commander, Lord of the Keep |
| Simirri | sim-er-ee | Acolyte of the Black Goddess |
| Lindin | | Illiah's foster-brother |
| Murryn | mer-rin | Mila's sister |
| Tarran | | Illiah's ward |
| Caeri | ker-is | King of Jullayah |

## THE TARM

| Cotoch | koh-tok | Lord of Mahlas |
| Stone | | Prince Arrain, Eva's amourii |

| Easra | ez-ruh | Cotoch's captain |
| Rory | | Soldier |
| Hawk | | Soldier |
| Geral | | Guard |
| Kullin | | Guard |
| Redi | | Cotoch's servant |
| Yeri | | Cotoch's mistress |
| Tsuga | soo-gah | Earth spirit |

## THE MIDLANDS

| Maclais | mak-leyz | Master of Fishtown |
| Davis | | Maclais's partner |
| Captain Seagrass | | Ship's Captain |
| Cutless | | crewman on Seagrass's ship |

## RODAN

| The Muro | | Earth goddess of the *heera* |
| Mute | | Spirit of the varing |
| Imal | | Emperor of Rodan, *heera* |
| Aiyan | ahy-uhn | Imal's assassin, *heera* shapeshifter |
| Tilley | | Aiyan's slave, Kitarran |
| Day | | Aiyan's slave |
| Cliff | | Aiyan's slave |
| Wani | | Aiyan's slave |

| | |
|---|---|
| Beic | rodaeri |
| Nulla | Slave |
| Dart | Slave |
| Cresa | Slave from Kitarra |
| Allia | Princess, *heera,* Imal's sister |
| Jagu | *Daeum* captain |
| Jeka | Rodaeri, Nulla's master |
| Killor | Slave |
| Presdian | Rodaeri |
| Grendal | Rodaeri, Master of the League Men |
| Valint | *Daeum* |
| Waffa | Rodaeri |
| Feros | Slave |
| Padra | Slave |
| Brental | Beric's slave |
| Lis | Slave |
| Letti | Slave |
| Pena | *Heera,* Cotoch's mother |
| Stara | *Heera* |
| Yala | *Heera* wisewoman |
| Herta | *Daeum* guard |
| Nyamish | Aiyan's former master |
| Ben | Aiyan's brother |
| Wynne | *Daeum* |

# PLACES

JULLAYAH      joo-ley-uh
Caer Andri    kair an-dree    Capital of Jullayah
The Keep
Dwelllor's Knoll


KITARRA
Kilev        kee-lev        Capital of Kitarra
Withe        wahyth         Mountain city
Markeh       mahrk-ey       Border town


ALLATI
Attingard                   Capital of Allati
Windekeep                   Vagar's estate
Wanderling Mountains        Stronghold of the Shadow Guard


GREAT FOREST                Home of the Allmakers
                            and the velidar


RODAN        roh-dan        Land across the sea
Kara                        Capital of Rodan

| | | |
|---|---|---|
| Praedan | prey-dan | Rodan name for the realms |
| THE TARM | tahrm | The valley plain between Kitarra and the Midlands |
| Mahlas | maw-lahs | |

THE MIDLANDS:

Fishtown

StoneyHill

# WORDS OF INTEREST

| | | |
|---|---|---|
| Velidar | vel-uh-dahr | Old word for the Forest Folk |
| Forest Folk | | People who live in the Great Forest |
| Sanarii | san-ahr-ahy | Mages who use the *simul rami* |
| Candarii | kan-dahr-ahy | Sorcerers that use the varing |
| Simul rami | sim-yuhl ram-ahy | Life magic |
| Varing | vair-ing | Dark magic |
| Daeum | dey -uhm | Enslaved warriors controlled by the varing |
| Heera | heer-uh | People of the forest in Rodan |
| Vivus | vi-vuhs | Manifestation of the varing |
| Revenant | | A vivus |
| dicidium | dih-sij-yoo-uhm | An aura |
| Rauna | | An old spirit |
| Allmakers | | The old spirits who live in the Great Forest |

| | | |
|---|---|---|
| Vercuri | vur-kyoor-ee | Magical artifacts |
| Rodaeri | | Title of Rodan slave master, a Rodan aristocrat |
| Ro | | Rodaeri prefix |
| Cendari tree | | Special Kitarran tree that is a conduit for the *simul rami* |
| Stormspear | | The spear the vercuri were carved from |
| Culla | | Powdered herb used as a drug |
| Culla girl | | Prostitute drugged into slavery using culla powder |
| Shadow Guard | | Sorcerer hunters of Allati |
| Latha | | Kitarran weapon |
| Iudarii trail | yoo-dahr-ee | Trial of a Kitarran warrior |
| Muhala or | muamoo-hah-luh moo-ah | Kitarran word for mother |
| Polii | | Kitarran delicacy |
| The Dark Night | | Kitarran winter solstice festival |
| Uandian | | Kitarran guardian dogs |
| Kinadra | | Kitarran word for wife, or life partner. |
| Amourii | am-ohr-ahy | Kitarran honor body guard, one who owes his master a life debt. |
| Sicara | | A curved sword |

| | |
|---|---|
| Hisana | Kitarran word for rest, associated with combat training. |
| Ragwood | Herb that is refined into culla powder |
| Lamar | Rodan fibre animal |
| Golla | Rodan slave-pulled transporation device |
| Valisha | A herb |
| Gurdy Root | Herb for birthing |
| Bacara | A herb |
| Bojar | A herb |

# ACKNOWLEDGEMENTS

While writing this book, peices of my broken heart fell into the pages. I am not sure how it happened. It wasn't intentional, but it was healing. This book gave me a place to tell someone special what they meant to me.

To my readers: There are so many wonderful books, thank you for choosing mine, and joining me and my characters through this adventure. I hope you have enjoyed it.

To my amazing beta readers, you are the best. Thank you for taking the time to read this book and answer my questions.

To my editor, Jenn Sommersby, thank you for your hard work and for helping me evolve into a better writer.

To my husband, Quinton, thank you for being part of my fairytale (Still not sure if you are the prince or the loveable scoundrel) and for building me a beautiful home in the forest where we can live the Best Life Possible. Thank you to my boys, Robbie and Ben, for making me laugh every day.

All mistakes are mine.

# ABOUT THE AUTHOR

Andrea Gibb lives on Sumas Mountain, in British Columbia, with her family. She is an artist and book designer. And when not writing, enjoys long, misty hikes in the forest with her dog.

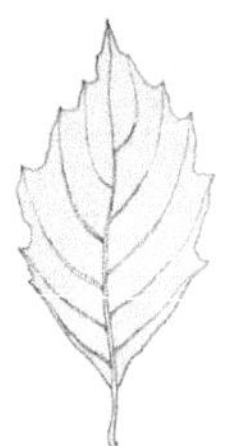

www.andreagibb.com

@andrea_gibb_author

# The Sanarii Chronicles

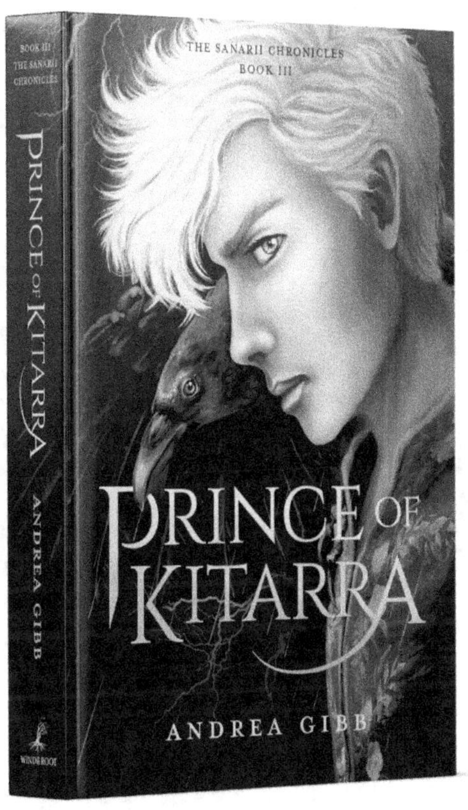


# Book III out now!
*Available in paperback
and ebook.*